The Sweetness of Tears

NAFISA HAJI

D0188473

WILLIAM MORROW

An Imprint of HarperCollins*Publishers*

This book is a work of fiction. The characters, incidents, and dialogue are drawn from the author's imagination and are not to be construed as real. Any resemblance to actual events or persons, living or dead, is entirely coincidental.

"My Friend" from *A Tear and a Smile* by Kahlil Gibran, translated by H. N. Nahmud, translation copyright © 1950 by the Estate of Kahlil Gibran. Used by permission of Alfred A. Knopf, a division of Random House, Inc.

Doctor Zhivago by Boris Pasternak, translated by Max Hayward and Manya Harari, translation copyright © 1958 by William Collins Sons and Co. Ltd. Copyright © 1958 by Pantheon Books. Used by permission of Pantheon Books, a division of Random House, Inc.

THE SWEETNESS OF TEARS. Copyright © 2011 by Nafisa Haji. All rights reserved. Printed in the United States of America. No part of this book may be used or reproduced in any manner whatsoever without written permission except in the case of brief quotations embodied in critical articles and reviews. For information address HarperCollins Publishers, 10 East 53rd Street, New York, NY 10022.

HarperCollins books may be purchased for educational, business, or sales promotional use. For information please write: Special Markets Department, HarperCollins Publishers, 10 East 53rd Street, New York, NY 10022.

FIRST EDITION

Designed by Diahann Sturge

Library of Congress Cataloging-in-Publication Data has been applied for.

ISBN 978-0-06-178010-3

11 12 13 14 15   OV/RRD   10 9 8 7 6 5 4 3 2 1

for Ali and Khalil

And the tears you shed, my grieving one, they are sweeter than the laughing of one seeking to forget, and pleasanter than loud voices in jest. Those tears shall cleanse the heart of hating and teach him that sheds them to be companion to those of broken heart. They are the tears of the Nazarene.

Kahlil Gibran, "My Friend," *A Tear and a Smile*

Part One

Through the night of doubt and sorrow
Onward goes the pilgrim band.

Sabine Baring-Gould (1867 Hymn)
Originally written in Danish by B. S. Ingemann

Jo

The first time I ever experienced doubt, I tried to climb over it. Literally. The way I'd been taught, doubt was a seed planted by Satan, the fruit of which led to disobedience. But my doubt had nothing to do with God or the Bible. My doubt was closer to home—though it would take me far from it, eventually, across oceans and continents, stretching bonds of love and loyalty to the breaking point before I could return again, finally, at peace with all of who I was. Back then, I did everything I could to avoid the hiss of that serpent—the temptation of knowing what I didn't want to know. At first, I simply ignored the whispers, pretending I didn't see what I saw, as if there were a way not to believe what your own eyes tell you. I knew how the story of original temptation ended and I had no wish to be cast out of the garden.

It was a struggle I kept to myself through the whole of tenth grade. To give voice to the questions—even in my own head—would have been to give them power, to confirm the presence of doubt, to risk eventual downfall.

The effort of denial drained me of words—a remarkable thing that did not go unnoticed.

"You're so quiet lately, Jo. What's wrong?" Mom asked me worriedly at dinner.

The second she did, Dad dropped his fork to reach over and put his hand to my forehead, shaking his head when he found it cool to the touch, running a calloused thumb down the length of my nose, tugging at my ponytail in that way that he did.

"No fever," he declared. "Only stops talking when she's got a fever. Normally. Never lets anyone else get a word in. Now's your chance, Chris," Dad said to my brother, who shrugged, flashing a brilliant smile, teeth, shine, and sweetness lighting up the expressive face that was all Chris ever really needed to communicate with, the face Mom always said was worth a thousand words. Dad was stingy with his—complete sentences being a luxury in which he rarely indulged. He wasn't so frugal with his ears, though, lending them to me generously through all the girly, childhood prattle I subjected him to as I grew up.

Mom listened, too, more actively, in fact, inserting herself into my monologues, upstaging me, in a way, with her anxious and worried engagement, always scanning for problems she felt compelled to help me solve, to pray over, quick to feel slighted on my behalf. Conversations with Mom were tiring. For her, I know, because of the effort it took to be so emotionally invested in the events of my life, in my successes and failures. For me, too, because her anxiety was contagious, making me want to hide things from her to spare her the worry. Though I never did. Until now.

"Is it school?" Mom asked again, unconvinced by Dad's reassuring diagnosis. "You can always go back to Christ Academy, you know. I never liked the idea of you transferring to Garden Hill High." She'd made her objections loud and clear in the summer before freshman year, wanting me to stay with my brother, Chris, at Garden Hill Christ Academy, which we'd both attended since preschool, instead of going to the public high school around the block, which is where she'd gone to school herself.

"Nothing's wrong, Mom. School's great." It was. But I wondered, still, if she hadn't been right in wanting me to stay at Christ Academy.

I felt Dad's eyes on my face and ignored the instinct to avoid them—the same way I had to fight not to avoid Mom's and Chris's for most of that year, still only managing to look *at* their eyes, instead of into them, like focusing on the glass of a window instead of seeing through it.

It wasn't until summer that I could admit the doubt that plagued me, even to myself. At camp. Pilgrims' Progress Summer Youth Camp, which Mom had founded when I was eight years old.

Pilgrims' Progress Summer Youth Camp—PPSYC, which Chris started calling Psych for short—was Mom's special project. The brochure—which Chris and I helped to stamp and label, sent out to churches all over Southern California—described it as "an experiential summer learning program for Christian children, firmly rooted in the teachings of Our Lord and Savior, Jesus Christ."

Spreading the Good News was a family tradition spanning four generations, a glorious one that I knew I would one day follow. My great-grandfather was The Reverend Paul Pelton. *The*. If you know anything about the evangelical world, you've heard of him. He was the son of an Oklahoma preacher, born just after the first world war, who took off to circle the globe as a missionary just after the second one, wife in tow. Their only daughter, Faith Pelton—my maternal grandmother—was born in China. When she was ten years old, her parents brought Grandma Faith to the States for a visit. It was her first time on American soil.

They arrived just in time to see Elvis Presley make an appearance on *The Ed Sullivan Show*—one of his first, before they decided to cut his pelvis out of the shot. There and then, shocked by what he saw that night in grainy black-and-white—Elvis making love to a bunch of screaming girls with his voice, swinging and gyrating in a way that must have looked, to him, like wild, simulated, non-missionary sex—my great-grandfather decided to stay in the States, realizing that while he'd been away, spreading the Good News to poor, ignorant souls who would otherwise have perished, the Christian nation he called his own—the land of the Puritans from whom he was descended—had itself been lost.

Two years after he decided to stay in the States, Great-grandpa Pelton's book, *Evilution*, was published. It was a bestseller, and made him a hero in conservative Christian right circles. Years later, Great-grandpa Pelton's fame helped to inaugurate his grandson's career in the same medium that had so horrified him when he returned to the States. Uncle Ron, Mom's brother, moved more than a hundred miles north from home in Garden Hill, a suburb of San Diego, to the suburbs of Los Angeles, becoming the youngest ever televangelist, launching a weekly TV show when I was still a kid. Uncle Ron said his mission was to turn Hollywood into *Holy*wood.

Mom carried on the tradition, too, in a more quiet kind of way. Her focus was children. My brother and me. Our cousins and all the kids from our congregation. From the beginning, the camp she founded—PPSYC—was a family affair. As the camp director, Mom practically became everyone's mother for the two weeks we spent in the hills of Southern California, making sure all the kids were well-fed, always locked and loaded with plenty of Bactine and Band-Aids. Grandma Faith, who was a nurse, spending most months of the year off on medical missions around the world, sometimes joined us, flying in just in time from someplace far away. Uncle Ron would make an appearance, even televising a sermon from camp once. Dad was in charge of the nuts and bolts of the operation—literally. He's a carpenter and handyman and he was the one who rigged up all the fun stuff beforehand. The construction of the elaborate obstacle course, under Mom's direction, was his baby. And the obstacle course was what did me in.

Every day, after breakfast, we'd jog through tires and try to swing over Sloughs of Despond—huge mud puddles specially hosed down so that there was no way to avoid getting covered in muck if we let go of the Rope of Faith. We ran through the woods, hiked up rocky hills, through "valleys" of Humiliation and Shadows. Most of the obstacles were named for the path that Christian's journey takes in John Bunyan's *Pilgrim's Progress,* symbolic landmarks on a trek of faith carefully designed by Mom every summer to illustrate a specific detail of the allegory of salvation that was one of Mom's favorite books—the reason, she said, that she was a Christian.

Before we even learned to read, Mom gave Chris and me our

own copies of the book at Christmas, stuffed into our stockings, explaining later how the March sisters in *Little Women*—another book Mom was a big fan of, chock-full of subtle and overt references to John Bunyan's seventeenth-century Puritan classic—had gotten the same gift from their mother in the frugal days of sacrifice during the Civil War. She always jokes that part of the reason she married Dad was that his last name was March. She named my brother Christian, after the pilgrim in Bunyan's work. She named me Josephine, after the tomboy in *Little Women*. Josephine March, aka Jo, just like my namesake.

I loved camp. But not as much as Chris did. He was the first to finish every project, every treasure hunt, every race. Except for one year, when we had a crazy, mixed-up race that Mom called The Give Place Race. The idea was to be last.

The race began right after breakfast. When Mom said: "Ready, set, go!" no one moved. Not one step was taken. Eventually, we all sat down. We sat and sat, giggling at first. It felt like hours passed, even if it was only a few minutes. We weren't allowed to talk. Some of us bowed our heads and prayed. Then Dad wheeled out a gas barbecue and fired it up just beyond the finish line. We watched him, hyperalert, as if we hadn't just stuffed ourselves at breakfast, while he carefully opened a package of hot dogs. Then another. Mom laid out all the fixings. Dad took out a cooler and propped it open so that we could see the delicious assortment of sodas it contained. Bags of chips were brought out, too, and displayed at one of the picnic tables near the finish line. And potato salad. One by one, taking each other's measure, most of the kids started to move, taking steps, slowly, haltingly, giggling again, toward the finish line.

Only my brother, Chris, sat patiently, still at the starting line, chalked in white at the beginning of the dirt track. I tried to hang in there with him for a while. But I was bored and hungry and more than a little hot. I crept forward, still hanging far behind the rest.

Pete McGraw was in the lead. This was no surprise: Pete had never yet managed to demonstrate any of the virtues of a spiritual pilgrim that Mom's carefully crafted curriculum required, destined to be sent home from camp the very next year, expelled permanently, for climbing up on a crate to peek into the girls' bathroom. When Pete reached the finish line, which was within sight of the start of the race, he hesitated for a long time before finally stepping over. Mom patted him on the back and congratulated him. Pete had been afraid before. Now he smiled and nodded happily. Mom handed him a hot dog, a Coke, and a bag of chips. The boy took them, muttering thanks, still painfully aware that by the rules that Mom had set up, he had lost the race. After a second, he ripped into the bag, popped open the soda, and took a big bite out of the hot dog.

The rest of us drooled at the sight. Within seconds, we were all right there beside him, claiming our own hot dogs, bags of chips, and cans of soda. Mom stood to the side, her eye on the stopwatch she had held and not yet needed. I had barely taken one bite of my hot dog, savoring the taste of the mustard and relish, only had time for one swig of pop, when Mom blew the whistle around her neck. Loudly. She advanced on us with a big trash can in hand, taking everything away from us to dump. Then she stood at the finish line and beckoned to Chris, the only one among us who had never wavered from the start. As Chris approached, she gathered the same treats for him as she had for us. She handed them to Chris, who took them warily. Mom led him to the picnic table, where none of the rest of us had bothered to sit.

"Take your time, Chris. There's no hurry. Not for you, who has had patience," Mom assured Chris. She watched for a moment as Chris dug into his meal and then whipped out her worn pocket copy of *The Progress*, opened the book to a marked page, and read: "Passion of the men of this world; and Patience, of the men of that which is to come. For as here thou seest, Passion," Mom gestured to all of us who had finished first, ". . . will have all now. . . . So are the men of this world; they must have all their good things now; they cannot stay till next year, that is, until the next world, for their portion of good. But first must give place to last . . ."

We, those who represented Passion—and lack of Patience— sat and watched as Chris finished his first hot dog and then had another. At that point, Mom decided that we had all suffered enough in the way of a good lesson and passed us all another round of hot dogs, saying, "You get it don't you? That this world is temporary? So are all the prizes in it. Here and gone before you know it. The real reward, the one worth waiting for—everlasting life in Heaven—is what it's really all about."

None of us were surprised that Chris was the one who "won" the race. He took himself very seriously at camp, embracing the identity of the pilgrim he was named for with a conscientious zeal that none of the rest of us could ever match.

By the time Chris and I were in high school, we were junior counselors at the camp—along with some of the other handful of kids who had come loyally since its inception. Now, PPSYC was a huge affair, with hundreds of kids attending from all around the country, hundreds more being turned away after Uncle Ron started to endorse the camp on his television show.

In the summer after tenth grade, we got there the night before camp began. Mom happily walked us through the Progress Course, or PC—as the obstacle course was now called—taking us through to the end, where her latest allegorical innovation had been rigged up by Dad the weekend before. The Wall of Doubt. In *Pilgrim's Progress,* Christian gets sidetracked from "the way" and imprisoned by the Giant Despair in the Doubting Castle. Because the construction of an actual castle would have been too elaborate a project (not to mention a little scary for the younger kids to be locked up in), Mom had compromised with a wall instead—ten feet high, with ropes attached on either side to help us climb up one side and down the other. I eyed the wall uneasily, wary of the doubt that had recently become a companion I refused to acknowledge.

The first day of camp, I couldn't get over it. I gave up after a few tries, walking around it to the end of the course. I told myself that I lacked the upper-body strength needed. Other girls at camp had trouble, too, after all. I brooded over my failure that night and the next few, failing again and again no matter how hard I strained. The few others who had failed managed to conquer it eventually. I started gulping down my meals, using free time to practice, doing pull-ups and push-ups to develop the muscles and strength I needed. On the day before the last day of camp, I had still not managed to conquer the Wall of Doubt.

Mom always explained what each challenge meant on the first morning of camp—the sloughs, the valleys, the ropes. About the wall, she said, "You have to understand that doubt is poisonous to faith. It eats away at it. It has to be overcome, climbed over, and conquered in order to complete the journey of faith."

After lunch, I snuck away to try to tackle the wall by myself. At the foot of it, I took hold of the rope and looked up, thinking about what Mom had said about doubt. I closed my eyes as if to avoid her words. The sound of footsteps crunching behind me made me turn, heart thumping, to see Chris, who stepped forward, offering advice I hadn't asked for.

"Just take it one step at a time, Jo. You can do it. I know you can."

I shut my eyes again, scrunching them tighter than before, trying to concentrate on the moment, to rise out of the haunting shadow of questions I had brushed aside. I saw a bright blanket of unidentifiable color, the sun, cresting over the top of the wall, which my eyelids weren't thick enough to block out, and the mental association of those words—"eyes" and "color"—made me sink back into the shadow and let go of the rope.

"What's wrong, Jo?" Chris was asking, his hand on my shoulder. I shook my head and shrugged him off.

"Nothing. I'm—I'm going for a walk."

"You want me to come?"

"No."

He was studying my face, but I couldn't meet his eyes. He tipped my chin up with his finger and tucked a lock of hair that had slipped out of my ponytail behind my ear. "You'll do it, Jo. You've got one more day."

"Yeah. One more day."

It's funny now, to think of how earnest he was—he really thought I was upset about not climbing the wall. But it was the allegory of the wall that was bothering me—and its real-life translation.

I left the Progress Course and headed into a wooded area beside it. It was cooler there, under a canopy of leaves and branches that gently shushed and crackled in the breeze that livened them in sudden spurts. As I walked around in the woods, stalked by the insurmountable wall of the Progress Course behind me, I heard a strange noise—a clicking from above—and looked up into the branches around me to find its source. I saw a bird, small and ordinary, and was watching him when he repeated the clicking, followed by a whole repertoire of varying kinds of bird calls, along with what sounded like a car alarm, woven into the song. It was a mockingbird. I sat down on the ground—slowly, carefully trying not to scare him away—and watched him for a while. I wondered who the concert was aimed at and looked around to find another bird. There was none. Maybe he was just practicing.

Mockingbirds made me think of Finches, capital F—as in Atticus and Scout, because I'd just read Harper Lee's classic in English class. Finches led me to Darwin—the different species he encountered in South America and the Galapagos Islands being one of the things that led him to consider the idea of variant species descending from one common ancestor. Until I was struck dumb by those darned Punnett squares, I'd spent much of the past year disputing Darwin with my biology teacher, Mr. Hicks, armed with all the arguments in Great-grandpa Pelton's book.

But Darwin hadn't been my problem in the end. Nothing Mr. Hicks said could shake my faith in the Genesis account of Creation. It was Mendel and his peas that I stumbled over—Mendel, the gardening monk, the man of God who believed in Genesis like I did. Specifically, dominant and recessive genes, phenotypes and genotypes. Detached earlobes. Blond hair. Hemophilia. And eye color. Mine are brown. My parents—they have blue eyes. Both of them do.

Here was the dilemma that had given birth to doubt. I had never heard anything against Mendel's Laws of Inheritance—not from Mom, not from my pastor, and not from anything I could find in Great-grandpa Pelton's book. No one disputed the fact that blue eyes are recessive, that two blue-eyed parents cannot produce a brown-eyed child. So I had to choose between not believing my own eyes and questioning everything I knew about myself.

The mockingbird, done with rehearsal, flew off in search, perhaps, of an audience more relevant than me. I stood up and tried to walk off the implications of Mendel's conclusions.

Exceptions. There were always exceptions to rules. That's what faith was all about. Miracles. They had no basis in science. The Bible was full of events that scientists dismissed as impossible because they went against the rules—the parting of the seas, the healing of the sick, resurrection, and the virgin birth. I was uneasy about lumping the color of my eyes into the august category of the Bible's accounts of God's work on Earth. But it was all I could manage on that walk in the woods.

It worked, I suppose. The last morning of camp, I made it over the wall, fueled by will—mostly Chris's. He yelled me all the way up—like Richard Gere in *An Officer and a Gentleman*, when he helps the girl recruit climb over the wall and graduate as an officer.

Getting over the wall seemed to clinch it. I'd conquered my doubts, climbed over them—with help from Chris. Left them behind. That's what I told myself.

Except, two years later, just as I was leaving home for college in Chicago, the doubts surfaced again, bursting their way out of my mouth, asking Mom for the truth as she helped me pack my suitcases. Then I knew I had been right to be afraid. The story she told me made my mother seem like a stranger. It made me a stranger to myself.

"Does Dad know?" was the only thing I could think of to ask when she was done.

"Of course he does. I didn't lie to him, Jo!"

But you lied to me, I wanted to say. *And you're asking me to lie, too.*

That had been two weeks ago. Now I was in Chicago, getting ready for classes to start the next day, trying not to think about what Mom had said, thinking I'd just plow over the whole story and pretend not to know. Instead, I found myself standing, staring at a stranger's building from across the street. The numbers on the glass door, etched in gold, were clear, matching the address I had found in the phone book that morning, next to the name I hadn't meant to look up, my fingers doing the walking that my mind didn't want to do.

I looked left, right, left. There were no cars to stop me from crossing over. But after a moment spent on the brink of the curb, I stepped back, staying on my side of the street, pacing up and down the sidewalk, my eyes on the windows of his building, wondering if he was home, if he was even the same person as the man—the boy—from my mother's story.

I sank my hands into the pockets of my jeans and, this time, didn't double back when the sidewalk ended, walking two blocks up and then two blocks over, circling the perimeter around where he lived in a two-by-two grid, like the Punnett squares that were the reason I was here.

I guess my feet were telling me that what I felt now was the same as what I'd felt back in Mr. Hicks's class, when who I thought I was ran up against Mendel. No matter how many times I had tried, filling out the worksheet that Mr. Hicks had passed out in class, erasing those letters and filling them back in, over and over again—capital and lowercase, dominant and recessive—I couldn't fit myself into those Punnett squares. Finally, I'd had to lie my way through the assignment, rearranging the letters, forcing them to make sense, pretending my dad had brown eyes instead of blue, faking a place for myself where there was none. But two years of lying to myself hadn't worked.

I completed my way around those blocks, was back in front of his building. This time, after looking both ways, I crossed the street and found his name on the intercom system outside the building.

Mubarak, S. A.

Finding his name in the phone book—the name my mother had so reluctantly shared two weeks before—had been too big a co-incidence. If he was the same person, his being in Chicago was another whopper, one of those twists in a story that's too hard to swallow. But I didn't believe in coincidences. You can't if you have faith.

Still, I hesitated, reluctant to raise my finger to the buzzer. Then I saw a woman come out of the elevator in his building, pushing a stroller. She struggled with the door, until I caught and held it for her. I watched her mouth make thank-you sounds, saw her turn and croon to the baby in the stroller, who clapped its hands at whatever it was she said, watched her make her way up the street, probably to the park I'd passed only moments before, my own attention focused on the door my hand still held open. In a flash of surrender, I walked inside, through the lobby, into the elevator and up to his floor. I went down the hall in search of the apartment number listed in the white pages. Finding it, I stared at the peephole, wishing it worked both ways. Faintly, through the door, I heard music—a high, woman's voice, singing in a foreign language. I lifted my hand and knocked hard, the sound drowned out by the beat of my heart.

Before he opened the door, the volume of the music went down. And then there he was. "Yes?"

"Uh—I—hello," I said, my eyes registering the dark, smooth chocolate color of his.

"Can I help you?"

Over his shoulder, I saw boxes. Lots of them. He was packing. Moving someplace, it seemed.

"I—uh—are you Sadiq Mubarak?"

"Yes?"

"I—is—is your mother's name Deena?" It was the only question I could think of to ask to make sure he was the right guy before getting to the point.

"Yes?"

"I'm Jo. Josephine March. I'm Angela's daughter."

"Angela?" I saw the flicker of something on his face. He remembered her.

It is the wisdom of the crocodiles,
that shed tears when they would devour.

Francis Bacon

Sadiq

My daughter, who is newborn to me and eighteen years old, knocked at my door last month. She identified herself. First name and last. Jo—Josephine—March.

She said, "I'm Angela's daughter," slowly, and then paused, her eyes seeming to measure the length of the space between my eyes, searching from one to the other of them.

I frowned at her. "Angela?" The way her face shifted, I gathered she was afraid that I had forgotten who Angela was. How could I have? Angela. My first American friend. A beautiful, blue-eyed girl—tall and slim—who I once thought I was in love with. The first girl I ever felt that way about, though certainly not the last. A mixed-up, miserable girl who I knew back when I was a pretty mixed-up, miserable child myself—also angry, resentful, sullen. No, I had not forgotten Angela.

Jo released the breath of air she'd been holding. And then told me who she was—in relation to me. After withstanding the long moments of shock that washed over me as we stood on either side of the threshold to my home, my hand gripping the door, my eyes blinded by the implications of what she said, I must have invited her in. That's where I found her, inside, standing among the boxes in my living room. I looked at her face, searching for traces of me. What I saw, instead, was something there that reminded me of my mother. Was it in her brown, wide-open eyes? In her lips, slightly parted and uncertain? Or in the symmetrical arrangement of the features on her face? A face as beautiful as my mother's.

Maybe the sense of familiarity had nothing to do with any resemblance she may have borne to my mother, nothing to do with *her* eyes and everything to do with mine. This was something I had experienced before—staring at a stranger who should not be one. I saw that she was staring back at me, looking for herself in a man she had just met, seeing a face browner than hers, more thickly browed, a nose a little too long, and black hair. Then, when her eyes were done staring, before I had a chance to process what I felt, if I yet felt anything at all, she said she wanted to know who I am.

How to even begin to respond to such a question—from such a source? Her very existence casts doubt on any answer I may have thought I knew. My name, Sadiq Ali Mubarak, she knew already. My address, too, or else she would not have been there, confronting me with what was worse than impossible—because it was possible and had been overlooked, concealed, and completely unexpected—leaving me breathless with the likelihood of other truths that I should own but which I knew nothing about.

Other pertinent information that I might offer—driver's license and Social Security numbers, marital status, educational creden-

tials, names of businesses I owned, and references, fill-in-the-
blank facts that I have written thoughtlessly a hundred times on
forms and applications: for the government, for banks, and car-
loan applications, bureaucratic questions of identity that helped me
claim what was mine, officially, in two countries, and to discard
what was not—was irrelevant to the deeper question she seemed
to be asking. I invited her to sit down on the chair where I had been
sitting before I stood to answer the door, and cleared a space for
myself on the couch piled high with possessions still to be packed.
On the coffee table in front of us was my passport, ready, alongside
the airline ticket I had bought weeks before she knocked—the beginning of a journey I have taken, in body, many times, to and fro,
unable to find my place in this world or that one.

Now, I hesitated before beginning that same journey back in a
different way, one paved with words. I hesitated because I knew
that no matter how hard I tried, I would fail to paint her a complete
picture of the scenes that suddenly, incomprehensibly, stood out in
my memory. Childhood scenes from before life changed forever—
pictures of and senses from a world of stories and rituals that the
young American girl who claimed to be my daughter could never
really understand. How could she? There was too much to translate, too much grounded in a context that no one in this world, the
one I am running away from again, has ever seen.

But I tried. I owed her that, at least.

The orbit of my childhood world was small and safe. It was a
woman's world, my mother's, located in the house where she
had spent her childhood—an old-fashioned, pre-Partition home
with a rickety, double-front door whose paint had long ago chipped

and peeled. A home from which another family, Hindu, had fled to newly independent India before my mother's came to live in it, in newly formed Pakistan, having left their own home behind in Bombay. The front windows were shuttered and screened so that there were no views to the narrow residential street in front. But there was no shortage of light in the house, because of the open courtyard in the middle of the once-stately structure, the floor laid with faded mosaic exposed to the elements—the brilliant heat and light of the Karachi sun, the heavy wetness of the morning dew, the sudden, soaking downpour of infrequent rains.

Along one side of the courtyard, a hallway led to bedrooms, one opening into another, mine and my mother's the second in a line of three. Another side opened to the living and dining rooms, all with the same rust-red mosaic as the courtyard, large square shapes inlaid with sun-colored flowers, sharp and angled in a geometric pattern that became roads for the dinky cars I played with, battlefields for the tin soldiers I lined up, making motor sounds and crashing noises for all the collisions and clashes that little boys delight in orchestrating. On the other side of the courtyard was the kitchen, a dark hole of a room furnished with cement blocks that had a countertop gas stove and a floor-level sink in the corner, where Macee, the aged kitchen servant who had been a part of the family since before I was born, would squat to scrub and wash the pots and utensils that emerged as the kitchen alchemy over which my mother presided produced delicious sounds of onions sizzling and throat-scraping vapors from dry spices roasting, which drove me just outside to the courtyard, where I would hop from one mosaic square to another, within sight of my mother, within hearing of the laughter and chatter that she and Macee exchanged.

The refrigerator, which was far from the kitchen, in the dining room on the other side of the courtyard—a vicious old clunker known as the "Machine"—had a pull-down handle that gave out a sharp electrical shock to anyone hapless enough to try opening the door without first wrapping a hand with a dishcloth. There was an L-shaped terrace above the house, spanning the length and breadth of two sides of the courtyard, built atop of the living room, dining room, and bedrooms. There, a table and low chairs were arranged, affording the view to the street lacking inside of the house. The walls around the terrace were low, something my mother constantly warned me to be cautious of, calling sharply if I ventured too near to them. When the heat of the day abated, I would climb the wobbly, wooden staircase, my hand firmly grasped in my mother's, and we would sit and watch the quiet life of the street go by, my mother sipping the tea that Macee would bring her, reading the newspaper, telling me stories.

"Tell me the one about the monkey and the crocodile again."

My mother would smile. "*Oh-ho?* Again? That one is your favorite, *nah?*"

I would nod.

She would close her eyes, as if to conjure up the presence of the characters I loved, and begin, "Once upon a time, there was a monkey who lived alone in a *jamun* tree."

"Why did she live alone, Amee?"

"She was a naughty monkey—strange and different from the others. They didn't like her. So she lived by herself in a big, leafy, green *jamun* tree, which gave fruit all the year round."

"A tree like that one?" I would say, pointing at the tree that shaded one corner of the terrace, a tall tree that grew up from the neighbor's garden, showering us with fruit, but only in season.

"Yes. A tree just like that one. Except the monkey's tree grew at the bank of a river and gave fruit all the time. She was never hungry, and the tangy, sweet *jamun*s were all she needed to live. But she was lonely."

"Until she met the crocodile?"

"Yes. One day, a crocodile swam out of the river and onto the bank to take shade from her tree. The monkey watched the crocodile for a while, having never seen one from so close before.

"Then she called, 'Hello there, Crocodile!'

"And the crocodile replied, 'Hello.'

" 'Where have you come from?' asked the curious monkey.

" 'Oh, from the other side of the river,' answered the crocodile.

" 'Are you hungry?' asked the monkey.

" 'I am a crocodile,' he said. 'It is my nature to always be hungry.'

" 'Here, have some *jamun*,' called the monkey, and threw a large number of the fruit down to the crocodile, happy to share.

"The crocodile ate the fruit and found it scrumptious. Sweet and crunchy and soft, all at the same time. 'Thank you,' he told the monkey. 'Those were delicious.'

" 'Any time,' said the monkey. 'Come again tomorrow and I shall give you more.'

"And so, the crocodile came again. Every day. And every day, when the crocodile came, he and the monkey would talk—he would tell her of his journeys on the river, and she would listen and share her fruit. Before they even realized what had happened, the monkey and the crocodile became friends. That was a glorious moment. For it was unheard of, for monkeys and crocodiles to be friends. But *this* monkey and *this* crocodile rose above their natures, taking pleasure in each other's company, the way that friends do.

"One day, they spoke of their families. The monkey told the crocodile of how she lived alone and separate from the other monkeys. And the crocodile told of his brothers and sisters and parents, who he lived with on the other side of the river.

"'But why didn't you tell me that you live with your family!' exclaimed the monkey. 'I would have sent extra fruit home with you for them.' And that was what she did that day.

"'This is so kind of you,' said the crocodile, truly touched by the monkey's generosity.

"'Anything for my friend,' said the monkey.

"That day, when the crocodile went home, he shared the gift of fruit that his friend the monkey had sent for his family. They all enjoyed the fruit and asked him where he'd found it. He told them of his friendship with the monkey, of how kind she was, and what pleasant company. They were all astonished to hear him speak this way about a monkey, who they had only ever thought of as food.

"Then one of his brothers, the eldest, began to laugh at him. 'What kind of croc are you? That you would be friends with a monkey! Crocodiles eat monkeys, don't you know?!'

"'I know that,' said the crocodile. 'But this monkey is different from other monkeys. This monkey is my friend.'

"'Your friend!' they all guffawed, following the eldest brother's lead. 'That is unnatural,' they told him.

"The poor crocodile was very hurt for his friend. He decided not to talk of her anymore. But it was too late. Every day, when he would return from his visits with his friend, they teased him.

"His older brother bragged to him of having eaten a monkey

once. 'Oh— their flesh is so tender and tasty— it makes my mouth water just to think of it! And your monkey, who spends all day eating that delicious fruit, must be especially tasty.'

"The crocodile would turn away from his brother and try not to hear. But his brother would not stop. 'You know what the best part of the monkey is? The very tastiest part? It is the heart— mmm, oh, so delicious! And your monkey's heart,' the crocodile's brother smacked his sharp teeth, 'oh, yes, your monkey's heart must be the most delicious in the world! But what does it matter? You are too cowardly to ever know that what I tell you is true. Only brave crocodiles can ever know the taste of monkey flesh. I wonder whether you are really a crocodile at all.'

"What his brother told him bothered the crocodile. His sense of honor was offended. He was torn. On the one hand, the monkey was his friend. Surely, all of her kindness to him required him to honor that friendship. But he was a crocodile after all. And every day, his brothers and sisters reminded him that crocodiles and monkeys cannot and should not be friends—that he was a cowardly kind of croc for not even trying to eat the monkey. In the end, what his brother told him was too much to bear. His mouth would water whenever he heard of the tastiness of monkey flesh, of the great delicacy of monkey heart. And his greed won out over his sense of honor as a friend.

"The next day, when he visited the monkey, he said, 'My friend! My family has made me realize that while you have been a good friend to me, sharing your fruit and sending gifts home for them, I have not been such a good friend to you. They have asked me to invite you to the other side of the river in order that they might meet my friend who has been so generous.'

"The monkey was happy. 'Oh, Crocodile! You and your family are too kind. But how can I visit them? I am a monkey. I live on the land.'

" 'Oh, that is no obstacle,' said the crocodile. 'Climb onto my back and I will take you to my family.'

"The lonely monkey was tempted out of her tree. 'Why not?' she said, and climbed down to mount the crocodile's back.

"The crocodile could hardly contain himself. Now that the monkey was on his back, he thought of all that his brother had said. His mouth watered at the prospect of eating his friend's heart. He swam out to the middle of the river and stopped.

" 'Why have you stopped here, my friend?'

" 'I have stopped, Monkey, because I am a crocodile. You are a monkey. And real crocodiles eat monkeys. I have been thinking about how especially tasty you will be—you, who eat delicious *jamun*s all the day long. I am very sorry, Monkey, but I have decided to eat your heart.'

"The monkey was silent for only a moment. Then, thinking quickly, she said, 'Oh, my friend! I wish you had told me your intent! I would have happily shared my heart with you. But I have left it back in the tree for safekeeping. Take me back to the tree, so that I can share my heart with you.'

"The crocodile's greed impaired his judgment. Without thinking, he swam back to the bank of the river, where the monkey's *jamun* tree was. His mouth was watering so that he could hardly wait to eat her heart. When they reached the bank, the monkey flew off the crocodile's back and ran up the tree.

"The crocodile said, 'Well, my friend, be quick, for I can hardly wait to taste your heart.'

" 'Foolish crocodile! My heart was with me all the time. You have betrayed our friendship and I lied to you in order to save myself. Now, I will no longer be your friend and will never share my fruit with you again!'

"The crocodile was shocked. 'So, you tricked me, my friend?'

"The monkey said, 'Yes, I did. Just as you tricked me. But your deception was out of greed. And mine was to save myself.'

"The crocodile thought about what his greed had cost him. His friendship was lost, and because of it he would no longer receive the fruits he loved and craved. He began to cry and ask for forgiveness. But the monkey refused to ever forgive and never trusted him again. She was lonely once more. But at least she was safe."

After the story was done, my mother and I would be silent—listening together to the sounds of the neighbors' houses on either side of us: a mother calling out to the young girls who lived on one side of us, the lady of the house shouting for the servant on the other. Before sunset, the last of the street hawkers would roll down the street, calling out the merits of their wares in a song they sang from morning till sundown, pushing carts filled with everything from toys and sweets to fruits and vegetables.

We never purchased any of the latter. Instead, several mornings each week, my mother would take me with her in a rickshaw to Sabzi Mandi, the vegetable market, drawing her chiffon *dupatta* over her head as we left the house. We walked to the nearest intersection to hail the putt-putting motorized tricycles that are everywhere in Karachi. There, venturing out of the small world of our home, I sensed how happy she was to be out and about in the hustle and bustle of a major metropolis. At the market, she would touch and smell the fruits and vegetables, as I clung to the hem

of her *kameez,* answering the *salaam*s of the vendors who recognized her and who laughed heartily when she shook her head at the
prices they quoted, saying to me, in a voice they could hear, that
she would have to make *ek pyaza* instead of *dho* if the cost of onions
continued to rise, using half the number of onions for the recipe
that called for an abundance of them. They called her "sister" or
"daughter," and she called them "brother" or "uncle," and I saw
how my mother enjoyed these interactions, anonymous acquain-
tanceships that must have felt safe to someone who spent most of
her life in a state of social seclusion that I was oblivious to. I don't
think my mother had any friends apart from these gentle men and
Macee.

I was an extremely shy child and rarely spoke to anyone outside the walls of our home. When a favored vendor, the one whose
prices my mother trusted the most, tried to talk to me on occasion, "Eh, Baba, what vegetable will you help your mother prepare
today?" I remember pulling on my mother's *dupatta,* sharing the
veil so that it shaded my head as well as hers, stretching the long
scarf over my face, looking out through a grainy lens of chiffon—
gray, dark blues and greens, brown, or white, depending on the
colors of the *shalwar kameez* suit that my mother had donned that
day, cotton lawns in summer and linens in winter, tailored from
sober-colored and subtly printed fabrics, widow's colors of mourning, dull but not black, which was a ceremonious color reserved for
only one season for Shia Muslims, which we were. I would cautiously assess the man's friendly eyes against the fearsome growth
of hair above his lips—a thick, dark mustache, curled villainously
at its ends. The vendor would laugh at me, revealing brown, betel
nut—stained teeth and smile at my mother, who would turn away,

also smiling, and earnestly resume the task of lifting and turning tomatoes, checking their ripeness, always careful to regulate these familiarities according to unspoken rules of engagement between men and women, between lower and upper classes.

When we came home, after cooking and showering the smell of spices and onions out of her hair and skin, my mother prayed, putting aside her chiffon scarf to don the thicker white *chadar* of prayer that veiled her hair and the shape of her body. When she bowed for *sajda,* I would sometimes climb up onto her back, my arms encircling her neck tightly, a passenger on the journey of her prayers. She would stay prone, her forehead pressed to the prayer rug, waiting for something else to distract me off my perch, before rising back to the sitting position of her *namaz.* Her patience was boundless—I was everything to her, I knew.

The only other outings we had were visits we paid, every week, to a giant fortress of a house—the home of Abbas Ali Mubarak and his wife, Sajida, my paternal grandparents, who sent their car for the ride every Friday. Their driver, Sharif Muhammad Chacha, who was also the brother of our servant, Macee, would announce his arrival with the honk of his horn before knocking at the door to visit with his sister while my mother combed my hair and washed my face in preparation for our departure. When we were ready, I would eagerly climb into the backseat with my mother, my hand tucked in hers, my eyes drinking in the sights of the city streets that lay between the house that I called home and the mansion to which the car belonged. Once there, we would sit, my mother and I, close together on one of four sofas—ornately carved, all of them, upholstered in blue velvet, in a grand living room lit with chandeliers that sparkled and gleamed. There, my grandmother—Dadi is what I called her—

would have special food laid out for me, along with toys and candies, gift-wrapped, like it was my birthday, every week. Dada, my grand-father, would speak to me. But I spent most of the visit stuck close to my mother, hiding my face in her lap whenever anyone tried to coax me away.

This would annoy Dadi, so the purse of her lips would tighten further than it had at first sight of my mother, her eyes narrowing as she gazed at this woman, the mother of her grandchild, who she clearly disliked, and said, "Surely he's old enough, now, to get to know us outside of your presence, Deena. It is not healthy, the way he clings to you."

Dada would interrupt, saying, "He's only a little child, Sajida. Leave them be." My shyness never abated, no matter how hard my grandmother smiled at me, no matter how many gifts she tried to bribe me with. Many times, my cousin Jaffer would be there with his mother—my father's sister, Asma, who I called Phupi-jan—and they would join in Dadi's effort to entice me away from my mother. I would watch him play with the toys laid out for me and tug at my mother to come join me on the floor. She always obliged, so that I made friends with Jaffer, silently, in the shade of my mother's shelter. I would talk about him all of the next day, but I was too shy to ever speak to him myself.

Every night, my mother would lie down beside me on the bed we shared and sing me to sleep—Urdu songs and English—in a voice that I knew was the most piercingly beautiful in the world. I would struggle to keep awake to hear it, her fingers running through my hair, my body cradled in the curve of hers, a nightly battle where defeat was sweet, a total surrender to sleep that only small children enjoy.

I was amazed to hear one of those favorite nighttime battle hymns on the radio one day—"Love Me Tender"—in my grand-parents' car, on the way home from one of our weekly visits to the big house.

"Amee, that's your song," I whispered, too shy to let Sharif Muhammad Chacha, the driver, hear me.

My mother laughed and put her hand on my cheek. "*My* song? No, Sadee. That's Elvis Presley's song."

I shook my head and frowned, because this didn't seem right and the song sounded strange in the baritone of the man whose peculiar name my mother knew.

There were two months of the year when my mother would not sing the usual songs to me at night. And what she did sing, I had to share with others by day. Suddenly, the boundaries of our sober world would become porous as the social life of all of Karachi's Shias—a life I didn't know, of dinner parties and wedding functions, of beach picnics and the constant flow of spontaneous, unannounced visiting, which I would probably not have enjoyed in any case—shifted into a period of ritual grieving so immediate and intimate that it was hard to believe that the deaths being mourned had occurred many centuries ago. Radios and televisions in Shia homes were mute and dark, for the first ten days of those two months at least. Solid black clothing was aired out of closets and donned for those days, giving way to black prints patterned with whites and grays for the rest of those two months. Jewelry was shed, makeup eschewed. During Muharram and Safar, the tales my mother told me in those afternoons on the terrace were different, her words weaving into the rituals and symbols and chanting of those strangely sensual days—the names and stories so tied into the sounds, scents, tastes, and textures that they blend together in my memory.

We wear black, Sadee, every year, for two months, my mother said. *We don't listen to music. We mourn what happened in this month, almost fourteen hundred years ago. As if it were today. We grieve for the family of our beloved Prophet Muhammad, peace be upon him, crying and mourning for them more than we mourn for our own troubles and problems. The family of the Prophet, who brought the Quran—a message of unity and justice. With it, he united the savage Arabs who used to fight and feud and kill one another, who worshipped stones and statues and buried their baby daughters alive. They were ignorant people, uncivilized. And while the Prophet lived, under his leadership, they had become one people, one community.*

I remember perfumed wisps of smoke that drifted through the living rooms of people's homes, where women of the community gathered—my paternal grandparents' house among them—emanating from the incense sticks that were lit daily during those ten days of Muharram. And the scent of roses gathered and arranged in vases set upon makeshift altars, peculiarly enhanced in the hot, humid climate of Karachi and later, a signal of the end of those gatherings, from the rosewater that was sprinkled on frenzied crowds of women from ornate, long- and thin-necked silver bottles, ready and at hand.

I remember hushed, whispered greetings exchanged between women as they arrived, dressed fully in black, slipping off their shoes, shuffling them carefully to the side with a gentle clatter before stepping onto the crisply laundered white sheets that covered carpets in rooms cleared away of furniture. Older women were usually the first to arrive, adjusting their *dupattas,* or the *pallo*s of their *sari*s, to cover their heads before sitting down on the floor—most of them with an audible crack of joints—to take up the coveted space along the walls, which would give their backs rest, admitting the passage of their youth in order to claim one of the few privileges of that loss. Prayer beads clicked softly, accompanying the nearly silent movement of lips as the piety of old age sought expression in the idle moments that came with being punctual in a community that had never submitted to the tyranny of timepieces.

Within a few years of the death of the Prophet, my mother told me, *the Muslims were beginning to forget what he'd taught them. A very bad man, Yazid, was the leader now. The people were afraid of him because he was a tyrant. He was power-hungry and greedy. Cruel and unjust. But he was also a coward with no honor. And there was one thing he was very afraid of . . . he was afraid of the righteous voice of Imam Husain—grandson of the Prophet, son of Fatima and Ali, who is our first Imam—who lived in Medina. There were some people who remembered the Prophet, still, and who remembered the goodness that he had taught them—to feed the poor, to take care of widows and orphans, to remember that this life is but a journey of return. That when it is done, we will be held accountable for the harm we cause to others and ourselves. Those who remembered these lessons were loyal to Imam Husain. And Yazid considered this loyalty a threat to his power. He demanded that Imam Husain pay allegiance to him as ruler, but Imam Husain, who knew what a corrupt man Yazid was, refused.*

Later, louder voices intruded on the quiet scenes of anticipation that the older women had set, as younger women, for whom the call of piety was a less immediate concern than the social need to be seen as pious, and wealthier women, whose day-to-day lives had little to do with the deprivation and sacrifice the gatherings were intended to honor, greeted one another warmly, lowering their voices only to exchange the latest news of community misfortune and scandal, which the congregation surreptitiously served the purpose of spreading.

The people of the city of Kufa, who like so many others had begun to forget, invited Imam Husain to their city as a spiritual teacher. He accepted their invitation, leaving Medina to make a pilgrimage to Mecca on his way there.

Husain knew that his life was in danger because he had refused to bow down to the will of the tyrant Yazid, but he traveled only with his family and friends, not with an army. Imam Husain's caravan, after leaving Mecca and on its way to Kufa, was forcibly stopped in its path by Yazid's army. They were made to camp at Karbala, near the banks of the River Furat—the Euphrates. There, Imam Husain told Yazid's forces that he had no wish to fight them, no desire for blood to be shed. He asked them to let him go home. Peacefully. They refused.

Three days before the tenth of Muharram, their access to the banks of the river was cut off by Yazid's forces, and they had no water to drink and no food supplies left. On the night before Ashura, the tenth day of Muharram, Imam Husain urged his friends to leave him to his fate, not to sacrifice their lives for his. Not one of them listened. Instead, one of Yazid's military commanders, Hurr, the very one who had arrested Husain's journey in the first place, forcing him to stop at Karbala, came over to the Imam's side, knowing full well what this decision meant— certain death. The next day, one by one, the men from among Imam Husain's companions battled forth, hungry and thirsty, in his defense.

A small group of women then gathered near the pillow placed in front of the carefully tended altar, a table dressed in black, which was set up at one end of the room—the back wall of which was lined with long poles, draped in rich fabrics and topped with hand-shaped sculptures made of silver and gold—around one of them, its fabric adorned with the figure of a lion, hung a *mushk,* a water bag, which everyone knew was for Abbas.

Husain's brother, Abbas, the standard-bearer, could not stand to see the plight of the thirsty, innocent children in the camp. When they came to petition him for help—their brave uncle who never denied them anything—led by Sakina, his beloved niece, he agreed to venture out, alone, to the banks of the river, to gather water for them in his mushk.

A preliminary rustling of yellowed pages from a worn school composition notebook, whose thread and glue binding had often long since retired from service, would be followed by an exaggerated throat-clearing signal from the usually middle-aged woman in the center, who, by now, would have soberly donned a thickly rimmed pair of reading glasses.

In a scratchy whisper punctuated by an exclamation point, the woman would say, *"Salawat!"*

On cue, the crowd of women, who by now sometimes numbered in excess of a hundred, would respond, in harmonious chorus, *"Allahuma sale ala Muhammad w'ale Muhammad!"*

The *marsia*s would begin, the nasal chorus of long-suffering notes usually leading to an exodus, the few children present standing up to leave the room. At the gatherings held in my grandparents' house, my cousin Jaffer would get up and gesture for me to follow him out. I never did, unhappy at the prospect of leaving my mother's side. Once, I was brave enough to wander a few inches away from the comfort of her space, to stand at the window and look out at the large garden, where a group of children had collected themselves, following Jaffer as I had refused to do. They were my cousins, my mother whispered to me: first cousins, second cousins, and cousins removed to all numbers of degree. They charged about, playing *baraf-paani*—ice water or freeze tag—and "red light, green light," running amok in the way that children do when their elders are otherwise occupied. Behind me, I heard another *salawat*, signaling the end of one *marsia* and the beginning of another. And then a multiple chorus of *salawat*s as the *zakira* took her place on the black-clothed chair set up for her in the corner to begin her sermon.

Abbas reached the banks of the river safely, filling the water bag but refusing to drink himself, not while his brother and the children and women of the camp remained thirsty. Alas, on his way back to camp, the enemy soldiers who had failed to prevent him from reaching the river now surrounded him. Abbas, beloved brother of Husain, was attacked from all sides, his arms chopped off as he strove to keep hold of the water he carried. When the enemy pierced the bag of water, along with the precious water, all hope to save the children gushed and spilled on the sand.

The *zakira*'s emphatic voice rose and fell with the delivery of each sentence, exhorting her listeners loudly and angrily—about what, I could not yet understand. I watched the children tag each other outside for a long while until, suddenly, the *zakira*'s volume increased dramatically, her voice, suddenly thicker, issuing forth from a throat heavy with emotion. And then the wailing started. Weeping sounds of misery, always disconcerting, no matter how expected.

They were outnumbered by tens of thousands and slaughtered by Yazid's army. Imam Husain lost all of his friends and all of the men in his family, seventy-two in all. His nephews, Qasim, Aun, and Muhammad. His son Ali Akbar, who looked just like the Prophet. Not even his infant son, Ali Asghar, was spared. While he had friends and relatives alive, no one would let him go forth and do battle. But in the end, he fought bravely. Alone. And when he took a break from the battle for the afternoon prayer, the commander of Yazid's army sent Shimr after him. While Imam Husain prostrated himself, his forehead touching the hot sands of Karbala—wounded, hungry and thirsty, broken from the grief he had suffered throughout the day—Shimr mounted his back, ready to kill him. He leaned forward to hear the words of Husain's prayers—and heard the Imam asking God for the forgiveness of those who would harm him. This made Shimr pause. But in the end, his heart was too hard, his belly too greedy for the riches that he was promised upon completion of his mission. He cut off Imam Husain's head. And the battle of Karbala was over.

The children outside heard the weeping, too. Their ears seemed to prick up as Jaffer shouted, "The *masaib* has started! Come on, let's go!" loudly enough for me to barely hear him. The game was abandoned and I saw that my cousins were excited. They had been waiting for the sounds of bitter grief that were getting louder and my eyes followed them as they ran up the garden steps and back into the house, screeching to a halt at the entrance to the living room. There, they abandoned their air of play to assume a solemn pose. All of the women were still seated, most of them with handkerchiefs clutched in their hands, stemming a steady flow from eyes and noses, or holding them up against their faces, like veils, to cover the sobs that made shoulders heave and hands slap against knees. The *zakira*'s voice was now a high-pitched kind of keening and her listeners responded to each of her barely intelligible words—words to a story so familiar that clarity was unnecessary—with the rise and fall of their own sobs, a mournful kind of duet.

Just as suddenly as the crying had begun, it was over. The *ʒa-kira's* voice, raised to a fevered climax, was muffled by the hand that she wiped over her face, murmuring again, *"Allahuma sale ala Muhammad w'ale Muhammad."*

And then another ritual began, the one my cousins had come running inside for. As the women stood up, a voice called, "Husain, Husain!"—that beloved name—and a circle formed in the center of the room as another woman opened another tattered notebook and began to sing. *Not sing, recite,* my mother would later correct me. The others took up the pulse of her melody, beating their chests with open hands in a rhythmic thud that sounded deeper than claps and somehow more powerful. Jaffer waved all the children forward, and I saw them push their way around taller bodies to the center of the circle, where I already stood with my mother. I watched them, my cousins, as they strained to pull collars and necklines aside and lower, to maximize the exposure of the skin on their chests, before joining enthusiastically in the chorus and the accompanying beat. I hesitated, my hand hovering awkwardly, flailing against my chest in a pale imitation of the confident pounding going on all around me.

The stridently mournful song, or *noha,* was over soon. And in the space of time it took for my mother to step forward, a notebook of her own in hand, the chest-beating continued to the sound of that name again, "Husain, Husain! *Ya* Husain! *Masloom* Husain! *Shaheed* Husain!" A leader called the words out and the others echoed her chants in a practiced rhythm that was familiar to all.

My mother would begin her signature *noha* in a voice soft and sweet at first, thick with the same emotion I saw reflected on the women's faces around her, then strengthening as the first verse shifted into the second—tender grief giving way to crescendos of fierce anguish, the beat of hands against chests strengthening in response, matching her cadence. The words of the song were rhythmic and rhyming, a loftier version of the Urdu we spoke daily. But it was her voice that set my mother's *noha* apart. None of the many that followed her recitations could match her expression. Now, the chanting in between the *noha*s grew more furious, more frantic, and more complicated as the morning progressed. After the last, the women at the center of the crowd became frenzied. The younger women and my cousins used two hands now, instead of one, reddening the exposed skin on their chests. The beat of their hands, no longer accompanied by song, hard and loud as that of a drum, could not be mistaken for some variant form of clapping now.

A voice shouted, *"Hai,* Sakina!," another beloved name, the name of a child violently bereft of her father, thirsty and hungry and lost in a world indifferent to her suffering.

"Hai, pyas!" the others replied, their voices desperate, grief-stricken, claiming her thirst as their own.

Oh, Sakina, oh thirst, my mother shook her head, wiping tears from her eyes. *After Sakina's father, Husain, was murdered in prayer, before her thirst was quenched, the enemy descended upon the women and children of the camp, looting and burning. They slapped Sakina's cheeks, snatching the earrings off her ears without undoing the clasps, so that her earlobes were torn and bloodied. They snatched away the veils of her mother and aunts, dishonoring the women of the House of the Prophet, stealing what little the modest household had in the way of possessions. In the end, it was the women from the enemy camp who took pity on them, bringing food and water on the Night of the Desti-*

tute. *Later, the women and children who survived, along with Husain's eldest son, who had been too sick to fight, were chained and bound and led through the streets of Kufa, and on to Damascus, where Yazid held court, beaten whenever they cried in sorrow for the beloved bodies they left behind.*

This, you understand, was the House of the Prophet! It was attacked from within, not by some invading force. Betrayed by its own people, men who called themselves Muslims, followers of the same Messenger who had carried Husain on his shoulders as a boy. It was the worst kind of tragedy. One that originated from inside.

And then, when the chants, the beating, the frenzy hovered for a few moments at the edge of hysteria, I would feel the fresh, soothing drops fall on my head, my face, my eyes—drops of rose-water that rained down on us, dampening the fervor of the crowd instantaneously, prompting loud *salawat*s from cooler heads at the outskirts of the crowd, which turned, in some mysterious chore-ography, and faced one of the walls as my grandmother, Dadi, in a voice still heavy with the tears that continued to make tracks down her face, would begin a long recitation in Arabic that was familiar, the language of prayer, but not our language—full of *sa-laam*s, the Muslim greeting of peace, interspersed with some of the names that had been chanted moments before with such pas-sion. In the middle of these *salaam*s, all the women would turn together, to change the angle of where they faced, and then turn back again to stand the way they had when they began—turning directions to match the locations of where the people they saluted were buried. Some in what is now Iraq and in Medina, the City of the Prophet, in the Arabian Peninsula. And one in Iran, which is why the women turned during the salutations.

When the *majlis* was done, the solemn fog of grief that still filled the room lifted slowly at first. Women greeted each other, the ones who had not had the chance before, those who'd come early meeting those who'd come late with kisses and hugs. Eventually, smiles were seen and laughter heard, from faces still wet with tears. While tea and snacks were served, my mother would take my hand and lead me to the altar, praying silently, touching the various objects there with a hand she then kissed. Sometimes, my mother would give me some money, a few rupees, to place in front of one or other of the symbols on the table—like the water bag—to be collected later by Dadi, for alms. I never hesitated about where I placed the money she gave me—in the cradle, a miniature one made of silver, only big enough for a small doll.

That is Ali Asghar's cradle, my mother told me, *who was Imam Husain's six-month-old baby. That is where the infant slept as his mother rocked him and watched over him when her milk ran dry, from lack of food and drink, and she saw that he was dying. Before Imam Husain went forth to battle, she begged him to take the baby to the enemy forces, to ask that they quench the innocent infant's thirst if no one else's. So, Imam Husain took Ali Asghar to the battlefield and pleaded with the enemy soldiers to take pity on Ali Asghar's innocent thirst. In case they thought it was a trick to gain relief for himself, Imam Husain laid his baby on the burning sands of Karbala, inviting someone from among them to take the child themselves to give him water. As savage as the hearts of Yazid's soldiers were, some among them began to cry, remembering babies of their own, safe and sound, far away at home. Seeing this, quickly, the commander of Yazid's forces ordered his best archer, Hurmula, to shoot an arrow into the baby's throat. The first arrow missed its mark when Imam Husain picked up Ali Asghar in his arms. The second arrow struck true, too big for the baby's tiny throat, digging into the cradling arm of his father.*

Imam Husain did not know what to do next—the only moment during all of the events of Karbala when he was unsure. Should he bury Ali Asghar so that his mother would not have to see what the cruel soldiers had done to her baby? Or should he take the body back to the camp so that she could see her beloved child for the last time and witness how they had responded to his plea? With the corpse of his baby in his arms, Imam Husain would begin the walk back to the tent where Ali Asghar's mother waited, hoping that the soldiers had taken mercy on her child, then he would pace backward in indecision and grief. Seven times he did this, back and forth, before finally delivering Ali Asghar back to his mother. And the empty cradle is how we remember him.

"But— they lost," I said one Muharram afternoon when I was old enough to begin to understand the story. "Imam Husain and his friends. They lost the battle."

My mother shook her head. "No. They stood up against tyranny. Their story is alive. And as long as it is, as long as we remember their sacrifices, they have won. We remember their bravery for the first ten days of Muharram—we recognize that Imam Husain's sacrifice was offered for us, we who are unworthy. And then for the rest of Muharram and for the next month of Safar, we remember those left behind—the captive widows and orphans who were marched through the streets of Muslim cities, in chains, to Yazid's court at Damascus, where Imam Husain's sister, Bibi Zainab, bravely challenged the tyrant, and bore witness to his oppression. We carry the story of what happened at Karbala with us in our hearts. Always. Do you know, Sadee, that my grandmother is buried there? All her life, she wanted to go to Karbala, on pilgrimage. Because she never went there, it was her dying wish to be buried there. So, her son, my father, made all the arrangements and took her to Karbala to lie at rest near the Imam. Her life had not been an easy one. She was a widow at an early age. And her stepson, my father's older brother, didn't treat her as well as he should have."

After a little silence, I asked, "What is a widow?"

"A widow is someone whose husband has died."

"That's what you are."

My mother was silent again, for a moment. "Yes."

"How did *my* father die?"

"He—he was not well. And then he died."

I waited for more, but let it go when I found that my mother had no more to say on the subject.

On the tenth day of Muharram, on Ashura, glued to my mother's side, I felt the story of Karbala in my heart, offering the special prayers of the day, walking forward and backward seven times, reenacting and honoring Imam Husain's moment of indecision, the grief and tragedy of the thirsty orphans, Sakina among them, and her baby brother killed in his father's arms.

H e has begun school now. He is old enough and can stand to be away from you, whether you like it or not," I heard my paternal grandmother, Dadi, say to my mother in the Muharram when I was five years old. "Send him with his grandfather for the *juloos* on Ashura."

Dada, my grandfather, turned to me and asked, "What do you think, Sadiq? Are you ready to be a man now? To join the men's Ashura procession through the streets of Karachi? All of your cousins will be there."

"Jaffer, too?"

"Of course. None of the other boys would miss it for anything."

I nodded nervously, unaware that what he proposed would expose me to the masculine side of Muharram rituals—the side that was gruesome and violent, where *matham* was painful and bloody.

I went with him on Ashura that year and heard *noha*s that sounded like battle cries, the beat of hands on chests like the blows of a choreographed kind of combat. Carpets of hot coals were raked over in preparation for bare feet to run across them. Carefully sharpened swords were struck in self-inflicted frenzy on bare heads and blood flowed freely from split scalps to drip down faces twisted in grief and pain. And small, curved blades hanging from chains were swung in lateral rhythm, whipping the air with a metal twang to beat upon bare backs from which horizontal rivulets of blood sprung and trailed stains onto hot pavements, shimmering in the heat of the sun.

There were other boys there, Jaffer among them, along with other cousins that I was a little less wary of than before, and they were excited. They had seen it all before. All of them, many of them younger than me, had been initiated in the practice of *zanjeer ka matham* with their fathers, using mini-size blades that were dull and relatively harmless and hung from smaller chains designed for use on smaller bodies.

My stomach clenched at the sight of blood dripping everywhere. The scenes of bloodshed struck me as all the more grotesque because the wounds were self-inflicted. Jaffer's father—my uncle, who was with us, too—thrust me into the circle of young boys, where Jaffer and the others had already claimed their spots, shed their shirts, and commenced an awful imitation of the swaying, chain-swinging motion that older men in bigger circles, which I could still see, only yards away from us, performed with far greater effect. In my hand, my uncle placed a new set of chains, the dull blades winking at me with the reflected light of the sun. My stomach unclenched suddenly, and though I had observed the half-day fast, the *faqa,* which is customary for the day of Ashura, a stream of bilious liquid stained my shirt before my head lightened and I fell, faint, to the ground.

I woke up in my grandfather's arms, crying for my mother. The other boys would have laughed at me, but it was Ashura, too somber a day for laughing. For hours, I walked on the sidelines of the procession, unable to participate, impatient and crying to be with my mother, back among the women.

One day, when my mother and I were on the terrace, the quiet of our street was disturbed by a small commotion outside of the house next door, the house with the *jamun* tree in its garden. A car had pulled up and the residents of the house spilled out onto the street with exclamations of joy that drew me close to the wall. My mother stood up to reel me back, but her eyes, too, were caught by the scene below. A man in a white shirt and black tie had emerged from the car, greeting the old lady next door, suit jacket slung over one shoulder. Servants were emptying the trunk, pulling out suitcases. I heard my mother gasp beside me. As if he heard it, too, the man looked up toward us, causing my mother to step backward, too late. The man had seen her. I saw him frown, his eyes on the space she had occupied. His gaze shifted to me, his eyes locked with mine. Then he walked into the house next door.

Something about the scene stayed with me. I found myself suddenly fascinated by that man—curious about who he was and where he'd come from. That side of the terrace, under the shade of the *jamun* tree, became my favorite. My curiosity made me less timid. Now I would steal away to the terrace without my mother, something I had been expressly forbidden to do. Until the day I saw the man sitting in the garden, drinking tea and reading the newspaper. I wanted him to see me. The *jamun* tree was in season, the ripe, nearly black, ovoid fruit on its upper branches within reach. I picked some and began to throw them down into the garden where the man sat. The third *jamun* hit closest to its mark, landing at his feet, catching his attention. But when he looked up, I lost my newfound courage and ducked. After long moments of listening to the thud of my own heart, I chanced a look over the top of the wall and caught his eye, briefly, before ducking down again.

"Is that a monkey up there? Trying to catch the attention of this poor, weary crocodile?"

This irresistible invitation, one I had sought, made me laugh and say, still crouched at the base of the wall, "Yes. A monkey."

"A lonely monkey, it would seem. Who doesn't know that tempting a crocodile with fruit is not a good idea."

"Why? Will you want to eat my heart?"

"Not today. Today, I have had a big lunch."

I laughed again. And then heard my mother calling from below. He heard her voice, too.

"Is that the monkey's mother's voice?"

"Yes."

"Well, you'd better go to her. She's calling."

* * *

One day, before I turned six, the car from my grandparents' fortress came for me alone. When the driver honked the horn, my mother kissed me and held me close for a moment. Then she walked me out of the house to the car. Over her shoulder, I saw Macee purse her lips. She looked at the driver, her brother, Sharif Muhammad, who had not come in the house for a visit this time, and shook her head at him angrily. Sharif Muhammad Chacha looked down at his hands, muttering something under his breath.

My mother, her hands on my shoulders, said, "Sadee, this is not the way I want things to be."

"Why are you crying, Amee?" I asked.

"Because, Sadee, now life will be backward for you and me. They are taking you away from me, my darling. Macee will take you to your *dada*'s house today instead of me. When you get there, Macee will come home. But you will stay there. With them."

"No!" I started to cry, louder than she, blocking out the words she offered to explain the unexplainable.

"From now on, the car will bring you to visit me for a few hours. Every week, the way we used to go and visit them. But at the end of your visit, you will return to your *dada* and *dadi*. Their home will be yours, too. It always has been, I suppose. But now, I have been told, our time is up. I have tried and tried to avoid this moment. To delay it at least. Never doubt that. But I have failed, Sadee." She tried to wipe the tears from my face, using her *dupatta*, but she couldn't keep up with the fountain that flowed. "This isn't my wish, Sadee. It is the way things will be. Not the way I want them to be. If I could, I would do anything to change it. But it's not in my power." Her voice was hard now, her hands on my shoulders tightening. She pulled me to her again and then pushed me away from her, toward the driver who handed me over to Macee, already seated in the car. Sharif Muhammad Chacha, avoiding his sister's angry glare, took the bag I had not noticed from my mother's hand.

I tried to get back out of the car, now howling, but Macee held me back, her face wet, too, her voice trying to soothe. Through the grip of her arms, I barely heard her brother, Sharif Muhammad Chacha, say to my mother, "Deena Bibi, forgive me."

"Forgive *you*? Sharif Muhammad Chacha, you, of all people, have nothing to ask forgiveness for. This is all the result of my own hastiness. If I had listened to you—" Her voice, muffled by the tears she was trying to contain, broke off. Then she shook her head vigorously. "No. That won't do. If I had listened to you, Sharif Muhammad Chacha, then there would be no reason for these tears, which I would not trade for anything. Whatever bitterness is in them is outweighed by their sweetness." She kneeled down and reached into the car to take my hand. With it, she stroked her own face, letting me feel the wetness of her tears. "These tears that we are shedding, Sadee, let them fall. Can you taste them, Sadee, these tears of love?" I frowned, my howls subsiding into sobs, not understanding what she meant, opening my mouth to test the salty wetness with my tongue. "No, Sadee, not with your tongue. Close your eyes, my son, close them as I close mine, so that you can taste the tears with your heart." I watched her close her eyes and then felt my own fall shut. "Go beyond the bitterness and the pain of this moment, Sadee." Her hand was on my chest, rubbing it and patting. "Shh— stay still as you shed these tears." There was a long moment of silence. Even my sobbing had stopped. "Do you feel it, Sadee? Do you feel what I feel? The sweetness? Hiding under the bitter? That's the sweetness of my love for you—of your love for me. Can you taste it? In the fullness of your heart?"

I understood what she said without understanding the words. My heart full, tears streaming down my own face, I nodded.

"These tears are the proof, Sadee, that there is love in the world. Tears are only bitter when we cry selfishly for ourselves. When we deny and forget the sweet love that tears are made of. When we let our sorrow turn to anger. When people cry for each other, it is a good thing. Always remember that and never try to suppress the tears that flow from the love in your heart. Let them fall, these sweet tears, and remember that you are a human being, connected to all other human beings. When you cry for others—remember how we cry in Muharram?—you are opening your heart to God, who must see what we do and weep for us, too, for the suffering we cause to one another and to ourselves. Do you understand, Sadee?"

I nodded.

"Whether or not you do now, you will someday. That is the secret we are born to learn. The secret of the sweetness of tears." My mother let go of my hand and stepped back to shut the door of the car.

Sharif Muhammad Chacha took his place at the wheel. I felt the driver's door slam shut, the engine coming to life at the turn of his key, and then we pulled away, my face turned backward, eyes fixed on my mother, already turning to go into the house, the corner of her *dupatta* raised to blot her cheeks.

On the day I became a part of his household, I remember my grandfather saying, "You are where you belong, Sadiq. You are a big boy, now. A man. You don't need your mother anymore. There is nothing to cry about."

That day, my grandparents initiated a strategy of distraction—calling on a servant to go out and buy me ice cream—that would form the foundation of my new identity, a rich little boy surrounded by a rich little boy's toys and indulgences. This was who I learned to be, which was different from who I had been before. My weekly visits to my mother were a source of agony for me and for her—a repetition of that first wrenching away. So, I became complicit in my grandparents' efforts to distract me, allowing them to devise excuses—special treats and outings carefully timed to interfere with those appointments with my mother—which made the time between those visits stretch until I hardly saw her at all.

Until, one day, my mother came to see me. I was struck by the difference in the way we sat, she on one of the giant sofas in the living room and I on another. She was still a visitor to this mansion, while I had grown to be one of its most important residents. She'd come to say that she was getting married. To the crocodile next door. She told me that she was leaving Pakistan to go with him to America. There were a few more tears then. Bitter, not sweet, shed only in passing. Luckily, my grandparents had many diversions planned to distract me from the pain of that final parting.

Instead of the old school close to the house that I had lived in with my mother, I began to attend the best school in Karachi. And realized that my family name—a name that could be found on billboards for various businesses and products around the city—was like what Kennedy might mean here. Or Rockefeller. The kind of name that evokes admiration, envy, respect, and resentment. I began to understand who my grandfather was—a man of humble beginnings, who had arrived in Pakistan after Partition, with his wife and son and daughter, with barely the clothes on their backs. Within a few years, he had created an empire of wealth.

But he still tried to be humble—as humble as his wealth allowed him to be. He was a philanthropist, opening schools for the poor, and hospitals. He prayed all of his five prayers, three times a day, as Shias do. And fasted in Ramzan. In Muharram, he slept on the floor and ate no meat, so strong was his love for the House of the Prophet. Wealth and piety—impossible, they say, to reconcile the two—my grandfather worked hard to balance both.

I never went to women's *majlis*es in Muharram anymore—the one at my grandparents' house took place in the mornings, when I was at school. Instead, I went to men's *majlis*es at night with my grandfather—to gatherings of men, some of whom cried as loudly and unashamedly as the women did by day. We would sit right in front of the *zakir*'s chair—not because we arrived early. Rather, because when my grandfather's figure appeared at the entry to the hall, men cleared a path for him, waving him forward, fawningly, until he was seated in the favored position, which, because of his wealth, he had grown accustomed to expecting. On Ashura, every year, my uncle, Jaffer's father, took us to the *juloos,* where I was now able to participate without fainting. I wasn't afraid anymore. Of anything.

At the side of those processions, I saw another way that people remembered Karbala—those who believed that the shedding of blood through self-inflicted grief was a waste, who organized blood drives every year. As we grew older, Jaffer and the other boys and I scoffed at those who donated blood at these stations, thinking them weak and afraid of the manly rituals of *matham* that those who we considered to be *real* men, brave and bold, practiced.

Abbas Ali Mubarak, Dada, rarely spoke of my mother and never about his son. His wife, my grandmother, was less reticent. "Your father was the sweetest boy—just like you, Sadiq. Losing him was like losing my heart. Until you came to live with us, I was only half-alive. Your mother kept you away from us, from your rightful place in your father's home, making you live in that hovel of a house that she came from. So we waited, Sadiq. I prayed and I prayed. And now, your mother has gone. To build a new life for herself. Over there," she waved her hand, "in America. With that new husband of hers, Umar, that Sunni man with his Sunni name. Ah, well, that doesn't matter. Your life is here, now. With us, in your father's home. The way it was meant to be. How happy I am, that the son of my son, my very own, is back where he should be. You *are* happy here, aren't you, Sadiq?"

"Are we going shopping, Dadi? You said you would buy me a bicycle. And that Sharif Muhammad would teach me how to ride."

"Yes, of course. Anything, Sadiq. It makes me happy to see you happy."

Already I had stopped calling Sharif Muhammad, the driver, *chacha*—a title of respect that means "uncle." I had no need to. I was the master of the house, above having to give respect to mere servants.

At first, Sharif Muhammad chided me, "You have stopped calling me *chacha*, Sadiq Baba. The way your mother taught you. The way she addressed me."

I ignored him and his references to my mother. I had to. To remember her, with him, was also to remember how he took me away from her.

Almost every day, Jaffer would come to visit. I had not realized before that he lived just across the street, in a mansion that was a smaller version of the one I now lived in. Together, we would take over our grandparents' garden, shouting and running wildly in a way I had been too timid to do before—building forts and holding battles, sometimes as brothers in arms and sometimes as mortal enemies, using flower petals for weapons and unripe mangoes, jungle *jalebi*s, and *badaam*s for booty as we waged war, against each other and also against other children, whose parents dropped by to visit my grandfather and pay their respects—supplicants who came to curry favor, to ask for advice, jobs, guidance, references.

The first time my mother came back to Pakistan, a year and a half after she had left, she came to see me at my grandparents' house. She didn't come alone; she was carrying a baby with her, who she said was my sister. The baby cooed at me and cuddled up to my mother, tugging on her *dupatta* for a game of peekaboo. I was filled with rage and refused to speak. She came again the next year, this time without the baby, Sabah. But the same rage filled the room and she cried when she left. I refused to see her after that, refused to speak to her when she phoned from America.

In my grandparents' home, I had the world at my feet—quite literally. Every day, a different hawker was invited into the gates of our compound. Jaffer and I would inspect the wares they laid out for us, taste of their goods, or avail ourselves of their services, with no worries about who would pay—this was a house where the adults set no limits on the children, and all accounts, the hawkers knew well, were settled with no questions asked. There was the *kilona-walla* on Monday, the toy man who sold old-fashioned string tops; squirt guns; paddle balls; ugly little baby dolls with blond, plastic, painted-on hair; cap-guns; balloons; and little pieces of junk that would pass no safety regulations that any sane person would have ever subjected them to. We bought slingshots from him, which we practiced at every chance we got, aiming for a line of old cans that Jaffer ordered the servants—a full retinue of them, assigned to follow us around and see to our needs and wants—to set up in the driveway, hoping to perfect our skill enough to shoot at something live one day.

Jaffer even managed to do it once, killing a bird—a sparrow, I think it was, a small, undistinguished specimen—which the driver, Sharif Muhammad, lectured Jaffer against killing, telling him that hunting was only allowed in Islam if you ate what you killed, because life was sacred and even the lives of the lowliest of God's creatures could not be taken lightly. So, I remember with disgust, Jaffer asked the cook to marinate and grill the dead little bird and managed to swallow a couple of bites before throwing up all over the new shoes his mother had sent for from London.

The horse handler passed through our neighborhood on Tuesday afternoons, giving us slow, plodding horses to ride slowly, ploddingly around the neighborhood, while the servants followed us on foot to make sure that no one stole us away to sell to a beggarmaster who would maim us in order to increase the return on his investment—this was more Jaffer's worry than mine. Jaffer had never been anywhere on foot, nor commuted by rickshaw, like I had with my mother. Without the glass windows of chauffeur-driven cars to keep him safely separate, he was afraid of the evidence of poverty that was everywhere in Karachi's streets.

On Wednesdays, we'd wait for another hawker, who would sell us *buddhi ka baal*, old-lady hair—a wonderfully disgusting name for cotton candy. On Thursdays, it was the *kulfi* man, who sold a heavenly sort of ice cream on a stick, set and frozen in aluminum molds, sold from a pushcart loaded with wooden barrels that smoked when he opened them. The monkey-man came on Saturdays—twirling a handheld drum and jerking on the poor monkey's leash to make him dance, bow, scrape, and gesture to accompany the silly story his master narrated. Whatever pity rose up in my heart for the monkey, I smothered, trying hard not to remember the favorite old story and the voice—my mother's—that had told it.

Those vendors and what they had to offer were merely the daily, routine indulgences that now defined life. My grandparents also took me to Europe every summer. We shopped at Hamleys, in London, for remote-control cars and train sets and racetracks, watched movies in Leicester Square, and fed pigeons in Trafalgar. In Paris, at the top of the Eiffel Tower, I looked down at the world and wondered at how small it was.

One year, Jaffer and his family went to America, a place I longed to see and yet hated the thought of at the same time—its whole population, in my mind, reduced to one woman, my mother, and one man, the crocodile. Jaffer told me about the buildings, the big cars, the roads, the freeways, and the bridges. Once, he made the mistake of telling me about the toll roads and booths he'd gone through. I was intrigued with the idea of charging money for the use of roads. One lazy afternoon, when there were only servants around to stop us—which was no impediment at all—I suggested that we build a barricade in the road in front of the house that no one would be able to pass through without paying the requisite toll—money we had no need for at all, but that was beside the point.

We used big, heavy rocks, which we found a few houses down, in the plot where construction for a new house had begun and been abandoned, and spent quite a bit of time and energy lugging those rocks, boulders really, closer to the house, drafting the labor of the servants in our effort, directing them to line the rocks up, effectively blocking passage for any car that might drive by. It's amazing, now, to think that no car actually did pass through during the whole time it took us to complete our ragged blockade. After we were finished, we sat down at the side of the road and waited.

Some minutes later, a car came by—most private cars in the area that I lived in were driven, during the day, by chauffeurs rather than by their owners, and this, we could tell by the shabby and traditional clothing of the man behind the wheel—was one of them. The driver of the car stopped abruptly upon seeing the barricade of rather treacherous rocks in his way, as well as the little boys—Jaffer and me—who flagged him down using an old piece of red cloth that Sharif Muhammad used to polish the car. Jaffer explained the situation, speaking with an authority that comes with class and privilege—throwing in enough English words to make everything sound official—and the poor, old, bearded driver moved his skull cap around on his head for a few seconds, scratching, before pulling out a wad of notes from the dirty side pocket of his *kurtha* and peeling a *paan*-stained one-rupee note to hand over to Jaffer, who took it and scratched *his* head, as he realized it would take some time to clear the way, since it was blocked with rocks instead of the striped hydraulic arm that he had described to me. The poor old driver waited patiently while Jaffer and I made the servants earn the rupee we had just extorted, lugging a portion of those rocks out of the way with heavy breaths—just enough for the skilled old driver to wave his hand cheerfully and shout: *"Bas. Teek heh,"* before pulling through with a screech into first gear.

The next driver was a little more skeptical, but still polite. And the one after that—for whom Jaffer raised the toll to two rupees, given the relative ease with which these men seemed to be convinced of our authority, and the amount of labor moving those rocks back and forth entailed, for the servants, not for us—cursed at us, using language that made my ears turn red, involving, as it did, both our mothers and our sisters. Jaffer met the volley with a string of equally colorful epithets, and the two of them rallied back and forth for a bit before the driver jerked the car into reverse and bumped backward up the street, waving his fist at us all the way.

Altogether, we made about fifteen rupees before Phupijan, Jaffer's mother, came running out, screaming and yelling, having been informed of our activities by the big-mouthed cook, who must have come out for a smoke and seen what we were doing and knew that *his* job, at least, depended on pleasing adult taste buds rather than allaying children's tantrums. The money was nothing to us, but well worth the effort for the number of times we laughed later, marveling at our own audacity.

When I was fifteen, I learned the truth about how my father had died, though I didn't accept it as the truth then. And not for many years after. Jaffer and I got into a fight, a very bad one—I don't remember over what. We were trading insults of the usual kind lobbed back and forth between boys. I pushed him, hard. He fell on his wrist, breaking the new watch Dada had given him for his birthday. A digital watch, with a calculator on it.

He was furious, standing up to rush at me with his fists stretched out in front of him, shouting, "You bastard! Look what you've done! You're a bloody, mad bastard, Sadiq! Just like your father! And your mother is a whore, marrying that son-of-a-bitch Sunni bastard. No wonder your father killed himself!"

I didn't even hear him. Not at that moment. I was fending off his blows as he shouted the words. Dada came running at the sound of the commotion we were causing in the lounge.

"Jaffer! Shut your mouth! Get out! Go home! Now!" Dada shouted as I'd never heard him shout before.

The expression on his face, the fury in his voice, made me stop and turn, my anger at Jaffer suddenly dissolved, to look into Dada's face very carefully. His eyes would not meet mine. I reviewed what Jaffer had said, what I hadn't really listened to as I warded him off. Dada turned and left the room. It took me a few hours to go and find him, to ask him about what my cousin had said.

"Don't listen to him, Sadiq. It's all nonsense, what Jaffer said. You boys! What horrible things you'll say out of anger. Lies, all lies."

I pretended—to him and to myself—that I was convinced and reassured. If Dada was lying, covering up the truth, a part of me decided that I didn't want to know. Jaffer came over later and apologized. I told him I was sorry about his watch. He never raised the subject again.

Neither did I, too distracted by the gift Dada bought for me the very next day. A car of my own, though I was still too young to legally drive it. Dada sent Sharif Muhammad to obtain a license for me—illegally, bribe in hand—and, after Sharif Muhammad taught me to drive, Jaffer and I were free to wander around town on our own, to pursue a suddenly feverish social life that began to involve other licenses that my grandfather did not approve of when he found out. I am ashamed, now, to think of how I fought with him—an old man who had given me everything and anything I wanted. But I thought I was a man. He himself had told me I was. I spent the money he gave me as if it were no object, buying gifts for my friends, picking up the tabs at restaurants, buying booze and hashish for everyone. Soon, Jaffer was no longer allowed to go out with me. But no one could stop *me*. I was the youngest at every party and felt I had something to prove. The slightest provocation was all it took for me to come to blows. I deserved the reputation I had—racing my car against others', equally indulged—for being wild and reckless.

One day, I drove home from a party in the early hours of the morning, in a thoroughly inebriated state. I was veering and swerving my way home, missing turns and running stoplights. I turned fast onto one street, too fast and too late to stop when I saw them. A woman and a small child.

I remember the sound of the screech of the brakes. I remember her face, caught in the headlights, her scream, the sickening thud of steel hitting vulnerable flesh, her body flying and then disappearing off to my side. The car was stopped. I pushed open the door and stood to see what—who—I'd hit. The woman was crumpled on the ground, the child kneeling beside her, howling. Men started to spill out from a mosque up the street, where the dawn prayer had just ended. I heard shouting. Someone stopped to check on my victim. The rest of the men gathered menacingly into a clump, heading in my direction. I didn't think. I jumped into the car, turned the engine, and fled, remembering nothing of the rest of the way home.

When I got there, I honked for the *chowkidar*—the gatekeeper—to let me in at the gate. Bleary-eyed and resigned—he was used to my odd-hour homecomings, along with the regular payments I made him to lie to my grandfather about them—he opened the gate. I drove in and parked on the driveway, noticing, for the first time, the race going on in my chest, between heartbeats and ragged breaths. Sharif Muhammad came in from his prayers just behind me, walking into the compound by the pedestrian gate. He saw me sitting in the car, my head pressed against the steering wheel.

"Sadiq Baba? Are you all right?" he asked loudly, knocking at my window.

I raised my head and looked at him. I must have looked wild-eyed. I didn't answer him. He reached to open my door, which was unlocked, not even properly closed.

"What's wrong, Sadiq Baba? You look like you've seen a ghost."

I sat there, unable to move.

He sighed, a long, hard sigh of disapproval. The *chowkidar* had not felt obligated to keep my secrets from Sharif Muhammad, who lectured me regularly about my drinking, words I ignored, words I laughed at, in his face. Sharif Muhammad reached into the car and helped me get out, mistaking the reason for my shaky state, understandably—the smell of my breath must have been all the evidence he needed. He was walking me toward the door of the house, trying to get me to speak all the while, when he stopped, suddenly, at the front of the car.

"What's this, Sadiq Baba?" he asked sharply.

I looked down at where he was pointing—at the front bumper of the car, bashed and bloody. I heard myself moan and realized that I had been moaning all along.

"That's blood! Whose blood, Sadiq Baba?" He squeezed the arm of mine that he held, hard enough to hurt. "What did you do?"

I started crying, unable to answer. I closed my eyes and saw them again. The woman on the pavement. The child kneeling beside her.

Sharif Muhammad shook me and asked again, "Whose blood? Who did you hit? Where did it happen?"

I mumbled an answer, suddenly remembering the street I'd been on. In Karachi, directions are given by landmark, because most of the streets have no name. So, I gave him directions that way—naming an ice cream shop, a newsstand, a bakery as signposts for him to follow.

"Did you run away, Sadiq Baba?"

His question was a formality. Later, I would be ashamed at the presumption in his words. He knew damned well I had run, without having to ask. And it didn't surprise him that I had.

He left me at the front door of the house, shoving me inside.

"I will go. I will see what happened." His voice was harsh and gentle at the same time, waylaying the objections he thought I might offer.

This time, at least, I didn't lower myself to his expectations. I nodded gratefully, still shaking. This was a line that he offered, I knew, to keep me from drowning. "Yes. Yes, go see, Sharif Muhammad. See if they need anything." As soon as I said the words, I moaned again, out loud. The tone of my voice sickened me. The privilege in it. The patronage.

I made my way to bed and fell asleep in my air-conditioned room, oblivious to the heat of the rising sun, oblivious to the life or death of the woman I'd hit, to the grief of the child I may have orphaned.

I woke up from my dreamless, pampered sleep and made my way out into the lounge. Both of their backs toward me, I came upon Sharif Muhammad, returned from his errand, filling my grandfather in on the consequences of what I'd done.

"She's dead. Leaving behind a little boy."

"How old is the boy?" Dada asked.

"Four or five. Younger than Sadiq Baba was when he came to live with you."

Dada stopped short his pacing, his hands behind his back. He frowned at Sharif Muhammad's words.

Sharif Muhammad didn't flinch. He said, "I left the boy, still crying, in the care of the old imam of the *masjid*. The *masjid* on the street where his mother was killed. They will try to find out who she is—was. Who her people are."

"Hmm. Yes, the boy must be restored to those he belongs to. We'll do what we can for him." Dada resumed his pacing, already moving on from the matter of the boy.

Sharif Muhammad, too, switched gears. "And what about Sadiq Baba?"

My grandfather frowned again, unhappy with his servant's tone of voice—a tone I had never heard him use before with his employer. Defiant. Interrogative. Peremptory.

"It seems you have an opinion you wish to express, Sharif Muhammad."

Sharif Muhammad took a step forward. He took his skull cap off his head and crumpled it in his hands. "Yes, Mubarak Sayt. I have something more to say." He stopped, as if to line up words he had amassed in an arsenal he had long waited to deploy.

"Then say it, Sharif Muhammad. Say what you will." Dada's voice was menacingly stern, belying the invitation he offered.

"It is time, Sayt. To reckon with the dirty deed you sent me to do for you more than nine years ago. This is something I should have said then, but I didn't. You have been a good master. Fair and just. I have not forgotten any of your generosities over the years. I carry them with me, always, in a heart that is grateful. You took care of my sister, found her employment when Deena Bibi left for *Amreeka*. But what you made me a party to, when you took Sadiq Baba away from his mother, was not right."

"Sharif Muhammad. The matter is none of your concern." Dada's voice was final. I thought he would stop there. Sharif Muhammad didn't budge. He stood, silently, forcing Dada to utter more. "I was in my rights. The boy belonged here. You are a religious man. You know that what I say is true. Ask any mullah. Your Sunni ones will tell you the same, I am sure."

"I don't care what any mullah says," Sharif Muhammad said. "I have a mind. And I know how piety and religion can mask the truth of what justice calls for. You took that boy away from his mother. That was wrong. You caused his mother grief—a good woman, who did nothing to deserve what life handed her. And now *kismat* has played out its retribution. Your grandson is the reason another boy's mother has been taken from him."

"These are matters you don't understand, Sharif Muhammad. The law was on my side. The law of the nation and the law of God."

"The law of the nation? What is that? Nothing but a plaything of big people. The law of God? When law is separated from justice, Sayt, that is not the law of any god I worship. That is when the true test of faith and wisdom comes—that is our opportunity to shine the light of humanity and compassion on the misfortunes we inflict on one another. There are no laws you can quote me that will change the way I see it. And what have you done with the boy? By separating him from the love of his mother? If heaven, for him, lies under her feet—as the Prophet, peace be upon him, said—then you have kept him far away from heaven, casting him on the path to hell. Send him to her, Sayt. He is out of control. Even Asma Bibi, your own daughter, will not let her son spend time with him anymore. The tragedy he has caused today is only the beginning—this, I promise. The boy needs his mother. Has needed her all these years. Send him back to her, I beg you. It may be too late already to undo the damage. But give him a chance at least. All your wealth and possessions *have* done and *will* do nothing for him. He is a coward. He ran over a mother and ran away from what he did. He will always run away."

"Enough, Sharif Muhammad! You are a good man. You have always served me well. For this, I will forgive you today's impudence. Leave me now!" Dada roared.

But what Sharif Muhammad said must have had an effect. Two weeks later, Dada put me on a plane to America. At the airport in Los Angeles, I saw my mother for the first time in six years. She was with her husband, the crocodile, and her daughter, Sabah. When she hugged me—her stiff-backed stranger of a son—her face was wet with tears. She took my hand and put it on her face, smiling through them. "See? These are sweet tears, Sadiq. So very, very sweet." I stepped back from her, because she was so unfamiliar. Even the smell of her was foreign. But she welcomed me into her home. She and Sabah and Umar, the crocodile. But it was *their* home. Not mine.

While I was there, only a year—until I graduated, early, from high school and went away from them to college—I met Jo's mother. Angela. I was still fifteen, new to America, living with my mother though I had already, long before, learned to live without her.

When I was done telling Jo my story, on that day she was born to me, I looked up to catch an expression on her face that was plain and easy to understand, despite my having never learned to read her stranger's features. She had come to ask who I was. And the answer I had given her was one that she did not understand. I realized, almost immediately, that what I had told her would drive her away and out of my reach.

Since then, I have tried and tried to call her. I keep thinking of more I should have said and also of what I shouldn't. Her departure had been abrupt, as sudden as her arrival, coming before it was my turn to listen. That, too, keeps me awake at night—the questions I would have asked, which surely I had the right to ask, but which she gave me no opportunity to voice.

The boxes in my living room are all gone. I have delayed my trip twice already. Today, when I called her, she picked up. She was sorry, but there was nothing more she wanted from me. She was glad to have met me, she said, very graciously. But that was it.

Drop, drop, slow tears,
And bathe those beauteous feet,
Which brought from Heaven
The news and Prince of Peace.

Phineas Fletcher, "A Litany"

Jo

For a while, that day with Sadiq, I lost myself—dizzy in the spiral of his stories inside of stories. It took a lot to keep my face clear of all that I felt in response to what he told me—pity, disgust, revulsion. Until the end, when his eyes—dark brown and dominant—came back into the room and found mine, staking a claim I had no intention of granting. I left him as fast as I could, chased away by the questions I didn't give him a chance to ask.

I knew what those questions would have been. About my mother. But I didn't want to talk about her. I didn't want to hear about her, either. Not from him. To see her through his eyes would have been too much—making her as alien to me as he was.

He might have asked about Dad, too. Scenes with him flashed through my mind. Going into his workshop when I was little, when I knew Mom was too tired to listen to me. He'd be sawing or hammering away. When he'd see me, he'd put down his tools, clear a space on the counter for me to sit on, lift me up to place me there. I'd start talking. He'd resume working and listen—his hands busy, his head nodding. His hands would pause as he looked at me, from time to time, smiling, laughing, or frowning to let me know he was still paying attention. He didn't talk much himself. His favorite joke was that I never gave him a chance to. Eventually, the sight of those hands working would catch my attention so fully that I'd run out of words.

One day, when Dad and I were in the car on our way to the library, we stopped at a red light and saw a homeless guy standing at the corner. He was holding up a sign—HOMELESS VET. Dad pulled the car over and took the guy with us into the coffee shop around the corner. My father bought him a meal, me sitting next to Dad, sipping on a milk shake, my eyes staring at the long-haired, bearded, scary-looking stranger across from us at the table. When we were done, we took the guy back to his corner and went on to the library as if nothing had happened.

Except, when he turned the key to start the car, Dad said, very softly, "That could have been me. It would have been. But for your mother. She saved me. Brought me to Christ. Gave me a reason to live. Two reasons. You and your brother."

My brother. Sadiq would have asked if I had any brothers or sisters. And Chris was off-limits. Because of what I'd promised Mom.

The minute I got back to my dorm room from Sadiq's place, while they were still fresh in my mind, I wrote down all the words I could remember, the foreign ones from his story, adding them to the lists of words in my special notebook, which I'd packed and brought with me from home, on a fresh page, under a new heading: Urdu—though I remembered he'd mentioned Arabic, too, and wasn't sure which words were which.

Amee	mother
Dadi	grandmother
Dada	grandfather
Zakira	preacher?
Rickshaw	motor tricycle
Majlis	?
Mushk	water bag
Noha	religious song—sad
Muharram	month
Shia	
Sunni	
Jamun	kind of fruit
Chacha	uncle
Dupatta	scarf?

I wrote down names, too, which was something I hadn't done on any of the lists I'd made before. Sharif Muhammad. Deena. Jafar. Abbas. Husain. Sakina. I wrote them as a way to unpack the images Sadiq had loaded on me, not because I wanted to remember the people he'd talked about.

When I was done with the new list, I turned over the pages to look at the old ones—collections of words in Tagalog, Mandarin, Swahili, and Spanish. These were gifts from my grandmother—

not the paper or the notebook I had written them in, but the words themselves.

Grandma Faith, whose husband left her when my mother was little, began traveling the world when her son—my uncle Ron— was away at college, and when her daughter—my mother— started high school. She left Mom behind in Great-grandpa and Great-grandma Peltons' care.

Mom said that Grandma Faith was a gypsy at heart. "I suppose it's in her blood." She sighed. "She was born out there," Mom said, waving her hand around vaguely, lumping all places beyond our borders together—all of them a little scary. Borders were some- thing we were acutely aware of, living in the suburbs of San Diego. But only as something that should be sealed tighter than they were. We'd never been across to Mexico. Never gone out of the country at all, until the big trip Chris and I took that summer, before I started college.

Grandma Faith was an oddball in our family, exuding an exotic air that she must have absorbed from years of traveling. She didn't like to be called Grandma. At least not in English. She gave herself a new title every year, teaching me and Chris the word for "grand- mother" in whatever language she'd spent time learning on her most recent travels.

One year, she was Abuela Faith. She'd been in Central America that year. The next year, the year she spent some months in East Africa, she was Bibi Faith, which is how you say "grandmother" in Swahili. Another year, coming back from the Philippines, she was Lola Faith.

Every time Grandma Faith came home, she taught us the new

word we were supposed to call her and listened to us repeat it, wincing a little at the way Chris mangled the words, nodding her approval at the sounds I made.

"You've got an ear for languages, Jo," she'd tell me. "It's a gift. Some people have got it and some don't." Then she'd quiz us on the words she'd taught before. The different words for "grandmother." Numbers, one to ten. Colors. Hello and good-bye. I always remembered the words, making lists in my notebook from when I was ten, studying them before Abuela/Bibi/Lola Faith was due home for a visit. Chris never did. It was a game to him, the novelty wearing off quickly so that he'd forget and slip back into calling her Grandma after a day or two. Not me. I'd keep it up until she'd leave on another trip.

Last year, just home from Taiwan, she was Wàipó Faith.

"That's maternal grandmother, mind you," Grandma Faith had said. "There's another word for your grandma on your dad's side. A lot of languages are like that—you can tell exactly how someone's related to you, on your mother's side or your father's, by blood or by marriage—by what you call them, all the relationships very specifically defined, the words themselves like a family tree. I guess that says something about the importance of family in some cultures. Something we could all stand to emulate. Instead of just talking, all the time, about *family values*—only thing I ever saw being valued when I've heard those two words getting thrown around is the act of not minding your own business."

That comment, like a lot of what Grandma Faith said, set Mom's eyes rolling in her brother's direction. Once, I heard Uncle Ron say to my mother, "Mom just has a talent for going native, Angie. I suppose that's a good thing, in her line of work. But I know how you feel. I worry sometimes. Just like you do. That she goes too far—approaching her work like some kind of evangelical version of Margaret Meade." That was a reference that went over my head, until I looked it up later. Margaret Meade, the woman who made anthropology as much about learning *from* other cultures as learning *about* them, making all values relative, leaving no room for the absolute. "It also makes her a bit of a stranger to us, I suppose. I love her. But I don't always understand where she's coming from." He chuckled. Mom just shook her head.

Grandma Faith was the reason I'd transferred from Christ Academy, where the foreign language program wasn't that great, to the public high school, where it was. I'd taken four years of Spanish and French there and counted myself as pretty fluent in both. Grandma Faith was also the reason I had decided to go to college in Chicago, to a university famous for the wide choice of foreign languages it offered—ready to venture out of Europe, linguistically speaking, and into more exotic, less Romantic languages involving whole new sets of letters and sounds that I'd have to memorize and master.

I ran an eye down the list of words I'd collected in Swahili, one of the classes I was enrolled in, which was starting the next day, a long list because of a trip Chris and I had taken earlier in the summer.

Right after high school graduation, before I'd asked Mom the truth about the color of my eyes, Chris and I had gone to Africa with a bunch of kids from church and camp, Uncle Ron in charge, to meet up with Grandma Faith and the missionary organization she'd been working with for the last few years. Grandma Faith coordinated the trip on the African end, to a slum town on the outskirts of Nairobi in Kenya. They spoke Swahili there, so, of course, Grandma Faith made us call her Bibi Faith. The mission had been simple. To give shoes to kids.

"It's not that there's anything wrong with going barefoot," Grandma Faith had said. "I think there's something true and honest about having your bare feet grounded on the earth. Huck Finn had it right when he resisted getting 'civilized' by the widow, kicking off his shoes every chance he got. Except, for some of these kids, here in this town, it's a matter of life and death. This isn't the banks of the Mississippi. Right near here, there's a huge garbage pit, where a lot of trash from the city gets dumped. Some of the kids have to go through those garbage pits, looking for food and stuff to salvage and sell. And in those pits, there are needles—infected needles. These kids get stuck by one of those and they can get AIDS or all kinds of other diseases. So shoes are important for them. I know that foot-washing has become a fashionable thing to do on missions. But here, it's not just about humbling yourself, or reenacting a scene from the Bible—though that's definitely part of the experience. Here, you're providing a necessary service, a real-life mission, not just something symbolic."

Before we handed out the shoes, we washed and disinfected the feet of those little kids, the way Jesus washed the feet of the disciples at the Last Supper. It *was* humbling. Beautiful. Like something right out of the Bible. Some of the kids would laugh and laugh, because our hands on their feet tickled. And, at the end, the way those kids' eyes lit up when we showed them how to tie their shoelaces!

I helped Bibi Faith—all the kids here called her that—with her work in the mobile clinic on wheels, parked in the slum. She saw patients and vaccinated kids, making even the most frightened ones, the little babies, laugh at the voices that she put into the mouths of the silly puppets she used to distract them. I knew this was what I wanted to do—not the nursing, because needles made me queasy. Just the interaction. The communication across languages. I understood why Grandma Faith had such a hard time staying home.

I didn't want to go home, either, deciding not to leave with Chris and Uncle Ron and the other kids from church, as we'd planned to do at the end of two weeks in Kenya.

During the second week of our stay, I told Chris, "Bibi Faith is going up north, to Ethiopia. To some villages out in the Omo River Valley."

"I know," said Chris—red-faced, nose peeling from sunburn, the same way mine was. He was thinner, too, because he'd had a hard time with the food.

"I want to go with her."

"What? PPSYC's starting right after we get back. You've got to come home."

"I'll skip camp this year."

"But— Mom and Dad need us at camp."

Mom and Dad hadn't come with us to Africa. Not that Mom had seemed interested anyway. She'd used camp as an excuse—all the preparations that needed to be done before it started, all the activities she was planning for the Progress Course this year. "They'll do fine without us."

"Us?"

"Stay back with me, Chris. I already talked to Bibi Faith and Uncle Ron. They're okay with it."

"But— I want to go home. I mean— it's been a great experience. But I want to go home now."

Chris had been more homesick than me. But he'd enjoyed himself with the kids—able to communicate with them without words. By the time I'd find the words in my phrase book to ask them their names, he'd already be cracking them up with his funny faces, kicking a ball around with them in the dirt.

"Come on, Chris. It'll be awesome to stay back. They speak different languages out in the villages. We'll get to learn new words."

"You mean *you'll* get to learn new words. I'm not the nerd with the notebook. No way, Jo. I'm going home. Just like we planned. Two weeks. That's enough for me."

In the end, I wasn't the only one to stay back. Uncle Ron stayed, too—along with the team he'd unexpectedly brought with him. His camera crew, his makeup man, his production team—a whole media entourage that I hadn't realized his television show had grown into. They were the reason the trip ended on a bit of a sour note.

Everything was fine at first. I saw Bibi Faith crinkle her nose only a few times when she watched some of the interviews that Uncle Ron's team was engaged in filming and collecting for broadcast later. Once, while we were still in Nairobi, on the shoe mission, we found her in the clinic, muttering to herself, and then to me and Chris when she saw we were there. "Complaining! Actually complaining, because the kids are smiling too much! *Get me some kids that look sad*, he says! Did you hear him? That idiot who calls himself a producer? *They shouldn't look so happy*, he says!"

Chris shifted his feet around and said, "Uncle Ron said

they're going to show some of this stuff on TV to get people to donate money to your mission. Guess people give more if the kids look sad."

Grandma/Bibi Faith nodded, furiously, raising her voice out of mutter mode and into pure indignation. "Pity! That's what they want people to feel!"

"Well—if it works, why not? If it gets people to give more?" I asked.

"But it's not the truth! Do you know I actually heard that man ask one of the children to *make* a sad face? One of the most amazing things about these children—and others like them all over the world—is their capacity to smile and laugh. They live in garbage pits for God's sake! That's what they should do a story about. To get people to think about how these children, who have none of the things that people back home think are absolute necessities, how they can smile and laugh and look so damned happy." She trailed off, falling back into a mutter.

Later, in one of the villages on the Ethiopian side of the border with Kenya—an amazing place, with people right out of *National Geographic,* half-naked, bodies painted in all kinds of colors, and those women with plates in their lips—Bibi Faith really blew up. This time, at Uncle Ron and one of the reporters, who was doing an interview with her. He kept asking Bibi Faith about how many children had been saved. Three times, she answered, telling him how many vaccinations she'd given and from what diseases they'd now be protected.

Frowning and shaking his head, the man said, "No, Mrs. Rogers. I'm asking about how many kids were *Saved*. In the Christian sense." It wasn't the first time he'd asked. It's what he'd been asking every day, keeping a tally that seemed to be the focus of all the filming.

Right there, on camera, Grandma/Bibi Faith started yelling, "I've had it up to here with this obsession with numbers—with all you mighty 'Christian soldiers' and your body counts! I told you to lay off of that here, in this village. They don't take kindly to it. We promised the elders here that we wouldn't proselytize. They'll kick us out and nobody else from our group will be allowed back and if these kids die from lack of vaccinations, it'll be all your pushy, pushy, fault!"

"Take it easy, Mom," said Uncle Ron, stepping in with a forced smile and a hand on her shoulder meant to soothe, but which only made her more mad.

The reporter said, "I think you've forgotten the reason for this mission, Mrs. Rogers. It's not about the shots or the shoes. It's about Jesus."

Grandma—Bibi—Faith stomped off in a tizzy. I found her muttering to herself again, way up one of the dirt paths in the village.

"Nothing worse than the smug smell of certainty—they're all reeking with it." She waved her hands wildly, in a way that indicated not just the reporter but her own son as well.

I was quiet for a moment. "But— isn't certainty a good thing? It's the opposite of doubt," I said, thinking of the wall at camp that had been so hard to climb. "It's what faith is all about."

"Not when it makes you willfully blind to the truth. That's not faith. That's belief. A decision. A line in the sand. It's telling yourself, this is what I believe in. And anything—or anybody—that doesn't fit is the enemy."

"If faith isn't belief, then what is it?"

"To me? Faith is revelation. And in order to receive revelation you have to be open. *Belief* is about closing yourself off—a lie you tell yourself to make the world fit in with how you've decided it should be. Real faith is an action—a verb. It's truth unfolding. You have to let yourself be vulnerable to let that happen. You can't hide from it. You can't run away from it. You can't drown it out, covering your ears while you shout out declarations of *belief.* That's not faith. That's cowardice—a fear of truth, which is only scary when you're fighting to keep yourself from knowing it. Do you know what the first phrase I learn is when I go to a new place where they speak a language I don't understand?"

I shook my head, still digesting what she'd already said.

"I don't understand. I don't know," Bibi Faith said. "It's the most liberating bunch of words you can learn in any language. When you admit your own ignorance, to yourself and to others, you open the door to the kind of revelation—real faith—that I was talking about. The strangers I meet in foreign places slow down when I say those words. They start paying attention to my face, to see if I get what they're saying. It brings out the kindness in folks. I've had people—all kinds—men, women, children—literally take my hand and guide me to the place I'm asking directions for. Miles out of their way. Waiters in restaurants have chosen my meal for me—and it's always the best stuff on the menu. People will help you shop. They'll take care of you. If you let them know the truth. That you don't understand. That you're ignorant. That you're lost. It's the best part of going to a new place. Because you've admitted something that's true for all of us—whether we admit it to ourselves and to each other or not—that we're all vulnerable. It's

like—it's like going back and getting to be a kid. You're not afraid of breathing through your mouth, of letting your eyes drink everything in, wide-open—that cynical slit of the eyelids that we all have to practice and perfect in front of the bathroom mirror disappears and all those muscles in your face that you have to flex to look smart get to relax. And it's wonderful. All the pretense of adulthood melts away. It's all crystal-clear—that I don't know a damn thing about anything and that's okay. Good, in fact. Kind of like what Jesus said in Matthew: *'Unless you change and become like children, you will never enter the kingdom of heaven.'* Diving into a new place, a new language—that's the closest I've ever come to understanding what that verse means," Bibi Faith said.

After that trip to Africa, Grandma Faith decided not to work with religious organizations anymore, taking up a position with a secular medical aid group instead.

She said it was something she'd been thinking about for a long time. "With these guys, at least, I'll be able to just do the work that needs to be done," she said, "without constant interference from ignorant fools who're too much in love with the sound of their own preachy voices to really understand what Christ is about. They think evangelism is about spreading the Word by talking about it, while I think it's about *doing* it, as best I can."

I suppose that talk with Bibi Faith, back in Ethiopia, was the reason I finally asked Mom the questions that took me to Sadiq's door.

When Sadiq called that last time, I picked up. I was relieved to hear him say he was leaving. I pretended to write down the number he gave me, in Pakistan, so that I could reach him if I ever needed to. As if I ever would. I felt bad, but I think he got it. That I didn't really want to have anything to do with him. I already had a father. And even though I couldn't pretend, anymore, not to know what I knew, I didn't have to let it affect the rest of my life.

Except that it did, of course. I didn't tell him. That I dropped out of the Swahili class I'd enrolled in during the first week of school. That I signed up for an Arabic class and an Urdu one instead. I only dropped in to audit the classes at first. But I fell in love with the letters—mostly the same alphabet for both languages. The curves and the dots. The unfamiliar sounds.

The Arabic department had an assortment of professors that I got to know over the next few years. The first class I took was taught by a British man, Professor Crawley—a large man with an intimidating, snooty attitude dripping from the lines of his jowls and the sacks under his eyes, topped off with thick, black-out-of-a-bottle hair—who was old-fashioned enough to never address his students by their first name. In my first semester of Arabic, I went to his office one day to ask a question about an assignment. After he'd answered me, he leaned forward at his desk, put his chin on his hands, and asked me, in that lazy, British drawl of his, "Are you a convert?"

"Excuse me?"

"I am asking, Ms. March, if you are a convert? To Islam?"

"Oh. No. I'm Christian."

"I—see," he said, as if he'd just tasted something sour. "Then you have an Arab boyfriend?"

"Uh—no."

"That's good. They're handsome devils, some of them. But barbarians, the lot, when it comes to women. May I ask, then, why exactly you are taking Arabic?" he asked, frowning a little.

"I—uh—I love languages."

"An admirable sentiment," he said, his voice dripping with the kind of sarcasm that only a British accent could convey. "But why Arabic?"

"No particular reason."

"Hmm." His eyes, under the shadow of a pair of straggly eyebrows, narrowed with amusement. "An Ian Fleming fan, Ms. March? Or is Le Carré more to your taste?"

"Excuse me?"

"Russian would have been the choice only a few years ago. How circumspect of you to choose Arabic. See me when you're ready to discuss career options, my dear. I have some connections that might be helpful."

For Urdu, there was just one professor. A native of Minnesota, with a much milder, gentler personality than Professor Crawley. Professor Dunnett—who was tall and thin-faced, with soft, white hair—had spent many years in India and some in Pakistan. Some of the other students in his classes, Indian and Pakistani Americans trying to reconnect with their roots, said his accent was amazing. That if you listened to him with your eyes closed, you'd never know he was white. He was the one who introduced me to Devon Avenue—a long street on the other side of the city, cut up and nicknamed in sections that represented a diverse range of Chicago's ethnic populations. At the end of the first semester, he took me and the other students there. We passed the Mahatma Gandhi and Golda Meir sections of the avenue to eat in a restaurant on the Muhammad Ali Jinnah block, where the stores and restaurants had as many signs in Urdu as in English, a great place to practice reading. The restaurant, which Professor Dunnett said was his favorite, became one of mine, too

Unlike Professor Crawley, Professor Dunnett never asked why I was taking Urdu. And because he didn't, I told him one day, in my second year in Chicago, over chicken *biryani* at Mashallah Restaurant. "I want to be a missionary."

"Ah," he said, smiling, with none of the smugness of Professor Crawley. "My parents were missionaries. You're taking Arabic, too?"

"Yes."

"Well, you'll have to tread carefully. They don't take kindly to proselytizing in the parts of the world where Arabic and Urdu are spoken. Can't blame them really—given the history. Missionary work in the Muslim world is necessarily cloak-and-dagger. You've certainly chosen two very challenging languages to learn. Though you're doing quite well, I must say, in Urdu at least. You have the ear, which is important—you can never really master a language until you learn the rhythms of its intonations. And your tongue is flexible enough to master the sounds."

"Thank you." I flushed with pleasure, remembering Grandma Faith saying almost the same thing.

"Of course, the real test of proficiency comes when you get to the stage of poetry—in any language one undertakes. Poetry touches on truth beyond words. Almost impossible, really, to ever fully understand poetry in a foreign language. Almost. It's too difficult to translate, you see, because there's so much more to it than the definition of words. In poetry, words are meant to bypass our normal ways of understanding—to skip the mind altogether and pierce the heart. One must fully live in a language before truly comprehending its poetry—to know it from the inside, to feel it rather than understand it. In the Eastern world, this is even more true, because poetry there is a living thing. Not something you learn about in a class in college. Here, when we think of poetry, we think of dusty old sonnets and verses written long ago by people no longer living, or by strange, solitary people who write their words in privacy, to be read privately, too, out of a book, silently, to yourself. Poetry in the East has to be recited and sung out loud in public to be considered really alive. The written form of it is only a record, to help people remember how the words go. Here, you don't see people writing music to go with Shakespeare's sonnets or Wordsworth or Yeats. A pity. In India and Pakistan, the *ghazal*s of Ghalib are still sung out loud. In Iran, Hafez comes alive in the mouths of children, through songs that everyone knows."

While I was at college, I went home as little as possible. I took a trip to Northern India one summer, volunteering at a Christian mission—an orphanage—to practice my Urdu. I went to the Middle East, too. Professor Crawley, who seemed to take a liking to me though his sarcasm never softened, arranged for me to stay with some friends of his in Lebanon, wealthy Christians who showed me around Beirut. From there, I went to Syria and Egypt, my eyes wide-open, breathing through my mouth the whole time, just like Grandma Faith had talked about. When I did go home, when I had to, I tried my best to slip back to a time before Mendel, living with Mom and Dad and Chris as if nothing had changed. If Mom wondered why I was studying Arabic and Urdu—she must have!—she never said anything about it.

Chris was attending Shepherd's College of San Diego, having

decided, after that trip to Africa, that there's no place like home, no food like Mom's, and no other place he could have gone where his bed would be made for him, his laundry folded. To call him a mama's boy would have thrilled Mom and not bothered Chris at all, since nothing really ever did. School had never been a priority for him anyway. He was serious only about one thing—his music and the Christian rock band he'd formed when he was still in high school. Christian March, it was called, which was his name, and which his friends, the other guys in the band, had decided was too good not to use. Chris was the lead singer, and they were working on getting enough material together to do an album.

He came to visit me in Chicago for a long weekend at the beginning of my last year in college. I showed him around the city— Navy Pier, the Sears Tower, the Magnificent Mile, and the Field Museum. And talked him into trying Pakistani food, taking him to Mashallah Restaurant on Devon Avenue.

The restaurant was crowded and we had to wait a few minutes before getting a table. When one opened up, Zahid, the restaurant owner, who I'd gotten to know over the past couple of years, seated us, handing us menus. I showed off my Urdu, asking him about his family—his mother and father in Karachi, his sister in New Jersey. Chris looked obligingly impressed.

Zahid asked, "The old professor isn't with you?" referring to Professor Dunnett.

"No."

He looked at Chris, curiously, and asked, in English, "This is your boyfriend?"

"No. You've seen my boyfriend. This is my brother, Chris. He's visiting from California."

Zahid nodded and then turned, in a hurry, to put some tables together for a huge Pakistani family that was waiting at the door.

Chris said, "You and Dan getting serious?"

"I don't know. I guess." Dan was a friend of Chris's from high school. He'd asked me to the prom at Christ Academy and we'd been together, chastely, ever since. He was going to school at Wheaton and came out to spend the day with me, now and then, in Chicago. He'd spent most of the weekend with us.

Chris said, "He's a good guy. But I'm kind of glad he couldn't come tonight. Haven't had a chance to talk to you alone all weekend."

I looked at Chris, smiled, and nodded. I'd invited Dan along with us everywhere on purpose.

"What's up with you, Jo?"

"What do you mean?"

"You're so— far away. You have been, really, ever since you started college. Haven't been to PPSYC since high school. You used to love camp."

"I'm not a kid anymore."

"Oh, so I am?"

"I didn't mean it that way."

"You hardly ever come home. When you do, it's like you're not really with us. Everyone's noticed. Mom and Dad, I mean."

I had no answer. None that I was free to share. "Has— did Mom say anything about this?" I knew the answer. She'd never raised the subject of the silence that had grown between us since she'd told me the truth. And I'd never told her about meeting Sadiq.

"No. But I know she's hurt about it. It's like you're avoiding us or something."

"I—I don't know what you mean, Chris," I lied.

I was relieved when Zahid came to take our order.

Chris scratched his head doubtfully at all of my suggestions, saying to Zahid, "Not too spicy, okay?"

"Oh, but Pakistani food *is* spicy, my friend," said Zahid.

"Well, go easy. I can't take spicy food."

"It's good for you, my friend."

"Maybe so. But it's not in my genes."

Zahid laughed and said, "Your sister. She can eat food so spicy that it would make *me* cry. Isn't that so?" It took me a second to rustle up the chuckle he was expecting in response. My mind was still on what Chris had said about his genes.

Zahid left to pass our order on to the kitchen, and I brightened up, forcefully, saying, "So, tell me about the new version of 'Onward, Christian Soldiers' that you and the band are working on."

That kept Chris talking until dinner arrived. I had another little conversation, in Spanish this time, with the Mexican waiter who served us.

As I helped myself to some curry and tikka and naan, Chris said, "I'm proud of you, Jo."

"Huh?"

"I wish I could be as focused as you are. I mean, you decided what you wanted to study right from the get-go. You stuck with it. And you have something to show for it. Four languages."

"Five," I said. "English counts."

"Well, five then. That's how many times I've changed majors. So far. I have no idea what I'm doing at school. And you're gonna be done at the end of the year."

"You have your music."

"Yeah. But who knows if that'll go anywhere? And I have no idea what else to do with my life."

A little later, my plate nearly empty, my belly full, I watched Chris cautiously pop some naan into his mouth. Then he pushed some curry around on his plate.

He said, "So. You really like this stuff?"

I realized that apart from some naan, he hadn't eaten a bite.

"We're going to have to stop and get you a burger on the way home, aren't we?"

He grinned. "Yup."

I finished my last bites in silence, slightly annoyed with him, and even more with myself for dragging him there.

When Zahid came with the bill, he stopped to chat some more with Chris, teasing him about how little he'd eaten. Then he asked, "Which one of you is older?"

"She is," Chris said. "But only by a half an hour. We're twins."

"Twins?" Zahid stared at both of us more closely.

I asked, "How do you say 'twins' in Urdu?"

"*Jurwa.* It means 'joint.' Half-hour's difference, eh? But you don't look like each other! Except for the eyes, of course. Both brown."

I knew Chris was rolling his at me, the way we always did when people said things like that, not getting the difference between identical and fraternal. But I couldn't look up to roll mine in response. I studied the bill carefully, hoping that Chris wouldn't see through the careful blankness of my face.

Suddenly, before I could stop myself, I asked, "Do you know who Mendel is, Chris?"

"Nope. Should I?"

Hesitantly, I asked, "You took biology in high school, didn't you?"

"Sure." Grinning, he said, "You know I was never very good at paying attention in science. Or math. Or English or history for that matter. What's the deal?"

I stared into his eyes, brown like mine, on the edge for a few long seconds—before backing off, shaking my head. "Never mind." It was the closest I ever came to sharing the secret that belonged to him as much as it did to me.

Days after Chris came to visit me in Chicago, the flight path of four airplanes changed the world.

When I talked to him on the phone that week, Chris said, "Everything's different now, Jo."

"I know."

"Remember how I said I didn't know what I wanted to do with the rest of my life?"

"Yes."

"I do now, Jo."

I heard the conviction in his voice and envied it. In a world now flooded with fear and doubt, I wanted what he had, dismissing what Grandma Faith had said about the dangers of certainty.

Professor Crawley called me into his office a few weeks later. He told me about the career options that were more lucrative now, and more in demand, than when he'd first mentioned them. I grabbed at the sense of conviction that he offered, leaving behind all the reasons I'd wanted to study languages in the first place—to do what Grandma Faith did, to connect with people so that I could help them. What I'd intended to do before—Grandma Faith's whole approach to life—seemed suddenly naïve, too simple for what the world had become. Because now, among the people who spoke one of the languages I'd stumbled into studying—fresh from the strangeness of Sadiq's story—there were some who were even less comprehensible than he had been, the source of a hatred I couldn't fathom, no matter how well I understood their words, the source of mass murder in the name of a god that could have nothing to do with the One I worshipped.

Language, Professor Crawley told me, was a weapon now. And I could use that weapon to help in a war that my country hadn't asked for. I applied for the job. And got it.

Signing all the contracts was scary. Confidentiality clauses galore. All the secrecy involved made me hesitate, wondering what exactly I was getting myself into—national secrets, now, on top of the personal ones I already kept, buried deep inside the color of my eyes and Chris's. But I didn't dwell on the doubts hidden in that hesitation. For the second time in my life, I climbed over them, taking on a role I'd never imagined I'd want. And, just like before, the doubts came with me, eventually forcing a reckoning far more difficult than the one I'd dealt with before.

The sinning is the best part of repentance.

Arabic proverb

Angela

I t seemed like a lifetime ago, that weekend when Chris went to visit Jo in Chicago. I worried my heart out that she would give away the secret I'd asked her to keep—the truth that had driven Jo away from me no matter how much we both pretended things were the same. Now, both of my babies were gone. For the first time in more than twenty years, I was back where I started. Confused. Not knowing who I was, now that I didn't have either one of my children around to define me. I had nothing to do but mope around the house, dwelling on the past, on the life I had before I had them, on the details of that life, which I'd shared with Jo, laying them all out for her, hoping she would understand.

How lonely it had been, before I became a mother. How dull.

D on't be so dull, child! No one buys a dull-looking doll. Put a smile on that face of yours—paint it on if you have to!" my grandmother, Grandma Pelton, used to say to me when I was young. She'd clap her hands. "Liven up, liven up, Angie!" Dull was the very worst thing a person could be in Grandma Pelton's eyes. She herself was anything but—a bustle of noise and energy that wouldn't tolerate any dullness around her.

To "liven" me up, she'd hustle me into the kitchen and scoop me up some ice cream—with a look over her shoulder to make sure the coast was clear. Grandpa Pelton didn't approve of snacking between meals. He didn't approve of a lot of things. Not that it mattered. He spent most of his time in his study—reading and writing, preparing the sermons he delivered every Sunday in the nondenominational, evangelical church he'd founded when he settled back in the States. He was from another time—old-fashioned and formal. I never saw him out of his shoes and socks, not even first thing in the morning. And he never left home without a tie around his neck.

In the kitchen, Grandma Pelton would tell me all about her and Grandpa Pelton's travels around the world, about China, where Mom was born. Her words sparkled, bouncing off the kitchen walls, like light reflecting off the sequins of one of her favorite Sunday sweaters—always pink or baby-blue. Grandma Pelton's head was a smooth, shellacked helmet of steely gray, stiffly flipped just above her shoulders. The whole package of her appearance might have looked ridiculous to someone who didn't love her like I did. To me, she looked sweet as candy.

I spent more time with her than I did with my own mother, more nights at my grandparents' house than at our own small apartment three blocks away, because Mom, after she went to night school to get her nursing degree, mostly worked the night shift: the pay was better.

Grandma Pelton was the only one who ever talked about my father, who'd left my mother when I was a baby. The subject was off-limits with Mom. The few times I'd asked her about him, the shadows in her eyes made me feel bad for bringing him up.

Grandma Pelton told me that Mom was a junior in high school when she met my dad—Todd Rogers.

"It was love at first sight," Grandma Pelton told me. "They got engaged right after high school. Your grandfather didn't like him at first. He thought he was too coarse. Too common. But Todd's people were good, churchgoing folk and your grandfather came around, eventually. Your father joined the Marines, like his father and grandfather before him. I remember Todd's graduation from boot camp—we all drove down together to attend. Oh, my—he was so handsome in his uniform. And your mother and he were so in love. They got married a few months later, living like gypsies for a while, on bases all over the place, coming home for Christmas sometimes. They were so happy. Even happier when Ron came along. When the war in Vietnam started, you were barely on the way. Your father got sent over right at the start. That's how it is with those Marines, first ones to get sent in when there's trouble in the world. So he wasn't here when the stork flew you in. Your mother came home with Ron to be with us while he was over there—I took care of Ron when your mother went to the hospital to have you.

"I don't know what happened when your dad came back. But he was different, that was clear. Todd's father had died while he was away. He might have been able to help with—whatever it was that was bothering him, having fought in a war himself. Your mother never talked about any problems they were having. Instead of staying on in the service, like he'd planned to—to make a career for himself in the Marines—Todd decided to get out. Your parents got themselves an apartment around the corner—same one you live in now. He was barely home—two months, maybe three?—and then, suddenly, he was gone. It was a real shock to all of us. Faith, naturally, was brokenhearted. And none of the rest of us could make any sense of it. Not even Todd's mother. Your grandma Rogers. She died a couple of years later. We didn't even know how to get in touch with him to let him know his mother had passed, so he missed the funeral. I tell you, the man just packed up and left everyone and everything behind, no looking back. It was a hard time for your mother. Divorce is a mighty serious thing—a tragedy. A national one now, the way it's spreading through homes today. Like a wildfire. It's all because women won't let men be men anymore. But with Faith—it wasn't her fault, I know. She was a good wife to him, the way we'd raised her to be, following his lead, giving him the respect she owed him as a good Christian wife, never trying to be the boss. And he repaid her by abandoning his duty as a husband and a father. Broke our hearts, too—your grandpa's and mine—to see her marriage crumble. Well, your mother went through a dark patch. Stayed away from church for a while. Said she couldn't stand all the pity. As if sympathy were a bad thing! She moped around for a couple of years, trying to put the pieces back together. But you can't do that when one of the biggest pieces is gone, can you? And moping doesn't get you anywhere. Don't you become a moper, Angie. Didn't raise your mother to be one, either. She got through it, eventually. Picked herself up after a time and made the best of it. Went back to school. Got a job so she could support you and your brother. Not the way things should be. Not even close. But she made the best of it." Grandma Pelton always nodded approvingly at that part.

I don't know when the Christmas cards started coming. From my father. But it was years after he left us. No return address. Same message every year. *Dear Ron and Angie, thinking of you and hoping you have a wonderful Christmas. Love, Dad.*

"Christmas is easy," Grandma Pelton said one year to Grandpa Pelton when they didn't know I was in the room. "Everyone remembers Christmas. Notice how there's never a card for the kids' birthdays? That would be something. To actually remember when they were born."

By the time I was in high school, when Mom started going off on her missions, and my brother, Ron, was away at college, I was too old to be cheered up with ice cream and stories. I was restless, angry at my mother for leaving me behind, acting out. Grandma Pelton didn't know what to do with me. I'd get in trouble at school. She'd keep it from Grandpa and never told Mom when she came back. I'd be good for a while. Then, when Mom would take off again, so did I.

I fell into what Grandma Pelton called a "wayward crowd." It began with the boy I started seeing—an older boy who lived up the street. Denny. He wasn't the first boyfriend I'd had, but he was the worst: a high school dropout who rode around town on a motorcycle. Grandma couldn't stand him. She tried to stop me from seeing Denny. But I didn't care. I used to sneak out at night to be with him—one of those secrets that Grandma kept from Grandpa, when she found out. I started to cut school. And smoke with my friends in the bathroom. I was suspended for that. Twice.

But I settled down whenever Mom came home.

It might have gone on like that and eventually been all right. Except that Grandma Pelton died at the beginning of my senior year in high school. I took it harder than anyone realized. Whatever shaky kind of faith I claimed to have at the time became even shakier. Growing up the way I did, in the heart of a good, Christian family, rooted in the kind of faith that should have been a guiding light from early on, I have no excuses.

I remember how horrible that Christmas was, without Grandma Pelton. Leading up to it, Mom and I fought all the time, about everything. She was leaving on another mission—to India—in a few weeks, and I was terribly unhappy about it. Christmas morning, I remember, I threw a tantrum over a pair of jeans I'd been expecting and didn't get. Jordache, as I recall, the must-haves of the time.

"I'm sorry you're so disappointed, Angie. I just couldn't afford them. Fifty-dollar jeans!"

"That's all I wanted for Christmas! The only thing I asked for."

Mom was shaking her head. "Do you know, Angie, how disappointed I am that you would even want them? Do you know what fifty dollars can buy? In terms of food and medication for the kids I work with? I'm talking about saving lives. Even if I had the money, I wouldn't spend it on a pair of fancy jeans for your behind. I know better than that, even if you don't."

Looking back, I can't say I disagree with her. But I hated the way I felt. Dismissed. Thrown over. I begged Mom not to go away on her next trip, not to leave me with Grandpa Pelton.

"I have to go, Angie. You know I do. I've made a commitment. And I'm needed."

"Then let me come with you."

"You have school. You can come with me in the summer. After you graduate."

That was no consolation. Mom hadn't seen my report card. She didn't know that there was no way I was going to graduate in June.

The Christmas card from Dad came a few days late that year. For the first time ever, there was a return address, in Los Angeles, on the envelope—something Mom pointed out to Grandpa Pelton before handing the card over to show him.

"Looks like he didn't go far," Grandpa said, handing the card back. He shook open the paper to read with his coffee, putting the matter away from him.

Mom fingered the writing in the card and gave a sigh before handing the card back to Ron, who, without a word, gave it to me to read.

I dug the envelope out of the trash later, wiped the wilted lettuce off it, and put it away. Before going to bed that night, I wandered into Mom's room and asked, "Why did Daddy leave?"

She sighed and put down the book she was reading. "I told you before, Angie. I don't know why he left. I wish I did. I wish I had an answer for you. But I don't."

What she said made me furious. I didn't believe that she didn't know. Only that she wouldn't tell me. When Mom left me in Garden Hill that time, I got into more trouble than ever before, trying to shake the dull off me. Only this time, Grandpa was in charge. No ice cream from him. Just lectures, at first. He'd pace, hands behind his back, throwing words in my direction, words that washed over my head without cleansing any of the anger and confusion in my heart. One night, I took Mom's car for a ride with Denny and some of his friends. Somebody had some liquor. We got pulled over. Denny was driving—he was drunk and they threw him in jail for the night. But I didn't stop seeing him. Not until he dumped me for another girl in the neighborhood.

When I got suspended from school a third time, it wasn't tobacco I was caught smoking. Mom was still away. Grandpa Pelton had no idea how to handle me. I see that now and I don't blame him. He said some nasty things. And I said even nastier ones back.

One of which was: "You're not my father! You have no right to tell me what to do!"

He lifted his hand at that one, but managed to stop it before it got anywhere near my face. Teeth clenched, he yelled, "I thank God for that! You have the morals of an alley cat and if I hadn't promised your mother to take care of you, I'd say that's where you belong!"

I took that as an invitation to run away. I wanted to start fresh, to get away from all the trouble I was in at school, to be somewhere I could belong without having anything from the past hanging over me. I knew where I was going without having ever really planned it.

I took Greyhound to L.A. It was scary being out on my own, and I had to work hard to resist the urge to go back home, thinking about how worried Mom would be when Grandpa told her I was gone. But Grandpa Pelton had a temper that, though slow to rise, could be fierce, and knowing that I'd tested it enough lately, I didn't want to turn around and bear up to the hollering I'd be in for back at home.

It was easy enough to find the house on the map I bought at the bus depot, a little place, not far from the freeway in the San

Fernando Valley. I stood outside of it for a long time, too scared to ring the bell. It was early evening, maybe five o'clock, and it didn't look like anyone was home. What was I supposed to say if he answered the door? *Uh—hi, I'm Angela. Your daughter. Remember me?* I retreated from the porch and walked up and down the sidewalk for a while. Pretty soon, a beat-up old station wagon pulled up in the driveway. A woman was driving. She got out and hustled a couple of kids out of the car and into the house I'd been casing for almost an hour—a boy carrying a guitar and a girl, younger, in one of those ballet tutus and slippers. For a second, I wondered if I had the wrong house. It took a while before the truth even crossed my mind as a possibility. The woman was his wife and those were his kids. The moment I realized, I hated them.

Eventually, I worked up the nerve to ring that bell. A tall man with fading, sandy-blond hair answered. It took me a moment to recognize him from the photographs in the old family album at home. It was my father. Apparently, he was a schoolteacher and had been home since four o'clock, inside all the time that I'd paced the sidewalk. It was even more awkward than I'd been afraid of. After a few minutes of me stammering and him stuttering back, he let me in the door, still dazed. I met his wife. Connie. Their son, Cory. He was thirteen years old. And their daughter, too—Michelle, who was seven. They didn't know about me—Cory and Michelle, I mean. Connie did. She pretended to welcome me, smiling and saying how glad she was to finally meet me. As if there had ever been any wish or plan to ever meet me before.

We all stood awkwardly in the living room for a while. Then Connie asked my father to go with her into the kitchen to help get dinner on the table. I would have offered to help, except I thought what she really wanted to do was get him alone for a second. To talk about me.

Cory turned the TV on so loud it hurt. And Michelle stood and stared. After a few seconds, I asked to use the bathroom, mainly to get the crazy beat of my heart under control, to splash my face with water, and try to get some air into my lungs. Michelle led the way without a word. When I came out, I traced my way back down the hallway and stopped outside what I thought was the kitchen to hear Connie's louder side of a whispered conversation—my father was better at whispering, so I couldn't hear anything from him.

"Well— I mean, I just think a phone call ahead would have been— I mean, it's such a shock. How long do you think she wants to stay here?"

Dad's answer sounded like air.

"Well, don't you think you should ask her what her plans are?"

More blanks from Dad, short enough to indicate that he used fewer words than Connie.

"Of course, I know that, but I just need to know how long."

"_____"

"What about her mother? Does she know she's here? Or did she just run away?"

"_____"

"Well, maybe you should ask. How old is she, Todd?"

"_____"

"You don't know? You don't know how old she is?" Connie's whisper had some voice in it now. I decided that what I'd heard, and hadn't, was enough.

Cory was still on the couch. Michelle left the Barbie dolls she was playing with to stare at me some more. Pretty soon, Connie called us into the kitchen for dinner, as bright and cheerful as she'd been before. She didn't ask me any of the questions I knew she wanted to. Instead, she kept up a flow of bright-eyed conversation that was saccharine-sweet enough to give lab rats cancer—asking me about "my trip," about how long the bus ride had been and all. Michelle was still staring, making it even harder to swallow the bites that would have stuck in my throat anyway. Cory shoveled food into his mouth without looking at anyone. My father did pretty much the same.

When dinner was over, I offered to do the dishes.

Connie said, "Oh, no. You go and rest. You must be tired. Thank you." She smiled so wide I could see the pink of her gums. I wondered what she looked like when the smile actually reached her eyes. I hadn't seen that happen yet.

Cory was back in front of the TV. But he got up when Connie came in and said, "Go get your homework done, Cory. Michelle, put those Barbies away and finish your spelling sentences. I'm going for my walk with Deena."

Michelle skipped out of the room backward, still staring. I sat down on the couch and waited for my dad. I wondered if Connie's walk was a way to give me some private time with him. It wasn't, I found out later. She went for a walk every day with the lady who lived across the street.

Dad came in, wiping his hands with a dish towel. I stood up to switch off the television. The sudden quiet was a relief. I wondered whether Cory had hearing problems. And then the doorbell rang. Dad opened his mouth and closed it a couple of times, like a fish, and then went to answer it. A few seconds later, he was back with a man wearing a tool belt and carrying a toolbox.

"I sure appreciate it, Todd. I—I haven't worked for a while."

My father nodded. "Don't mention it, Jake. I know how it is. Let me show you what we want done." They went into the kitchen. In the silence of the living room, I heard them discussing creaky doors and squeaky hinges. Then they moved on down the hallway. There was a light switch that needed to be three-way. A faucet leaking in the main bathroom. A tilting dresser in the master bedroom. My father had stuff for Jake to do in every room. Cory and Michelle were quiet. The TV was still off. I listened to every last one of Jake's assignments. It took my father almost forty-five minutes to go through them all. When they came back to the living room, they were talking about paint colors. Navajo White. No—maybe something with a little yellow in it. Better to ask Connie. Jake was nodding, writing it all down in one of those little memo pads you could get for nineteen cents at Thrifty's. At least you could back then. Back when ice cream was fifteen cents a scoop. I watched him tuck his pencil back behind his ear without really looking at him, waiting for my father to remember I was there. When he finally led Jake out, he turned and came back to the living room, catching sight of me with a startled look that was proof of what I had begun to think—that he'd forgotten all about me.

Connie came back just then. She helped me make up the couch in the den, explaining that I should feel free to sleep in—that they'd all be out of the house by seven in the morning.

"I was off from work today. I'm a nurse."

I blinked. And stared. A nurse. Same as Mom. If I gasped, Connie didn't seem to notice.

She was still talking. "Tomorrow, my shift starts at six o'clock in the morning and I won't be home until six in the evening. Todd will pick Michelle up from school. Cory takes the bus. And then he'll take 'em for their after-school stuff." She was chattering away. I could tell she was uncomfortable. "Just make yourself at home, okay? Here's a towel for you to use. Is there anything else I can get for you?"

I shook my head, said thanks, and wandered back into the living room where my father was. He was watching TV now, and Connie was with her kids, checking homework and running a bedtime bath for Michelle.

I stood and waited for him to notice me for a few minutes. Finally, when that didn't work, I said, "Maybe I should call home?"

My father looked up and blinked a few times. Then he said, "Uh— of course. There's a phone in the den. Feel free."

He didn't ask about Mom or Ron and hadn't mentioned them since I'd gotten there.

That was when it hit me. The failure. I'd come looking for a way out of my troubles and confusion—a happy ending that wasn't going to happen. I wouldn't have come if I'd known about Connie and her kids. My father wasn't some tragic hero, wandering and lost—the way I guess I'd pictured him from my grandmother's description—pining away for the family he'd left behind, someone I could save who could then turn around and save me. He had picked up and moved on and there wasn't ever going to be a happy ending that involved him coming back to a family he'd never been a part of in all the years of my life.

I woke up the next morning to the bustling sounds of that family, the one he *was* a part of, getting ready for its day. I may as well have not been there at all. I didn't bother getting off the couch I'd slept on, just waited until the house was quiet before getting up to get dressed. I thought of my phone call to Grandpa as I did—he'd been relieved to hear from me. And quiet when I told him where I was.

I could hear him sigh into the phone. "Won't you come home, Angela?"

"No."

"I've spoken with your mother. She's worried sick. Trying to get a flight back as soon as possible. If you're not coming home, she might as well stay in India. What do you want me to tell her, Angela? Should I tell her to come home?"

Yes, yes! I wanted to shout, thinking of the man in the next room who was my father, who didn't have anything to say to me and no interest in anything I had to say, either. Choked up, I said, "No. I'm not coming home."

Remembering that call, I started to cry. The simple truth was that Mom was all I had. Mom and Grandpa Pelton and Ron. This home, the one I woke up in that morning, was the home of a family that I had forced myself on. I wasn't stupid enough not to know that. But that didn't mean it didn't hurt.

I was still crying, half-convinced that I should leave, when the doorbell rang. I wiped my face and went to answer it.

A woman was standing there, holding a carton of eggs.

"Hello. I'm Deena. From across the street. I wanted to return some eggs I borrowed from Connie."

"She's not here."

"I know. You must be Angela."

I nodded. She spoke with an accent. I couldn't figure out what kind. She looked like she could be Spanish or Italian, but she sounded British. Sort of. Iranian maybe—there had been a lot of stuff about Iran on the news. About American hostages being held there and pictures of an angry-looking old man with a beard that Grandpa Pelton had said might be the Antichrist. I'd seen it on TV, big crowds of people, women with their heads covered, waving their fists angrily around, burning American flags.

"Will you put these in the fridge for me?"

I took the eggs from her. Her eyes were dark and beautiful. And full of sympathy.

"You're alone. Why don't you put those in the fridge and come over to my house for a visit? I'll make us some tea."

I couldn't think of any reason to say no. I put away the eggs and followed her across the street. She led me into her house—painted yellow on the outside, with white trim—and into her kitchen. I watched her put the water to boil. She opened cabinets and drawers, laying out teacups, saucers, and spoons.

She gave me a quick glance. "You were crying? When I rang the bell?"

I nodded.

She sat down at one of the chairs at the kitchen counter, pointed to the other one for me to sit on, and asked, "How old were you when you last saw your father?"

"I was a baby—like one and a half—when he left my mother."

She shook her head as the kettle of water began to whistle, and stood to turn the stove off. Then she frowned. "The tea. I can make it any way you like. But our way is different. I cook it with milk and spices."

I frowned back. "Where are you from?"

She smiled. "Pakistan. Which is next to India."

"Oh."

I watched her scoop tea leaves into the kettle, along with whole spices that she named out loud. "This is cardamom. See? These pods?" She split them open as she dropped them into the kettle. "A very good breath freshener. And these are cloves—not too many of these. They're strong. Cloves are good for a toothache. They numb the pain. And cinnamon. Now, I'll let the water boil again, with all the tea and spices. Then I add the milk and let it all simmer together. That's the way to have tea." She rocked her head side to side and sighed before sitting down again. She propped her face up in her hands and focused her eyes on me, sparkling eyes that reminded me of Grandma Pelton's.

"My mother's in India," I said.

"Is she? India and Pakistan used to be one, you know. Before Independence. Before Partition. What is your mother there for?"

"She's a missionary."

"A missionary? Oh." There was a long moment of quiet. "Catholic?"

"No. Just regular Christian. My grandfather's church—he's evangelical—it's nondenominational."

She said, "Ah," with a frown, but I don't think she knew what I was talking about. After a second, she said, "I went to a Catholic school. A convent school, for girls. Run by nuns."

"You're Catholic?"

"No, no. I am Muslim."

"Oh." Now I was the one who didn't know what she was talking about.

"Tell me, Angela, how old are you?"

"Seventeen."

"Seventeen? Only two years older than my son." She stood up

and turned off the stove. I watched her use a little strainer to catch the spices and tea leaves as she poured out two cups and brought them to the kitchen table, where we sat. "Normally, the tea is made with the sugar boiled in also, but I have stopped taking sugar myself." She pushed the sugar bowl in my direction and watched me put in a spoonful and stop. "Oh, no, no. This is your first cup of *chai*. Have it properly. With lots of sugar." She was doing the job herself, adding another two heaping spoonfuls to my cup as she said, "*You* are a skinny little thing. No need to worry." She stirred my tea for me and then wrapped her hands around her own cup and sat back to wait for it to cool. "It was brave of you to come to see your father."

"Brave?" My voice croaked. My face crumpled. She stood to get some Kleenex and patted me on the back. After a few minutes of bawling, I said, "He—he won't even talk to me."

"Hmm." She put her hand on her chin and stared out the window. She seemed to be speaking to herself. "Yes. That's the thing. When so much time has passed in silence—so far away—it is hard to know what to say. Too hard. He was probably shocked to see you. You were so young when he left. And now—you are already grown up. You know, when you are older, it is easy to look in the mirror and live in denial—you don't see those wrinkles, you tell yourself that those white hairs are just a trick of the light. But children—there is no escaping the truth when you have children. That time is passing. They grow so fast, mocking the best of intentions. I imagine your father always meant to come back for you, to get in touch. But time—and circumstances—got away from him. And then you showed up—not the little baby girl that he left behind. A grown lady instead! With what kind of ideas and opinions about him, he has no idea. What could he say to you? What explanations would answer such a gap?" She turned to face me again and smiled. "Listen to me—philosophizing about what is none of my business! There is this, also—Todd is a very shy man. Very quiet. He probably needs time to figure out what to say. Time—such a cheap word for one as young as you, I know. But so precious to those of us who have seen its wings spread in full flight."

"You know him really well? Him and Connie?"

"Todd, not so well. Connie and I are friends. We go for a walk together every day."

"She's mad, isn't she? About me coming?"

"Not mad. Surprised, I think." She was frowning a little, shaking her head again. "Was she— did she make you feel unwelcome?"

I didn't answer her.

After a minute, she picked up her cup and took a sip. I did the same.

"Mmm. This is delicious."

"You like it? Very good. You come tomorrow also. I'll make it for you again, okay?"

My dad came home around three o'clock that day. Michelle was with him. A little while later, Cory came home on the school bus. By the time Jake the handyman showed up with his toolbox, the house was beginning to feel like a train station—like any second a whistle would blow. My father waved Jake off into the bathroom to start work, made the kids a snack in the kitchen, and then hustled them out to the car, remembering me on the way out the door.

"Uh— I've got to run Cory out for baseball practice. And Michelle has piano lessons. You want to come?"

I nodded and followed them all out to the car. We dropped Michelle off first. Then, when we got to the ball field and Cory jumped out of the car almost before we were parked, my dad didn't follow him. He sat with his hands on the steering wheel, tapping his fingers for a minute, eyes on the field in front of us, and then reached behind him to get his wallet out of the back pocket of his pants. He flipped it open and passed it to me, saying, "I—I want you to see this."

It was a picture—the kind they take at Sears, Ron holding on for dear life to a baby version of me, both of us awkwardly arranged on a block of green carpet in front of a big-screen picture of bright green, leafy woods. Mom had a bigger version of it framed and kept on the mantel. There was a white paper crack running right through the middle of this copy that hers didn't have. I stared at it for a long time, waiting for him to say something.

Finally, he did. "I—I know that I didn't—welcome you yesterday. Not the way I should have. That picture—your mother sent it to me in 'Nam, after you were born. I carried that picture around with me there—and ever since. It was—it was like a lifeline. What kept me going." He was tapping his fingers on the wheel again, his eyes straight ahead. "I—I don't know what your mother told you about—about why I went away." He paused to look away from the field to me—for just a second—and then his eyes were back on the boys throwing, catching, batting, and running. "I came home from the war in kind of a fog. I—I wasn't paying much attention to what was around me. To you and your brother or your mom. I was lost. In my head. I couldn't talk about it. About anything. I—I didn't think anyone would understand. And I didn't have it in me to try and make them. But what was inside was dangerous. Bottled up and toxic. Did your mother tell you about the time I hit her in the face?"

I shook my head vigorously, my jaw dropping a little before I pulled it back up again.

"One time, in the middle of the night. I was asleep. She must have moved or something. The next thing I know I'm sitting up in bed, on my knees, my fist pulled back to give her another one and she's crying and there's a mark on her face that got darker the next day. I didn't even know. I wasn't even awake. That terrified me. I couldn't stay there and be that guy who put the fear in her eyes. So, I left. I don't want to make any lame excuses. My leaving had nothing to do with your mother. Or you guys. It was—it was what I had to do. I had to get away and be by myself to try and figure things out."

"But you did? Figure things out?"

"No. Not really. But I learned to live with that."

"Why didn't you ever come back?"

"I—I couldn't. I couldn't come back."

"How did you meet Connie?" I was making an accusation.

"We met in Washington. At an antiwar rally."

I frowned. "Antiwar?"

"Yes. I don't know how I ended up there. It wasn't like I started out to make some kind of statement. I hated all those rich college kids trying to get out of serving. But I—I didn't disagree with what they had to say about the war itself. That was part of why I left. Everyone I knew—when I came back—everyone thought I'd done this great thing. Serving my country. And I did do that and I was damned proud of it, too. I went to Vietnam to do what my father had done. And his father before that. To serve and honor my country. And I did what I had to while I was there." He stopped talking for a long time. And then started again, suddenly, "You know, the truth is that war isn't complicated. It's about killing. Killing is the whole purpose of it, avoiding getting killed yourself and killing others in order to do that. But no one ever wants to talk about *that*. It doesn't make for polite dinner conversation, you know? Heck, I wouldn't have wanted to talk about it anyway. All I knew was what I *didn't* know. Before I went to 'Nam, the world was black-and-white. And when I came back, all I saw was gray. Everything I'd seen and done came back with me. No one understood. And I didn't want to have to make them understand either—how could I, when I didn't understand it myself?"

"And Connie? She understood?"

"Yes. Yes, she did. I didn't have to explain anything to Connie. Because she was there, too."

"In Vietnam?!"

"She was a nurse. She served over there. She'd seen it all. She knew."

"Oh."

"But that," he pointed to the picture in his wallet, still in my hand, "was always with me. All these years. It's—it's how I remembered you both. Yesterday—it was a shock to see you. That you're—that you're not that little baby anymore. That was hard." He took a deep breath and closed his eyes. "You have every reason to be angry—to hate me for not being there for you for all these years. I have no right to ask you anything. About why you ran away. About why you're not in school. But I want you to know that I'm glad you're here."

He didn't say anything else. Neither did I. We just sat there and waited for Cory's practice to be over. Then we went back to pick up Michelle.

What Deena had said that morning—about time—had already made me decide to stay. What my dad said in the car—that just seemed to prove her right. I don't know if Deena ever talked about our conversation with Connie. I think she may have. Connie was really nice to me that night, telling me I was welcome to stay for as long as I wanted—that both she and my dad wanted me there. I'm not sure I believed her. But her saying it made me feel better—even if it made no difference to how I felt about *her*.

That time I spent with my dad in the car was the only time we ever talked about him walking out on Mom and us. It wasn't some kind of corny magic moment—that point in a movie or TV show where everything falls into place and becomes all right. But it helped make things more normal. It got us over the awkwardness. The next day, when he got home from work, he went out into the yard to do some weeding, trimming, planting. At first, I thought he was just trying to avoid me. But then he asked me if I wanted to help him. And we talked—a little. Just about stuff we were doing right then. He told me about what he planned to do in the yard next. Then he put the radio on—tuned to K-EARTH 101, I remember, and we listened to oldies from the fifties and sixties. It was nice.

Until Connie came home. I was glad to have that afternoon and others without her. No matter how nice she was and in spite of what my dad told me about her, I couldn't really be comfortable around her. I'd get real quiet and watchful when she came home. Like I was trying to find something that would justify how I felt about her. She and my dad seemed to have a real good marriage. That didn't make her any easier to like. They never seemed to fight or even disagree at all, except once—about Jake the handyman.

"You have to talk to him, Todd. He's taken more than a month already, and he said he'd be done in a week."

"I'll talk to him."

"The other day, I smelled liquor on him. He could fall off a ladder and get himself hurt. He could sue us. I understand what you're trying to do, Todd. Helping these guys out. But I don't think we should be inviting every one of these strays you pick up into our home."

"Jake's a good man, Connie. It's not easy for him. You know that."

Connie sighed and shook her head. "You're the one who's a good man, Todd. Honestly. Impossible to argue with, which can be darned irritating. But a good man for sure." I saw them smile into each other's eyes and had to look away or be sick.

Connie had good reason to complain. Jake never turned up when he said he would. And when he did, he started things and then left them unfinished for days—leaving a toilet out of order once so we all had to use the master bathroom. Another time, he took a door off its hinges and left it propped up against a wall for days before showing up to put it back on. The windows and doors in the living room were taped off for weeks with no sign of him showing up with any paint.

One time, in the yard, my dad told me that Jake was a Vietnam vet, too. He'd served at the very end of the war. "By the time he came home, most people didn't even remember that we were still in a war, much less think that there was any way left to win it. He had it even tougher than I did."

"How'd you meet him?"

"I check in with someone I know at the VA hospital every once in a while," my dad said. "To see if there's any way I can help out. There's too many of these guys—like Jake—walking around, wounded in a way that no one notices."

The next time Jake came over, I saw him in a different way. Before, I'd avoided him as much as possible, taking off for Deena's house whenever he showed up in the mornings, so I guess I hadn't really seen him at all. Now, I noticed how much younger he was than my dad, in his late twenties. He had blue eyes and straggly, long hair. He was shy and kind of mumbled when he talked. It was hot that day and I made him some lemonade. He was so grateful, you'd have thought I'd cooked him a five-course dinner. After that, I made a point of saying hi to him when he came.

My mother called a couple of times from India, in the mornings, when no one else was home.

"Are you okay, Angie?" she asked.

"I'm fine."

"And—your father? He—he must have been happy to see you."

"Yes."

"Well. I'll be home in a bit, Angie. I hope you're home, too, when I get back. I'll be there in time to celebrate your birthday."

I didn't say anything.

"What about school? Are you going to school?"

"No."

"Angie?"

"What?"

"Do you have any plans? For the future?"

"No."

"Well. There's time, Angie. I hope you think things over carefully. In the meantime, maybe it's a good thing. This chance you're getting. To get to know your dad." I had already told her everything about him—about Connie and the kids. She'd asked, "Is he happy, Angie?"

"I don't know. I guess so," I'd said grudgingly.

"I'm glad."

Every time I went over to Deena's, we'd have tea. It was funny—but those visits kind of stood apart from everything and everyone else. I mean, she was Connie's friend—that alone was enough reason to hate her as much as I hated Connie. But I didn't. Right from that first morning, I couldn't. Having tea with Deena is what I remember most about the time I spent in Los Angeles. I went over only in the mornings, so I never hung out with her family—I don't even remember seeing her husband. She had a daughter, older than Michelle and younger than Cory, and a son. I only remember what her husband looked like from the family pictures on the mantel.

Sometimes, she was cooking when I came over. I'd watch her slice onions—so fast, I worried she might chop off a finger—and fry them, tossing in bright red and yellow spices that crackled and popped. She would always apologize for the smell.

"I am so sorry—I got a late start cooking today. Our food is delicious. But it stinks when it's cooking. Frying onions and spices. The smell gets into hair and clothes—be sure and take a shower when you get home. Or you will smell like a spice shop!"

I would whiff it all in with pleasure. "I think it smells good!" I'd say.

She'd laugh and give me some to try with a warning that I would ignore. "You are not used to the spices—your mouth will burn."

The first time I tried one of her curries, with some rice, every opening in my head sprang a leak. I waved my hand in front of my mouth, trying to fan down the flames, and tearfully asked for a glass of water.

"No, no. If you have water, it will be worse. Try to resist. If you must have something, put some yogurt on the side of your food and mix it in with each bite." She was scooping some, plain, onto my plate.

Without thinking, I did what she said.

"Yes, you see? The yogurt dampens all the heat, but adds to the flavor instead of drowning it out. Water would only intensify the spice—making your mouth fight a battle against itself. You cannot fight the spices—if you want to eat spicy food—you have to let yourself feel the pain and then your mouth will adjust. Eventually, you will be able to taste the other flavors, too. And peace will reign!"

One day, when she had me sit in the living room while she brought out the *chai,* to get away from the fumes of food simmering on the stove, she said, I found a book half-hidden behind one of the pillows on the couch. It was *Little Women.*

"Ah—you've found Sabah's book! She was looking for it all day yesterday." Deena set the cups of tea down on the coffee table and took the book from me. "For a whole year I have tried to get that daughter of mine to start reading this book with me—it was my favorite when I was a girl. But no—every day there is an excuse. 'My favorite TV show is on, Mom; I have too much homework, Mom; I'll start it tomorrow, Mom.' And now that we have begun, she can't wait for bedtime so that we can read together! She was convinced that her brother had hidden it from her . . ." Deena's voice trailed off. "Ah, well. You have found it for her. She will be very grateful. She was so mad at my son."

"I've seen the movie on TV."

"But you haven't read the book? Oh, Angela! That is not the same thing. You *must* read it to know what it is about! Such a beautiful story—oh, how I cried when Beth died. You remember? Which movie did you see? The one with Katharine Hepburn or Elizabeth Taylor?"

"I—I don't know."

"Was it in black-and-white?"

"No. Color. But it was old."

"The Elizabeth Taylor version, then. Ah, well, it's not your fault. Your whole generation—I feel sorry for you. Television has robbed you all of your imagination. When I was young, we read and played. We invented our own toys and plays—just like Jo in *Little Women.*"

I laughed. "But Deena—you're not that old! You had television when you were a kid!"

"Not in Pakistan, Angela. Not until after I was married. And I consider myself lucky." Deena gave me a quick sideways glance before picking up her teacup. "You— forgive me for asking, Angela, but you have finished school?"

I turned red. "No. I quit. I was no good at it anyway."

"I see." Deena's lips twitched, like she wanted to say more but didn't.

On another day, she said, "You must be getting bored. With nothing to do all day until Connie and Todd come home."

I shrugged.

The next day, when I went over, she had her purse in her hand and was ready to go out when she answered the door. "Come, Angela. I am going to the library. You'll come with me?"

"Uh— sure. Why not?"

She made me get a library card, watched me fill out the form, and made me check out a copy of *Little Women*. As we left, she pointed out a hiring sign on display at the checkout desk. "What a wonderful job this would be for a young person! To work in a library."

I finished reading *Little Women* in two days. She took me to the library again the next week. I wanted to check out more books. While I was there, I filled out a job application. A week later, I got the job. The library was walking distance, and I worked only a couple of days a week, in the afternoons usually, stacking books back on the shelves. Sometimes, I dropped my dad off at work so I could keep his car to drive. I proudly showed him my driver's license without being asked, to prove I could drive, and hoped he'd see that my birthday was coming up. But I don't think he noticed. I started driving the kids to their after-school stuff sometimes. Michelle was really friendly. But Cory was a tough nut to crack. Not that I tried very hard.

One day, when I'd worked at the library in the morning, I

walked home just at the time that the school bus was dropping Cory off from high school. Deena's son—I recognized him from the picture in her family room—got off the bus, too. A bunch of boys were yelling at him out of the windows of the bus. "Sad-Dick! Hey Sad-Dick, the I-raynian! Watch out, Sad-Dick! We're gonna kick your ass!" One of the boys spit at him, but missed. Cory was walking home real fast, trying to keep his distance. When I got home, I did something I had already tried to do a couple of times. I started a conversation with Cory. "Hey—that boy—the one the others were yelling at, he's Deena's son, isn't he?"

Cory looked around like he was making sure I wasn't talking to anyone else and then barely looked at me as he nodded.

"Why were they picking on him?"

Cory shrugged and shuffled into his room.

That night, I saw Deena's son out in front of her house, sitting at the curb and lighting up a cigarette. I hadn't smoked since I left home. Suddenly, I was dying for a puff. I went out and asked him for a cigarette. He squinted up at me for a long second before fishing the pack out of his shirt pocket and offering me one.

After he lit me up, I asked him, "Does your mom know you smoke?"

"She knows."

"She doesn't mind?"

He shrugged.

I stared at him through the wisps of smoke that rose up from the tips of our cigarettes. He had the longest, thickest eyelashes I'd ever seen. There was a bit of a five o'clock shadow on his jaw, which made him look older than fifteen. I didn't think I'd started the conversation off right, so I decided to try again from scratch.

I stuck my hand out at him, real formal. "My name's Angela Rogers."

He stared at my hand for a second before taking it to shake. "I'm Sadiq. Sadiq Ali Mubarak."

"Sah-dik? O-oh." That explained the "Sad-Dick" from the other kids. "I saw the boys on the bus giving you a hard time."

He scowled and took a suck on his cigarette. "They're assholes."

He had even more of an accent than Deena. "What about your dad? Doesn't he mind you smoking?"

"My dad is dead."

"Oh. So— Deena's husband is your stepfather?"

His scowl went fierce. I understood. Until that second, I hadn't thought of Connie that way, either. She was my stepmother. It was hard to think of the word without adding "wicked." I figured Deena's son must feel the same way about her husband.

I went out there and smoked with him a few times after that. I did most of the talking—about what, I don't know. He'd listen and nod. I felt kind of guilty about the smoking. He was younger than me. And Deena was so nice to me. I felt like I should try to be a good influence on her son. Try to be his friend. I don't think he had any. But he didn't seem to care whether he did or not.

One thing I do remember talking to him about was religion. I asked him tons of questions.

"Do you guys believe in Jesus?"

"Yes. But not the same way that Christians do."

"What do you mean?"

"We believe he was a prophet. Not the son of God."

"A prophet?"

"Yes. Like others before him. Moses. Abraham. Noah."

"So, you don't accept him as the Messiah?"

"Oh, yes. We do."

"As your Lord and Savior?"

He frowned. "I don't know what that means."

"It means that he died on the cross. For our sins. To save us."

He looked at me like he still had no idea what I was talking about. Then he said, "Why do you eat his flesh and drink his blood?"

"Huh?"

"The bread and the wine. The priests say it's his body and his blood."

"Oh. Catholics do that. And some others, I think. Not regular Christians." I shrugged and changed the subject, one *I* wasn't comfortable with either, having been more than a little confused about religion myself over the past few years. I thought I'd been born again twice, once when I was six and then again when I was ten. But each time, whatever it was that made me stand up in church for the altar call and say the words of the Sinner's Prayer along with others who stood when Grandpa Pelton invited them to, faded pretty fast. I'd begun to suspect that what other people described feeling when they testified to their experiences—a feeling of surrender, of lightness—had nothing to do with anything I had felt. The way they talked, I could tell—it *seemed* like they were caught up in the moment, like I was, but their moment seemed to last, while mine just fizzled.

About a month after I first got to L.A., on my eighteenth birthday, I woke up early, with knots in my stomach. Kind of expectant. Even though I had no reason to be. Just as I'd figured, even if I'd secretly hoped for something different, no one said anything about my birthday. I wasn't scheduled to work. And I didn't go to Deena's either, spending the day moping instead. Jake came over around noon and started hammering away at stuff in the kitchen. I hid out in the den with a book from the library.

Afternoon came. And evening. Nothing special happened.

Mom called after dinner. I spoke to her in the den so no one could hear. She wished me a happy birthday and sounded sad. "I got home yesterday, Angie. I was disappointed that you weren't here."

Grandpa Pelton came on the phone, too—the first time I talked to him since the day I'd run away. "Your mother is miserable, Angela," he said. "I hope you know that."

That bummed me out even more. After we hung up, I asked my dad if I could borrow the car.

"You got plans?"

"Yeah. With a friend from work."

"Knock yourself out."

"Have a good time," Connie said, waving cheerfully as ever.

Sadiq was at the curb. I pulled up to him and told him to get in the car. He looked kind of surprised, but did what I said.

I drove us around for a while. All over. I had a vague sense of direction to go on—Connie and my father had taken me on a kind of drive-by tour: Beverly Hills, Hollywood, a couple of beaches. That's where we ended up—at the beach. We got out and walked for a while, lighting up cigarettes. We both stopped and stared at the ocean for a bit.

"It's my birthday today," I said, to the ocean, like I was making some kind of announcement.

Sadiq turned and stared at me for a minute. "Happy birthday, Angela," he said, as he leaned in to kiss me. One kiss led to another and another. It was strange. I'd had boyfriends, Denny being the last of them. So this wasn't my first kiss. But it kind of felt like it was—better, though. That first one had been with the pimply, brace-mouthed boy who lived next door in Garden Hill. With Denny, it had been all about doing what it took to make him happy. What Sadiq and I did was nothing like the first wipe-my-mouth-off experience and definitely more mutual than with Denny. Eventually, breathing hard, I put my hand on his chest and pushed him away.

"I— I can't think, Sadiq. This isn't right."

His eyes flashed at me by the light of the lamppost in the parking lot behind us. He looked as dazed as I felt. He put one of his hands in my hair, pulling me back toward him and whispered into my ear, kissing it between each feathery word, "Do you believe it's a sin?"

"Huh?" I couldn't think. "Mmm. No. Yes. I— don't— know." My mind wasn't doing a very good job at finding enough words to fill a sentence.

He kissed me again, on the lips, making my mouth too busy to help my mind anyway, and I kissed him back with everything I had.

Then, after a moment of both of us breathing raggedly, he said, "In my religion, it *is* a sin. But we also have something called *mut'a*."

"What's that?" I didn't really care.

He stopped talking to kiss my neck, making it even harder for me to focus on what he was saying. "Temporary marriage."

"Temporary?" I was distracted by his hand, which held mine. He raised it to his face, and bent to put his lips on the inner part of my wrist, moving them up, slowly, into the palm of my hand. My fingers curled around his mouth, his face, moving to the back of his head and into his hair, guiding him back upward.

"A marriage with a beginning and an end." He took both of my hands in his, his words muffled in the hollow at the base of my neck.

I might have said something like "Mm-hmm."

"The point is . . . it's not a sin. It's a commitment. For a set period of time."

"A commitment? Not a sin? So— how do you— what do you have to do?"

He pulled away and locked his eyes in mine. "We make an intention. I say: Angela Rogers, you are my wife for tonight. And you say: Sadiq Mubarak, you're my husband for tonight."

"Sadiq Mubarak: you're my husband? For tonight?"

"Just for tonight."

"What's the point of that?"

"It means . . . I am responsible. If anything happens."

We ended up in the backseat of my dad's car. It was the first time for him, I think, so mechanics were what he focused on more than technique. But that was a good thing. He kept stopping to check in with me. To make sure I was—well—enjoying myself. That was something Denny had never bothered with. When we were done, we held each other close. Temporary husband and wife.

After a while, I put my hand on his cheek and asked, "How old were you when your father died?"

"I don't know. A baby."

"How did he die?" I tried to imagine Deena young and widowed with a baby version of Sadiq in her arms.

Sadiq laughed. "Depends on who you ask. There are some who say that it's all my mother's fault."

I sat up. "Fault? What do you mean? Like, she killed him?! You don't believe that!" I know I didn't, whether he did or not.

He laughed again. "No. Not murder. Some think that my mother drove him to it."

"What— what do you mean?"

He wasn't laughing now, just shaking his head. His scowl was back. "I don't know what I mean. I don't know what anything means." After a minute, the scowl faded.

I wanted to ask him more, but he started kissing me again— lighting everything back up between us all over again. This time, it was all about technique.

I didn't feel like going to Deena's house the next day. But she came over around ten o'clock in the morning. She had a wrapped present in her hand—for me.

"You didn't come yesterday. I wanted to give you this. And wish you a happy birthday." She was smiling.

"How— how did you know it was my birthday?"

"I saw it when you were filling out your job application. At the library. You are eighteen now. A young woman—all grown up! You can vote. You are the mistress of your own future. Isn't that so?"

"You remembered?"

"Of course, I remembered!"

"No one here knew it was my birthday."

Deena put her hand on my shoulder. "Silly girl. You should have told them." She pointed to the present she'd put in my hands. "Go on. Open it."

I ripped open the wrapping and looked at what she'd given me. A book. *Pilgrim's Progress* by John Bunyan.

"It's what Marmee gives to Meg and Jo. Beth and Amy. In *Little Women*," Deena explained.

I nodded. "I remember. Thank you, Deena. I— thank you for everything."

By the time I knew I was pregnant, I'd read *Pilgrim's Progress* three times—the first part anyway, about Christian's journey. It wasn't an easy read, and the part about his wife, Christiana, wasn't as good.

That book changed everything for me. I understood, for the first time in my life, what faith was all about. I thanked Deena over and over again and told her she should read the book, too.

"We have our own stories, Angela. About faith. They all mean the same thing, you know."

I thought about what she said. But I didn't agree. I couldn't because I knew better. Jesus said, *I am the way and the truth and the life. No man cometh unto the Father but by me.* I knew that now. Like Christian, I'd had to leave home and go on a journey, get sidetracked and make mistakes to figure it out. I still had a long way to go on the journey, I knew, but at least now I understood what it was.

It took forever for my father to come home on the day I decided to tell him that I was pregnant. I thought I'd be nervous and afraid. But I wasn't—not compared to how I would have felt if I'd been home and it was Mom or Grandpa Pelton I had to break the news to, which I guessed I'd have to, some time or another. This was easy, compared to how that was going to be.

When I told Dad, he was quiet for a long time. Then, without asking me anything, about who the father was or anything, he came and put his arm around me. I started to cry.

"Shh. It's all right, Angie. It's gonna be okay. I promise."

He was hugging me and stroking my hair, a little more clumsily than I had imagined he'd do when I first decided to run away from home. He held me for a long time, until I cried all the water out of me. He got me a glass of some more and held me again. I drank the water almost as thirstily as I soaked in the embrace.

Then he said, "It's okay, Angie. You've got your whole life ahead of you. We'll figure out what to do. You rest, okay," he said, laying me down on the couch, pulling a blanket up to tuck in around me.

I nodded, feeling vulnerable and taken care of, like the little girl he'd never known, asking, "Are you mad?"

"Oh, Angie, no. This was just a mistake. I love you and I'm here." I closed my eyes, happy and relieved.

A few minutes later, I heard him talking on the phone. To Connie. He was filling her in. I was furious. He came back into the room when he was done talking to her. Taking my hand in his, he said, all soft-eyed and sympathetic, "Connie will take care of everything, honey."

"Connie?"

Not seeing the resentment in my eyes, he nodded. "She's making an appointment for you. Right away."

"An appointment?"

"For an abortion." Dad squeezed my hand. "I'll be with you the whole time."

My hand in his went limp. "An abortion?"

"It'll be fine. I promise. No big deal." He gave me another hug, tight and quick, then looked at his watch. "I've got to go pick up Cory from guitar class and Michelle from ballet. I'll be home soon, Angie. We'll talk about this some more. But you don't worry about anything. Okay?"

I stared at him without nodding, not saying a word. I listened to the clink of his car keys, heard him go out the door, start up the car, and drive off. I took deep breaths to calm myself. It didn't work. Without thinking, I jumped off the couch and ran out after him, knowing he was already gone. After a second, I came back into the house and heard the phone ringing. It was Mom.

"Angie? Oh, baby, come home!"

"What's wrong, Mom?"

"It's Dad—your grandfather. He had a heart attack. I—I did CPR, but Angie, he didn't make it. He was dead before the ambulance came and they couldn't revive him, either. Will you come home, Angie? You will, won't you?"

I said I would and hung up. I started to cry. Sandwiched between death and birth—and more death if I did what my father wanted—I didn't know what to do. I left the house, crossing the street to ring Deena's bell, thinking of Grandpa all the time, remembering all the things he'd ever said to me, appreciating what a good man he was, now that he was gone, thinking of what a trial I'd been to him. Knowing, without having to wonder, what he would have said about Dad's idea to get an abortion. Sin on top of sin. The opposite of the path to redemption.

Deena's daughter, Sabah, answered the door.

"Is your mom home?"

"Yes."

I pushed my way into the house.

Behind me, Sabah said, "She's praying."

That made me stop. "Praying?"

"In her room. She'll be done in a minute. You can wait in the living room."

I was already in the living room, standing at the edge of it, at the end of the hallway that led to Deena's bedroom. Her door was open. I saw her standing on a rug laid at an angle on the floor. She was draped and covered in a big white sheet of cloth. She bent at the waist, stood again, put her hands up to her ears, then folded her body all the way down, touching her forehead to the floor, her lips moving the whole time, her backside in the air. I'd never seen her pray before. I couldn't take my eyes away. She was my friend, she was Sadiq's mother, the grandmother of the life inside of me, a stranger, too, with strange, foreign ways—she was all of these things at the same time. I thought of Grandpa—of how he would have seen her. As someone who had to be saved, praying, in this strange way, to the wrong god, not the one I'd just come back to. After a few minutes, she was done. She folded up the little rug, stood, and turned, catching sight of me. She came out of the room, loosening the sheet that still draped her body, smiling like what I'd seen was no big deal.

"Angela!" She was happy to see me. She came closer and saw my face. "Angela? Is everything okay?"

I didn't say anything for a second. Then I nodded. "Everything's fine. I'm sorry. I didn't know you were busy."

"Oh, that's okay. I'm done with my prayers. Shall I make us some tea?"

"No, thank you. I—I've got to go."

She frowned. "Is everything all right, Angela? You look—upset. Has anything happened?"

What could I say? I was ashamed of myself. She'd been so kind—this woman with her strange, misguided faith. And I had fallen so short of all that *my* faith required. I'd had sex with her son, who was younger than me and still in school. I was carrying his child. My grandfather was dead. There was nothing I could say that would express everything I felt. All I knew was that I had to get home. Dad, with his and Connie's murderous plans for abortion; Deena, with her foreign god and alien prayers—these people were strangers, alien to the way I'd been raised. I had to find my way back home for the same reasons I'd left. To wipe the slate clean and start all over again.

I said, "Everything's fine. Thanks," heading for the door. "'Bye," I called over my shoulder, running out of the house.

I ran into my father's house, got my bag out, and started to pack. I was sobbing out loud, not realizing that someone was in the house, listening.

Footsteps. A mumbled voice. "Are you okay?"

It was Jake. Jake March, the handyman. I saw him, but I couldn't stop crying. I screamed, "No! No, I am not okay! My grandfather's dead. I have to get out of here! I have to go home! But I can't! I'm pregnant! I'm gonna have a baby! And I have nowhere to go!"

He stepped into the den and took me in his arms, less clumsily than my father had done before.

I came home a married woman. After kissing and hugging and fussing over me, saying how worried she'd been, Mom said, when we were alone, still shocked, "Angie. I spoke to your father. This baby. It's not Jake's."

Because she hadn't asked me a question, I didn't answer her.

"You married the handyman, Angie. So much older than you." She'd barely met him and already she didn't like him, that was clear. "Did you tell him the truth?"

"He knows."

"And what are you going to tell your baby, when it's old enough to ask?"

"There won't be anything to tell it. It'll grow up with a father. He—or she—won't ask."

"And the real father? Who is he, Angie? Doesn't he have a right to know the truth?"

"He's nobody. There's nobody. Just Jake," I said, and just by saying it, willing it, living it, I made it true. At least until Jo came to me and asked me about the color of her eyes—something I had never considered, something I'd never learned about, even though I went back to school, got my high school diploma, and earned a degree at the college Chris had just dropped out of in what should have been his final year.

When the babies were born—Jo pushing her way out first, big and healthy; Chris, a half hour later, so small that the doctors had worried, frail in every way but will, all through his baby years— Jake was right beside me, praying and holding my hand the whole while.

We worshipped those babies together. Jo, the strong one, who was cautious, not learning to walk until she was fifteen months old. But she never toddled, never fell once she started. Not like Chris, the weak one—always the first to get sick, worse than anyone else, and the last to get well—who was up and off at nine months, before he had any sense of balance, falling and picking himself up before giving a thought to the next step. He willed himself out of the fragile health he started life out with, a football star in high school.

Talking was another story. Jo was communicating before she had the words to do it—babbling out sounds that sounded like questions. She'd point to everything and look at me and say "Ah?" with a question mark that let me know she wanted to know the names of things. Of *everything*. She couldn't say anything yet. But she wanted *me* to name everything—animals, people, colors, numbers. She reminded me of Helen Keller in that old movie *The Miracle Worker*, when Helen finally figures out what Anne Bancroft has been trying to teach her—that the sign for water means "water." Then she grabs Anne Bancroft's hand and points to everything, so she can learn the words. That was Jo. By the time she was two, she wasn't just speaking in sentences. She was talking in whole paragraphs. All day long. Sometimes, in my less-than-patient moods, it took a lot not to want to yell at her to shut up. She never let anyone else talk! I used to joke about it. That I had to ice my ears at night because they'd get sore from having to listen to Jo go on and on all day.

The one person who never got tired of Jo's yapping was her father. It was so strange to see. He's not much of a talker himself and you'd think he wouldn't have patience with anyone else's chatter. But Jake came alive when Jo started to talk. As a father. And as a husband. Her voice erased the awkwardness between us. When she called him Daddy, she made our marriage real. He would listen and nod through the whole length of Jo's baby-voiced monologues. It was a lovely thing, soothing away the last trace of any doubts I may have had about marrying him.

Even Mom warmed to him, over the years, never again raising the subject of what we'd spoken of when I first brought him home. Once, in the earliest days, when Jake and I had just handled a loud double-diapering session, working as a team, getting the twins settled down and smiling after they'd both been screaming at the top of their lungs, Mom had let herself in without us noticing, and watched the four of us cuddle up on the sofa. Surprising us, because we hadn't known she was there, she said, "Treasure these moments, Angie. Don't let them slip away without appreciating them. Those babies of yours aren't going to remember any of it when they're grown. I guess they're not supposed to. It's their job to grow up and away from you. And yours to remember."

I'd bitten my lip, thinking she was chiding me for being ungrateful to her.

Things between Mom and me were never smooth, something we didn't talk about, not since I'd run away. But her relationship with me had nothing to do with the kind of mother I wanted to be, I'd told myself, shrugging off the distance between us. *My* babies had a father—a good Christian man, the gentle head of the household we created, slowly, together, quietly providing the strength and guidance that is a man's duty to give. I had tried my best to be a good wife, too, looking up to him in a way I had not been sure I could when we first met. Only now is the first time we'd ever really been on our own, just husband and wife—apart from those few weeks when the twins went to Africa. But that didn't count. Then, they were coming back. Now, who knew what would happen?

The doorbell rang. It was Mom, unexpected, home straight from the airport, from wherever the heck she'd been this time.

"Is he gone?" she asked, a little breathless, as if she'd been running.

"To boot camp. He called to say he was okay." On the phone, Chris hadn't sounded like Chris. "It was like he was reading from a script. Like a robot."

Mom nodded. Of course. She'd know what I was talking about. She'd been through this before, with the man who'd been her husband. But that's not the same as when it's your baby.

"What about Jo?"

"She's fine. Worried about Chris, I guess."

"Has she discussed her plans with you? About what she wants to do when she graduates?"

"Be a missionary. Like you." I heard the resentment in my voice.

"No. Not anymore."

I frowned.

"She didn't tell you about this job she's got lined up?"

"A job?" I shrugged. "She's busy with school. She'll tell me eventually." I didn't say anything else, realizing suddenly that the way things were between Jo and me, I had no right to be smug with Mom. Not when Jo obviously talked to her more than she did with me. When she'd told me about the languages she was studying, three years ago, with a lift to her chin, daring me to raise that old subject, I hadn't said anything. She was learning *his* languages. Sadiq's. And I didn't want to know why.

"Well, I'm worried," Mom said. "You should talk to her, Angie."

We were in the kitchen. I was putting on some coffee. "You

came back early," I said, trying to change the subject. "I would have come to the airport if you'd have let me know."

"Won't you let go, Angie?" Mom said suddenly. I didn't know what she was talking about and looked at her, confused. "I don't blame you for being angry with me. You've carried it around on your shoulders since you were a girl—since I went back to school to get my nursing degree, when I finally managed to climb out of the hole of darkness I crawled into when you were barely done crawling yourself, because of your father leaving. Later, when I started going away on my missions, you just got madder and madder. I know you don't think I was a very good mother, Angie. That may be so. I'm a better one now, but you haven't let yourself notice in all these years. You've been so wrapped up in the role of being a mother yourself that you won't let me be yours. The truth is, you've been a good mom. I know I've never said it out loud. But I've noticed. You've been the opposite of what I was. Focused. Always present in the lives of your children. When they were little, I saw how in the middle of adult conversation, you'd turn and answer a question no one else noticed being asked, tuned into those baby voices, which, for you, always came first. But now— any fool could see it—there's something wrong between you and Jo. Whatever it is, Angie, don't let it fester. Not the way things have between you and me for all these years."

I didn't say anything, just closed my eyes to try to keep the tears from falling.

Mom sighed. "I didn't tell you I was coming home because I didn't have time, Angie. I was in the biggest hurry. I dropped everything, right where it was, as soon as I heard about Chris. I came back for you. I'm here, Angie. I'll stay for as long as you want. For as long as I'm needed."

My eyes still closed, I whispered, "I'm scared to death, Mom. I don't want him to go to war."

"I know, baby," she said, turning me around to face her, taking me in her arms, stroking my hair like I had so desperately needed her to do before I ran away all those years ago.

٢

Part Two

I held my tongue, and spake nothing: I kept silence, yea,
even from good words; but it was pain and grief to me.

Psalm 39, v. 5

Jo

By the time I got home from Washington Dulles Airport, it was the middle of the night. I let myself into my condo, dumping my bag just barely inside the door before kicking it shut. I went straight to bed, like I always did, fooling myself into thinking I'd actually be able to sleep when I knew I wouldn't. Not after the kind of assignment I'd just come home from. After a couple of restless hours, I gave up and made my way into the kitchen to make myself some tea. But I was hungry, too. And there wasn't any food. I went back to the bag, abandoned at the entrance, and rummaged through it to find myself a granola bar.

While I waited for the kettle to whistle, I went to the dining table to sift through the mail that the woman next door had collected for me, neatly stacked, and looked around at the plants she'd watered while I was away, green and thriving. Colleen was a wonderful neighbor—a retired secretary who had worked for years for various congressmen, up on the Hill—quietly vigilant on my behalf. She spent more time in my apartment than I did.

The kettle whistled. I left the mail where it was, went back into the kitchen, dunked a tea bag into a mug of steaming water, and carried the mug and the granola bar into the living room. I clicked the television on. And swore. Nothing but snow. I must have missed the cable bill. I kept forgetting to set up the automatic payment online. This wasn't the first time this had happened.

I leaned my head back on the couch and thought about the movie collection in the cabinet next to the TV. In my bag, there was an Urdu television drama I'd picked up at the Karachi airport. But that was work—more useful for keeping up my command of Urdu than anything I encountered on the assignments they sent me on. High-quality Urdu, no subtitles. And they were good, too. Hours and hours of drama, heavy on the dialogue and light on the action. One I had enjoyed in the past was an adaptation of Ayn Rand's *Fountainhead*. I had some Arabic TV shows on DVD, too. But I wasn't in the mood for either.

I looked at the clock. It was 4:45 A.M., 1:45 on the West Coast. Dan would be fast asleep. Last time I'd called him in the middle of the night, he was mad. Not like when we'd first started dating, when he'd wake up to talk and listen, in love with the sound of my voice. After college, I'd come to Washington, D.C., and he'd gone back to California, to L.A., which made our relationship a long-distance one, still nice and chaste and Christian, with hardly any physical temptation to get in the way of our plan to really get to know each other. In the last year, he'd tried to make things more serious between us, even mentioning marriage a few times.

His timing was terrible, pushing for commitment right when

work was causing me to lose all perspective. I didn't know how I'd lasted as long as I had. I sighed with relief. At least it was over. I took a bite of the granola bar and a sip of my tea, my mind still floating around, landing on scenes from the assignment I'd just come home from.

When Artemis Intelligence Services, the private defense contractor I worked for, had recruited me through Professor Crawley, I thought I would be one of the good guys, helping to catch terrorists bent on killing Americans. I would aid and assist in the investigations and interrogations that would prevent those bad guys from ever hitting us again. I didn't know what I knew now—that the line between good and bad would get so blurry. That other line— the one between *us* and *them*—getting more distinct. It had to be, for us to be able to do what had to be done. But there were visceral moments that stayed with me, fueling my imagination, disorienting me, making it hard sometimes to remember the role I was assigned to play, to stay detached from the things I had seen—the things I had been a part of.

In those moments, I saw men in hoods or goggles, the snip of the scissors sharp in their ears as they were shorn of their clothing, before their hearing was muffled. Deprived of sight and sound. Before that, beaten, bound in shackles and chains. Drugged with tranquilizers, administered roughly, through the rectum. Diapered.

I only really saw this a few times. The initial softening-up process, when I was an unnecessary appendage, there only in case I was needed. The loud noise and music, the orders to stand or squat or hang from the bars of a cell. Pain and humiliation need no translation. Sometimes, the team's assignment was just to pluck men off the street and fling them into prisons in places they'd never been and would never see. Other times, our assignment was only a transfer. Picking up detainees from one level of hell and delivering them into another. Often, too often, the target was already broken before we got him, at the hands of those who had him before. Sometimes I witnessed the breaking myself. Once, we picked up a detainee from a place to which I had been a part of delivering him only months before. The man we'd handed over and the man they handed back were not the same. And the differences—mental and physical—were shocking. The team took pictures—they always took pictures. The marks on his body were in places that made me shudder. Cuts and burns.

This was not what I thought I had signed up for. Back when I was still in college, Professor Dunnett, my Urdu professor in Chicago, had asked me to see him at the beginning of my last semester there.

"That interview with those recruiters that Crawley set you up with? Have you accepted the offer, Jo?"

"Yes," I said, surprised that he knew of it.

He had paused for a moment, resting his chin on a triangle made of hands and fingers. "I'm not sure this is the right thing for you to do, Jo."

"But— I just want to help. To do my part."

"Did they say what kind of work you'd be doing?" Professor Dunnett asked.

I nodded warily. "I'll be working as an interpreter. Under contract to the government. They're really short. In all areas. And— I know two languages they'll be needing."

"But what will you be interpreting? Will you be on the battlefield?"

I shook my head. "No. Intelligence work. They're running background checks. To get me a security clearance. It'll take about six months. So I'll be able to start right after I graduate." I was eager to start, was planning to cram all I could into those last months of study.

"Intelligence work? As in, paperwork? Correspondence? Or— in person?"

I'd shrugged.

"This isn't what you planned to do, Jo. With what you've learned. I thought you wanted to be a missionary?"

"I do. But the mission, for now, has changed."

In the process, so had I. In the grand scheme of things, I was nothing, I knew. Nothing but a translator. An interpreter. A human dictionary. That's what I told myself in the beginning, trying to absolve myself of any of the responsibility of what I'd taken part in. But the trick was the human part. A *human* dictionary.

I didn't work in any of the places that became famous. Guantánamo or Bagram or Abu Ghraib. I worked in the dark. Initially, in prison cells in Pakistan. Sometimes in hotel rooms. Other times, in other places—secret locations. Black sites, the newspapers started to call them. In Africa. In Asia. And Eastern Europe. A beautiful island in the Indian Ocean.

In the course of my work, I had been to Pakistan many times. Mostly to cities in the north, but to Karachi, too, a few times. Landing there, in the city that Sadiq came from, I couldn't help but think of him. Looking down at the lights of Karachi from the window of the plane as we'd make our descent, I'd wonder if he was there. On the road, driving from the airport to secret locations in Karachi and other cities and back, I would look out from behind the tinted glass of SUV windows that no one on the streets could look into, like a woman from behind a veil. I only experienced the place in fleeting moments and snippets, always in a hurry, usually on the ground for merely a few hours and in the dead of night. I wondered sometimes if I'd ever go back and see those places in daylight.

My language skills narrowed—I knew how to ask questions— over and over again, the same ones. I knew how to translate the same repeated answers and assertions: "I am innocent. No! That's not true. That's a lie. Who told you that? I don't know. I don't know what you're talking about. I am *not* a terrorist. I am *not* a bad man. I am a good person." I couldn't translate the sobs and the screams. I didn't have to.

How was I supposed to know? That these cries and pleas would all sound the same, whether or not the person who formed them was telling the truth. That the people I worked for couldn't tell the difference either. They thought they could. They thought that pain and confusion could be a filter for lies and truth. So they were liberal in handing out both. Along with threats. Involving children and wives and families left behind.

Once, I'd been assigned to an interrogation of two little boys. Eight and six. Their father was a big catch. And the mission was to get intel from them that would help to convince their dad that we had them and that they were in danger. Their mother was in our custody, too. I did the best I could to make myself understood, to understand them, but I wasn't used to talking with children. I'll never forget how scared those little boys were.

When we were done with them, the guy in charge took one look at me and said, "Don't let yourself get all dewy-eyed for those kids. Their father is a murdering monster. They're murderers in training. They don't deserve those tears threatening to fall out of your girly eyes."

I put my hand up to my face in shock. I hadn't noticed the wetness. That was how good I was at doing what had to be done. I was numb, totally cut off from the source of those tears.

On my very first assignment, the people I'd be working with— government interrogators, not military—had offered the old joke, "If we tell you who we work for, we'd have to kill you," as if it wasn't crystal-clear. The lead interrogator, the night before our first mission, had given me lots of advice at the bar in the hotel where we gathered, in Barcelona, getting ready to fly somewhere else the next morning.

"Don't get caught up in any of the bullshit they'll feed you. They'll cry and talk about how innocent they are. I mean grown men. Weeping. Be ready for that. They'll tell you their sob stories. About what a big mistake we've made. That's not your problem. Your job is just to translate. To tell them what we tell you to tell them. To tell us what they tell you."

The others had nodded, raising their glasses to their lips. Wide-eyed, I'd sipped my Coke and tried to prepare myself. In the morning, over breakfast, before our flight, I'd asked if I could say a prayer for our mission. The guys all nodded their agreement. I closed my eyes, bowed my head, and said, "Lord, we ask You to be with us, to guide us in our mission, to let our hands be Your hands, our words be Your words, our works be according to Your will. In Jesus' Name, Amen."

"Amen," everyone said; big, brawny guys who swore too much and drank too much, led in prayer by me, with my quaky, shaky, scared-of-what-was-next voice. After that first assignment, I couldn't look at them anymore without flashes of what they'd done streaking through the air at odd moments. I regretted praying with them. But they asked me to, again, before the next assignment, and then, again, before the next. So, I did, always unsure about whether it was the right thing to do.

You'd think I wouldn't fit in. I don't know what it says about me that they accepted me as they did. I wasn't even that good at my job, not as good as some of the native speakers who were also on contract, far better interpreters than I was. I think I was more trusted than they were. Simply because I *wasn't* a native speaker.

Despite the pep talk and the prayer, that first time and all the others, it was impossible to ever really be ready for our assignments, even after dozens of missions. Each and every one of them was recorded. Sometimes literally, by one of the guys, in a mask, holding a camcorder, but always in my memory. There was a room in my head, where the scenes played repeatedly. I could be in my apartment. Could watch TV and laugh at a sitcom. Have dinner with friends. Or listen to Dan on the phone, telling me about his day. But the images were my constant companion.

It was strange, too, the tricks my memory played. That when I remembered, my perspective changed. The mask on my face, which we usually all wore on assignment, would fall off, leaving me exposed to the pain, sometimes the hatred, raw, of the people we questioned. But the masks on the faces of the people I worked with remained. So that my nightmares were filled with them, faces of violent people in ski masks, their eyes hard and cold, looking at me, at the detainees, utterly drained of anything recognizably human. That was a scary feeling, one I couldn't escape at times—like now, just home, with fresh memories to assemble into line with all of the old ones.

F our hours later, the phone rang.

It was my boss. "You okay?"

"I'm fine."

"Your contract is officially up."

"I know. Two years. Time flies when you're having fun."

"Well?"

"Well what?"

He sighed heavily. "Come on, Jo. The offer for renewal? The one you said you'd think about?"

"*You* said I should think about it. *I* said I wasn't interested."

I heard him sigh again. "Is it the money? Because I've been authorized to up the offer."

"No. It's not about the money."

"Come on, Jo. You know this is important. You know how much we need you."

"I don't want to do it anymore. I told you."

"Look, I know it's a crummy gig, but someone's gotta do it. It's a matter of national security."

I decided that silence was the way to go. He argued some more, not noticing that he was only arguing with himself, trying to convince me to renew. Finally, he gave up, but not before telling me to call him if I ever changed my mind.

I was still on the couch, too tired to get up and too wound up to bother trying to sleep where I was, when, a little while later, I heard the key jiggle in the lock before the door creaked open, and a hand reached in to flick the lights on.

Colleen was already inside, mail in hand, when she saw me and gasped, "Oh! My! You scared me, Jo."

"I'm sorry, Colleen."

"I didn't know you were home. I've got your mail here, from yesterday."

"Thanks, Colleen. Come in."

She put the mail down on the dining table before taking the few steps into the living room.

"When did you get home?"

"Last night. Late. Thanks again, Colleen. For taking care of everything. All the plants are thriving. Doing better than they would have if I'd been the one watering them."

"That's because I talk to them. You look exhausted."

"Bone-weary. Too tired to move. I just want to sit here and do nothing."

"Poor baby! You gonna be going away again soon? For work?"

"No. I quit."

"Oh." She paused. "Should I leave the keys on the table, then?"

"Nah. You keep them, Colleen, if you don't mind. I'm going home for Thanksgiving next week. To California."

"Oh, that's nice. You haven't been home for a while, have you?"

"A few months ago. But only for a day or two, when my brother came home from his tour in Iraq. I'm going to stay longer this time. While I'm there, I'm going to think about moving back home. To try and make the savings last as long as I can, now that I'm officially unemployed. You going anywhere, Colleen? For Thanksgiving?"

"Nope. My daughter's coming to visit me. With her kids."

"Oh. Well, feel free to use my place if you need more room for them to stay."

"Aw—bless your heart, Jo."

"I mean it."

"Do you? That's not a bad idea. If we get too crowded in my place, I might take you up on it. Well, I'm sure I'll see you before you go. But if I don't, you say hi to your family for me. And give your brother a big, giant hug from me!"

"I will." Colleen had met Chris, once. When he'd come to visit me before being deployed.

"See ya later," Colleen said, leaving, taking her cheery energy out the door with her.

I went through the mail when she left, seriously this time. Got out my checkbook and caught up on my bills. I called the cable company. If I was going to continue to be sleepless, I needed my cable.

I got through the day. Went out to stock up on some groceries. I called Dan. And Mom and Dad and Chris. Thanksgiving was going to be a big deal for Mom. The first one we'd all be at in a long time. Uncle Ron and his family would be there, driving down from Los Angeles. Grandma Faith would be coming home, too, just in time, back from a quick mission, the first one she'd gone on since Chris was at boot camp, going only after he'd come home from Iraq.

By evening, I was unpacked, stacking the new Urdu and Arabic DVDs in the cabinet with the rest of my movie collection. I cleaned up, wiping away the dust that had settled on the surfaces of tables and counters while I was away, and did some laundry. Took a hot bath. Made myself some cocoa. And took up my place on the couch again, a book in hand. After a while, I put it down, giving up the fight.

It wasn't the parade of images that was getting in the way now. Just one—one bewildered face. There were plenty of reasons for him to be memorable. He'd been rounded up in a house raid in Karachi—one that had netted some pretty big fish and made it into the news. Everyone caught in that net was considered high-value, and the team had been pretty excited. These were some really bad guys. Most of them had been shot during the raid, and the Pakistani authorities hadn't bothered to treat any of them. So they came to us with wounds, festering. His was in his thigh. He'd also been beaten up pretty badly. He couldn't walk and had to be held up and frog-marched.

His name was Fazl. The guys called him Fuzzy, behind his back, and then, eventually, to his face. That was against protocol. We were only supposed to refer to detainees by their numbers. But in Fuzzy's case, for some reason, everyone broke that particular rule. He was only a few years older than me. And something he'd said, more to himself than to me, mumbling, had stayed with me, striking a chord of memory—like déjà vu. It was a spectacular coincidence. It had to be. But it had nothing to do with what the guys on the team wanted to hear.

There'd been some hesitation about taking him with us at all. We'd walked through the cell block in Karachi, doing the usual preliminary screenings. The biggest fish, the one whose name was on the front page of the *New York Times* that week, spoke English, so I wasn't called in to help with him. Outside of Fuzzy's cell, we stopped, trying to get his story. About what he was doing in the house that had been raided.

One of the Pakistani agents came up to us and said, pointing at the guy we'd soon be calling Fuzzy, "This one is retahded." We'd stared at him blankly. "He's—not right in the head. An idjit. Stchupid, you know. The mind of a child. He says he was only a gatekeeper. He didn't even have a gun on him. The others say the same thing about him."

One of our guys said, "So—he was a bodyguard, eh? And the retarded thing—it's an act. It's standard op with these guys. To pretend not to know anything."

The Pakistani agent shook his head. "He's not pretending. He's retahded, I tell you. Poor bahstard. You'll get nothing out of him. And he's not one of *them*." He pointed his head in the direction of the cell block where the biggies were. "He's Pakistani. Not Arab."

The lead interrogator stood and stared at Fuzzy for a moment, unsure. This was unusual, to have a local agent discourage us from taking a detainee. The Pakistanis would have given us a lot more guys if we let them. There was a lot of money to be made, handing them over for American taxpayer-funded bounty.

Then the lead guy said, "We've got to be careful. They're telling us that we're bringing in too many of 'em who have nothing to give us."

Breaking another rule, unwritten, I used a word we weren't even supposed to think, saying, "You mean— they're innocent?"

"I didn't say that!" he snapped.

"Look," one of the other guys on the team said, "we've got our orders. This was a big raid. Everyone in that house has something to tell us. Even this fuckin' loser."

That had settled it.

I was the interpreter assigned to Fuzzy's interrogation. If he was acting, he was really good at it.

No matter what we asked him, he'd always go back to the beginning, speaking in a very soft voice, so soft that I had to lean in close to hear what he was saying. "When I was little," he'd say, "my mother died. We were in the city. And she died. I was all alone."

"What the hell's he saying?!" the interrogator, my least favorite to work with, thundered.

"He's talking about how his mother died when he was little."

"What am I, fuckin' Freud, now? I don't give a shit about his mother. Ask him about his boss. Ask him if he's ever met Bin Laden."

I did what I was told. But Fuzzy just started over again, still barely audible. "When I was little, my mother died. I was very, very little. We were in the city. The big city. We'd left home. She died. And I was all alone."

He made the interrogator furious. Fuzzy suffered for that fury. But nothing that they did to him got him on the track they wanted him on. It wasn't that he was being uncooperative. It was just that he seemed not to understand how to start in the middle of the story. He *had* to start at the beginning. After a while, after Fuzzy had been punished a lot for what the interrogator considered to be un-cooperative behavior, the team tried a new tactic. They let Fuzzy start at the beginning.

"When I was little, my mother died. I was very little. We were in the city. I was all alone. Then Uncle came to see me. He said he would take care of me. He took me to a school."

"What's that he said?!" the interrogator interrupted. "Some-thing about a *madrassa*?"

"Yes. But that's just a word for 'school'—he says he went to school."

"Yeah! Fuckin' jeehad school is what it is! Ask him about that! About where the school was. Did they have guns there?"

I asked Fuzzy about the school. But the interruption had caused him to start at the beginning. "When I was little, my mother died . . ."

"Jesus Christ! This moron is fuckin' killing me!" The interro-gator threw his hands up, curled them into fists, and waved them around for a second, and then sat down again.

Fuzzy, again, started at the beginning. It took a few moments for him to catch up to where he'd been before. That's when I re-sumed my translation.

"Uncle took me to school. I learned there. But it was a hard school. They used to beat me. I learned to read the Quran. Uncle used to come and visit sometimes. When he found out that they beat me, he was angry. He took me out of that school and put me in another. He wasn't really my uncle, he told me. He paid for my fees. Bought my clothes and books. Uncle was good to me. Sharif Muhammad Uncle."

My eyes widened. I—I remembered that name.

The interrogator said, "What's that he said? He gave you a name?"

"Yes," I said reluctantly.

"Sharif Muhammad?"

"Yes."

"Ask him who he is. Ask him how he's connected."

"He says it's his uncle. Who took care of him when his mother died."

The interrogator worked hard to bite back another outburst. With an angry exhale of breath, he let Fuzzy go on talking.

"Go and ask him," Fuzzy said. "Find him. Sharif Muhammad Chacha will help me. He has always taken care of me. When others were unkind. He will come again to save me, I know," Fuzzy said.

Finally, Fuzzy got to the point in his story that we were interested in, telling us that when he was done with school, he'd gone to work. In a series of jobs. Finally, through someone he knew, he'd been hired as the gatekeeper for the raided house.

"I was the one who opened the gate when people came. I was the one who shut the gate when people left."

"What people?"

"I don't know."

We were at the end of the line of Fuzzy's thinking. After that, he just went back to the beginning again. "When I was little, my mother died . . ."

When he caught up to the present the second time, the interrogator shot out more questions, a little more gently than before. He tried to come back to that name a couple of times. Sharif Muham-mad. But all Fuzzy ever said was that he was his uncle. Not his real uncle. But an uncle who took care of him.

I broke the rules once more, asking Fuzzy a question that didn't come from the interrogator.

Pissed, the interrogating agent barked at me, "What'd you ask him?"

"I asked him how his mother died."

"Don't go encouraging him! Who gives a shit about his damned mother?" After a pause, almost in spite of himself, the interrogator asked, "What'd he say?"

In a whisper softer than Fuzzy's, I said, "He said she was hit by a car."

I did what I was supposed to for the rest of that interrogation. But I wasn't there anymore. *It couldn't be,* I kept telling myself. They say the world is small. But Karachi is a city of 14 million people. It just couldn't be related. To Sadiq. To my brown eyes and the story behind them.

Eventually, they gave up on Fuzzy. But they didn't let him go. They sent him to Guantánamo Bay. Leaving me, in the midst of all the other crap I carried around, wondering about coincidence, which I used to believe was just another word for Providence—God's plan for the universe.

Two days later, my boss—my former boss—called again.

"What the hell are you playing at, Jo?"

"I don't know what you mean."

"Don't bullshit me. The Department's got your application for clearance. They cross-checked you and realized you were one of ours. They're furious!"

"Oh. That."

"Look, Jo, I know you've been unhappy. But that's no reason to turn your whole life upside down."

"I don't see that this is any of your business. I've been thinking about this for a long time. And I applied for the other position months ago."

"Well, I'm not gonna let you do this, Jo. Losing your nerve is one thing. But you can't flip over and out like this."

"I'm not flipping out. I'm straightening myself up. And I'm not losing my nerve. I just got it back."

"Look, I know this whole thing has been messy, that some of your assignments have been a little—unconventional. Too much John Wayne, and not enough Jimmy Stewart. It's what the times called for and there's talk of some of that changing. Maybe. For the better. In the meantime, you can't go off and start working for the other side!"

"The other side?"

"Hell, yes! That's exactly what you're doing, Jo."

"I don't see it that way."

"Oh yeah? Well, good luck paying the rent!"

This time, when he hung up, I could tell he wanted to slam the phone down. Too bad you can't do that with a cell phone.

He was right about the last thing he'd said. I looked around at my apartment, and thought about the salary the lawyer had quoted, a fraction of what I'd made on contract. No benefits, either. And another six months or more before I was cleared, again, for security. From a different angle. They'd drag their heels this time. Standard Stalling Procedure. It felt good to think about all of this, to calculate my own redemption.

When the phone rang again, it was my *new* boss calling. "Hi, Jo. Just calling to catch up. All the paperwork's in," she said. Her name was Cheryl. She was a lawyer.

"I know. My former employer just called to scream."

"Oh? Yeah. Well, this is unusual. To come from your line of work into mine."

"I know."

"It's gonna take a while, though, to get in the door."

"I'm ready for that."

"Good. And— that other matter you were asking about?"

I knew right away what she meant. This new boss of mine was a little paranoid about talking openly on the phone. She was convinced that the government was listening in. She was probably right.

"Yes?"

"I'm still making inquiries. But I've got nothing for you, yet."

"Oh."

"They're being impossible, Jo. It's like playing Go Fish. 'Have you got a two? No, go fish,' if you get what I mean. But I'll keep my ears and eyes open. Keep talking to the other habeas lawyers, trying to see if anyone—uh—if—oh, what the hell!—if anyone's heard of him. Or takes his case. I'll let you know if I get any information."

"Uh-huh."

"There have been some releases. Your guy could be one of those. But they don't give those names out, either." If someone *was* listening in, I don't think Cheryl was fooling anyone.

"Well, keep in touch. I'll keep you posted. And I'm really looking forward to working with you, Jo."

"Me, too."

"Sooner, I hope, rather than later. It all depends, though. These are strange times we're living in. Tragic times for anyone who gives a damn about the Constitution. Are you okay? For money? 'Cause this is going to be a long haul. It could be a year or more before I can use you. I could give you an advance."

"I'm good for now. Thanks for everything, Cheryl."

All the code stuff was to let me know that she hadn't been able to trace Fuzzy. I hoped he was one of those sent home. He should never have been taken to begin with. One of the reasons I'd taken the job with this lawyer—had offered my services as a translator for her and any other of the habeas lawyers who'd been fighting tooth and nail, with no success so far, to get into Gitmo to meet with clients that the government said had no right to lawyers in the first place—had been Fuzzy. Not just him, of course. I wanted to go and try to help undo what I'd helped to do—because I was no longer willing to pretend that doing the right thing could involve doing anything wrong. Somehow, Fuzzy had become the face of the salvation I sought. I thought about it for a long time. Then I pulled out my laptop and did a search that I'd tried already, after my encounter with Fuzzy. As easy as it had been to find Sadiq in the white pages years before, Googling him now was proving to be fruitless. Well, there was another way to find him. A way that would take me back into his story—the one I'd run away from before my life had become so diverted off the path I'd planned to take—from another angle. Something I had to try, because Sadiq's story had become weirdly entwined with mine. At least, that's what I had to assume, based on what I knew about Fuzzy, which wasn't much and which still could turn out to be a smaller coincidence than it seemed. Not the same person at all. Just someone with a similar story. Who'd been taken care of by another man named Sharif Muhammad, not the man who was Sadiq's driver.

I went to my bookshelf and pulled off my copy of *Pilgrim's Progress*. Tucked into the back pages was a Christmas card from Todd Rogers. He still sent them. One for each of his children now—for Mom and Uncle Ron—always, with that same return address in L.A. where Mom had found him. Uncle Ron had met him a couple of times, over the years. Not Mom, though. I wasn't planning to, either. My destination was the house across the street from his—a house my mom had described as yellow with white trim. I hoped she still lived there. Sadiq's mother. Deena. The grandmother I'd never met.

See what the drop must pass in order to become a pearl,
The open mouths of a hundred crocodiles,
circling a trap with every wave.

Ghalib

Deena

I almost didn't answer when the doorbell rang. I was making a grocery list. *Halal turkey, croutons for stuffing, mushrooms, celery, marshmallows, yams, cranberries*—a list of ingredients that no recipe I had learned at home ever called for. The first few Thanksgivings that we celebrated, when Sabah was young but old enough to want to celebrate with turkey, I had cooked it into a *salan*—pieces of turkey, not the whole thing at once—curried with spices I knew: red chili powder, garlic paste, ginger, saffron, cumin, and coriander. We had rice instead of stuffing and *cachumber* instead of salad. The meat of the turkey was tough and stringy and I could not understand why Americans would eat such an unappetizing bird. Later, when we began to have an "American-style" Thanksgiving, at Sabah's insistence, I grew to like it—the blandness of the meal made a nice change and I found it easy to prepare, cleaner, without the mess and fumes of *masala* frying that our normal cooking required.

I made the list, but I didn't plan to go grocery-shopping until night, after opening my fast. Going shopping for food in Ramzan, during *roza*, is not a good idea. The cart quickly fills with all kinds of unnecessary treats, which end up going mostly uneaten. Ramzan makes your eyes grow and your stomach shrink. I sighed. Ramzan and turkey. Culinary culture clash. I wondered if fruit *chaat* would be okay to serve. How about cranberries in the *chaat*? Mmm. I was feeling my *roza* and hoped the resulting menu wouldn't be too strange for Sabah's latest boyfriend. The last one had been adventurous, even eating the *achaar* I had served when she'd brought him home to meet us last Christmas, picking up the pieces of unripe mango, richly marinated in spices, with his fingers, gnawing his way through the sour flesh and olive-green skin of the fruit. The one before, not so much. He'd turned red and coughed with the first bite of chicken *khorma*. But then, I had stopped accommodating the delicate taste buds of these guests long ago.

Umar had said, "As if it isn't bad enough that we have to meet a different man every season. We have to suffer through spiceless food, too?"

It was a joke between us. That first bite the poor boy took. How long would he wait before reaching for the water? Umar and I made bets.

"Two bites for this one."

"No, this one looks like he has some balls. Five bites at least," we would whisper to each other in the kitchen, while Sabah did the usual tour of the house, sneaking up to her old room to smooch.

Later, when dinner was served and the boy reached for his

water, Sabah would say, in the same way I used to, "No. Water will only make it worse. Have it with yogurt instead," making me laugh. It's always a little strange to hear your child voice the old lessons you have taught them.

In Sabah's case, I think that is the only thing she ever learned from me. The things I have put up with for that daughter of ours—from birth to breast-feeding to boyfriends and beyond! Every moment of it has been a joy. But I hope that this one sticks, I thought to myself. My lap is aching for a grandchild.

The doorbell! Yes—it rang, and I almost didn't answer it. Who would be so rude as to come unannounced? Only a salesperson or a Jehovah's Witness, I was sure. Back home, unannounced visits were the only kind ever paid. Though that changed for me. No one ever came to visit in the last years I spent in Pakistan. Here, in the very beginning, I used to answer the door always. I even invited many of those Witness people in. But it became a nuisance. Anyone who is so very sure of themselves and their beliefs runs the risk of being a nuisance. I admit, I admired the tenacity of those people, who must know that everyone groans when they see them through the peephole and yet go on anyway—pushing doorbells, knocking away—knowing that the only people who will welcome the sight of them will be those desperately lonely enough to be even more of a nuisance than themselves.

Then I thought, it might be a package. Amazon.com has given new clout to doorbells.

There was a young woman standing there. No package in her hand. No uniform or clipboard for me to sign. No pamphlets, either. But there was something about her that made me relax the air of dismissal I had quickly cultivated in light of the absence of these things. She was not here to sell me anything. She was here to receive.

She told me she was Angela's daughter, hesitantly, with a question mark, as if she doubted I would remember who Angela was.

"Angela's daughter?! Oh! Come in, come in," I said. Angela. I knew there was something familiar about her.

She told me her name. Jo. And then said nothing more, expecting me to fill the space of her silence.

I obliged, pretending not to notice the monosyllables of her replies—that is, when she replied with words at all. She was staring at me and looking around the room, making me feel very uncomfortable. "How is your mother? She's well? She was such a nice girl. So sweet. Did you come to visit your grandfather? Across the street? No? You've come to see me? How nice!"

I invited her to sit down and said, trying to hide how annoying I found it that she only nodded and hardly said anything at all, "Your mother was my good friend. I still remember her, every time I go to the library. Did you know that she worked there while she lived here? You did? She told you that? Yes, she was my friend. Will you have some tea? Yes? Your mother told you about my tea, huh? Let me put the water on. You sit. I'll be right back."

In the kitchen, I filled the kettle, wondering at the uneasiness of this unexpected visit. I had not invited her into the kitchen, something I normally would have done. Most of Angela's time in this house had been spent here. But there was something about this girl, Jo. From the moment I opened the door, I felt under inspection—my words assessed and analyzed. I didn't think it was conscious, the watchful, wary distance she maintained. But it was strange. She had knocked on my door, saying she came to visit me.

Why? Who am I to her? I asked myself, lingering in the kitchen without realizing that I did. Boiling the water, simmering the tea, taking my time, leaving my guest unattended—something that was against the rules of etiquette I normally followed.

When I took the tea out to her, I didn't tell her why I wasn't having any with her when she asked. I said, "No, I've had mine already." It would not have been proper to tell her that I was fasting, to make her feel strange about my abstinence. It would have lengthened the distance between us, I thought. Which was strangely long enough already.

I said, "You don't look like your mother." As soon as I did, I realized how odd this was, that she had looked familiar to me and did not look like her mother.

She took a sip of her tea and said, "No. I look more like your son."

It was a good thing I was fasting, that I had no cup of tea in my hand. Else I would have dropped it, letting it clatter to the floor loudly, like a melodramatic character in an Indian movie.

After a long, long moment, a moment I spent remembering— Sabah, at eight, telling me that she'd seen Sadiq get into a car with Angela, something I had found curious at the time, because neither Angela nor Sadiq had ever told me of their friendship—I asked, "Does Sadiq know?"

"I went to see him a few years ago," she said.

"He didn't tell me." That was a silly thing to say. As if he would have. As if I was someone he would have ever confided in, the son whose name made my heart ache, still, at the memory of leaving him behind. Our relationship is perfunctory at best—which is better than it once was.

The girl, Jo, said, "He was going away when I saw him. Do you know where he is?"

"Going away? Yes, he is always on his way here or there," I said, "rarely staying in one place long enough to know where he is himself. But I spoke to him last month. He was here, in the States. In Boston. But on his way back to Pakistan in a hurry. His grandfather has had a stroke."

"Oh."

I tried not to stare, but couldn't help myself. There was no doubting the truth of what she said. It was clear, in her eyes, in the line of her jaw and chin. "You're looking for him? You want to see him again?"

She nodded.

"He—he welcomed you? When you went to see him before? He spoke to you?"

She nodded again. "Yes. He told me about his childhood. About his life with you—the house you lived in with him, the terrace and the fruit tree. And the story of the monkey and the crocodile."

"Oh? He did? I thought those were things he had deliberately forgotten. I thought his memory of life began when we were separated."

"He told me about that, too." Her voice was soft, gently nudging. "Why *were* you separated from each other? What's the story behind that?"

This was an unsettling question—one Sadiq himself had never bothered to ask, one that had undermined my faith for a time. I asked, "You want the short version or the long?"

The girl closed her eyes, which struck me as a strange thing to do. She tilted her head and then opened them again. "The long, please."

"That will be very long. You have time?"

"As much as you're willing to give me," she said.

I tried to think of how to begin. And then seized on the most innocuous of the references she had made.

The monkey and the crocodile. My father used to tell me that story when I was very young. But the version he told me was different from the tale I told Sadiq. In my father's story, the crocodile is put up to the betrayal of his friend, the monkey, by his greedy wife. She deceives him, feigning illness to get him to do what she wants—to bring back the monkey's heart for her to eat so that she might become well. Same ending, though. When I was eight or nine years old, older than Sadiq was when he was taken from me, I told my father that I didn't like his story.

I said, "That's not right. The crocodile himself made the decision to kill his friend. Why should his wife be blamed? Women are always the ones being blamed for everything!"

My father laughed. "Oh? So this is a subject you've given some thought to?"

"Yes. When a man is bad to his mother, it's his wife's fault. When a man is bad to his wife, it's his mother's fault. When is a man ever responsible for himself?"

"Hmm. This is a very good point. *People* tell stories. And *people* listen to them. The way a story is told says something about the one who tells it. And the way it is understood, the lesson drawn from it, tells something about the one who listens. How would *you* tell the story, Deena?"

"Me? I would say that the crocodile himself was greedy. That he was never really the monkey's friend. He only liked her for the fruit she gave him."

"Ah. But I don't like your version."

"You don't?"

"No. For me, the beauty in the story is that the crocodile and the monkey were able to be friends, even if for a brief time. That they rose above their own natures and the way they had been taught to live—to live by fear or to live by greed—and became friends in spite of it all."

"But their friendship didn't last."

"No. That doesn't matter. They were friends for a time. For me, that is such an important part of the story that I'm not willing to change it."

I was quiet for a long time. Then I said, "All right. What if it's the crocodile's brother who tempts him?"

"His brother, eh? All right. *That* I'm willing to accept. That is the new tale of the monkey and the crocodile. Deena Iman's version."

"And yours."

"Oh? You'll share credit with me? So kind of you, little Deena. All right then, Deena and Iqbal Iman's version of 'The Tale of the Monkey and the Crocodile.' Shall we tell it together? Yes? I'll begin . . . Once upon a time . . ."

And so it began. My father and I, together, gave each other permission to change old stories, to challenge old ways of understanding. Monkeys and crocodiles. Fear and greed. Who hasn't succumbed to those old temptations? And how many can claim to have risen above them?

When I was nine years old, I used to spend time on the terrace of our house. There was a *jamun* tree in the neighbor's garden. You are nodding. Sadiq told you about the tree? Well, remember, I am speaking of a time long before he was born. The tree was younger then, not so tall, its branches not so wide, as when Sadiq knew it, its fruit spread from branches that shaded one corner of the terrace, within easy reach for him as it was not for me. When I was a child, the top of the tree was level with the top of the low wall of the terrace. To get any fruit, I had to lean down at a dangerous angle, to reach for the one branch that stretched out to meet my grasping hand. That didn't stop me. The fruit was tasty enough to make the risk worth it. One day, when I had already consumed all of the fruit from the tip of the branch, I leaned farther than I should have, too much of my weight hanging over the wall, and gravity had its way. As I lost my balance, in the second before I fell, I heard someone call, "Look out!" A child's voice, from the garden below. The voice of someone who was there—in the right spot at the right time—to break my fall and save me from certain death.

He was a boy, only two years older than myself, who sat, playing near the base of the tree, and looked up in time to shout his warning. I literally fell on top of him, felt him flatten as he absorbed the shock of my impact, the wind whooshing out of him, the sound of bones snapping with painful pops. Members of his household came running and screaming. His mother shouted, "Umar! Umar, my son! Wake up!" Someone pulled me off him and I saw that he was unconscious, his leg and arm twisted behind him at angles that looked painful. They rushed him to the hospital, after checking to see that I was all right, sending me home with a servant, where I wallowed in miserable guilt, thinking the boy must be dead for sure. He wasn't. He came home in a few hours, his leg and arm in casts. My father went to see his parents, to offer his apologies on my behalf.

When he came home, he saw the look on my face and said, "He's fine. His leg and arm are broken. But he will mend." I burst out crying and my father took me on his lap and dried my tears, trying to make me laugh with his words. "Well, Deena, this is a new twist on the old story. The monkey falls on the crocodile in a preemptive strike, breaking his bones and frightening him away before he ever dares to look upon her heart as a meal for himself."

His words made me cry louder as he laughed, until I had to laugh, too, after first reassuring myself that the boy really was all right. When the tears and the laughter faded, I said, "I thought he was dead."

"That's what the boy thought, too, when he woke up in the hospital. That you must have died in the fall. He was glad to know that his bones were not broken in vain."

This was not the first interaction between the boy's family and mine, although it was the first in a long time. When I was very little, the only telephone on our block belonged to these neighbors. And anyone who needed a phone would knock on their door. It was a service the lady of the house was not very happy to share, and even though everyone in the neighborhood tried not to take undue advantage, insisting on paying for the calls they made, no one entered the house without hearing Mrs. Yusuf's grumbles and complaints—that was her name, the mother of the boy I had fallen upon—who stood guard over the phone, within inches of the caller, able to hear every word of every conversation, and

making no secret of the fact that she did. Everyone breathed a sigh
of relief when others on the block, better-mannered and less abra-
sive, finally had phones installed—though we were not among
those who did.

Our own relations with the Yusuf family became even less
friendly, long after we began to use another neighbor's phone, and
the fact that my father went to their house to apologize was not a
small matter. Several years before, you see, a young girl, maybe
fifteen or sixteen years of age, had knocked on our door. She
was the daughter of Mrs. Yusuf's washerwoman, next door, and
wanted to know if my mother would hire her for work around the
house. This was a time of relative prosperity in the ups and downs
of my father's ongoing serial of business ventures, and my mother
decided that it was time to hire a second servant, someone to help
in the kitchen, to wash the clothes, which were getting harder for
Macee, our old servant, to handle. Things worked out well with
the girl. Until the ten days of Muharram approached. I see you
are nodding. Sadiq told you about this—about Muharram? And
about Sunni and Shia? I would say I am surprised. But the rest of
what you have told me he shared with you has dulled my capacity
to be surprised.

Well, as Muharram approached, the girl suddenly wanted to
leave. My mother was taken aback, asking her if she had been unhappy working for our family. The girl said no, that everything
was fine, but that she must leave on an urgent matter to go back to
her village. My mother probed deeper and found that the girl had
been told, by our neighbor, Mrs. Yusuf, that we were Shia.

"Is that true?" she wanted to know.

My mother told her that it was.

She hesitated for a moment. And then said, "You see, my mother's employer, the lady next door, she says that you Shias celebrate a great sacrifice on Ashura, the tenth day of Muharram. Is that also true?"

My mother said, "We remember it, yes. The battle of Karbala, when the Prophet's grandson Husain and his family and friends were slaughtered by the forces of the tyrant Yazid."

Another moment of pause was followed by a great rush of words. "You see, the lady of the house next door wants me to work for her, with my mother. She has convinced my mother that it's dangerous for me to be here. To work for you. That you Shias kill young people, Sunnis, on Ashura. That you kill them and cook them up and eat them as a sacrifice. I didn't believe her, *Bibi*, but she went on and on and has persuaded my mother, who is very frightened. The lady said all kinds of horrible things about you. About Shias. She said that you are not true Muslims, that you are evil. And that you eat Sunni children."

The girl wanted to be reassured. And my mother did manage to do so, eventually. Poaching for the servants of another household was not unheard-of among neighbors. Perhaps, because the mother of the girl worked for her already, Mrs. Yusuf felt she was entitled to do so in this case. But the virulent propaganda directed against us due to who we were was striking. And exceptional. From then on, my mother referred to Mrs. Yusuf, lips pursed, with a dismissive wave of her hand in the direction of the house next door, as "That *Wahabbi* woman." You know the word? Yes. It's a common term now, isn't it? For Shias, it was always an epithet of intolerance—a way to label Sunnis who were particularly hostile. Most Sunnis were not. None of my school friends and none of the other neighbors.

Not that there wasn't another side to the story. Now, I am embarrassed to recall how every year, during Muharram, the sounds of shameless sermons were broadcast in the streets, shrill and shrieking, from loudspeakers set up in Soldier Bazaar—Shia sermons that raised the blood pressure of all the Sunnis who lived within earshot. Sermons that were deliberately antagonistic—filled with thinly veiled venom directed at the first three *Khalifa*s of Islam, who the Shia saw as usurpers and the Sunni saw as rightly guided. Can you imagine? Fourteen-hundred-year-old views of history determining how neighbors interacted in the twentieth century? No. You can't. Because history here is a dead thing. Something captured in books that schoolchildren have to endure and which they forget about the moment the books are closed. In Pakistan, every conversation, however personal, is punctuated by the raspy, decrepit gasps of the past breathing down your neck; every generation has to fight out all the old arguments that have been fought before.

All I knew was that the mean lady next door didn't like us. That is what I was thinking, the next day, spying on the woman whose offspring I had inadvertently assaulted, as I crouched down next to the terrace wall. I watched as Mrs. Yusuf set her son up in the garden below, fussing over him, going in and out of the house to bring food and drink for him to enjoy, getting him a comic book, and games to play to divert him from the pain in his arm and leg. He wasn't complaining. On one of her trips back into the house, the boy rested his head back on his chair to take the nap his mother had been urging him to take. Before he closed his eyes, they caught sight of me, hovering anxiously from my perch.

"You're the girl on the wall."

"My name is Deena." My tone was wary. Who knew if the boy had views similar to his mother's?

"Hello, Deena On The Wall. My name is Umar." Umar. A Sunni name—the name of one of those much-maligned *Khalifa*s that a Shia would never bestow on a son. His tone was friendly. Which was remarkable, given that there was every reason, his arm and leg among them, for it not to be.

"I'm sorry about what happened."

"If you were truly sorry, you wouldn't be standing there again, making me queasy at the thought of seeing you fall."

Contritely, I took a step backward.

"Wait! Come back. Now I can't see you, Deena On The Wall."

I stepped forward again so he could see me.

"That's better. Did you get any fruit?"

"I'm sorry?"

"It would have been worth it, if you'd gotten any fruit."

"Oh. Yes. I had a bunch of *jamun* in my hand when I fell. I didn't notice it in all of the commotion. Not until I was home again. I had squeezed it so hard that the juice ran down my sleeve. My mother thought I was bleeding. That's when I realized I was still holding the fruit."

He laughed. "Did you eat it?"

"No. I couldn't. I felt so bad."

"And you'd mashed it all up."

"Well, yes. That, too. Does it hurt very much?"

"Only a little."

"I'm sorry, Umar. And thank you."

He frowned. "For what?"

I paused awkwardly, aware of the drama of the words I then uttered, "For saving my life."

"Is that what I did?"

"Of course! If you hadn't been there, I would have fallen straight to the ground! I would have died for sure!"

"Who knew that I was such a hero?"

"A hero? I wouldn't call you a hero."

"No?"

"No. You just happened to be there. At the right place and the right time."

"Or the wrong ones, if you take my broken limbs into account. And if that's the way you think, then there's no reason for you to thank me, is there? Since you give me no credit anyway."

"I— that's not what I meant. I just meant that— well, a hero has to do more than just stand there and break someone's fall. A hero is someone who has to *do* something. Not just *be* there."

"How do you know I didn't take action? I called out, didn't I?"

"Oh. Yes. You did do that."

"And I stretched out my arms to catch you."

"You did?"

"I don't know. Maybe I did. Yes, definitely. That's what I did."

"I don't believe you."

"You don't believe me?! I saved your life—according to your own words—and now you accuse me of lying?"

I had nothing to say to this. I *had* thanked him, after all.

"Besides, it was your own greed that made you fall. It seems a bit harsh that the one who fell should question the one who saved her. I could have stepped aside, you know. And there you'd be. Splat."

"I hadn't thought of that. I guess, then, that you could be called a hero. For not stepping aside. If *not* doing something counts." My tone was doubtful. Then I asked, "Why didn't you? Step aside?"

"I didn't think of it. I didn't have time to. But even if I'd had time to think, I wouldn't have stepped aside, Deena On The Wall. I would have stood my ground, spread out my arms, and caught you."

Less effusively than I had the first time, I said, "Well. Thank you. You saved my life."

His mother came out again, making me duck, for some reason.

"Why are you laughing?" I heard her ask Umar.

I held my breath, afraid he would give me away and that she might scold me for talking to her son—me, the Shia girl who had caused him pain.

"The comic book. It's very funny."

At the same time the next day, I watched him again be settled in the garden. When his mother went inside, he called up to me, knowing somehow that I was there.

"Tell me a story, Deena On The Wall."

I did, telling him the story of the monkey and the crocodile. Then I made him laugh, telling him what my father had said about the monkey falling on the crocodile to scare him away. That was how our friendship began. We were only children. Neighbors. Young enough for it to be all right, despite the fact that he was a boy and I was a girl, he a Sunni and I a Shia. Even so, there were limits we knew enough about already for us to keep our interaction secret—or try to, at least, though we had no chance of succeeding, considering that the volume of our interaction had to accommodate the distance from my terrace to his garden, and that there was no real way to hide from these vantages, despite the constant ducking I grew accustomed to. Once, I ducked late enough to catch a look on his mother's face—cold and hostile, enough to make me want to keep ducking.

Normally, Umar's afternoons would have been like those of the other boys in our neighborhood. As a boy, he would not have been confined to the boundaries of home. Boys could spend their time in the street. Riding bicycles and playing cricket. Umar was still young, so he would not yet have been allowed to travel far, by bus and rickshaw, to the movies and around town, like other, older boys in the neighborhood. Without my parents, I went only to school and back—by horse carriage, no less—a two-wheeled *tonga,* with a driver contracted for that purpose, always accompanied by Macee. My world, a girl's world, was smaller than his. But now, Umar had to stay home, too. And I was his only company. By the time Umar's casts came off, our daily conversations had become a habit. While he returned to the larger world that was his as a boy, now he still spent time at home every afternoon. Time with me. No one said anything about this for quite a few months. But, eventually, it became an issue between my parents—a regular argument, circle-shaped, that sounded remarkably the same no matter how many times it occurred.

"A daughter running wild and not one word to say about it. Soon, the whole neighborhood will be talking! Something must be done to stop it. Something, before the boy's mother, that *Wahabbi* woman, finds cause to insult us again," my mother would say to the back of my father's newspaper. She would wait for a response, less and less patiently as time passed and the words became rote. When none was offered, she would say, less than gently, "Is no one listening to me?!"

"I'm listening. Merely trying not to," my father would finally sigh, giving up on his attempt to read the paper in peace.

"It must be stopped," my mother would say again.

"They're only children."

"Yes, children. Children who will grow up soon enough."

"So you keep reminding me."

"Well, what's to be done?"

"Surely not what has been done before? You won't have me act as fathers do in the silly, tragic stories of old? An often overlooked fact about those stories is how badly such fathers end up being regarded in the annals of history."

My mother never laughed. "This is no time for your philosophizing. Something needs to be done."

"What would you have me do? Ban them from conversing? Again, taking history as our guide, that will only make matters worse, don't you think?"

"*Something* must be done." My mother was not to be diverted.

"Must it? What if we do nothing? Most likely, the friendship which began innocently will continue in that vein. And then, they'll grow up and out of it."

"And if they don't? Then what?"

"I don't know. I don't have the energy to plan for that kind of battle, let alone to fight it. We're the old parents in this story. And we always lose in the end."

"This is not a joke. This is a question of your daughter's future."

"She's only a child."

"Now. *Now* will become *then* before you know it, you stubborn man. And then this little terrace-to-garden friendship will start to look like balcony scenes from *Romeo and Juliet*."

"Worrying about it will not make it come slower. And what you worry about is not a matter of *when*. It's a matter of *if*."

"*Oof!* Can no conversation be had between us without playing some kind of game? All right—what will your response be, *if*?"

"I don't know. Maybe I will offer my congratulations."

"Be serious! Their community and ours are not the same. You—surely you would object if—God forbid—something happened in the future?"

"There are a lot of things I object to. Friendship in any form is not one of them."

My mother would purse her lips and shake her head. "How very modern of you! How very reasonable! How very lucky for you to be able to live at such lofty, reasonable altitudes. Too bad for the rest of us, who live in the real world, the practical one where reason is a luxury we can ill afford. Like the food on our table, the clothes on our backs." This line of argument was one of my mother's that predated my friendship with Umar.

"Yes, yes. Everything has a cost, not a day goes by without you reminding me of that. No food am I allowed to digest without hearing from you about it—the daily price of flour, potatoes, onions, rice, eggplant, and okra—this is what passes for conversation in this house," my father would say, following the script of old.

"You think I take pleasure in this? In being the one to try and keep your feet on the ground? *Someone* has to be practical. *Someone* has to think of these things."

"Is there an accusation there somewhere that I should respond to? Can we not be happy with what we have, without pining after what we have lost?"

"You think I am unhappy?" my mother would ask.

"Aren't you?"

"No. No, I am not."

"How can that be? In the face of all we have lost?" My father's tone would shift—from accusation to wonder.

"We have a home and our daughter. We have all that we need and more. I have no complaints."

"You are a good woman. A good wife and a good mother. Leave aside these worries of yours. The future will take care of itself."

That our family had once been wealthy was something I knew from Macee, our old servant, who had been with our family since before Partition. Macee loved to speak of the taste of old luxuries lost.

"You don't remember the days, Deena, when my brother, Sharif Muhammad, was *our* driver instead of working for that friend of your father's. There was a car. And a cook. A big house and lots of servants. Back in Bombay."

"How many servants?"

"More than I can count. The family was rich."

"Then what happened?"

"It was all left behind at Partition."

"Why?"

"Because *he* told us to. Your father's older brother. His *brother*. He tricked your *abu*. He told him that the times were too uncertain. That it was better for half the family to come to Pakistan. And half to remain in India. Just for a while—until things were settled. He sent your *abu* here. And kept everything for himself."

"Everything?"

"Everything but some. A little money—enough to live on in the beginning. Barely. But all of the rest—the house and the business, buildings and property all over Bombay, all of which he should have shared with your father, by right, he kept for himself, betraying his younger brother. That is what he had planned all along. To get him out of the way."

"How hurt Abu must have been!"

"And your mother. She had to sell all of her jewelry. To help your father start his first business here in Pakistan. The battery factory. A total failure. Until Abbas Ali Mubarak bought it and made it a success. He is the one who hired Sharif Muhammad." Macee sighed. "Now *that* man is a lucky one. Not like your father, whose hands are allergic to money." Abu had a knack for losing money—the anti-Midas touch—beginning a multitude of businesses that sucked him dry, only to sell them off and watch them flourish in the hands of others. From year to year, they varied— steel, guar, trucking, and textiles—a series of ventures begun with high hopes, yielding fruit only after he gave up on them.

I sat and mulled this over, thinking of what it might have been like to be rich. "Were we as rich as Abbas Uncle?" I asked.

"No one is as rich as Abbas Uncle, Deena," said Macee darkly.

Abbas Ali Mubarak was my father's oldest and closest friend. Every week, for as long as I remembered, Abbas Uncle would come to visit, his booming, bass voice, originating from somewhere in the region of a barrel-shaped belly, preceding his entry into the worn, paint-thirsty double wooden doors of our home.

"I would have phoned, my friend, before I came, but I don't suppose you have resolved your differences with the telephone-*walla*s, eh?" he greeted my father.

"You would insult our old friendship, Abbas, if you ever stood on such ceremony—modern conveniences should not hinder a man's freedom to pay and receive the pleasure of unexpected company. And no, to answer your question, the battle with the telephone-*walla*s rages on. They sent a new man, last week, whose request for a bribe was at least more suitably delicate than his predecessor's shameless demands. He hemmed and hawed, round and round, and had the decency, at least, to look embarrassed. I give him a week before he is fully acculturated to the corrupt climate of Pakistani bureaucracy," my father said.

"What do you think you're proving by all this fuss, Iqbal? If you won't shell out the money, let me give the bribe for you. Think of it as a wholly inadequate repayment for all the advice you have given me."

"That would be a strange form of repayment, Abbas, if any is required. To undermine the principle I have chosen to stand on in these matters. I do not pay bribes. And neither should you."

"Did you hear that, Rukaiya Bhabi?" Abbas Uncle said to my mother, who entered the room with a tray of tea and biscuits. "Did you hear what your *sadhu* of a husband would have me do? How do you live with this impractical man?" He took the cup she offered him and scooped and stirred sugar into his tea with vigor. "These little niceties—bribes and *baksheesh*—these are merely the cost of doing business, Iqbal. Merely a means of spreading the wealth."

"Spreading the wealth? It's a disease you spread—your dirty hand greasing all the outstretched palms it encounters."

"I didn't make the world so, Iqbal. I take it as I find it."

"Is that how you console yourself? I thought ambitious men like you were in the business of reshaping the world. Try that for a change."

"Ah, Iqbal, my friend, your sour sanctimony would be insufferable if it wasn't accompanied by the sweet, uncanny wisdom of your business forecasts." Abbas Uncle turned to me, always to be found eagerly skulking in the shadows, waiting watchfully for his big hand to reach into deep pockets, as they did now. "Did you know, little Deena, that your father is a prophet of profit? A brilliant man—I owe my whole fortune to him. If he hadn't failed so miserably at his battery business—letting his high and mighty self be robbed blind by the kind of men he seeks to save from my corruption—he would never have sold it to me. And in all the years since, his advice has been golden, directing me to every project I have undertaken. See these sweets that I bring for you?" The hand withdrew from the pocket, filled with foreign chocolates, already soft and melting in a climate alien to their origin, a weekly luxury I had come to cherish. "I can afford them thanks to your father. Who should take his own advice—not the nonsense he tries to reform me with, mind you, but the shrewd, clairvoyant acumen he refuses to feed his own hunger with."

The barbed exchanges between the two men were typical—the kind that only a friendship born in childhood could withstand.

"You confuse hunger with greed, Abbas. The one, by the grace of God, I have never suffered. The menacing growl of the other,

I agree, I refuse to nourish," said Abu, with a sincere sigh of contentment.

"Ah, well. I owe you. Of that, there's no doubt. Tell me, Deena," Abbas Uncle would turn to me again, "how many marriage proposals have you had to refuse this week?" Here, inevitably, was the teasing moment when I paid the price for the Cadbury-flavored sweetness that would, by now, have made its way into my mouth, my tongue and teeth chocolate-coated, empty wrappers crumpled in the fists of my greedy, little-girl hands, heedless of the lesson that my father had just delivered to his friend.

"Have you finished those chocolates already, Deena?" my father would laughingly ask. "If you *will* join the ranks of those corrupted by your uncle, at least set your price a little higher than a few moments' pleasure."

"Ah—leave her alone, Iqbal. She's a sweet girl, your Deena. Have some more, *Beti*. More sweets for the sweet." His hand would make its way temptingly back into the pocket. "How fast the girl is growing, Iqbal, and how lovely. Don't count on her to support you in your old age, my friend. And don't forget—when those proposals really do start to pour in—she's already spoken for. Such a sweet bride she will make for my son, Akram," he would joke, only when I was young, before such teasing would have been unseemly, making the second serving of chocolate less easy to swallow than the first. Though I was too young for him to be serious, I frowned all the same.

We rarely visited Abbas Uncle where he lived. Although his house was a gathering place for women during the ten days of Muharram, the *majlis*es were held in the morning, during school hours, so I hardly ever attended. His daughter, Asma, was my classmate in school, but not my friend. She was a difficult girl to like. Occasionally, Abbas Uncle would bring her with him on his visits to my father.

I would invite her to come and play with me on the terrace, and she would reply in a sour, sullen voice, "I'm not allowed to play in the sun. My mother says I am too dark already." Any pity this might have given rise to would be quickly relieved by her next words. "I'm surprised *you're* allowed. You're even darker than I am, Deena."

At school, she was always accompanied by a servant. Unlike Macee, who left me at the gate every morning, Asma's chaperone, her *ayah*, would accompany her beyond the gate and onto the school grounds, under strict instructions to follow the girl around, a prettily painted parasol in hand, which she would carry over Asma's head at recess, to protect her from the sun, as if she were some kind of royalty. This did not endear the girl to her classmates.

Her brother, Akram, was not the despised figure that she was. Like all the girls at school, I knew him by sight. And by reputation. When we were younger, he used to come to our school straight from his to pick up his sister.

"There he is," the girls would say as Akram rolled up in a big-finned American car, driven by Sharif Muhammad Chacha, Macee's brother, "the crown prince coming to pick up his sister, the princess."

Akram had a reputation for being wild. He was a subject of fascination to the girls who were senior to me, the ones who were closer to his age and whose brothers were his classmates. These older girls affectionately called him Akram the *chakram*—a word that comes from *chakr*, which means "dizzy"—staring and giggling at him from afar, the way that girls always do at boys who seem bad. And he *was* bad. His school pranks were famous, going far beyond the typical frog-in-the-teacher's-desk and tack-on-the-teacher's-chair level, achieving heights that made us laugh even from our girls'-school distance.

Once, we heard, he'd dressed up in a tattered old *burkha*, pretending to be a mad beggar woman. In this guise, he'd gained entry to the grounds of his school, saying he'd come to ask the headmaster for alms, frightening the poor man and chasing him around the school buildings, shrieking all the while, pretending to have fits—causing all the boys in the school to gather and gape and giggle—until the guards finally caught and threw "her" off the grounds. On the other side of the gate, now safe, still panting, the headmaster caught sight of the schoolboy shoes sticking out of the bottom of the *burkha*. That was the second time that Akram was expelled from one of Karachi's finest boys' schools. Rumor had it, confirmed by Abbas Uncle on his visits to my father, that Akram had been kicked out of three of them by the time he was thirteen.

One day, when Asma and I were still young, eight or nine at the most, Abbas Uncle announced that he was sending Akram abroad, to a boarding school in England.

"Boarding school?" I was horrified. Boarding school was the ultimate childhood threat in our world, a last resort brandished when the promise of a spanking was not enough to frighten badly behaving children—like the bogeyman. It was a form of banishment that we knew, from books and stories, was a matter of course in the culture of those who had ruled over us before Independence, when children of the Raj were sent back to cold, gray England, far from their mothers and *ayah*s, in order to become properly English, but which was incomprehensible in the child-centered world that was ours.

And so, Akram the *chakram* was banished, causing the girls in school to have to find other boys to giggle and drool over.

By the time I was twelve, my mother had decided that I should learn how to cook. Every day, after school, she would have me watch her and help her and Macee in the kitchen. Trying to stone two birds at once, I think. Keeping me busy was one way to keep me away from the neighbor's son.

"It is for your own good, Deena, that you should learn to cook. I didn't learn until we moved to Karachi. Imagine! I couldn't even boil water for tea. I grew up in a house where we had a cook and my mother never imagined a life for me without one. But you should be prepared for whatever the future brings you. Who knows what kind of household you will marry into? Rich or poor—it will not harm you to know your way around a kitchen."

"Is it true, Ma? What Macee says? That we had a cook and car and driver in Bombay, before I was born? And a big house? That we were rich?"

"Yes. It's true."

"Do you miss all of that, Ma?"

"Miss it? Of course not! The cook—he was a very good cook. He knew how to make everything. His *shaami kabab*s were excellent, perfectly spiced and melt-in-your-mouth. He knew how to make Chinese food, too—noodles and egg rolls. He had worked in one of the best hotels in Bombay before he came to work in your father's house. We used to have lavish dinner parties there—back in Bombay—and everyone who was anyone would come and comment on how delicious his food was. But, oh, that man was a bully in the kitchen, never letting anyone near him while he prepared dinner, guarding his recipes so jealously that you would think they were magic potions. Remember, Macee? What a cranky fellow he was? It has taken me years to figure out how he made certain dishes—through trial and error and taste alone. But I like it better now. Being the mistress of my own kitchen, humble as it is. No, I don't miss it at all."

I asked my father about these matters, too. "Abu? Macee says that your brother cheated you? Is that true?"

My father looked up at me, from the book he was reading, a frown on his face. "Do you know, Deena, that there is an old Arab Bedouin saying: *I, against my brothers. I and my brothers against my cousins. I and my brothers and my cousins against the world.* That is jungle law. It is the way of the world when the world is thrown into chaos. It is our job to avert that chaos, to fight against it, to resist the urge to become savage. Because the problem with such law is that if you follow it, you are always fighting against someone. There are some who will seize upon any convenient sign of chaos in order to justify descent into such thinking. My brother, it pains me to say, is one of those. Partition was just such a time of chaos. He took advantage of it. Like many do and always will."

"But that's wrong! It's not fair. Why didn't you fight to get back what was yours?"

"Fight? Against my brother? Then I would be what he is, following jungle law. The only way to rise above is to rise above. The only way to respond to wrong is with right. The only way to deal with injustice is to be just."

I told Ma what Abu said. "Hmm. Abu carries a lot of wisdom around in his head. But the problem is that in the real world, wisdom is very hard to distinguish from foolishness."

"What are you saying, Ma?! That Abu is foolish?!"

"I am saying that most people would consider him to be so."

"Do you?"

My mother sighed. "No, Deena. Don't tell him I said so—but I think he is wise. It's the rest of the world that's foolish."

This assertion of my mother's tied in very nicely to the way I saw myself in relation to other students at the convent school that I attended, which was run by nuns. In school, the hierarchy of who was who was determined first and foremost by who your father was, just as it would later be determined, in adult life, by who you married. In this sense, Asma, Abbas Uncle's daughter, was in a class by herself. But I was never ashamed of my father's fiscal failures, because while being rich counted for something, how well you spoke English counted for far more in the game of class and status in school—in all of Pakistan, for that matter. All of our lessons were in English. Among my classmates, the nouveau riche were those whose parents spoke either no English at all, or a broken, heavily accented form of it that the rest of us secretly mocked. We took pride in the fact that we studied Urdu as a *second* language. Can you imagine? The fact that I spoke English better than Urdu, like my parents, meant that I was among the social elite at the school, where there were many girls both richer and poorer than me. Two among the latter in my class were so poor that their parents had to give them up to become boarders at the school, subject to the nuns' religious education.

The convent school I attended was one among others in Karachi, along with similar boys' schools, run by priests, which were considered the best source of education at a reasonable price. It is strange to think about now. Of the nuns who were our teachers. We girls were fascinated by them, constantly speculating over their lives, harassing the boarder students with questions about life after school hours and what they knew of the private lives of our teachers, who lived in quarters behind the classroom buildings where we were never allowed to go. Their clothes were so strange—old-fashioned wimples that covered their hair, full-length habits, you understand, that drowned the shapes of their bodies in voluminous folds of black and white fabric, which led us to wonder about what they hid underneath. Did they wear bras? Underwear? These questions never failed to give rise to giggles among us, a natural tendency among girls of our age. Our own clothing was decidedly less modest by design—the *kameez*es of our uniforms tailored tightly, darted to emphasize the budding breasts that began to blossom as we waded into adolescence, cinched at the waist to imitate the hourglass figures we admired in actresses like Vivien Leigh and Elizabeth Taylor. The *dupatta*s of our uniforms were starched and folded into narrow sashes, veiling nothing; those we wore at home, twisted ropes of chiffon that were all the rage, stretched open minimally, even less so.

The curiosity was mutual. I remember how the nuns, equally inquisitive, would quiz us with questions about our lives at home—about what we ate and where we shopped, how we worshipped, and who we lived with.

I was one of those rare teachers' pets who did nothing to earn my favored status, willful and wayward, rarely applying myself to my lessons, muddling through them with passing grades all the same. My priorities were social rather than academic.

Once, when I was fourteen, I led the way to convince Reverend Mother Borden, an American woman who was the principal of the school, to let us hold a fund-raising jukebox session during recess for our Charity Club. One of the girls brought in a record player, and we all brought in our favorite rock-and-roll records. Rehana, my friend, was put in charge of playing requests at a cost of four annas per song. With the opening guitar strike of "Jailhouse Rock," my tapping toes led me into the middle of the courtyard, pulling whichever of the girls were at my side at the time along with me and without even realizing it, we were dancing—girls with girls, swaying our hips and rocking our heads, responding to the rebellious undertone of Elvis's voice, in imitation of the American girls in his movies and others. Almost everyone joined in, erasing the superficial distinctions between us: rich; poor; Christian; Sindhi Hindus, native to the province Karachi was a part of, whose families had not migrated to India during Partition; Muslim, Sunni and Shia, whose differences were only an issue, a mild one at that, during Muharram; with a sprinkling of Parsis—Zoroastrians—among us, too.

Sister Catherine, a young Irish nun, new to the school, put her hand up to the *O* of her mouth for a moment, in response to the dancing frenzy that erupted right before her eyes. Then, after giving a cautious look to either side, she smiled. By the visible and rhythmic twitch of the hem of her gown, I guessed that her toes were tapping, too. We danced through two or three songs before our squeals and shrieks drew the attention of Reverend Mother Borden, who came out of the building behind us, marching into the scene to grab the ear of the first student her fingers could reach, pulling her along as she stomped over to the record player and lifted the needle off the record with a piercing scratch that made us all cover our ears. I was at the center of the melee, impossible to single out as the instigator in what had become mass mischief, but somehow the reverend mother knew enough to train her eyes on me with a frown and a finger summons. In the stark, sudden silence, I gulped my way over to her.

"You. You were the one who asked permission for this indulgence. And you are the one I hold responsible for this unseemly behavior, Deena. I suppose I should blame myself, too. I should have known better than to give in."

Her eyes next found Sister Catherine, who was wringing her hands nervously. Sister Catherine hurried over, visibly pale, the freckles on her face, which we found so strange, standing out more than usual. The reverend mother looked like she wanted to reach out to pull on Sister Catherine's ear, too, prevented only by the fact that hers was hidden safely out of sight under the wimple of her habit. We watched them retreat into the staff building and waited for the summons, which came twenty minutes later. Rehana and I and a few others sat in the reverend mother's office for a long while as she paced and lectured, finally drawing to a conclusion with the assignment of an essay to be titled "On Dignity, Decorum, and Duty in the Delicate Sex"—the reverend mother had a poetic streak with a penchant for alliteration—to be handed in the next day.

On another occasion, my transgressions crossed the line severely enough to garner an invitation for my father to the reverend mother's office. It was Ramzan, the holy month of fasting, when Muslims abstain from food and drink during daylight hours. England's cricket team was visiting Karachi for a test match and Pakistan was winning. The fifth and last day of the match, my friends and I decided, would be too exciting to miss. It also happened to be the twenty-seventh of Ramzan—the holiest day of Ramzan for Sunnis. For Shias, the important day was the twenty-third, but that would not signify in the plans we cooked up, which had little to do with religion, except to use it as an excuse, and everything to do with loving cricket.

We had skipped class before, many times, to indulge this particular passion. Unfortunately, this time, there was a test scheduled, too important to miss. We knew that if no one came to school, the test would have to be rescheduled. So, we instigated a mass bunking—urging all of the girls in our class to join us, on religious grounds. "Who do these nuns think they are?" we asked the other girls indignantly, those who would normally be too timid to participate in the kind of uprising that we were planning. "To plan a test on such a holy day! Just because they are Christians and have no respect for our religion! Scheduling tests without consulting *our* calendar—it's an outrage!" The Shias in my little gang of friends winked at one another as we talked up this angle. Eventually, we got most of our classmates to agree with us. Those who didn't, we cajoled and bullied to stay home anyway. Of course, one among those we pressured tattled—none other than Asma, Abbas Uncle's daughter, in fact, the only one to show up at school from our class.

The reverend mother was furious. "This time you have gone

too far, Deena. Make sure it is your father that comes. Not your mother. I know how it is with you girls. Your mothers are too soft with you. Only your father will have the will to discipline you as you deserve to be disciplined."

The sexism of her demand escaped my notice at the time. Perhaps it was too much a part of the world in those times to be striking. Or I was secretly too relieved to reflect on it. In my house, Ma was far more to be feared in matters of discipline than Abu. When he came home from his meeting with the reverend mother, I asked him anxiously what she had said.

"The reverend mother said that you are a very bright girl, Deena. That your intelligence is matched only by your high spirits. You are a natural-born leader. That's the trouble. If you applied yourself, she said, you would be at the top of the class. She wants me to tell you to concentrate your—how did she put it?— your powers of persuasion for good instead of mischief, to be a role model instead of a ringleader. Despite all the trouble you cause her, Deena, I believe she has great affection for you. She praised your English, too. I told her of how you love to read. From now on, she will make a point of keeping you busy with all the books she can manage to get into your hands. From her own personal library."

I clapped my hands at this news. This would be a treat instead of a punishment. The regular school library was horribly stocked. One year, I remember, we girls had gotten terribly excited at the news that boxes and boxes of new books had arrived from America, a donation from schoolchildren there. We waited eagerly for the day when they would be opened and shelved, available for us to read. When the day came, we were very disappointed. The books were all torn and marked, half of them with pages missing. And none of them were good books to begin with. Our teachers made us write thank-you notes for those books anyway, words of gratitude that we did not feel, muttering angrily, under our breaths, at the spoiled American children, anonymous, who thought that torn and marked books could be counted as a gift! What the reverend mother promised my father—that I would have access to her personal library—was tremendous news, because everyone knew that the best books in school were those housed on the shelves in her office. It was news I couldn't wait to share with Umar. Before I could run off to find him, Abu had one more thing to add, making me frown.

"Don't be *too* excited, Deena. You will be expected to write essays on each and every book she lends you."

Yes, Umar, the boy from next door. We had remained friends for all the seven years since my fall from the wall. Everything I thought and felt made its way to his ears. And one of my other childhood passions, the one Abu had told the reverend mother about, was one I shared with him.

"Page?" Umar would call out.

"One hundred twenty-seven," I would answer from my perch at the wall.

"How did you get so far ahead?" he would complain as he rustled the pages of his book to catch up.

We read books in parallel fashion, sharing passages out loud from terrace to garden and back again. *Alice in Wonderland* was one of the first. Umar refused to read *Little Women,* though he listened to me read quite a bit of it out loud before shutting me up with a taste of my own medicine with Stevenson's *Treasure Island*. Beginning with Arthur Conan Doyle and moving on to Agatha Christie and Erle Stanley Gardner, we outdid each other with wild guesses and reckless bets on whodunit that changed as we twisted and turned our way through mysterious plots until unlikely culprits were revealed by Sherlock Holmes, Hercule Poirot, Miss Marple, and Perry Mason, Umar with his copies of the titles we read and me with my own, both of them rented from the book man who came to our street every week, on bicycle, renting comics for two annas and paperbacks for four—that is an eighth of a rupee and a quarter—knowing us well enough to make sure he kept two copies of books by authors we liked, because we couldn't wait for each other to finish and had to read our selections together, at the same time. We laughed out loud, in concert, at the antics of P. G. Wodehouse's Jeeves, saved the world from outlandish villains out to dominate it with Ian Fleming's James Bond, which we read at Umar's insistence, and for which I had my revenge with *Gone With the Wind*. Somerset Maugham kept us busy for a while. And then we ventured into Russian literature. *Anna Karenina* first, whose title character I could not forgive for having abandoned her child in pursuit of a passion that proved to be so self-destructive. Then *Dr. Zhivago*. That one we loved so much we were compelled to buy our copies instead of renting them.

With *Zhivago*, we talked, as we had on that first day of our friendship, about whether Yuri was a hero or whether he just happened to be always in the right place at the right time—or the wrong one, depending on your point of view.

"So you think that Yuri's infidelity was all right? And Anna Karenina's was despicable? That won't do, Deena On The Wall. To sympathize with one and condemn the other."

"How can you compare the two, Umar? Yuri was the victim of history and fate. Anna was nobody's victim but her own."

"So—Anna is less of a heroine because she chose the direction of her life? And Yuri is a hero because he didn't? And what kind of choice did she really have anyway? She was no less a victim of circumstance than Yuri."

"Come on, Umar. She wasn't separated from her family because of war and chaos."

"But she was a woman. The life she left behind was predetermined for her. Her passion for Vronsky was the first time she ever had a choice to make for herself."

"The same was true for Yuri. But he didn't make that choice. To walk away from his duty and obligation to his family. Even when passion arose, he turned away from it. At first. Until there was nothing else left—no choice but to surrender to fate. He did the right thing, the honorable thing—until every other road was closed to him. And when that happened, he didn't let himself be devoured by selfishness and self-involvement. He wrote poetry. His passion for Lara became the source of something great. He created something and left it behind for others. Even then, he made his life about something more than himself."

"This is heavy talk. Too heavy to be had at such a distance." My father had made his way up to the terrace so stealthily that I had not heard him behind me. This had become a new habit of his, instigated by my mother, worrying enough now that I was well into my teens, to send my father up to the terrace for tea, to keep an eye on things and try to avert potential disaster. It was the wrong move on her part. Instead of dampening our discussion, Abu did what Ma would never have allowed.

He invited Umar up from the garden. "Why don't you come up for some tea, Umar? This is an interesting discussion, better conducted at conversational volume, rather than having to shout up and down at each other in this unseemly fashion. The hawkers in the streets have a hard enough time as it is, making ends meet, without having to compete with the sound of your disagreements."

Neither Umar nor I said anything for a moment, both of us surprised, the distance between us one we were used to and hesitant to bridge. I saw him shrug off the significance at the same time that I suppose I did. Within minutes, Umar had gained entry into our home and was up there, on the terrace, with Abu and me. The literary argument that had flowed so naturally before was now stifled, both Umar and I suddenly shy in light of the formality of my father's presence.

I sought ease in the familiarity of teasing and said, "This is the first time that you and I have been so close, Umar, since my fall seven years ago. No wonder you are so quiet. You must be afraid of what happened last time—that I'll be the cause of a broken bone or two at least!"

Umar smiled, his eyes sparkling, at close range, in a way I would not have been able to notice from the usual perspective of terrace to garden.

Abu sent me down to call for tea. When I came back, tray in hand, the conversation was flowing, Abu and Umar immersed in politics, my copy of *Dr. Zhivago* held firmly in Abu's hands. I knew that it was a good thing I was finished with it, because he looked like he had every intention of reading it himself.

I poured Umar's tea and handed it to him, only to watch it grow cold in his hands as the afternoon wore on, he and Abu moving easily from politics to history, reliving Partition and the decisions it had occasioned, and worrying if war was imminent with the country in which both had been born. It was almost dinnertime when Abu said, "I believe you two were on the subject of poetry when I interrupted your argument."

"Yes," I said, my hand brushing Umar's as I reached out to take his copy of *Zhivago* from him. I flipped to the last section, to the poetry of *Dr. Zhivago* that Pasternak had included after the epilogue. "You see, Umar. This part. This poem, 'Parting'—it's my favorite. It tells exactly what I meant when I said that Yuri's love for Lara is something that happens in spite of himself, outside of his control. Especially this verse:

> *In the years of trial,*
> *When life was inconceivable,*
> *From the bottom of the sea the tide of destiny*
> *Washed her up to him."*

I sighed.

Umar said nothing for a long moment. Then, quietly, he said, "My favorite poem is 'The Wedding Party.' It's not a romantic poem, like the one you read. It's about life and what it means." Umar reached toward me to reclaim his book, found the page he was looking for, and said, "Here's the verse I like:

And life itself is only an instant,
Only the dissolving
Of ourselves in all others
As though in gift to them."

"' . . . *the dissolving of ourselves in all others . . .*' Hmm. Lovely. That is lovely," Abu said. "I think I like Umar's verse better than yours, Deena."

Neither Umar nor I said anything, falling strangely silent. Soon after, Umar left.

Predictably, Ma fumed to find that the battlefield had shifted and that the enemy had been invited into the gates. She bypassed Abu—who she believed had crossed over to the other side, and focused her fury on me.

She sat me in front of the mirror in her bedroom, the only one in the house that wasn't too splotchy with rust to still serve, as she did every night, combing out my hair to braid it with rough yanks that were unusually fierce. "What am I to do with that father of yours?! Inviting the boy up instead of—instead of— *oof!*—instead of doing what I sent him to do."

"Instead of scaring him off?"

"Exactly!"

I had to wince at her emphasis, my head snapping back as it suffered its way through the stroke of the comb in her hand. "But—Ma—ouch!—why does he have to be scared off? He's just a friend!"

"A friend? There's no such thing between a girl and a boy. Besides, we cannot confine ourselves to worrying about what he is and what you are—we have to worry, also, about what people will make of these things. It would be bad enough as it is. For word to spread about you being friendly with a boy. But the boy is a Sunni. And not just any Sunni. His mother is one who hates us. Whatever I think, and your father, *she* would *never* approve of her son marrying you."

"Ma! I don't want to marry him!"

"You be quiet! You don't know what you want! You are only a child—you don't understand the way that the world works! And your father?! He's no better! Acting no better than a child himself." I watched her in the mirror, muttering to herself as, mercifully, the work of the comb was set aside and her fingers wove their way down the length of my hair. When she was done, she put her hands on my shoulders, lowered her face so that it was next to mine, and gave me a little shake, loving but stern. "Look at you, Deena." She paused to do what she asked me to do, studying my face, putting her hands on my cheeks, her thumbs cradling the nape of my neck. "You have grown up into a woman. Right before my eyes. No longer a child."

"But you just said that I was."

"Yes. A woman who is still a child. Think, Deena. Think about who you are. About who you will be. You cannot remain friends with him. With that boy whose very name stands for who we are not. Sooner or later, you will be married, *Inshallah*. What will you tell your husband? That you are friends with another man? No. That is not the way things are. Nor the way they should be. Men and women cannot be friends. *Bas*."

Bas, she said. Enough.

And what did my father have to say? That night, after my hair was braided, when I went to him to say good night, he said, "I like this boy, this friend of yours. Umar. He's a gentle soul."

"Yes," I said, thinking of what my mother had said.

"Your mother is upset?"

"Yes, Abu. Absolutely livid."

It turned out that Ma's fury was in vain. The next day, when I went up to the terrace, Umar was nowhere in sight. Nor the next. Weeks passed.

Abu, who still made his way up to the terrace daily to stand guard with renewed vigor in light of Ma's fervent chastisements on his unforgivable lapse, observed, "It looks like your mother was wrong. I did drive him away after all."

I put down the teacups I was carrying, sat on the chair where Umar had sat, and began to cry, softly, to myself. "Why do you think he is angry with me, Abu?"

"What makes you think that he is?"

"Why else would he avoid me?"

Abu had no answer for me. After a while, he said, "Perhaps it's for the best, Deena. Perhaps his mother has convinced him of what yours has failed to do. That this friendship is impractical. That it will have to end eventually. Better now, before it is too late."

"Too late?"

"Yes. You are nearly grown. A young woman. Be practical, *Beti*. As it seems that Umar is trying to be."

"*You* are saying that, Abu?"

"Keep it a secret. Just between you and me. That perhaps there is *one* practical bone in my body—contrary to all of your mother's assertions. The fact is, Deena, that you and Umar are no longer children. Your mother is right. You have gone from sharing fruit to sharing poetry. It is time to set this part of your childhood aside, before you also move from broken bones to broken hearts. It seems that Umar is wise enough to realize this. You should, too."

After a while, I stopped looking for Umar at the wall of the terrace. I learned to read my books without his company, alone, as perhaps books are meant to be read. But poetry, I knew, was not the same. Poetry was something that had to be shared. Out loud. Something I left behind. Except in Muharram, when I began to recite *noha*s, the rhythmic poetry of sacrifice and tragedy that cannot be translated from one language to another because it is too specific, too much a matter of the heart and faith.

A year later, while I was on the terrace reading a book, my father climbed the rickety stairs, Umar following closely behind. "See who I found knocking on our door, Deena? Your old friend has come to see you."

I closed my book. I remember what I was reading at the time. Harper Lee's *To Kill a Mockingbird*.

"Sit, Umar." My father didn't join him, his eyes moving back and forth from my averted face to Umar's. Instead of sending me down to ask for tea, he said, "I'll go and have some tea made and brought up."

When Abu was gone, Umar asked, "What are you reading?"

I held the book up in silence, so he could read the title himself, my eyes forcefully focused on the roof of the house across from ours.

"Won't you talk to me, Deena On The Wall?"

"Why should I?"

"You're angry."

I didn't answer.

"I don't blame you."

I still said nothing, wondering why he was there and why he had disappeared from sight for a year.

I didn't have to wonder for long.

"I'm going away, Deena."

That brought my eyes up to his face. But only for a second. Enough to see that he had changed—the shadow on his face the shadow of a man's beard, the lines of his jaw and brow hardened and wide.

"Won't you ask where I'm going?"

I shrugged.

"I'm going to America. To study. But I couldn't leave without saying good-bye."

"When someone stops saying hello, I don't see that there's any need to say good-bye," I said, my eyes firmly fixed, again, on the house across the street.

"Won't you look at me, Deena?"

Reluctantly, my eyes met his.

What I saw there explained everything—the reason he had stayed away, why he had come to say good-bye. I can only describe what I saw by its effect on me. Every woman should be looked at in such a way, at least once in her life. With a longing that cannot be contained—with love that goes beyond mere feeling because it transforms and—like the verse of the poem he had read—it dissolves, as an offering, a gift. I felt my face flush and waves of knowing suffused every pore, every cell of my being. I was loved. And in that love, I felt beauty—my own, unrealized until that moment, suddenly rising to consciousness in a way that made everything in me come alive to the beauty all around me. Nothing more needed to be said.

Have you ever felt that way, Jo? Have you ever been looked at with such soulful longing that you are transformed, the object and the subject of Love, capital L? You look frightened, as if you didn't know what I was talking about and were afraid of it somehow.

There was nothing I could say in response to the look in Umar's eyes. I put my hand up, as if to ward off words that he had not uttered.

His eyes fell away from mine, severing the connection between us, but not the power of its effect. "I am going away," he said. "I— I cannot ask you to wait. I cannot ask you for anything."

My father came up the stairs. Umar stood up. He didn't say good-bye before he left. And what he left behind made me wish that he hadn't come at all—feeling, at the same time, a profound sense of gratitude for what I now knew. That every moment of life is as significant as that one was for me. The only difference is in knowing it. We squander the moments of our lives away, without realizing their worth. Oh, the tragedy of it. Truly, it is the human tragedy—to let ourselves be the victims of our own sense of irrelevance.

But one man loved the pilgrim soul in you,
And loved the sorrows of your changing face . . .

W. B. Yeats, "When You Are Old"

Jo

Deena's words stopped. Silence swayed over us, making me suddenly aware of what she was saying about the worth of every moment, as this one, here, now, rose up and made itself felt. I took a deep breath and remembered what she'd said a few seconds before. That I looked frightened. When she asked me that question: *"Have you ever been looked at with such soulful longing that you are transformed, the object and the subject of Love, capital L?"* That was because of the answer that came to mind—the image that rose immediately out of my recent memory. No. Dan had never looked at me like that. But I knew what it must feel like, from having experienced its opposite. I'd been looked at with such deep, soulful revulsion that I was transformed—the object and subject of Hatred, capital H. A little time in Deena's company was enough for me to know that she deserved the look *she'd* gotten. What made me afraid was knowing that the look I'd gotten was also deserved.

Her question reminded me of why I'd come here, to her house, something I'd forgotten in the act of listening.

Then the suspended silence between us was broken as the grinding noise of a garage door opening jolted us both out of the moment.

Deena looked at the clock on the mantel and exclaimed, "Oh, my! Is that the time? That's Umar. Home from work. And I haven't even begun to prepare the *ifthar*!"

As she spoke, I heard the door of a car slamming shut, the opening and closing of another door, leading into the house, followed by footsteps. I sat up straighter, eager to see the face of the man who had looked at Deena with such longing. He came into the room, stopping short when he saw me sitting on the couch across from his wife.

Deena stood and turned, repeating, for his sake, "Oh, Umar! I have not even begun to prepare *ifthar*. See? I had an unexpected guest. Umar, this is Jo. You remember Angela? Connie's stepdaughter? She was my fr—no—Sadiq's friend," she finished, on a bit of a broken note. Then said, "Well, Jo is Angela's daughter. She came. And I've been talking and talking."

Umar smiled and finished his way into the room. "Oh. Yes," he said, putting his hand out, taking mine in a firm hold. Shaking it. "Connie and Deena are very good friends."

He turned to Deena. "Don't worry. There's another half hour until *ifthar*. I'll get it ready."

"No! Together. We'll do it together."

That's when it hit me. What they were talking about. "It's Ramadan? Are you—are you fasting, Deena?" I thought about the tea she'd served when I got there. The cookies she'd brought out at some point. That was why she hadn't had any herself. "I'm so sorry. I don't want to intrude. I should go."

"Sorry? Go? No! Why? There's no reason for you to go. Stay! Come. We'll just move into the kitchen. You'll stay for dinner. You won't mind watching us get everything ready? Come, come." Deena was already leading the way, guiding me along with her, her hand on my shoulder. She sat me down on a chair in the kitchen, washed her hands, and started moving, gathering plates and dishes, collecting food out of the fridge, getting out a cutting board and knife. Umar was working right alongside her, their movements so fast and so coordinated with each other's that I didn't even offer to help—not wanting to get in the middle of the wordless rhythm that flowed between them, like the steps of a dance they had practiced many times before. I thought of warning Deena—that I spoke and understood Urdu, just in case she decided to speak it to Umar while I was there. But I didn't have to. She was too polite to try to speak over and around me.

I enjoyed watching them together in the kitchen, imagining both of them in the story that Deena had told me so far. Childhood sweethearts. Sadiq hadn't told me that. He probably didn't know. I was glad to accept Deena's invitation to stay, couldn't bear the thought of leaving now, completely hooked into the story of her life. There were twists coming, I knew. Because Sadiq—who was Deena's older son—was the son of another man, not Umar.

After a few moments of silence, Deena said, "At this time, in the last moments before breaking the fast, in Pakistan, the kitchen would be filled with the crackling sounds and salty, hot fumes of frying. *Pakora*s, samosas, *kabab*s. Umar and I avoid all of that. We prefer to keep things simple, now. We have to watch our cholesterol. And all that fried stuff is murder on the digestion. Especially at our age, eh, Umar?"

"Speak for yourself, old woman," he teased. "I wouldn't mind a *pakora* or two." He put his hand on her cheek, on his way to the sink, a quick, tender gesture, delivered with the flash of a smile on his face that lit hers up, too.

"Where is your mother, Jo? Tell me."

"In San Diego."

"So she went home? When she left here?"

"Yes."

"And—?"

"She got married. My father is Jake. He used to work for Todd Rogers."

Deena turned to look at me for a long moment. Then she nodded, turning back to the cutting board in front of her, slicing fruit—apples and bananas—which she laid out on a plate, along with something else, something pruney and brown. "She was young. To be married. She's happy?"

"Yes."

"You have younger brothers and sisters?"

"One brother. Chris." I didn't say anything else, wondering if she could hear what I heard in my voice. I was less sure of my right to silence on the subject of Chris than I had been with Sadiq. Whatever she heard, Deena didn't ask any more questions.

Within an amazingly short amount of time, the table was set, laden with food. The fruit she had cut. Meat sandwiches, made with finely sliced tomatoes and spread with some kind of green paste—a mint chutney, Deena explained—cut neatly into triangles with the crusts trimmed off, the way Mom used to do for Chris, who is a fussy eater. There was some kind of bean salad—Deena said it was called *chola*. And rice and curry.

When it was all ready, Deena and Umar looked at the clock. "It's time," she said. And then turned to me. "Excuse us for a moment, Jo. It's time to open the fast. Umar and I like to say our prayers first. Afterwards, we feel too lazy and full. Make yourself at home. Don't wait for us to start, if you're hungry. We'll be right back."

They went upstairs and stayed there for some time. I made my way back into the living room, taking a look at the pictures on the mantel. There was one of Sadiq, grown up, the somber expression one I remembered. A couple of him, I think it was him, when he was a little boy—smiling, laughing. In one, he stood against a wall, the branches of a tree with small, dark, plum-colored fruit hanging low, within his reach. There were also pictures of a girl—Deena's daughter, obviously—a series of them, randomly scattered, charting her progress from child into woman. A laughing woman, happy, her eyes crinkled with mirth, very different from Sadiq. I stood in silence, listening for sounds of prayer upstairs. There were none. I knew the movements of the prayers that Deena and Umar must be offering. Remembering, I thought again of the reason I was here and considered, again, the implausibility of what I suspected. And yet, here I was. Acting on instinct, wondering what it would mean if it turned out that I was right.

Umar came back downstairs first. Deena, a few minutes later. We sat down at the table. Deena picked up the plate of fruit and offered it to me and then to Umar. He took one of the pruney things.

As she took one for herself, she said, "It's traditional. To open the fast with dates." She pointed to the brown fruit. "These are my favorite. Locally grown, here in California. As sweet as chocolate. But be careful. They have pits."

I watched both of them hold their dates up to their mouths, whispering for a few seconds before taking their first bite. Very solemnly, they took sips of water. Then we ate in silence. Passing the food around. Neither one of them ate nearly as much as I did. After a while, Deena pushed herself back from the table and said to Umar, "Could you bear to go to the grocery store for me?"

"Of course," Umar said.

"You'll regret saying yes. The list is very long. I made the menu for the day after tomorrow."

Umar nodded, smiling. "Did you speak with Sabah today?"

Deena also smiled. "Yes."

"And? Did she tell you the name of the one she's bringing this year?"

Deena shook her head. "No. She's being very mysterious."

"Hmm. How were classes today? Anyone show up for the eight A.M. class?"

"Yes, surprisingly." Deena turned to me, explaining, "I teach at UCLA. I got dragged into academia through Umar, going back to school when Sabah started high school. I got my bachelor's and kept going. Now, I teach in the Women's Studies Department. Classes on South Asian women's issues. And Islamic culture and law." She turned back to her husband. "How was your day?"

"The usual. Papers were due and now I have a stack of them to grade. After class, I held court, hearing the usual excuses for those who needed an extension. They're getting more and more creative as the years go on."

Deena laughed and, again, explained, "Umar is a professor. Full-fledged, not merely a lecturer like me. His focus is Russian literature."

Umar pointed accusingly at his wife. "All her fault. I came here, to the States, to study engineering, like all good Pakistani students who came in the late 1960s. Her taste in literature, which she bludgeoned me with when we were neighbors, as children—" I nodded. "—led me down a different path. Less lucrative. But far more satisfying." Umar popped another date into his mouth, pushed himself away from the table, and started to collect plates and dishes.

Deena put her hand out to stop him. "No. You go. I'll take care of this. Jo will help me."

I stood up eagerly, taking plates to the sink, scraping them free of debris before putting them into the dishwasher.

Deena bustled around behind me, sealing up food, leaving some of it on the table. "Umar and I will nibble on this for the rest of the evening. In Pakistan, *ifthar* is followed by another complete dinner later. But Umar and I prefer to graze."

When we were done in the kitchen, Deena made another pot of tea. She served herself some as well as me this time. Then led me back into the living room. I couldn't wait for her to resume her story, thinking she'd sent Umar out shopping in order to give herself space and time to tell me the rest.

After a few moments, Deena asked, "Does Angela's husband know the truth? About you?"

"My father," I said, surprised at the defiance in my voice. "Yes. My mom says he knew right from the beginning. But I've never spoken with him about it."

"He was older than her."

I nodded.

"He's been a good father?"

"A very good father."

"And your mother told you the truth? When you were little?"

The defiance in my voice dwindled into defense. "No. I—I kind of figured it out. Partly. By the color of my eyes."

"The color of your eyes?"

"Yes." I explained to her. About Mendel. About asking Mom the truth right before I left home for college.

"So. If it weren't for the color of your eyes, you would not have known that Sadiq is your real father."

I winced at her choice of words.

She must have noticed, using a different phrase to refer to him in her next question. "How long ago did you meet him? My son?"

"It was 1998."

Deena frowned. "He was in Chicago?"

I nodded.

"You said he was leaving?"

"Yes. His apartment was all boxed up. And he told me he was going away."

"Nineteen ninety-eight? Yes. He was going to Pakistan. To be married. He invited me to the wedding. And I was planning to go—after many, many years away. With Sabah. And Umar. But Sadiq broke off the engagement when he got there. Before we even left America to attend the wedding. With no explanation."

"Oh."

After a few moments of silence, Deena said, "So. You want to hear more? You're not bored?"

"How could I be bored?" Then I noticed how tired she looked. "But— I don't want to impose. I mean, more than I have already. If you're tired? I—I could come back another day?"

She smiled and shook her head. "No. Stay." She was sitting closer to me than she had been before. Now, she reached out and put her hand on my cheek. I didn't mind. She asked, "Do you know what I was thinking before you came? When you rang the doorbell?"

I shook my head.

She laughed to herself. "Never mind. You wouldn't believe me if I told you. Now. Where was I?"

I said, "Umar left for America."

"Yes. He left." Deena paused, taking a few sips of her tea. Then she picked up where she left off, drawing me back into the story of her life.

It's a heart, after all, not a stone or brick,
Why shouldn't it fill up with pain?
When we cry, as we will—a thousand times!
Why should anyone bother us?

Ghalib

Deena

Six months after Umar left for America, my father died, suddenly, of a massive heart attack.

Ma was devastated—the ritual confinement of a widow's mourning was no effort for her. She could barely get herself out of bed.

All I remember of that time was darkness. There was hardly any money. I stopped going to college, a year shy of completion, and took over the care of the house. The second servant had to be let go. Only Macee stayed—though there were months, in the beginning, when we didn't have enough to pay her.

I know that this sounds strange—to complain of having only one servant instead of two. The idea of servants is so foreign here, to most people anyway. But life was harder in Pakistan at that time—as it still is, for most. Laundry was now my job—there was no machine to do it for me. Many of the spices needed in the kitchen were hand-processed. The things I can get in the Indian grocery stores now are amazing. Garlic and ginger paste. Ground spices. Macee and I did this all by hand. With a mortar and pestle, mind you. We had no blender. And what we take for granted from the supermarkets here! Lovely food, packaged and ready to eat. Back home, we set our own yogurt and pasteurized our own milk. We had "meatless" days in Pakistan, days when no meat was sold in the markets, when all were supposed to abstain—because meat had to be prepared fresh, the day it was purchased. Though we had a refrigerator, our freezer was small and, like most people, we were still in the habit of buying meat daily, so that "meatless" days really were meatless. Unless you were rich enough to afford chicken or fish instead.

Now, here, we are many degrees removed from the labor involved in living. Even when I use machines, I think of who made the parts for them. I think of where everything I use came from. Before I bought it. It is easy to forget. That someone picked the fruit and vegetables. That someone slaughtered the animals we eat—even if it was with the help of machines. That someone sewed the clothes. I used to do that, too, for a time. We had an old Singer, the kind with a pedal and a wheel. It would probably be worth money today. As something strange and antique.

Still, our lives were not deprived, by most standards. We had electricity. We had running water, a roof over our heads, and soft beds to sleep in. We managed to get food on the table—less of it, to be sure, and strictly budgeted. But I had no right to complain. Because the labor I engaged in was for myself and my family. Macee and the girl who had worked for us labored for others, which must have been unimaginably hard—something I had given no thought to before.

I remember, one day, watching from the terrace as a little girl and a little boy walked down the street. The boy could not have been more than two. The girl, older, wore a red tunic and baggy trousers, *shalwar kameez*, so drab and faded that the color that remained seemed a dusty ghost of its original. The boy wore a ragged shirt, but no pants. He paused behind his sister for a moment, to squat and shit in the street, then ran a few steps to catch up to her. They made their way to the empty plot on the corner that served as a garbage heap. I watched them as they picked through the garbage for food and things they might barter, both of them golden-haired, a sign of beauty when it wasn't one of malnutrition. These kinds of scenes were so commonplace that to remark on them feels strange. In Pakistan—in many parts of the world, I suppose—no matter how bad life gets, there is always evidence of how much worse things can be.

Abbas Uncle used to come and visit to see how we got on, though less often than before. He was the one who took Abu's accounts in hand, the one who told us that Abu's debts far outnumbered any assets that remained.

"The man who worked for him—like the men before—was robbing him blind, Rukaiya Bhabi. I am doing what I can to track him down and hold him to account. But I don't have high hopes." Abbas Uncle began to loan us money, monthly, to tide things over, and we were able to resume Macee's salary—though to call this support a loan was ridiculous in light of the fact that there was no way to repay him. "I don't want you to worry yourselves. You and

Deena," Abbas Uncle told my mother. "I am here. Iqbal was like my brother. Taking care of you both is my duty and my honor."

But my mother was uneasy. She said, shaking her head, after his visits, "Nothing comes without a price."

Now, sometimes, when Abbas Uncle visited, his wife, Sajida Auntie, came with him, though she hadn't before. One day, their son came, too, Akram the *chakram*, all grown up and home from his studies abroad.

The very next afternoon, Abbas Uncle sent someone—a friend of his family and ours—with a proposal of marriage for me to be his son's wife. It was unsuitable for me to be present, so I was sent out of the room before the message was delivered. But the nervous manner of our visitor was enough to make me pause outside of it, out of sight, able to see the way my mother's lips pursed in response. I knew why, of course. Why she looked frightened rather than flattered on my behalf. This was a proposal that could not be refused.

Akram had stared at me at first, when he came—with handsome, hungry eyes that hinted at the sizing-up purpose of the visit before the official proposal arrived. I had observed him through the veil of my lashes carefully. His long, straight nose—a beautiful nose!—was nothing like his sister's. What features they did share, Asma and Akram, lived more harmoniously on his face than they did on hers. In the brother's features, too, unlike the sister's, there was *namak*—salt—which flavored his expressions with a spark that livened his face and shone out of his eyes, especially when he spoke, directly to me, for much of the visit. While there was nothing improper about that—we were more than adequately chaperoned—there was something daring about the way he addressed me so openly, which added to the favorable impression he made.

Abbas Uncle's messenger began his task with an acknowledgment, "Abbas Sahab is aware, naturally, that—in light of the loss of your husband, his friend, so recent—this matter may appear to be too hasty in timing. But the boy is ready for marriage. The girl, if she is willing, is of age as well. And, he believes, there is no reason to delay future happiness in the shadow of past grief." When he added, "Of course, the boy and girl must meet each other. So that Deena can decide. Say the word, and Akram will come and visit," my mother's lips relaxed in agreement, easing the strain that had taken root in the lines around her eyes since Abu's death.

When the guest finally left, I reentered the room and sat, in silence, waiting for her to speak. I could sense her happiness. But also her worry. I knew the quandary she was in. We were under Abbas Uncle's *ehsaan*—under his obligation, the weight of it carried on our shoulders as a burden of debt, heavier than normal because it was a debt incurred through the favor of friendship, the interest for which is incalculable, according to the computations of honor.

I waited for a long while, but my mother said nothing for the next few hours. In silence, she retreated to her prayer rug and raised her hands in a plea for guidance. That is where she was when the knock came at the door. "Who could it be at this time?" Ma roused herself from her prayers to ask. "Macee! Please go and see who's at the door," she called.

A few moments later, Macee came in the room, bringing Abbas Uncle with her. I stood quickly to leave the room again, wondering, as my mother's face told me she was, at this breach of etiquette—a proposal was not to be forwarded by the family of the boy, should not even be referred to by them, in the usual course of things.

Abbas Uncle's first words told us that he was well aware of his break from protocol. "Forgive me. I realize that I have come out of turn. But there are things I must say." He put his hand out to stop me from leaving. "No, Deena, don't leave the room. Try to put aside the modesty that this occasion would normally require of you. Listen to what I have to say to your mother."

At Ma's indication, he sat on the armchair that had been my father's favorite. Ma sat on the sofa, while I remained standing, off to the side. Abbas Uncle never looked in my direction, making it easier for me to bear the embarrassment of having to go against convention, to be present in the room with the man who sought to be my father-in-law during the process of that seeking.

"Rest easy, Rukaiya Bhabi. I have come not as Akram's father, to plead and persuade on his behalf. Rather, I have come as Iqbal's friend—the friend of your late husband, the friend of Deena's father. I understand the dilemma that your earlier visitor must have caused. There are questions to be asked and answered, as there always are when the matter of a boy and girl's marriage is at stake. But . . . there are things that must be said in this case, things which are not—well, easy—for me to say." Abbas Uncle fell silent. And remained so for quite a long time, looking relieved when Macee came into the room with cups of tea rattling on a tray. The sound drew his attention, so that he turned to Macee and uncharacteristically asked, "How are you, Macee?"

Macee flushed. "*Alhamdulillah*, Abbas Sayt. I am well, thank you."

"Your brother—? Sharif Muhammad? He is expected back soon? It is difficult to get on without him, you know."

"You know that better than I do, Sayt. It is the first time he's gone home in ten years. To see his wife and our family left behind."

"And you? Will you be joining him? To visit your family in Bombay?"

"Not now, Abbas Sayt. I could not leave my mistress at this time," Macee said, handing Abbas Uncle his tea, and then my mother hers.

When Macee left the room, the awkward silence she'd interrupted descended again.

Until my mother said, "You were saying something, Abbas Bhai? Something difficult you wished to share with us?"

Abbas Uncle looked at Ma as if he'd forgotten she was there. Then he opened his mouth and licked his lips, but still said nothing. Finally, he spoke. "Yes. What I was saying. That the situation here is unique—the relationship already established between your family and mine is one which I realize might cause you unease. But I hope that you will put those matters aside. And treat this proposal as you would any other.

"Akram's mother has been very impressed with Deena, has watched her carefully, especially last Muharram, and speaks very highly of her beauty, and the grace and modesty with which she reads *noha*s. She wanted Akram to see Deena, convinced that she is exactly—uh, suited—that they will do well together, and insisted that he come with us on our visit yesterday. And Akram was even more impressed than his mother."

Abbas Uncle had been stirring his tea as he spoke. Now, he paused again. Then raised his eyes to my mother's as if to get to the point. "I have to say that I agree with Sajida—there is nothing so valuable as the love of a good woman. I have watched Deena grow up, have observed the liveliness of her mind, the fairness and strength of her temperament, develop right before my eyes. I know how much her father loved her. And I know how difficult your position is. I want you to understand that your answer will in no way affect any other ties between us. I will remain your friend. I will continue to look after your interests and those of Deena as if they were my own. I am the boy's father. But I valued my friendship with Iqbal too much to ever dishonor it by allowing you to be moved by unimportant and insignificant matters of status and means. I am the friend of Deena's father. That is why I have come today. As the guardian of her well-being as well as my son's. If— in the case that what Akram desires comes to pass— she will not merely be the wife of my son. She will have the love and protection of a father under my roof. This, I promise."

Ma said, "Thank you, Abbas Bhai. For all that you have done for us. Out of friendship, as you say. And since you have come as the friend of Deena's father, I have a question for you."

Abbas Uncle inclined his head, as if at my mother's service. "Please. Don't hesitate."

"You know Deena better than I know Akram. Are they truly suited in temperament? If you were in my place, knowing all that you do about both children, would *you* say that they will do well for each other?"

Abbas Uncle's only answer was to close his eyes for a long moment. To take a ragged breath. When he opened his eyes again, he put his palms up in supplication and said merely, *"Inshallah."* It took a few more moments of silence before my mother realized that this would be his only answer.

She said, "Thank you, Abbas Bhai. Again. For being such a good friend to us."

"There is nothing to thank me for, Rukaiya Bhabi. If you have no other questions, I—I will take my leave. *Khudahafiz*."

Abbas Uncle saw himself out.

After a few moments, Ma said, "That was a strange visit. Why did he come?"

I didn't answer, because Ma seemed to be talking more to herself than to me.

She looked up then, and asked, "Did you not get the impression, Deena—as I did—that what your Abbas Uncle came to say and what he actually said were not the same thing?"

I frowned. "I'm not sure what you mean, Ma."

"No? Never mind, then. It was just a feeling I had."

"You—you're unhappy, Ma?"

"Unhappy? No. Why should I be? The boy seems like a good boy. He is handsome. Young."

"And rich."

Ma's eyes on me were sharp for a moment. Then she nodded. "Yes. And rich. From a good family, known to us. Known to everyone. There is no home in the whole community that would not welcome and celebrate a proposal like this one, Deena. No family of sense and practicality."

"Yes. But you seem unhappy, Ma."

"Not unhappy. Uneasy. I wish your father were here. Practicality is not the only thing to consider. You must be careful, Deena. When you meet the boy. You must be sure. We are—we are not in a strong position. You must not allow yourself to feel pressured. You must realize that this is not some fairy tale out of a book. That marrying this boy will determine your whole future, the reality of your life."

"Yes, Ma."

"There will be other proposals if you decide to refuse this one."

"Yes, Ma."

I met Akram twice before I said yes, knowing that to do so was to lift us up out of the darkness that had descended since Abu's death. Despite what Ma had said, it *was* like a fairy tale come true.

In those two meetings with Akram, my first impression was confirmed. So was the mystique of the fairy tale. He was charming. A veritable prince, arriving with a flourish in his American car, bestowing respectful kisses on my mother's hand, keeping the hunger decorously out of his eyes whenever they rested, briefly, on me. Eventually, his parents and sister—newly engaged herself—were invited, officially, to receive an answer to the proposal, along with their closest relatives and ours, cousins of my mother's and father's who had not been able to help us as Abbas Uncle had in our time of need. *Sharbat* was served—glasses of milk, heavy with nuts and rose-syrup pink, the sweetness of the drink a traditionally coy affirmative to the question that had been posed a week before, because sweet was the taste of good news, the flavor of happiness. Akram's mother, Sajida Auntie, took the necklace hanging from her neck and placed it around mine, sealing the pact.

A week later, our engagement was celebrated with all the fanfare one might expect when the scion of a wealthy household becomes betrothed. It was to be a short engagement, and the preparations for the wedding began immediately.

Asma's wedding came before mine. Akram and I were a couple at all of his sister's wedding functions, our eyes meeting across rooms crowded with guests in a way that made me feel more and more comfortable at the thought of him as my husband.

Did I love him? No. But that was not to be expected, not yet, in the format of an arranged marriage. I liked him. I enjoyed his company. I was attracted to him, mind and body. And I saw, in his eyes, that he liked me, desired me in a way that was different from what had taken my breath away when I saw it in Umar's eyes, which had never made any claims on me, the way that Akram's did. Of course, I thought of Umar. But only in passing. As I thought of many scenes from my childhood, most of them involving Abu, whose absence I felt keenly. But childhood was something that was slipping away, as it was meant to.

Two months later, in the celebratory days leading up to my wedding, I was daily draped in jewels and rich fabrics. Those were exciting times, for me and for Akram, who threw himself joyously into all of the ceremonies and rituals, making my mother, who he courted more vigorously than he did me, laugh and smile in a way I thought she had forgotten how to do since Abu's death. That effort alone was enough to endear him to me.

Two days before the wedding, Sharif Muhammad Chacha, Abbas Uncle's driver, knocked at our door. Rather than visit with his sister, Macee, in the kitchen, he asked to speak to me.

"Sharif Muhammad Chacha! You're back from Bombay! Just in time for the wedding," I said, hearing the sound of happiness in my own voice, which only made me happier.

But Sharif Muhammad Chacha didn't return my smile. His face was set in stone, his eyes fixed on the pattern of the tiles on the floor, at our feet.

"Is something wrong, Sharif Muhammad Chacha?"

He shook his head, the seriousness of his face beginning to frighten me.

"Is everything all right at home? With your family?"

"Yes, Deena Bibi. My sister tells me that your mother has gone out."

"Yes. She has gone visiting. Did you want to see her?"

"Yes. No. I want to speak to you. I wish I had been here earlier, Deena Bibi, to tell you what I have to say."

"What is it, Sharif Muhammad Chacha? Tell me."

"Deena Bibi. I came back from Bombay. And they told me you're to be married. To my *sayt*'s son. To Akram Sayt."

I nodded, not sure I wanted him to continue.

"Deena Bibi. You must not marry him."

"What? What are you saying? Why not?"

"He—Akram Sayt—it pains me to say this, Deena Bibi. They should have told you. But my sister says they have not. This is not something I am proud of. To speak against my employer's son. What I have to tell you, I've never even told to my sister, until today. If she had known before, it would have been better. My master has been good to me, and I owe him my discretion. But before I worked for him, I worked for your father, Deena Bibi. That also counts for something. And if he had been alive—your father—I would have come and spoken to him. He would not have allowed this marriage. If he'd known what I have to say. But he's not here. And it's my duty to tell you. Deena Bibi, Akram Sayt is not a suitable husband. For you. He—he's not right. He's not well. In his mind. He's mad. He's crazy. They sent him away. To big doctors abroad. And now he's back. He's better. But still— you cannot marry him, Deena Bibi. You cannot."

I couldn't say anything. What could I say? What could I believe? This couldn't be true. Sharif Muhammad Chacha was wrong. He had to be. In a voice totally devoid of the happiness I'd been so conscious of moments before, hard and cold, I said, "Be careful, Sharif Muhammad Chacha. Be sure of what you're saying."

"Don't ask me to explain. These are not matters that I understand. Only that he's not well. When I realized—that they had told you nothing—I knew I had to come and tell you."

I was silent. Standing in the ruins of a broken fairy tale. Trying to pretend that I didn't hear what I was hearing. There were only two days left before the wedding. No. No. Sharif Muhammad Chacha was wrong. I knew the truth. I knew Akram. Nothing about him had anything to do with what this old, bearded man in front of me—only a servant, after all—was saying. It was slander. Yes, that was what it was.

"Sharif Muhammad Chacha. No. What you say isn't true. I don't know why you're doing this. What you have against Abbas Uncle. Against Akram. But you're lying. Go away. Go, now. And don't repeat what you've told me. Never repeat it. If you do, I'll tell your master. I'll tell him what you've said."

"No, Deena Bibi. Please don't do that. I've come to you, risking everything. Please."

Gentling my voice with an effort I felt in every muscle, I said, "No. I don't know why you've said what you've said. But I won't tell, Sharif Muhammad Chacha. Just leave. Pretend that this conversation never happened." His skull cap crushed in his hand, giving me one last beseeching look over his shoulder, Sharif Muhammad Chacha went away.

After a long while, Macee came and stood beside me. She put her hand on my shoulder and said, "My brother is not a liar, Deena

Bibi. He speaks the truth. You must tell your mother what he said. Let *her* decide."

"No! No, Macee. Leave it be."

"But—Deena Bibi—*Beti*—you are not thinking clearly."

"No, Macee! Don't tell her any of this nonsense. That's what it is. Nonsense! Some kind of misunderstanding. Leave it alone. And keep it to yourself."

I wonder, sometimes, what might have happened if Macee had disobeyed my command. Would anything have changed? Would I have wanted anything to be different? What an impossible question to ask! The kind of question that consumes us, if we let it. What if Sharif Muhammad Chacha had never come to say what he did? Would I have later luxuriated in my innocence? It would be easier, I think, to play the victim. To see myself as some kind of Rochester, duped into a marriage I would never otherwise have consented to, to let myself feel as powerless as I would have been then. But I was never powerless, no matter how I would have liked to think of myself as so later. It would have been so convenient—to blame everyone but myself. By telling me what he did, Sharif Muhammad Chacha made me a party to all that happened. He saved me, in a way, even though he felt he'd failed at trying. If I was deceived, I had a hand in the deception. As it was, both Macee and Sharif Muhammad Chacha did as I asked—no, commanded—them to do. Both of them kept silent. Just as I did.

On my wedding day, I spent the afternoon at the beauty salon, primped, pampered, and robed, like a living doll, only to find myself unrecognizable in the mirror. At the *nikkah* ceremony, I was seated on the floor of a raised platform at the front of a room full of ladies at the *mehfil*, having already signed the relevant documents earlier in the day at home. Before the mullah took my verbal permission to represent me and my interests—through a crack in a curtain beside me, on the other side of which sat Akram, similarly seated in front of a crowd of men—Akram's mother came and whispered in my ear, "Deena, my dear, I don't know if anyone told you. But there are two times when Allah especially listens to the prayers of a woman. One is during her wedding ceremony and the other is during the pains of labor when she gives birth. Please, Deena, when the *nikkah* begins, please pray for Akram. For all of us. For our health and for yours. And for Akram." Akram's mother put her fingers gently under my chin, tilting my face up so that my eyes met hers, as they were not supposed to meet anyone's on this day of my wedding. "Please, Deena. Don't forget. Especially for him."

I nodded wordlessly, suddenly frightened at the possibility that what Sharif Muhammad Chacha had said was true. Frightened at what I had already agreed to by signing the documents in the mullah's hand.

Someone placed a copy of the Quran, open, in front of me, instructing me to keep my eyes on it, on the words of the page my eyes had fallen on, during the ceremony. Around my wrist, my mother had twisted a string of prayer beads, a *tasbeeh*, the color of dried mud, made from the sand of Karbala, where the blood of Husain and his family was shed, a somber contrast to the sparkling bangles, red and gold, that tinkled when I moved my hand. Then everyone fell silent for the exchange of words between my mullah and Akram's—all in Arabic and therefore unintelligible to me, the groom, and most of the guests. When the solemn interaction between mullahs was done, all of the women in the community came to give their congratulations, embracing me with kisses and hugs, greeting my mother and Akram's with cries of *mubarak*. It was too late to be frightened. I was married. *For better or for worse,* as they said in the American movies I had seen at the Capri Cinema.

From there, accompanied by a distant young cousin who played the part of the brother I didn't have and carried a velvet-wrapped Quran carefully over my head for every step I took, my bridesmaid, who was another cousin, a young woman, recently married, and Akram's best man, a cousin of his, ushered us to the familiar, finned American car, which was dressed, like I was, in flowers and tinsel, driven by Sharif Muhammad Chacha. He drove us to the Beach Luxury Hotel, where guests gathered for a dinner reception. There, on the stage, Akram's mother tied an *Imam zamin* to my arm—a silk, embroidered armband with money sewn inside, which would later be distributed as alms. Ma did the same to Akram. We exchanged rings. Guests made their way up the stage to greet us, to wish us well, and to pose for pictures.

"Ye-es. Ple-ase," the photographer sang out in warning each time he clicked the camera, the giant, old-fashioned flash blinding me hundreds of times throughout the evening. At the end of the reception, though Akram's mother invited Ma to come home with us and witness the ceremonies involved in welcoming me to my new home, Ma refused, saying good-bye tearfully as my bridesmaid stepped forward to quickly mop up the tears that threatened to spill out of the wells of my own eyes. She went home with the sudden abundance of loving relatives who had stepped forward when news of my engagement to the son of Abbas Ali Mubarak had circulated, the same relatives who had been especially scarce when Abu died, when we had needed them most.

When we entered the compound of Abbas Uncle's house, there was a white goat tethered in the side garden, which Sajida Auntie, who I now had to remember to call Mummy, made me and Akram touch. It would later be slaughtered, its meat distributed to the poor, our touch casting off the evil intentions of jealous eyes. At Akram's side, I turned and was about to enter the house when I found myself suddenly lifted up in my husband's arms.

"Akram! What are you doing? Put her down!" his mother shrieked.

"It's tradition, Mummy."

"In Hollywood, maybe. Not *our* tradition!"

Abbas Uncle stood inside the doorway, next to me, when Akram finally carried me over the threshold and set me down inside of the home that would now be mine, too. "Never mind, Sajida." He laughed. "It's a good tradition, I think."

We were led into the living room, filled with Akram's closest friends and relatives, and seated on a sofa. A large tray of one-rupee coins was placed in front of me and I gathered as many as I could in both hands, to be given away for charity, to invite abundance into the lives of those who lived in this new home of mine. Everyone in the family lined up to give me jewelry, though I had been given much already. Another round of food and drink was served to the Mubarak relatives by the house servants. Akram's cousins teased him, telling him to eat up for the strength and stamina he would need for what was still to come. Finally, my bridesmaid and Akram's sister, Asma, now my sister-in-law, led me into the room that would be mine and his.

Every piece of new furniture was perfectly placed, polka-dotted with the red of rose petals that seemed to have drizzled down on the dresser laden with French perfumes and on the large bed, where my bridesmaid now artfully arranged me, too. The air was pregnant with the cloying, clashing scents of perfume, sandalwood, and tuberoses. When my bridesmaid and Asma opened the door to let themselves out, I heard the loud negotiations going on just outside the door—Akram's cousins rowdily refusing him entry until he met their monetary demands. I was too nervous to be flattered by how little he haggled, by how soon he was allowed admission. He closed the door carefully behind him, bolted the lock, and turned to face me. It was past three in the morning. We were alone for the first time.

"Are you tired?"

I had a hard time looking at him, focusing instead on the bangles on my wrists as I shook my head and said, "No."

"Neither am I. I know I should be. But I'm not. Does your foot hurt? Stiletto Auntie should be banned from all wedding stages in the future."

I laughed, remembering the friend of his mother who had unknowingly planted the pencil heel of her shoe in my foot, offering hearty congratulations as I tried not to wince. Akram had heard my soft sigh of relief as the woman turned to leave the stage, had leaned close to ask me what was wrong, and smiled sympathetically when I mumbled my complaint under my breath.

"Let me have a look," he said now, lifting my foot, gently unbuckling the strap of the golden sandal I wore, before setting my foot on his lap to examine it carefully. "Oh, Deena. You didn't tell me she made it bleed!"

The touch of his hand on my foot made me breathless. I looked at his fingers, noting the track of dried blood that they traced, a darker shade of red blending in with the fiery henna patterns on my feet. He stood up to get a damp towel and cleaned the wound. When he was done, he sat up, suddenly straight, and said, "This is what I'm supposed to do anyway, isn't it? Where's the basin? Ah, here it is." He had found a steel bowl on a table beside the dresser, which he took into the bathroom to fill with water. When he came back, he bent to lift my other foot, removed the sandal, and washed my feet. "Now, what am I supposed to do? Save this water? To sprinkle in all the corners of the house?"

"That's the custom."

"Yes. For *barkat*, they say. For blessings and prosperity. Well, I must say—I, for one, enjoyed it. What's next? Shall I wash your hair? Scrub your back in the bath? I like these traditions!"

I laughed. "No. No more washing or bathing."

"Did you have the *mehndi* lady hide my initials in the pattern of henna on your hands?"

"Of course."

He took my hands in his, but didn't begin the search. Instead, he leaned his head in close to my face. "Does my hair smell like *biryani*? One of the aunties came and put her hand on my head to bless me after dinner. I don't think she had washed her hands after eating," he said with a shudder that made me laugh.

"No. I don't smell any food."

"It was a grand wedding, wasn't it? Giving all the old gossips enough to talk about for weeks to come. Did you see Gulnaz Auntie? The way she bent forward to gape at your jewelry and then reached out to touch your necklace, to lift it and gauge its weight and value? I thought she would fall into your lap!"

I fingered the necklace, part of a diamond set that had been sent over with the clothes I was wearing, on the day before the wedding. I wondered what my mother's wedding jewelry had looked like—part of what she had sold off to finance my father's business. Normally, the gifts I had received from Akram's family would have flowed both ways. But no explanation was needed in our case. Everyone knew that our source of income was dry. The only gift my family had given to Akram was my father's old watch, polished and shined, to be sure, but secondhand nonetheless. I had been surprised to see it on Akram's wrist when he'd slipped the ring on my finger, never imagining that he would actually wear such a modest piece when I knew, from having seen them, that he owned far more expensive watches already.

Suddenly, Akram was on his feet, pulling me up along with him. "Did you look around the room? While I was paying the kids off outside? No? Do you like the furniture? I ordered it myself." He ran his hands along the dresser and then began to open drawers. "Come, see what's inside. Beautiful clothes for you." He opened the doors to the wardrobe and pulled out *sari*s and *jora*s. "I chose most of them myself. And you should thank me! You should have seen the old-fashioned stuff my mother would have liked."

"It's all lovely."

"And the bathroom? Did you see that?" He led me to the door of the attached bathroom, our own private one, pointing out the fixtures, all imported, which he had chosen, the high ceilings, the intricate tile work. "You like it?"

"Yes. It's beautiful," I said, thinking of the long walk across the courtyard at home to the one bathroom we shared, with its rough, cement finish, the antique geyser mounted at the top of the wall that worked less often than it failed, which Macee or I had to climb on a stool to relight, and the rusty chain-pull that operated the flush suspended from the tank overhead.

"One more thing—a matter of business before pleasure," Akram said, reaching into a drawer of the dresser. "It is tradition, also, I believe, for me to give you your bridal settlement before I make any demands of you over there." He jerked his head, with a charming wink of his eye, toward the bed.

"What? What's this?" I asked, fingering the little book, the size of a passport, that he handed me.

"It's your bank book. For the account we've opened in your name. You'll see the balance is in order." He was all business now.

I didn't say anything, didn't open the book.

"Deena. It's your *meher*."

"But— I— an account?"

He laughed. "Didn't you read the *nikkah-nama*?" That was the marriage document I had signed before the wedding.

"No. I didn't."

"Shame on you, Deena. No one ever taught you that you should never sign anything without reading it in full? All the fine print."

"But—" I didn't know what to say. I had not read the document for our marriage before signing it. The traditional *meher*— a prenuptial settlement that is supposed to be a bride's security against the possibility of a failed marriage—was often, in our culture, only a symbol. There were exceptions. I had even heard of weddings aborted over haggling, which turned to feuds, between the families of brides and grooms, about definitions of what was fair and what was extravagant. Among the people I knew, girls were encouraged to "forgive" these settlements, to tell their husbands on their wedding nights, "Never mind what you owe me." This—an account in my name—was not something I had expected.

Akram took the book from my hand and opened it, pointing to a balance that made me gasp. "My father is a stickler for these things, Deena. He believes that these laws of religion should be taken seriously. That money is yours. To do with as you wish."

It was enough money to pay off Abu's debts. Enough for Ma to live on—if she was frugal—for years and years. I was thrilled at the thought of it. That this money was mine to give to her if I wished.

"Thank you, Akram."

"You can't thank me for what is your due," Akram said gently, his hand on my shoulder, his eyes holding mine for a moment before I dropped them, overwhelmed. He let go of me and walked to the record player in the corner of the room, which I had not noticed before. He picked up the stack of albums there and shuffled through them for a moment, found the one he was looking for and held it up, saying, "You like Presley?"

I nodded and watched him flip a switch, put the record on the turntable, and carefully place the needle to fill the room with the sound of "All Shook Up," making school and the reverend mother seem suddenly a lifetime ago.

Then Akram came back toward me and held his hand out, like a hero in a movie, an unmistakable gesture that made his next words unnecessary, "Would you care to dance, Mrs. Mubarak?"

I took his hand and let him take me in his arms, dancing with a man for the very first time, fast, then slowly, and then fast again, matching the pace of the rhythms and melodies that filled the room, an unexpectedly lovely prelude to what followed. As the record ended, he led me to the bed and lay down next to me.

"What is your favorite Elvis song?" he asked me.

" 'Love Me Tender.' "

"Can you sing it for me, Deena?"

I did, while he kissed and caressed me and began the journey of consummation. How overblown had been my fears of that first time! Akram was sweet and soothing and gentle through the whole of it, holding me in his arms afterward.

Falling victim to the illusion of closeness that such moments foster, I asked, "What is yours? Your favorite Elvis song?"

" 'Wooden Heart,' " he said, before singing it to me—the words of the song seeming a heartfelt plea, from Akram to me, to safe-guard his heart, making my own fill with tender, protective urges.

How overrated physical intimacy is; the more preciously guarded—virginity and chastity sacredly preserved—the more false its promise. Physically, I had never been closer to anyone else in my life until that night. It made me believe what wasn't true—what could never be true—that I understood something of the man I married, that I had begun to know him, his mind and his heart, as a wife should. It made me able to put aside Sharif Muhammad Chacha's words, releasing the breath I had held since he'd uttered them. I knew that what he'd said had been untrue.

But I knew nothing. Absolutely nothing.

For the days that followed, a strange routine was set. Mornings, when Akram and his father left for work, were excruciating. There were too many servants for any work to be left for me to do. My mother-in-law spent the mornings in her room, breakfast and tea delivered there daily. I should have been happy with all that time to bury myself in books, the way I had scarcely had time to do since Abu's death. But I wasn't. Leisure is only fun in contrast to its opposite. In the afternoons, I joined Akram's mother in visiting or receiving visitors—there were condolence calls to be made, and congratulations to be offered for engagements and weddings, duties I had never had to perform before, because my mother's social circle was smaller and, until I was married, I was exempt from such grown-up obligations. Every day, there were petitioners who came to seek a share of the Mubarak bounty—mostly former servants and employees who had fallen on hard times.

It was the evenings I looked forward to, when Akram came home bearing even more gifts for me—flowers, chocolate, perfume, and jewelry. At night, we were the guests of honor at dinner parties all over town, where I wore the outfits and jewelry that Akram enthusiastically laid out for me. After the parties, our bedroom was a sanctuary from the strangeness of becoming part of a new household, a rich household in which I wondered whether I would ever feel comfortable. There, it was just Akram and me, in retreat from others, resuming what had begun on our first night of marriage. Music and dancing and pillow talk filled those nights, pleasantly at first. Eventually, exhaustion would overtake me and I learned to fall asleep to the sound of his voice talking or singing along with the records he played. It took a while for me to notice that there was something wrong. That after I was asleep, Akram would get up and pace the room. As the nights passed, when we measured the time of our marriage in weeks instead of days, his pacing became frantic. He stayed awake, drawing up itineraries for the honeymoon he was planning for us, a trip to Europe, a few months away. On more than one occasion, he woke me up, dragging me out of bed to go out and look at the stars, or go for a drive, so late that even the nocturnal streets of Karachi were deserted.

I didn't understand the clues that my in-laws eventually noticed, casting looks at their son filled with more and more worry as the days passed. The accelerated rate of Akram's speech turned into frenzied monologues. When I was too tired to dance with him at night, he danced by himself, long after I pretended to be asleep. Within three months of our marriage, I knew two things. I was pregnant. And what Sharif Muhammad Chacha had said about my husband was true.

Very quickly, I was educated on the technical terms to describe what ailed him. He was a manic-depressive—what they call "bipolar disorder" today—now flying high in a hyperexcited state that his father finally challenged in a conversation I overheard from the hallway outside of the lounge.

"What do you mean? You stopped taking your medication?!"

"I mean what I said."

"But— why? *Why*, Akram? You were doing so well!"

"I was dead, Papa. My heart was dead."

"But, Akram—you heard what the doctor said as well as I did—it's dangerous to stop your treatment this way. You know what can happen, Akram, please. Be reasonable."

"Don't you see, Papa? I was dead! A puppet! Made of wood, with a wooden heart. No joy, no life in me. That is not the way I want to live. It was my wedding time, Papa, and I had to experience it. Fully. Alive. With a heart of flesh and blood. Alive and beating, not numb from drugs. Dangerous? What is life without danger? Without risk?"

"Akram, stop it. Please! You know where you are headed. You know what will happen."

They knew. Akram and Abbas Uncle. Sajida Auntie and Asma. But I had no idea. How low Akram would fall from his heights. When it happened, it was so bad that drastic measures had to be taken. For Abbas Ali Mubarak's son, the psychiatrist made house calls. He came, with his machine, his wires, his rubber bands, and his assistants. He gave Akram electroshock therapy. Again and again, over the course of a few weeks. By now, no one pretended any longer that this was something they hadn't known about.

"We had hoped," Abbas Uncle said, "that this would never happen again. He was doing so well."

Sajida Auntie sniffed. "I thought his marriage would be the end of these episodes." There was an accusation in her tone. The line was drawn between her and me—never to be erased. I was somehow responsible, in her eyes. I was to have been the cure for her son—one of a series she had tried over the years, from herbal medicines to *hakim*s, faith healers, and quacks. In her eyes, I had failed him just as all the others had.

After I lost track of the number of electroshock treatments the doctor administered, Sajida Auntie said to her husband, in tears, "Enough! We have tried all these doctors. None of it works. This time, we will do as I say."

"As if we haven't tried things your way already," Abbas Uncle said, without looking at me.

"We will take him to Karbala. On *ziarat*. We will go on pilgrimage, to give our *salaam*s to Imam Husain, who will cure him. I know he will! If we have enough faith."

Abbas Uncle said nothing. In a week, he had arranged for the trip. They would go—Abbas Uncle and Sajida Auntie and Akram—on pilgrimage to Karbala and Najaf in Iraq. Because I was pregnant, I was not allowed to go. Instead of going on the honeymoon that Akram had planned, I went home to Ma.

Ma asked me what was wrong. Again and again. I said nothing. Merely the facts, with none of the details. "They've gone for pilgrimage to Karbala. I couldn't go. I'm pregnant." Finally, frustrated, she sent Macee to visit her brother, Sharif Muhammad. To find out the details I wouldn't share. After that, Ma left me alone.

When my husband came home from pilgrimage to Karbala, nothing had changed. More electroshock treatments. So many that his memory was broken. He didn't recognize me when I put my hand on his cheek, didn't even know who I was. Finally, Abbas Uncle sent him away. To the clinic in Switzerland, where he'd been treated before. Uncomfortable in my in-laws' home, I went back to stay with my mother while he was gone, heedless of the gossip that this must surely have caused.

What people were saying didn't matter to me. I didn't go anywhere. I didn't see anyone. Except Asma, who came to visit me a few times. She was pregnant, too. We should have had much to talk about. But we didn't.

The day I first felt my baby—Sadiq—move inside of me, as soft as the flutter of a bird's wings inside my belly, was the first time in a long time that I was happy. I wasn't alone. In that instant, I knew I would never be alone, no matter what else happened.

Akram came back to Pakistan when I was only weeks away from delivering Sadiq. I went back to be with him. He seemed better, able to smile again. But not at me. Toward me, his eyes were those of a stranger. I slept alone, in the room where Akram had danced with me less than a year earlier. He slept in the room that had been his as a boy, the room that was to be our child's room when he was born.

When my birth pains began, I went back to Ma. It was tradition—for me to go home to give birth, to stay in my parents' house for forty days after. It was a relief, too, to be away from Akram and his stranger's eyes.

Sadiq was born, filling the hole in my life with a purpose that I clasped close to my heart, making everything else fade in importance. Abbas Uncle and Sajida Auntie came to visit. Asma was at their home, having given birth to Jaffer a few weeks before. Her new home, a brand-new house that her father had built for her and her husband, across the street from her parents, so that she would never have to live under the rule of her in-laws, was ready for her when her forty days was up, a few weeks before Muharram was to start.

When Muharram was about to begin, Sharif Muhammad Chacha came to fetch me and Sadiq. I had spent more days of my marriage in my parents' home than in my husband's. It was strange to go back there. But I had no choice. Sajida Auntie's Muharram gatherings were to begin. And she was worried about what people would say if her daughter-in-law was not present. About what more they would say than they must have already.

Sajida Auntie hired an *ayah* to take care of Sadiq. "Let *her* take care of the baby. You must try to make Akram remember. That will be easier without Sadiq always in your arms." This was not something I could do. Sadiq was mine. He knew it, too—crying in everyone else's arms, soothed and sated only in mine.

Akram had begun to interact with his parents. Around me, he was still quiet. And Sadiq was of no interest to him. Sajida Auntie tried to convince him, to remind him, of who we were. Abbas Uncle said that the doctors in Switzerland had reassured him—it was an unusually long-lasting effect of all the shock treatment, this loss of memory. That in time, he would remember. But it wasn't in time.

On the second day of Muharram, just as I recited the last words of my favorite *noha* at the gathering of ladies in Sajida Auntie's grand hall, bereft of furniture for those ten days, Akram came into the room, a man trespassing on the space of women. He was agitated, looking for something. His eyes caught mine. He marched up to me and shouted, "Your brat is squalling!" In that second, I saw Akram's mother step forward. She hesitated, the calculation of her thoughts clearly visible on her face. How to rescue the situation? How to stop Akram without giving him away? But Akram wasn't finished and that hesitation of hers was enough to let him go on, too far, too late. "Go and shut that child up! And then take him and go back where you came from! Take your brat—that son of who-knows-what and get out of my house!"

I put my hand up to my mouth and sank to my knees. My mother was there to see the whole thing. All the women of the community were there to hear what my husband said. Ma came to my side and lifted me up.

"Enough, Deena. It has been enough. Go and get your son. I'm taking you home. This time for good."

* * *

I was not alone. I had Sadiq with me. Two weeks later, a few days after Ashura, Sharif Muhammad Chacha came to tell me that Akram was dead. That he'd hung himself in the beautiful bathroom of our wedding suite.

I went to my dead husband's house, a widow at nineteen, where people were gathered to give condolence, some of them the same women who had witnessed my humiliation two weeks before. Sajida Auntie, driven by grief, I know, shrieked at me to get out of her house. The same way her son had. I understand. Now, at least. What grief can do. How hungry it becomes—when combined with bitter anger and denial—how blind, looking for a target at which to cast blame. I was merely that—a convenient target—chosen without regard for fact or reason.

And I was not alone. I had Sadiq with me.

When Ma died, Sadiq was eight months old.

But I was not alone. I had Sadiq with me.

Abbas Uncle came often, urging me to return to live under his roof. But I told him what Ma had said before she died. That Abu would have wanted me to stand for myself. That my life was my own and no one else's. God's gift to me. Not to be squandered.

It never occurred to me. That Abbas Uncle would later use the name of that same God against me. That he had consulted with lawyers and mullahs—all of them men. That they had told him that Sadiq belonged to him. That after he was weaned, I had no right to my own son.

He didn't say any of this out loud. To me, he said, "I cannot force you, Deena. To come and live with us. Even though that is the way it should be. You have suffered enough. But we have suffered, too. Your mother-in-law was bitter. And wrong to blame you. Time is what is needed. For all of us to heal."

Time was what he promised. And time was what he gave. More than five years. He must have planned and plotted for all that time, mercilessly torn between his guilt and his grief. Between what he owed me and what he wanted. To take back his grandson, who was mine, no matter what his mullahs told him.

In those years, amazingly enough, I was happy. I lived with Sadiq, alone in the house where I grew up, with only Macee for company. Every week, dutifully, I took Sadiq with me to visit his grandparents. I never begrudged them that right, no matter how painful it was for me. No matter how much I would have preferred not to go there.

I put up with Sajida Auntie's barely veiled dislike and resentment—something she swallowed at the end of the first year of her grief, coming to see me. Urging me to attend her *majlis*es when Muharram came again. It was an act of atonement for what had happened in the weeks before Akram's death—carried out not for me but for her grandson, whose legitimacy her son had put in question, repudiating him in front of the busiest body of witnesses to be found. She made a great show of walking me into that first gathering, her arm around my shoulders. Perhaps it made a difference in the way some of those women perceived me. I wouldn't know. I shunned them before they could shun me, interacting with them with only my voice, in the *noha*s I recited. Those were for the love of the Imam. Those were not subject to their approval. And the grief we shared, together, made those gatherings neutral ground. There was room for me there.

I miss that—the special power in those congregations of women.

I have been unable to find a replacement for it over the years in this country, where women have to enter the mosques from back doors and sit in the less favored spaces of worship because the space and time for worship is shared and women often get the shorter end of the stick as a result. In Pakistan, we were so separate from the men, our gatherings held at different times and in different spaces, that we didn't have to share anything with them. Space, time, power. The spirit of Bibi Zainab was there when we gathered, the sister of Imam Husain—you know the story? All of it? Of Karbala? Sadiq told you that, too? It was Zainab that everyone turned to after that day of tragedy—Ashura. She led the captive women and children, gave them comfort, and spoke for them in the court of the tyrant, her feminine voice bold and strong for the cause of justice.

But in all those five years, when I attended *majlis*es at the home of my in-laws and visited them with Sadiq, there were signs I should have seen and been prepared for. How often Abbas Uncle and Sajida Auntie would complain—about how much Sadiq depended on me, how much he needed me. How unhealthy it was, that he should be afraid of them and everyone else. I remember how upset Abbas Uncle was when Sadiq cried inconsolably on his first outing without me. It was Muharram again. And Sadiq couldn't bear to be with the men in the Muharram procession, afraid of what he saw there. Abbas Uncle said that he was too sheltered in my feminine shadow. That children, especially boys, had to exit the womb, after all, in order to survive in this world. But I didn't understand what he was getting at. How could I?

I was there the day that Umar came home, on the terrace with Sadiq. I had no idea. That what went on in my neighbor's house, in the home of my old friend, would have such an impact on the life I was living and which I thought, with no complaints, would never change. From Macee, who heard it from the washerwoman who worked for Umar's mother—that *Wahabbi* woman, Ma had called her, always with an angry shake of her head—I learned that Umar was home for six months. Done with his studies in America, with a job as a professor waiting for him when he went back. A great success, by all measures. That he was still unmarried, his mother anxious to change that, the reason he'd come home.

I had no interaction with him. None whatsoever. In fact, unconsciously, I avoided the terrace altogether, drinking tea in the lounge, letting Macee hang the laundry to dry—normally one of my favorite chores, as the line was there, on the terrace, where I'd spent so many happy hours of my childhood. So, I was shocked by what Abbas Uncle came to say one morning, while Sadiq was in school.

"Your neighbor—the woman next door, Mrs. Yusuf—has come to see me, Deena."

"My neighbor?"

"She's very angry. An emotion, it seems, that she is on very familiar terms with."

"Angry? With me? What on earth for?"

"She's worried that her son will do something impulsive. You know him?"

I didn't say anything for a moment. Then, "I used to. When we were children. I don't anymore."

Abbas Uncle's eyes were slit-sharp in their study of my face. I had nothing to hide, meeting them with my own.

"She says that he's in love with you. That he always has been. Did you know this?"

"He——?" Suddenly, I found it difficult to find enough air to fill my lungs. "She—but—that's nonsense! I haven't even spoken to him. And what reason did she have to come and see *you*?"

"She seemed to think that I could stop her son. From making a mistake. That he was at risk of doing something about how he feels. She wants me to keep you away from him. And assumes that I will agree with her. That a marriage between my son's widow and her son, a Shia and a Sunni, is something I would wish to avoid at all costs."

"You should have told her, Abbas Uncle. That there's no risk of such a thing happening."

"Why not? Maybe she's right, Deena. How do you know that she's not right? That the boy loves you and wishes to marry you. And this Sunni-Shia thing." Abbas Uncle waved his hand dismissively. "I knew your father well enough to know that it would not have mattered to him. Especially now. When your options are—more limited than— before. How do you know what the boy's intentions are?"

"It doesn't matter what I know. That is not going to happen, Abbas Uncle. I told you, I don't even know him. Not anymore."

There was a long silence. Then Abbas Uncle said, "Nevertheless." Another long silence. "What she said is worth considering."

I let the confusion I felt make its way to my face.

"If not this boy. Then another. Don't you think, Deena, that it's time for you to think of yourself? That you've given up enough of your life already? For the mistakes of others?"

I remained quiet. Something about Abbas Uncle's tone made me wary.

"It's time for you to be married again, Deena. It's time to move on. For all of us to get out of this state of limbo and get on with life as it should be."

"As it should be?"

"Yes. Marry this man. If he wants you. If not, I'll find you another."

"You want me to marry? I don't see how this is any concern of yours."

"Everything you do is my concern, Deena. You're the mother of my grandson."

"If you're worried, Abbas Uncle, then you shouldn't be. My life is centered on Sadiq. I would never do anything against his interests. His life is mine."

"No, Deena. His life is not yours. What happened with you was not right. I made a promise to your mother. Before you agreed to marry my son. That for as long as you lived under my roof, I would protect you as if you were my own daughter. As it happened, the time you spent in my home was insignificant in amount. Regardless, I broke my promise—had already broken it, in fact, when I made it. What happened with you is not something I would have wished for Asma. And now, if she were in your place, I would want Asma to move on. Not to live in this prison of your past—unable to escape it and powerless to take the steps forward to be free. Not a day goes by that I don't think of you, Deena, with regret. Regret and shame for the position I placed you in. Regret and remorse for how you live now. In seclusion. The life of an old woman. Instead of the young, vibrant one I knew when your father was alive, the young, laughing woman who came into my home as a bride—

blooming and brimming with the joy of a future that I cheated you out of before it even began. You're still young, Deena."

I shook my head, rejecting this assertion of youth, feeling far, far older than the number of years in my age. Do you know how old I was? I was twenty-four.

"Yes, Deena. You are still young. Your father, who was my friend, would not have wanted to see you throw your life away, burdened with responsibilities that should be shouldered by others."

"Abbas Uncle. I don't understand what you're saying. Are you urging me to marry a man who lives in America? To leave Pakistan? This is something you would allow?"

"Of course, Deena. What do you take me for? Your well-being is everything to me. Your happiness."

I shook my head. "This is neither here nor there, Abbas Uncle. I have no intention of marrying Umar." Abbas Uncle raised his eyebrows, a question. "The neighbor's son," I clarified, feeling myself blush for no reason at all. "Nor is there any reason to suppose that he would wish it."

"If not him, as I said before, then someone else. I'll find you a husband, Deena. Just as your father would have done for you."

"No. This talk is ridiculous. I will not marry again. Sadiq is all I need."

"But Sadiq doesn't belong to you, Deena."

"I don't understand, Abbas Uncle. What you mean."

"I will not allow you to use Sadiq as an excuse for living your life as if you were already dead. I have decided. For your sake. Sadiq belongs in his father's home. And you will be free to move on. To make a new life for yourself."

That is when it hit me—the full force of what Abbas Uncle had really come to say—like a blow to my belly, making me wince in pain, wringing tears from my eyes, bitter tears of pure rage. "For my sake?! Please—be clear, Abbas Uncle. I want to understand you fully. Before I react. Your words—all of this contrition and concern—are you saying what I think you are? That you intend to take Sadiq away from me? From his mother?!"

"It's the only way, Deena. As harsh as it may seem. The only solution. There is wisdom in the laws of God. The laws that say he belongs in my house—in the home of his father. I tried to resist that wisdom, thinking that to take him from you would be too cruel. By rights, the boy should have come home when he was weaned. I realize now that this was the right thing. For everyone concerned. And I intend to fix it now. If I don't do this, you will never move on, forfeiting your future. I cannot have that on my head, Deena. That, on top of the pain of your past, which I am responsible for. Don't think I'm not aware of that."

"The laws of God? That's what you call it? You want to take my son away from me—to tear my heart, beating and alive, out of my chest—and then justify your brutal intentions in the name of God?"

Abbas Uncle bowed his head.

"Please, Abbas Uncle! Don't do this! If it's— if you want me to come and live under your roof, I will do it. Sadiq and I will move. I will give up this place. But don't take my son away from me."

"Deena. That will not solve the problem. If you think I do this for my own sake, then you'll see that I would have no problem with what you suggest. But that will not solve the problem of *your* future, Deena. Sadiq is a part of your past. I will not allow you to come and live with him under my roof—a sacrifice at the altar of my son's tragedy. That isn't fair to you. What I propose—it's for your own good. You'll see that. In time. I am sure that this is the right thing to do."

"The right thing? To separate me from my own soul? The reason I live and breathe? I—I'll do what you say, Abbas Uncle. I'll marry whoever you wish. Or not. Whatever you wish! But don't take Sadiq away from me! I am begging!"

"It is the best way, Deena. I cannot allow my grandson to be raised as the son of another. He belongs under my roof. And you must move on."

"But— I—I will fight you, Abbas Uncle. Surely I have some rights—?"

"You are free to do what you will, Deena. But I warn you, fighting me would be pointless. The law is on my side. And this is a fight I will not allow you to win. I will bring everything to bear in fighting and winning. Because I am right. I know I am."

I closed my eyes, letting myself imagine what such a fight would entail. Me—a mother, alone, widowed—fighting against the likes of Abbas Ali Mubarak. I felt faint at the thought of all his power and influence, at the knowledge of how justice in Pakistan worked—at the whim of a legal system enthralled with power, riddled with corruption. I remembered his talk of bribes with my father. This man—who threw God in my face, with no shame—he would buy judges and lawyers and clerks to do his bidding. What he said was true. The outcome of any fight between the likes of me and this man was already a foregone conclusion. Out loud, I whimpered.

Abbas Uncle stood up. "I will go now. And give you a chance to calm yourself. I will be back in a few days." He was at the door, about to see himself out. There, he paused for a moment, then said, "This is not the direction I wanted this discussion to take. I don't want there to be a battle between us, Deena. I only want to make things right in a situation where there are no good options for any of us. To make things right for you, my child, and to clear the way for you to have the future you deserve."

"I don't deserve *this*, Abbas Uncle. I don't deserve to have my son taken away from me," I whispered hoarsely, to myself, because Abbas Uncle was already gone.

I went to a lawyer. He told me that though it would be difficult and could take time, I had a case to be made. Then he asked me about the size of my bank balance. And laughed in my face when I told him who my father-in-law was.

I went to visit Abbas Uncle. At his office. In his home. I spoke with Sajida Auntie, appealing to her as one mother to another. To Asma, too. No one listened. No one cared.

Two weeks later, Abbas Uncle sent the car to take Sadiq from me. He had threatened to send the police, with a court order, warning me, "Don't do this, Deena. Don't make me bring strangers into this private matter. Making it into a spectacle."

What could I do? I couldn't let my son be dragged away from me in that way. For his sake, I let Sharif Muhammad Chacha take him, all the while racking my brains for a way to get Sadiq back. I couldn't find any.

I died that day. And waited, in death, for the day they would send him to visit. When he came, I came to life. For an hour, no more. The weeks passed. And there were days—so many days—when I waited in vain. This, too, I suppose, had been part of the plan. To wrench my son away, to keep him from me. I went to see Abbas Uncle again, to remind him of his promise. That Sadiq would visit me every week, the way I had let him visit them.

"It's better this way, Deena. You think I don't know? What I am inflicting on you?"

"If you knew, you wouldn't be able to do it."

"You have to move on. You must see this, Deena. It's for your sake. For you."

There was no one I could turn to. The few relatives I had would not help—no one wanted to become involved in helping to thwart the will of a man like Abbas Ali Mubarak.

In desperation, I searched through my English translation of the Quran, looking to see what it had to say about the custody of children. Nothing. Then I went to the mullah who had represented me at my wedding. He shook his head. "*Beti,* this is Sharia, the law of God, not to be trifled with."

"But there's nothing in the Quran that says so!"

"No matter. The interpretation of the learned ones is sound."

"The learned ones! They must all have been men!"

"Of course they were!" he said, shocked. "You think it's a woman's job to determine what the law of God is? The boy belongs in the house of his father. That is clear. It is God's will."

That day, I came home and knew the truth. I had lost Sadiq. Now, I *was* alone. Even God was gone. I took out my shears and hacked my prayer rug into slivers and slices, angry at the God I could see no sign of, railing at Him for His injustice, like a mad-woman. I *was* mad—as mad as my husband had been. I stopped eating. I stopped sleeping.

How to explain? What happened next. How the boy next door, who had rescued me from a fall when I was a child, saw the shell of what I had become—a brittle shell, about to shatter. He came to visit, prompted by Macee, who, in desperation, recoiling in horror when she saw the ragged ribbons of my prayer rug strewn about the floor of my room, sent him a summons through the washer-woman next door.

I don't even remember that visit. He came and sat with me in silence. Creating a space for me to just be, a space that was separate from the madness I had given in to. He began to visit every day. Bringing books with him, reading out loud. I drank in the sound of his voice. I savored the essence of his presence, remembering a time before this descent.

He made inquiries, confirming what I already knew. There was nothing to be done, any merits of my case outweighed by the power and wealth on Abbas Uncle's side. So, I yielded. Not to the injustice. But to the suffering it caused. I had no other choice.

In that moment of surrender, I also yielded to Umar. I agreed to marry him. To go with him to America, leaving behind what life had dealt me so far. In this new life that I began, there was a hole, too deep to ever fill. But it was right there in the open. Not hidden, or secret, waiting to trip me up in surprise. I learned to plant the garden of my life around it. To stop and look at it from time to time, standing at its edge. Even to descend, frequently in the beginning, into the hole—to lie down in it and let myself feel the pain of sepa-ration from my son, which was not by my choice. Though some may not see it that way. I could have stayed in Pakistan. Maybe I should have. But I don't regret leaving. Whatever regret there was, was not mine to feel. That belonged to someone else.

That regret was what eventually gave Sadiq back to me. But when he came, he was not the boy I had left behind. Nor was I the woman from whom he had been taken. We were strangers to each other—my baby boy, swallowed up by the sullen silence of manhood—the life I had built without him alien to his faded memories of a mother he had never had to share with anyone else.

Sadiq stayed with us for only a year, unable to adjust. Then he went away, no less a stranger than he'd been when he arrived. You, Jo, are the proof of that.

I let silence fall over the echoes of my story. While I'd been speaking, I'd heard Umar return from the supermarket. He'd quietly put away the groceries. Then, without intruding, he'd come into the room with his briefcase in hand, gesturing, telling me that he would be in his study, grading papers, if I needed him. A little while ago, I'd heard the movements upstairs that indicated he'd gone to bed. It was past my bedtime, too. Strangely, I was not tired.

After a moment, Jo asked, "And the reason that Sadiq was sent to you? The accident? You know about that?"

I nodded, a little surprised. "I know about it. I'm surprised that you do." I let another moment of silence pass.

Jo thought about that for a moment. "He's in Pakistan?"

"As far as I know." We had arrived, then, at the reason she had come—a reason that went beyond merely listening to the long story I had shared. "Why do you want to see him?"

"I—it's—it's complicated." She hesitated. "But—some of what Sadiq told me—when he did, I—I ran away from it. From the connection. It was hard. To acknowledge. But I realize, now, that there's a reason for it. And—I have some things I want to ask him. And some things I need to tell him about."

I nodded. Whatever it was, she didn't want to share it with me. I understood. We were strangers, after all.

Gently, I said, "I'll give you Sadiq's number."

"Thank you. You're in touch, then? Regularly? Things are okay between you?"

"That depends on what the definition of okay is. What was lost between us—that, we were never able to find again. But he is very dutiful. With his monthly calls. Letting me know where he is. I haven't seen him in many years." I sighed. "You can call from here, if you like."

"What I have to say, and what I want to ask him about— I have to do it in person. Over there. In Karachi, I hope."

I frowned. "You'll go to Pakistan?"

"Yes."

I felt my eyebrows rise. Then fall. I looked at my watch. "It's late. Do you live here? In Los Angeles?"

"No. I live in Washington, D.C."

"Where are you staying?"

"I was going to drive down to my parents' house. In San Diego."

"It's too late for that now. Stay here for the night. In the guest room. It was Sadiq's room while he was here."

After a while, Jo said, "Yes. I'll stay. Thank you."

"And, Jo. When you go—to Pakistan—to see Sadiq— I'll go with you."

٣

Part Three

Onward Christian soldiers,
Marching as to war . . .

Sabine Baring-Gould (1864 Hymn)

Angela

In the days leading up to Thanksgiving, I watched Chris carefully. And saw the effort it took for him to pull himself up and get ready for Jo to arrive. She'd come home for a short visit after he came back from Iraq, months ago. Was there when his bus pulled in at the base, with flowers and balloons and a great big hug and kiss, as big as the ones Jake and I gave him.

But Jo stayed only for a few days, not enough time to notice that anything was wrong, rushing back to D.C. to go on another one of her assignments. She said she wasn't allowed to talk about her job. But that didn't really explain how reserved she'd become, something that had started even before she took that job. The changes in Jo, since before she went away to college, were something Jake and Chris hadn't understood. I'd known the truth, of course. That she had less to say because of the answers I'd given her before she left home. But now, after coming back from Iraq, the changes in Chris were more drastic than the ones in Jo.

I didn't worry too much at first, giving him space, like the papers we'd gotten from the military said to do, assuming that some of what I noticed was just part of the process of readjusting back to life at home. At first, it was just that he kept to himself, in his room. I worried, but not nearly as much as I had when he was away. I was so relieved to have him home. So was Jake, even more relieved than me.

When Chris signed up for the Marines, right after 9/11, I saw how worried Jake was. For his son. He knew the danger. I'd thought of my dad and I'd worried, too. About what war does to a man—a word I couldn't even use for Chris. He was just a boy. He always would be to me.

Jake and I worried about Jo, too. But not as much. Jo had promised, when her father asked—after we realized that she was involved, too, somehow, in the War on Terror—that she wasn't doing anything dangerous.

"At least not dangerous to me," she'd said, and then refused to explain what she meant.

I knew Jake worked hard not to show how scared he was. He said that *this* time, it was different. I knew what he was talking about—that he was comparing the war about to start in Afghanistan to the one he'd fought in.

He said, "This one, we didn't ask for. It's a war that *they* came and started on our soil. We've got a right to defend ourselves. To get the people who attacked us."

He was reliving his past while I tried hard not to think of mine. When the war began, I looked Afghanistan up on a map of the world—a country I'd never even heard of until now. It shocked me to find out it was right next to Pakistan, the name of a place I *had* heard of, from people I had tried very hard to forget. Seeing that map made everything messier, more complicated, than I wanted life to be. I had to shrug off wondering where they were and what they were feeling—the boy I'd made love to, the woman who'd been my friend, people I'd been close to for one irregular moment of my life, yet hardly knew at all. It was the first time in all these years that I considered their connection to the lives I'd carried inside of me, the lives I'd nurtured and raised and kept from them—in the present tense instead of the past. Suddenly, I felt like the tie that I'd denied, my blood mixed with Sadiq's, was snatching my babies back to the part of the world where he came from. I wanted things to be simple and neat, a line drawn between us and them. But in my nightmares, it was Deena's face and Sadiq's that threatened my children, the faces of people who'd been kind to me, people I wanted to hate but couldn't. When Chris didn't go to Afghanistan, after all, I was relieved. I could put all those tangled old ties back into a box and turn my attention to another place, Iraq, which, I told myself, was far enough away not to matter.

But the shift, from one war to another, made Jake more uneasy. The day Chris was deployed to Iraq, Jake cried. In all our years of marriage, I'd never seen him cry. It was hard to see him suffer while Chris was away. He started to have nightmares. Something he'd never had before. He talked in his sleep, sounding terrified, whimpering. Sometimes, he'd wake up and get out of bed. I followed him once or twice. And found him sitting in the dark, in Chris's room. By the sound of his breathing, I knew he was crying. Once, I heard him say to himself, not knowing that I was there, in the doorway, "It's not the same. It's not the same." He sounded like he was trying to convince himself. And failing.

But that was Jake by night. By day, he was all gung-ho, up on every turn and twist of battle and strategy that I couldn't bear to hear about, because I was too afraid. He watched the news all the time. Kept the radio tuned to it in his car. He got a subscription to two newspapers, and started using the Internet to keep up with everything that was happening over there, in Iraq. All he talked about was the war, daring anyone—friends, customers, relatives—to say anything against it. Mom tried hard not to rise to the bait at first, her face all pinched up with the effort not to say anything—for my sake, I think. But I knew her well enough to know what she really felt. When she did start arguing with Jake, it was in a softer, quieter kind of tone than she normally used, making me think she'd guessed at Jake's nighttime secrets—that his furious, daylight optimism was a mask for a fear almost as big as mine was.

The truth is, I didn't care what either of them thought—Mom or Jake—didn't care about why or how this war was being waged, whether the reasons for it were sound or not. I couldn't let myself think about any of that, just keeping my head down instead, focusing on things I *could* control, putting together one care package after another for Chris and his buddies, praying, praying, praying. I'd lost a father to war and its aftermath. Now, I was afraid of losing a son.

Mom knew, somehow, that I needed her. She stuck by me, not going anywhere the whole time Chris was away, at home longer than she'd been since I was a kid. Whatever the arguments were between them, Mom and Jake and I were on the same page whenever we'd hear about casualties, all of us pacing the floor, waiting until we'd hear from Chris.

Nobody was happier than Jake when Chris came home. But, as time passed, my worry was increasing. Chris was taking longer to adjust to being home than I thought he would. He refused all invitations from his old friends, even the members of his old band, Christian March, who wanted him to come out and play with them. He'd go out alone. And come home alone. Chris had always been the center of a bunch of friends, all the years he grew up.

I was shocked, that first time it happened. To smell liquor on Chris's breath. He'd never had anything more than a sip of champagne at weddings before. I ignored it the first time. The second time, I asked him about it. He got angry. And told me to mind my own business. No big deal, I suppose. For a grown son to tell his mother off for babying him. But it *was* a big deal. To me. Chris had never once raised his voice to me before. When he got pulled over, for a DUI, I broke a cardinal rule in our dry house and begged him to bring home whatever he needed. But not to drink and drive. He'd been lucky. The officer who'd pulled him over was the brother of one of Chris's high school buddies. He brought him home instead of arresting him, giving him a stern lecture, telling him he wasn't going to haul him off to jail because he had too much respect for the fact that Chris was serving his country.

I regretted giving Chris permission to drink at home. Because he started to drink all the time. Finally, Jake put his foot down.

"Chris. You need help. You won't talk to us. That's okay. But you've got to find someone to talk to."

Jake called my dad for advice and to see if he still knew his way around the VA. I didn't object. I remembered how I'd met Jake in the first place. We'd only been in touch with my father through Christmas cards in all the years since the twins were born. That's all the contact I'd wanted to have. Ron had done more, though. Had even visited him in L.A., with his family. After that, Jake knew how to help Chris get an appointment at the VA. We drove him there together. The people there told Chris that he had PTSD, which is what Jake had suspected, and gave him a couple of prescriptions. What they talked about, what he said to them, I have no idea. I wasn't happy about the pills. Especially when I found out that there'd be no follow-up appointment for another six months.

At first, the pills seemed to help. But that was before I realized. That Chris, like Jake when Chris was in Iraq, was walking the halls at night. I'd wake up when it was still dark out, thinking I'd heard a sound in the kitchen. And there'd be Chris, getting himself something to eat. Keeping vampire hours. I'd make myself a cup of cocoa, offering to make him some, too. I'd ask him, beg him, to tell me what was on his mind. He'd shake his head and say nothing. The scariest thing was—there was no more light coming out of Chris's eyes, where before there'd been stars, suns, of light. Now, there was none.

I was looking forward to Thanksgiving. Was glad to see Chris make the effort to liven up. To shave. And shower. To clean his room, which was a place I didn't even try to set foot in because of how mad he'd gotten when I offered to clean it months before. I made a menu. And a list for groceries. Chris offered to do the shopping for me. He helped me in the kitchen. I felt like he was coming back.

Jo came a day later than she'd said she would. She told us not to come to the airport. That she was flying in through L.A. She drove home in a rental car. I asked her why she didn't bring Dan with her. I liked Dan. I was hoping to hear some kind of announcement soon. She said she didn't want him here for Thanksgiving. That she just wanted things to be like old times. Chris watched her face when she said this. He smiled, happier than he had been in a long time, I could tell. That Jo was home. That he'd have her to himself for a while. Sometimes, by the way he looked up to her, even when they were little, it seemed like there were years between them, instead of only minutes. She'd always been his big sister more than his twin. When she'd left for college, I'd seen the wedge come up between them. I hadn't done anything to stop it—something I regretted now. I'd been selfish, at a cost to their relationship that I'd pretended not to notice. Until now, when I knew he needed her. More than he'd ever needed her before. Chris was shaken and scattered and nothing I'd tried was helping.

Jo would help him put the pieces of the puzzle back together. She was good at that. Even when she was little, just a toddler, I saw how she made connections, fitting things together to make sense of the world around her. She'd sit there, with her tongue between her teeth, and figure out those wooden picture puzzles when she was two years old. At that age, Chris still thought the pieces just tasted good. If Jo couldn't understand what her brother was going through, and give him words to express it, then no one could.

On Thanksgiving, the house was bursting with people and laughter and love. Mom had flown in the night before. Ron and his family came early in the day. Jo and Chris and their cousins gathered around the television, watching the game, while I got the turkey ready in the kitchen, with the help of Mom and my sister-in-law, Lisa.

Everyone was still smiling when the meal was served. I asked Ron to say grace. And then we dug in. The turkey was the best I'd made in years. The stuffing, just right. And then, as the food on the table cooled, the conversation heated up.

What is it about Thanksgiving? That controversy always has to be on the menu? Like turkey can't be digested until someone around the table picks a fight. The one that day started before I served the pie. And, like every year when Mom was around, the fight started out being between her and Ron—both of them shooting biblical bullets at each other to defend their very different views on God and life and the world in general. Only this time, Jake, who had never before had anything to add to the spectacle that Mom and Ron seemed to enjoy making of themselves, had something to say, too. Something fierce.

"All I'm saying is that when I see your *friends*," Mom spit the word out at Ron, "on television, going around rubbing their hands with glee at the thought of Armageddon, it makes me cringe. All this talk of End Times! It's like they're playing some kind of board game with the Bible. Like the war and death they see happening in the world is just another move forward, roll the dice, and full-steam ahead. Yippee!" Mom raised her hands up, sarcastically, and waved them like a fan at a ball game. "Jesus is coming! And we're going to win!"

"These are biblical scholars you're talking about," Ron said, ignoring Mom's snicker. "They've done their research. They're just sharing what they see ahead of us. And it's not good."

"Biblical scholars! Puh-leeze! What does it take to be able to call yourself that? A certificate you earn off the Internet? You went to Wheaton, Ron. You know better!" Mom was even louder than usual. "You can't mean what you're saying. Giving these charlatans—these false prophets!—any credit for scholarship! The Bible can't be read that way. Picking and choosing passages. To support the twisted way they see the world. And what for?! To foster fear? As if there isn't enough in the world already!"

"Fear is good. Fear is what pushes people in God's direction," Ron said.

"Fear leads us into hate," said Mom.

"Watch it, Mom," said Ron scornfully. "You're starting to sound like one of those hippie Christians again." Ron was on a roll. "That lefty, liberal, mealymouthed version of Christianity that you preach, Mom—making Jesus out to be some kind of spaced-out, long-haired peacenik with no muscle in his words—it's just an attempt to make religion weak, to make God into something ineffectual and effeminate."

"As opposed to macho and muscular? I've got news for you, Ron," Mom said. "Jesus *did* have long hair."

"You know what I meant!"

"Here's a question, Ron," Mom said. "A simple one. When Jesus said, *'Behold, the Kingdom of God is within you,'* who do you think he was talking about? Only *some*? Or all? Do you think he only meant this group of *us* and not that group of *them*?"

"Luke. Chapter seventeen, verse twenty-one," said Ron, always eager to prove that he knew his way around a Bible. "That Kingdom, Mom, as you well know, can only be realized by those who are saved. Justified, by the blood of Christ."

"But—he was talking to the *Pharisees*, Ron. Not to the Disciples. Not to the *saved*. He didn't use the future tense. He didn't say the Kingdom will come into you if you accept Me. He said it's already there. Not just in those who followed and accepted his teachings. In *every* human being. What gives anyone, especially those of us who consider ourselves followers of Christ, the right to destroy, to kill, any other body that contains that Kingdom? Even if it's only in potential form, yet to be realized? Isn't that the whole argument against abortion? In war, we kill. We *kill*. People. Human beings who carry that same Kingdom in *their* hearts. I just can't stand the way those swindler friends of yours can talk about war and destruction—celebrating it!—with no sense of sorrow in their hearts."

And that's when the talk at the table turned more specifically to the war. In Iraq. I wasn't even listening to them anymore—to Ron and Mom—wanting to put my hands up to my ears as they carried on.

Suddenly, Jake pushed his chair back with a screeching scrape on the floor and stood up. "What the hell do any of *you* know about war? Huh? Nothing! Not a damned thing!"

I scooted forward to the edge of my seat, thinking I should say something to stop Jake, to explain his outburst, or apologize for it at least. But then I saw Jo's face. Her eyes were fixed, anxiously, on Chris. My eyes followed hers. And so did everyone else's.

Mom looked from Jake, still standing, fists clenched, to Chris. And said, "You're right, Jake. You're absolutely right. No one here has any right to talk about war. No one except you. And Chris."

The eyes that were already on Chris's face seemed to hold their breath, as if eyes can breathe. Chris shook his head. Said nothing. Stood up. And went upstairs to his room.

The rest of the evening was quiet. And awkward. Both Mom and Ron went to knock on Chris's door to try to get him to come out, apologizing through it when he wouldn't. Mom looked at me. Something she saw in my face made hers look worried.

Chris came out of his room the next morning as if nothing had happened, as if he hadn't locked himself away in the middle of a family gathering, not bothering to say good night to his uncle, his aunt, his cousins, and his grandmother. He was in the kitchen, eating cereal, when Jo came in, rubbing her eyes.

She took out a bowl and served herself some cereal, too, taking a seat next to her brother at the kitchen table, saying, "Hey."

"Hey," he answered back.

I realized, all of a sudden, that Jo, like Chris, had had nothing to say in the discussion the day before. I looked from one face to the other. Then turned back to finish unloading the dishwasher, wondering which of them I should be worrying about more.

Over the next few days, I watched them both like a hawk. Some of the tension eased out of my neck and shoulders as I saw them laugh together and joke. Jake's eyes, when he looked at me, were happier, too. It felt like old times, just the way Jo had wanted it to be. Like back when they were in high school, before Jo moved away.

At night, they'd stay up late, long after Jake and I would go to bed, watching movies and late-night talk shows. Laughing at Letterman and Leno. Both Jake and I slept easier than we had in a long time.

One night, they pulled all our old home videos off the shelf to watch. I walked into the room while they were watching them, Jo laughing loudly, at my expense, at the series of hairstyles that always look funny in hindsight. Chris's face was hard to read. When had he developed that skill? To flex the muscles of his face into a mask no one could see through? Was this something they taught in the Marines? In my heart, I cursed the Marines.

I fell asleep to the low murmur of their voices, when the sound of the home movies faded, talking softly and soberly. I hoped they were sharing their secrets with each other. I also worried that they were doing exactly that.

The next morning, I woke up early to the sound of the phone ringing. It was picked up before Jake or I could get to it. I got up and found Chris in the kitchen again. I smiled brightly at him and asked him if he'd answered the phone. He grunted a yes and glowered at me with doom in his eyes, the spark of light that had seemed to come back when Jo arrived totally extinguished. He grabbed a breakfast bar and, mumbling to himself, marched out the door. I heard the door of his car open and shut, the engine catch, go into reverse, and then pull away with a reckless squeal of the brakes. I sat down at the kitchen table and bowed my head and prayed.

I was still in the kitchen, stunned and scared, when Jo woke up. I turned on her, sharply. "Did you tell Chris?!"

She looked confused. "Tell Chris what?"

I knew, from that confusion, that she hadn't. I didn't say anything.

She repeated her question, "Tell Chris what, Mom?"

"Tell him about—what I told you. When you asked me—about the color of your eyes." We hadn't talked about it since before she left for college. I saw the surprise in her eyes. That I'd raised the subject.

"No! Of course not!" she shouted.

No. Of course not. What was it then that had made Chris fall back into the darkness? Was it the phone call?

Another one came an hour later. "Mrs. March? Christian March's mother?"

"Yes?"

"I'm sorry to have to tell you this. But there's been an accident. Your son's in the hospital."

My heart stopped. Oh, please God, please Jesus, please, let him be safe!

I have arrived where news of myself never gets back to me.

Ghalib

Jo

Chris was alive. All broken into pieces, but alive. The doctors induced a coma, to keep the swelling down in his brain. They kept him that way for weeks. Mom and I did shifts at the hospital, hoping some part of him knew we were there. Dad didn't do shifts. He stayed there. Only leaving when Mom or I dragged him out, kicking and screaming, forcing him home to take a shower and to change. Grandma Faith was with us the whole time.

I kept thinking and thinking, remembering what Mom had asked me. The morning of the accident. She'd known that something was wrong. She thought it was because of something I said.

We'd been having such a good time. I was scared at Thanksgiving. To see Chris's face when Grandma Faith and Uncle Ron were talking about the war in Iraq. But everything was fine the next day and the days after. More than fine. It was like going back in time. Like being a kid again, carefree. For both of us, I thought.

But then, the accident happened and all we could ask ourselves—

because we were too afraid to ask each other—was, why? The question presumed something that we all tried to deny, something that became harder and harder to do.

When the police officer who wrote the report on the accident came to the hospital, he said, "He was going pretty fast. The trajectory—it was straight into the tree. A pretty big tree, too. Hard to get the car untwisted from the trunk of it."

I shuddered. And then sat up straight at what Mom asked him next, "Was he drinking?"

"No ma'am. No alcohol in his blood, according to the doctor."

"Mom—why would you even ask?"

Dad said, "You don't know, Jo. Your brother was pulled over a couple of months back. For driving drunk."

"He what?! And you didn't tell me?"

"He didn't want us to tell you."

When the doctor had asked whether Chris had been on any medication, Dad rattled off a couple of names. I hadn't known about that, either, that Chris was on medication. Again, Dad told me, Chris didn't want me to know. That he had PTSD.

I pulled Mom out into the hall. "So— you just don't tell me? I'm not a part of this family? I get pushed out of Chris's life? Just like that?" I realized I was shouting, and stopped, stricken, when I saw Mom's face. I put my arms around her and we both cried. The thing is, all of us suspected. That Chris's accident wasn't an accident. That he'd driven into that tree on purpose. And all the facts that we didn't know at the time, the stuff that we learned, in pieces, over the course of those first few weeks, supported our suspicions. One day, while Chris was still in a coma, Dad went home to shower, shooed out of the hospital by me, Mom, and Grandma

Faith. There was a message on voice mail. For Chris. A reminder. They'd called him. That morning of the accident. To say that he was about to get redeployed to Iraq.

Dad called them back. And explained the situation. Chris wasn't going anywhere, thank God!

Then, another day, when I went home to sleep for a few hours, and couldn't, I got out my laptop and looked up the meds that Chris was on. For both of them, one of the possible side effects was suicidal thoughts.

Restlessly, I checked my e-mail, which I hadn't done since the day of the accident. Chris had sent me a message. That morning of his crash.

> Re: For Jo
> I'm sorry, Jo. Tell Mom and Dad I'm sorry. I love you. I love Mom and Dad.

There was an attachment to the e-mail. A document. When I opened it, I saw that it was a journal. A record of all of Chris's experiences in Iraq. All the stuff he wouldn't talk about.

I spent the next two hours reading. When I was done, when the numbness of shock faded, a fountain of tears sprang open, dripping onto the keyboard of my laptop. *Oh, Chris, Chris—why didn't you tell me any of this?* I knew the answer already. To give voice to the words, he would have had to listen to the sound of his own memories. So, none of us knew—not Mom or Dad or me—*none of us could see the death you brought back inside of you from Iraq.* I would have understood. But Chris didn't know that. *Because I'd stopped talking, too, long ago, never sharing my own doubts with you, the wall*

of them you helped me climb over, the truth I learned and put away
on a shelf before the war even began. Later, I had demons of my own,
screaming in my ears, too loud to let me hear that yours were louder and
larger—taking the form of friends blown to bits, of children howling,
of women sobbing, of old men's eyes filled with recrimination, the last
of these uttered in words I understood and which you couldn't, because I
refused to share the knowledge that was born of those old doubts that I
hadn't managed to overcome.

I didn't tell Mom what Chris had sent me. I didn't have to. She knew. So did Dad. They didn't need that final confirmation, the final proof. That Chris had attempted suicide.

Dan came down to visit. A couple of times. The last time, I broke up with him, knowing that he was ready to move forward and admitting, out loud, that I wasn't. I don't think he was surprised.

I also called Deena, to tell her I'd changed my mind. "I won't be going to Pakistan. Not now, at least."

Before she hung up, Deena said, "Jo? Please. Will you stay in touch?"

"I will. I promise I will," I said, and meant it. I didn't tell her what had happened to make me put off our trip. For a million reasons, most of them having to do with what I hadn't told her, what I hadn't told Sadiq. That he had a son, too. As well as a daughter.

I never prayed so hard in my life. All of us did. It must have worked, too.

When the doctors decided it was time to bring Chris out of his coma, they were hopeful. We waited for him to wake up for what felt like forever. When he did, it was hard not to shout and dance with joy. The doctors came rushing in, right after the nurses, to check the extent, if any, of the brain damage they'd warned us was possible.

They asked him his name. Right answer! They asked him to count backward from ten. Again, full points! And then, they asked him if he could remember what year it was.

In his weak, groggy voice, he said, "Nineteen ninety-seven?" with a question mark. The doctors asked him what he remembered happening to him last. What he described—a concert he and his band, Christian March, gave in high school—confirmed his first answer. He'd lost memory of more than six years of his life. Then, with a weak smile—oh, how good it was to see—Chris said, "Tired."

"Yes. You rest now, Chris. You're going to be just fine," the nurse on duty said. "You're a lucky guy."

The neurologist, my favorite doctor out of the crew that had worked on Chris over the past few weeks, an Indian woman with an accent like Deena's, said, "As he gets stronger, you'll want to fill him in on what he's forgotten. To try and jog his memory. It will help. But I want to warn you, he may never recover it fully. So it will be especially important for you to explain what he's lost."

When she left, Mom turned to Dad and said, softly, with a look at Chris's bed, to make sure he was still sleeping, "I want you to disconnect the cable out of that TV," pointing to the set mounted on the wall.

Months passed before Chris was ready to come home. During that time, I went back to D.C. and put my place on the market, packing up and having everything moved to San Diego, to put in storage. I was happier than ever about having quit my old job.

I kept in touch with Cheryl, the lawyer. Her clients' cases were moving forward at a snail's pace, my services still unneeded.

In one conversation I had with Cheryl, she brought up the subject of Fuzzy again.

"I've got some new information for you. About that—uh—situation that you were asking about?"

"Yes?"

"I think that particular case has been handled."

"Handled?"

"Mm-hmm. At first, like I told you before, it seemed like no one had even heard of him. Then I got word that someone had hired a lawyer for a client who met the description you gave me. The lawyer's a friend of mine. I'm pretty sure it's the same case you were asking about."

"Uh-huh?"

"Anyway, before the case could go anywhere, my friend said the matter was resolved."

"Resolved?"

"Resolved. As in home."

"Oh. Gotcha."

"Of course, that doesn't necessarily mean the bird's out of the cage."

"What do you mean?"

"A lot of times, that's one of the requirements for—uh—release. It's more like a transfer. Of custody. The child goes from his father to his mother. But he's still treated like a child, subject to guardianship. If you get what I mean."

"I think so."

So Fuzzy had been sent back to Pakistan. I could only hope he wasn't locked up in some jail there. In the meantime, the job I'd signed up for in search of redemption wasn't even close to starting. I had all the freedom and time in the world to be with Chris.

In the last weeks before Chris finally came home, I began to understand what Mom was thinking when she'd asked Dad to disconnect the cable in the hospital. Before they discharged Chris, his broken body having healed itself one bone at a time, Mom got rid of the TV at home. She unsubscribed to the newspapers. Got rid of Internet access. She went through Chris's room, removing all evidence of the last few years of his life—his uniform, his laptop, his cell phone with the numbers of the friends he'd fought with in Iraq. She called all his old friends and gave them strict instructions on how to deal with Chris. She contacted his newer ones, Marines, and told them not to call at all. She scrubbed his life clean of anything that might remind him of the things that drove him into that tree.

I understood her instinct, shared it at first. To protect Chris from remembering. But I knew it was wrong. That to be whole again, someday, Chris would have to remember. And assimilate all he'd gone through with who he was going to decide to be. Like Dad had, with such success, when he met Mom. I told Mom, the day before Chris came home. I told her what he'd written in his journal. Familiar stories—of house raids and checkpoint shootings, of buddies shot and killed and blown up by roadside bombs—the kind of stories that only made it into the periphery of the way the war was covered in the news, without any mention of its long-term effects, on soldiers and civilians. There was just no room for that kind of reflection, not on television, with its occasional rah-rah stories, pretending to honor the troops without wanting to understand what they'd gone through. By telling Mom, I think I only managed to strengthen her resolve.

"It won't last," I told Mom. "This bubble you're building. Sooner or later, he's going to find out. And it'll be worse if it's not from us."

"No. I won't let that happen. I'll protect him. The way I should have before. Can't you see, Jo? That it's back? The light in his eyes? Even with all the pain he's in, it's there. And I can't let it go out again. Which it will. If he remembers the reason it died in the first place."

"It won't work, Mom. You have to see that it won't work."

But she didn't hear me. I appealed to Dad.

He shook his head, deferring totally to Mom's judgment. "Angela—your mother—she knows what's best for Chris. Better than any of us."

Grandma Faith agreed with me. But she didn't do anything about it, supporting Mom by just being there, keeping silent. I stayed and celebrated Chris's homecoming, participating in the blackout, the willful state of amnesia that Mom made us all assume for Chris. For his own good, she insisted. All he knew was that he'd been in an accident and had lost six years' worth of memory, from high school until the day he woke up in the hospital. When he asked questions about what he was missing, Mom would put them off, telling him not to worry, that what was important would come back, all the while praying that it wouldn't.

A year after Chris's accident, he was physically almost back to normal. Mom's plan worked very well, at least at first. Chris was inwardly focused, he had to be, too busy with physical therapy, getting his body back into the shape it was in before the accident. But as time went on, the dam Mom built began to spring leaks. And she didn't have enough fingers to plug up all the holes in the dike.

Once, after a ride in the car with Dad, Chris came home and said, "Hey! I didn't know we were fighting in a war."

"What?" Mom asked.

"I just heard it on the radio."

Dad got in big trouble for that—letting the radio play in the car was something Mom had avoided, keeping plenty of Chris's favorite CDs ready and on hand whenever she took him back and forth to the doctor's.

Another time, it was one of Chris's friends, Sean, that incurred Mom's wrath by talking about a ball game on cable, which whetted Chris's appetite for television, something he hadn't had time to think about for a long while.

"Why don't we have cable anymore?" he asked, after that visit from his friend.

"We—uh—we just don't," Mom said, while Dad and I got suddenly busy with clearing the dining table after dinner.

"Why not?"

Mom shrugged. "We didn't have it before. When you guys were little."

"Yeah. But then we got it. When Uncle Ron went on the air."

"Well, we don't have it anymore."

"Uh—do you think we could get it? 'Cause the TV doesn't pick anything up as it is."

After a few desperate seconds, when you could almost hear Mom scrambling for something to say, she said, "Look, Chris, I didn't want to have to say anything, not wanting you to feel bad about this. But we're really strapped for cash. We just can't afford cable right now. All the medical bills—from your accident—they've been adding up, and—"

Chris interrupted her, his eyes full of remorse. "I'm sorry, Mom. I didn't realize."

It took a few hours before Dad and I could meet Chris's eyes that night.

Mom wasn't fazed at all. She just worked harder than ever at making sure that Chris was busily entertained, being more careful about keeping up the ban on TV and news. It had been a challenge, holding all the news of Iraq out of his reach—the first flare-up in Fallujah; the Abu Ghraib scandal; contractors beheaded, burned, and hung from bridges; the second, bigger battle of Fallujah—none of it good, but Mom managed somehow.

Instead of television, our family watched a lot of movies. Even those, Mom carefully vetted. No war movies or violence of any kind were allowed. With one exception. One night, we rented *The Passion of the Christ*. It was Mom's idea. We all joked about it—about being the last Christians in America to see the movie that whole congregations had waited for eagerly, going to see it by the busloads in theaters, or at private, church screenings around the country.

We watched it twice, back to back. I was amazed. At how much of the Aramaic I understood. It shouldn't have surprised me. Aramaic and Arabic are related, along with Hebrew. Aramaic was the ancient ancestor, old and dying, Arabic the young descendant, still alive and dynamic, vibrantly varied in its vocabulary and dialects. I didn't share my thoughts with anyone, or the words that jumped out at me, the ones that were so similar to words I knew in Arabic. But I wrote them down in my old notebook.

Wa for "and." *La* for "no." *Abba* for "father." *Anna* for "I am." *Be layla* for "by night." *Malika* and *malikin* for "king" and "kings." *Shahadu* for "witnesses." *Mowth* for "death." And what Jesus said on the cross, when he asked God if he had been forsaken: he called God *Illahi*—also a variation of the word *Allah. Illahi*, a word I'd heard in songs of praise and prayer, in Arabic and Urdu.

I also didn't share any of the blasphemous comparisons I couldn't help making—noting the tortured, pained, and shackle-bound way that Jesus walked, burdened with the weight of the cross. Remembering other people, who suffered far less, of course, but who were also shackled at the waist, the hands, the ankles, walking with a grimace, in a lesser way of pain, taunted, too, by guards who refused to recognize the vulnerability of their humanity, the way the Roman guards taunted Jesus.

Chris, too, was very quiet throughout the movie.

The next day, he said, "Jo. The scenes in the movie—of Mary— I—I feel like they're familiar. Not in some religious way. Like I've seen her. In real life. Her clothes. The way she's dressed, shrouded in black. From head to toe. The expression on her face, in her eyes, when she's watching the way the guards treat her son. I know that expression. I've seen it before. I feel like I'm remembering something that I forgot. But— that can't be? Can it?"

I couldn't answer Chris. I wasn't allowed to. Not by the rules Mom had set up for him, for all of us, to follow. I went back and watched the movie again—without him—trying to see it through his forgetful eyes, remembering the things he'd written about in his journal. About a woman he'd met, known, in Iraq. This time, when I saw Mary, I, too, was reminded of grieving Iraqi women that I'd seen on the news, which I only watched when I went to Grandma Faith's place.

It took me a while, but when it happened, it was sudden. To know, abruptly, one day, that I couldn't stay. I couldn't. Not this way. Not anymore—with these new secrets on top of the old ones I'd kept from Chris. I had to find a way to deal with the inevitable. The day that was coming. When Chris remembered, I wanted to have something to give him. To help him cope with the grief of what he'd seen and done. My own redemption was no longer enough. I had Chris's, too, to seek. I had no idea how to do that. I thought starting with my own might be a good way to begin. But the wheels of justice were turning too slowly. Now that I knew that Fuzzy was back in Pakistan, there was another way to go, tracing the connections to those other stories, Deena's and Sadiq's, which I had kept from Chris. Even those might mean something to him when he recovered.

I called Deena. And told her I was ready to go with her to Pakistan. She arranged a leave of absence for herself for the spring quarter, made all the travel arrangements, and called Sadiq to tell him we were coming.

Mom was furious. She didn't understand why I couldn't stay and keep lying to Chris. That's what I was doing—with every word I didn't say, with every smile I gave him, encouraging him to get well, when there was a big chunk of him that Mom hoped would never recover. Through my teeth, through the lids of my eyes, through every pore of my skin, I was lying.

I had to tell her where I was going, because this time I was on my own, with no one to back me up, to knock on her and Dad's

door to tell them if anything happened to me. I also had to tell her
who I was going with. That was a shock for her. I'd never told her.
About meeting Sadiq. And, now, Deena, too. It was a shock. She
didn't mean the things she said, the anger she expressed in fierce,
careful whispers of words so that Chris wouldn't overhear. When
he came in the room, a few minutes later, the anger on her face
receded back behind the mask of motherly smiles she offered him,
the kind that didn't come from inside, the kind that confirmed my
need to get away. She couldn't understand the reason I had to go
there, to Pakistan, because it wasn't something I could explain.
Not yet.

Most of all, I knew, she was scared. Of losing me. In a way that
was different from how she'd nearly lost Chris.

She said as much, when I told her that I regretted not having
told Chris the truth. About his eyes. That I didn't know how long
I'd be able to wait before telling him now. That it was just a matter
of time before the fort she'd built around my brother would come
under siege, from the inside, by his own memories. And that when
it did, I was going to tell him everything.

"Please, Jo. You can't tell him. I couldn't bear the thought of
it—of him looking at me that way."

"What way, Mom?"

"The way *you* do, Jo. The way you have. Ever since."

٤

Part Four

Again, in my heart, crying has caused an uproar,
As the unshed teardrop escaped instead as a storm.

Ghalib

Sadiq

I waited outside the airport, in the middle of the night, secure in knowing that the formalities of their arrival—immigration, baggage claim, and customs—would be smooth. I had made sure of that, greasing the right palms, those of my friend, and his friend, and, finally, his, who was a customs officer with clout. He would send a man to greet them the moment they passed through the concourse. This man—perhaps dressed in uniform, or, perhaps, in a suit and tie—would escort them through the official structures of bureaucracy, weakened at the foundation by the feasting of termites like himself, funded through the who-do-you-know network that is the real basis of Pakistani civil society and of which I freely partake. Bypassing the long queues, he would take their passports straight to the immigration desk, newly equipped with the latest technology, computers and webcams, gifts from the American taxpayer, courtesy of the War on Terror. Finally, the termite would snap his fingers, in a great show of power, summoning a porter to collect their bags from the baggage carousel and then load them onto a trolley, which the porter would push through customs without pausing, until my driver—now waiting with me at a respectful distance of four or five paces to my rear—took it over from him. If I'd paid enough, I could have met them at the door of the plane myself.

So, I was surprised to see them come out of the airport unescorted. And then resigned, realizing my own mistake.

"What do you mean, Sadiq? To hire a man to escort us through the airport? As if we were children!" my mother said, giving me a kiss on the cheek as she did.

I returned her embrace like an adult, instead of an awkwardly resistant adolescent, which was how I had greeted her on another occasion, at another airport, a lifetime ago. "What did you do? Whack him away with your purse?"

"No! I just told him—oh, I see—you're joking. No. I just told him, very politely, that his services were unnecessary. I hope you paid him a lot of money, Sadiq. Money you wasted and which you don't deserve to recover."

I looked from one face to the other, finding it difficult to reconcile the fact that they were here. Together. Ever since my mother's phone call, telling me she was coming and who she was bringing with her, I had wondered. How they had connected. What they had shared with each other, these two very different women.

I turned to Jo. "Welcome to Pakistan."

"Thank you."

"She's been here before, Sadiq," my mother said.

I lifted my eyebrows, not really hearing my mother, my eyes

still on Jo's face. She looked different from the girl who had come to see me in Chicago, years before. She was older, of course. But there was more to it than that.

With a wave of my hand, I called the driver over. He came, taking over the trolley that Jo had pushed out of the terminal. She looked at him with such curiosity, that I had the strange urge to introduce her to him.

Even he looked surprised when I gave in to the urge and said, cheerfully, "This is Usama. Usama the driver, not Usama the terrorist. Usama," I said, switching to Urdu, "this is my mother. Deena Bibi. And this is—? this is—?" I hadn't thought before speaking.

Jo picked up my sentence, saying, simply, "My name is Jo."

She spoke in Urdu. I stared at her. A phrase she had memorized? Yes, she *was* different.

On the way home, my mother said, "Is that the *azaan*?" She rolled down the window, letting the heat in. Jo rolled hers down as well.

"For the dawn prayer?" Jo asked, both she and my mother leaning out to listen.

My mother said, "Yes."

"It's beautiful," said Jo.

"For one second only," I said. "Before the other mosques chime in and all their calls overlap. Every mosque has a loudspeaker of its own, blocks away from the next one. And they never start at the same time, each one managing to be just enough seconds off from the next to clash with each other, making an unbearable racket."

Neither one of them answered, still focused on the calls of the muezzins, unbothered as the echoing clamor I'd described began.

When we arrived home, the sky was beginning to lighten. I showed them in, Usama carrying the bags behind us, with the *chowkidar*'s help. I took them each to their rooms. My mother hesitated, for some reason, outside of hers. She looked into Jo's smaller room and then whispered something to her. Jo whispered back. They nodded at each other.

With a smile and a hand on my mother's shoulder, a caress, Jo turned to me and said, "I'll share the room with your mom. If that's okay?"

"Of course," I said, completely mystified. The connection between these two women, related only because of me, seemed to have sprouted out of nowhere, outside of my presence, around my existence rather than through it. I felt a little besieged by their bond. A little jealous, too, like a child, wondering why they were here, if there was space for me between them, and, if there was, whether I wanted to occupy it or run from it.

I left them, then, still whispering to each other.

A few hours later, I met them in the dining room. We had breakfast in silence, broken only occasionally by a few attempts on my part to play the host.

Cradling a cup of tea, my mother said, looking around, "The room hasn't changed at all," putting me in my place. I had forgotten. This had been her home, too, once upon a very brief time.

Before we rose from the table, the nurse came to tell me that we were running out of one of Dada's medicines. I told her I would call for more.

When the nurse left the room, my mother asked, "How is he?"

"Not so well. It was a bad stroke. He is bedridden, a prisoner in a body that no longer serves him. His mind is all right. But his words are very slurred, sounding like groans and grunts, making it very difficult—impossible, really—to understand him."

"Does he know I'm here?"

I nodded.

"May I see him?"

"Of course."

"What about Jo? Does he know about Jo?" my mother asked, protectively, on Jo's behalf.

"Yes. I told him. Years ago."

I saw my mother's brows shoot up, and I looked away, down at my plate.

Jo asked, "So—he knows I'm here, too? With Deena?"

I looked at Jo from behind my cup of tea, swallowed a sip, and said, "Yes."

"Can I see him, too?"

"He would like that, I think."

Later, I led them into Dada's room. My mother went right up to him, taking a seat on his bed, picking up his hand. *"Asalaam alaikum,* Abbas Uncle. It's me. Deena."

Dada tried to speak. But his effort merely sounded like a moan.

"I was so sorry to hear of Sajida Auntie's passing. I hope you got my letter?"

Another moan. Dada's eyes were wide and sharp on my mother's face. They shifted from hers to mine.

I said, for him, "He was very happy to receive your letter. He planned to write back—but . . ." I ended the sentence with a shrug.

Dada tried to speak again, to my mother.

She looked at me with a puzzled frown. I shook my head, unable to help. Dada's slurs were not getting better.

"Should I go, Abbas Uncle? I don't want to disturb you. Or cause you discomfort."

He moaned again, unintelligibly. But I saw my mother smile. I could see why. His eyes, now on her again, had softened. His hand, quite deliberately, squeezed hers.

"Yes. I'll stay," she responded, understanding him completely.

I stepped forward. "Dada. This is Jo." She was standing next to me, waiting for an introduction.

In perfect, complete Urdu sentences, more than just a memorized phrase, she said she was happy to meet him, and spoke to him for a few moments. She called him Dada.

After visiting with my grandfather, Jo was overwhelmed with jet lag, no longer able to keep her eyes open. My mother sent her off to bed, but stayed with me in the lounge.

"Why is she here?" I asked my mother, as soon as the door shut behind Jo, wanting to ask the same question of her.

"She'll tell you herself, soon enough."

"You seem very close."

"Mmm. We've gotten to know each other a little. On the way here."

"She speaks Urdu," I said, still bemused by the fact.

"Better than Sabah does."

"How is Sabah?" I was ashamed for not having asked after my sister before.

"She's well. She's getting married."

"Oh? Anyone I know?" I was joking.

My mother laughed, heartily, surprising me with her answer. "Yes, actually, you probably do. After grazing around a buffet of different flavors and ethnicities, Sabah has found herself a Pakistani man to marry. You know the Farookh family? Hasan Farookh?"

"The insurance people?"

"Yes. She's marrying Hasan Farookh's grandson."

"Which one? Habib?"

"Yes. I didn't believe her when she told me. She brought him home last Thanksgiving. As a surprise. Such a small world it is."

"I know him. I know the whole family. Very well. How did they meet?"

"Who knows? Through friends, she says. Probably at some thoroughly disreputable place. A bar. Or a club."

"They're Shia."

"So?"

"So? That's all right with your— with— Sabah's father?" I heard myself stumble, as I always had, when referring to the man my mother had married. The man who, in my mind, would always be just "the crocodile."

"Umar has never let himself get caught up in such nonsense, Sadiq. Besides, he's just happily surprised that the boy is a Muslim. A Pakistani. We had long ago prepared ourselves to welcome whoever Sabah decided on. It's you, Sadiq, who cares for such things."

I didn't answer her for a while. Then I said, "Well. He's a good man."

"I hope so."

"From a good, respectable family." My mother didn't answer me with words, merely laughed, the way she always laughed, infectiously, making me smile, too, struck by the echo of my own stodgy words running through the thread of her wordless amusement. Then it was my turn to surprise her. "As it happens, I am also getting married."

"But that's wonderful news, Sadiq! Who is she?"

"Her name is Akeela. She's a widow with two daughters."

"How—fitting. A widow. And she has been allowed to keep her children?" There was no bitterness in her tone.

"What happened with you was unusual," I said.

"Hmm," she said. And then let it go. "Do they like you? Her children?"

"They seem to. I haven't asked them."

"You didn't like Umar. When you came to stay with us."

"I'm not sure I liked anyone then."

"You liked Angela well enough."

"Yes. I suppose I did. And look where that got me. A lifetime of ignorance. About matters I had every *right* to know."

My mother didn't say anything, merely looked at me with a disgusting amount of sympathy oozing out of her eyes.

Then I said, "I wasn't very nice to him, was I?"

"To who?"

"To the croc—to Umar."

"You were going to call him what you always called him. The crocodile!"

"It's a term of endearment. It's how he referred to himself when I first met him. You told me the story. You told it to him, too, I suppose."

"Yes. I did."

"Is it true, what they told me? That you knew him—that you loved him—before you married my father?"

"I knew him, yes. He was my friend. Before. And then, again, later. At a time when I most needed a friend."

Very slowly and carefully, I tried to air the thoughts and feelings that had taken many years to develop. "I realize now. The whole truth. All that I didn't know before and which I couldn't understand. About how they—Dada—my family—the Mubarak family—about how you were treated."

"Oh, Sadiq. I can hear how torn you still are, by the way your tongue gets all twisted. Between sides. In a tug of war that, for you, never ended. Don't you know, Sadiq, that the game is over? Long over. If you must see the past in terms of sides, then think of it as a coin. Two sides of one coin. It's all the same, in the end. Heads or tails. The winning and the losing only a matter of perspective. And the result of the toss, the way the coin landed, it's done and gone and finished, now. Isn't it?"

"But in this case it was a trick coin. The toss was rigged."

"Perhaps. But the game is still over."

"Have you forgiven him?"

The length of time it took for her to answer was an answer in itself, I thought. Until she spoke. "If you are asking, Sadiq, whether I'm still angry, then the answer is no. I stopped being angry long ago. For me, forgiveness is a silly question. The consequences of your grandfather's actions were ones we all had to suffer. He and I. And you, most of all. The question, Sadiq, is whether *you* have forgiven him. When you answer that question, I will. Besides, he isn't the only one you have to forgive."

I frowned.

"I could have fought him. I should have. No matter how hard it would have been."

I laughed. "You think you could have won?"

"Maybe not. But at least I could have tried." She paused. "Instead of leaving you behind, moving on to a life that has been a happy one. Despite the pain of having lost you. So, you see, I know how it is. That you have me to forgive as well as him."

Hearing her, I fought the sting in my eyes, acknowledging the resentment that might have melted long ago if I had allowed the tears to fall before now—tears that I believed I had outgrown. She moved from the chair where she sat to the sofa where I was, offering a hand and a choice. I took them both, squeezing like Dada had done, giving her a wordless answer that she acknowledged with tears that *she* was not—had never been—afraid to shed.

After a long, quiet while, she said, "Beyond the question of forgiveness, there's something even more important to ask—whether the burden of all that has been done to you, and all that you have done to others as a result, is one you still carry? Because if you do, then you are bound to go on sharing that burden with everyone you meet, everyone you love, everyone who loves you."

I closed my eyes. And then opened them to the sight of the woman before me, to the fact of the girl sleeping one room away. Between them, these women were the beginning and the end of my childhood. My mother and my daughter, two poles of a world from which I had been shut out. In response to that exile, I had pretended not to want what I'd lost. Now, I knew. That being a man meant returning to that world—embracing it. I had begun that journey before they'd come. Their presence, together, would help me complete it.

Again, I asked, "You won't tell me why she's come?"

"No. Why? Are you worried? That she's come to make a claim on all of your fabulous wealth?" That my mother was teasing was clear by the light dancing in her eyes.

But this was a subject I took very seriously. Without a smile, I said, "Not at all. Everything that is mine, I have already willed to her. As soon as I learned of her existence."

"Really? Does she know?"

"No. Of course not. When I met her before, she made it clear. That she wanted nothing to do with me. But I had to do what was right. She is mine. Legitimately. By God's law, anyway."

"By God's law? Forgive me, Sadiq. But I have an aversion to that phrase. Especially when it comes from the mouth of a man. Even if it is my own son."

"Yes. Her mother and I— it wasn't merely a casual encounter. We made an intention. Of *mut'a*."

"Of what?! Oh, Sadiq!"

"What? Would you have preferred it if I had— well— enjoyed Angela's company, without any sense of responsibility?"

"I would have preferred it if you hadn't enjoyed her company at all!"

"But I did. And I made a commitment. With a promise to be responsible for any unexpected consequences. I think that's a good thing."

"All right, granted—that your perspective is one way of looking at it. When two adults are single, what happens between them is their business. But you were only a child, making commitments which were above your head. And, Sadiq, you know that the institution you're defending—*mut'a*—is not fair to women. It's one-sided."

"What do you mean?"

"Not in this case, as I said. Where both you and Angela were not committed to anyone else. But what about married men? Because these so-called laws you're speaking of allow men to have more than one wife, married men get away with having affairs. All the while wrapping themselves in a mantle of piety. You know this very well. You've heard it all. What men do to women in the name of God. It is part of the same problem, the way your grandfather treated me, taking advantage of laws and traditions that don't apply anymore—laws that were meant to *give* rights to women, and which are now used to take them away. I have thought about this a lot, over the years—it is the subject that I teach, after all. And it's personal, too. When I think that anyone could have come up with the opinion that the just thing to do, in my case and yours, was to take you away from me—it makes me furious! In another time and place, in societies where women needed the protection of men in order to survive, this issue of custody was a way for a woman not to be burdened. For a man's family not to abandon the widows of their sons. But to hearken back to the way things used to be as a weapon against women now, that is not God's law. The only law that means anything—that can have *anything* to do with God—is one that is alive and that strives for justice given the circumstances of the present. Otherwise, the law is merely something dead, a weapon in the hands of those with power. Against those with none."

"I'm not disagreeing with you. And I'm not advocating *mut'a* for married men. Or polygamy in any form, for that matter. Don't lump me into the category of hypocrites. I was a boy. Playing a man's game. In my own way, I was trying to take responsibility for my actions. And I would have. If Angela had let me. Jo is my daughter. I am not ashamed. I wouldn't have been if Angela had told me back then. She's mine. And I will treat her the way I would have treated any children I might have had later."

"Might have had? You're getting married, Sadiq. You'll have children with Akeela. *Inshallah*."

"No. She and I have discussed it. I've told her about Jo. She already has two children of her own. And I want no more."

My mother sighed. "You told Akeela about Jo. You told your grandfather. It seems I am the only one you didn't tell."

"I—I'm sorry. This was not something I could say on the phone."

"So? Who told you to say it on the phone? All these years, Sadiq, and you never even came to visit."

"Neither did you."

She didn't say anything, and neither did I.

Then she broke the silence. "And? What about Akeela and her children? If Jo is to inherit all that you have?"

"She will have her *meher*. It will be more than generous. And I have opened accounts in her daughters' names. They'll all be taken care of. If I die."

My mother shuddered. "God forbid! How did we get onto this morbid topic?"

"You were teasing me. About Jo."

"Remind me never to tease you again. My God! What a somber

man you have become, Sadee. And when are you getting married?"

"After the Muharram season is over."

"Are the women's *majlis*es still held here? During the first ten days of Muharram?"

"Not this year. Not since Dadi passed away. Perhaps next year. When there is a woman in the house."

My mother yawned. "Oh—I am tired, too, now. Suddenly."

"Go and sleep."

"Yes. I will."

In the evening, Jaffer came to visit, from across the street, with his wife and children. Also with him were his parents. This was not unusual—they came often, just about every day, to see Dada. That day, I know they must have worked hard to contain themselves, to let the whole day go by without dropping in, curious to see my guests.

"Deena! It's so good to see you! After soooo many years!" my aunt, Phupijan, declared.

"Asma. It has been a long time," my mother replied, with a smile that could be described as mildly cautious.

"And this must be—"

"Jo. This is Jo," I cut Jaffer off, wary at the slight smirk lurking behind the friendly smile he flashed at Jo.

"Ah. Yes. Jo. It's a pleasure to finally meet you." Jaffer turned to me and said, in Urdu, "She's pretty, Sadiq, this secret American daughter of yours. The girl who has turned your life upside down and made you into such lousy company."

"That's not a bad thing, Jaffer," his wife, Haseena, said, also in Urdu. "I keep hoping that the new, reformed Sadiq will have some influence on you." Turning to face Jo, my cousin's wife said, "Come, children," pushing her offspring forward, a boy and a girl, "come and meet your cousin."

Before my relatives made total asses of themselves, I said, "Jaffer. Haseena. Jo knows Urdu."

Jaffer's face was fun to watch, as he reviewed his own words to see if anything he'd said might have caused offense.

Phupijan was sitting next to my mother on the sofa, lifting the fabric of her former sister-in-law's clothes, saying, "My *dear* Deena! We *must* take you shopping. You're looking positively dowdy in these old-fashioned clothes. Long *kameez*es are totally *out*. Mini, mini, mini is what everyone is wearing. And your baggy old *shalwar*—no, no. See these." She pointed to her own pants. "This is the trouser *shalwar*."

"The what? But, Asma, they're just regular pants!"

"Exactly!" said Phupijan. "Haseena," she called her daughter-in-law over, imperiously. "We *must* take Deena shopping. As soon as possible. My daughter-in-law has impeccable taste, Deena. She designs clothes for all the best boutiques. Has done exhibitions, too."

Her tongue in her cheek, my mother said, "But— it's still Muharram season, Asma."

Phupijan waved her hand dismissively. "Don't be so old-fashioned, Deena. Besides, clothes are a necessity."

My mother said, "What do you say, Jo? You want to go shopping? Tomorrow?"

"I'd love to go shopping," said Jo.

***

Two days later—after several trips to boutiques and tailors with Phupijan and Haseena, my mother's clothes now updated and Jo blending into the environment, as if in camouflage, with the new wardrobe my aunt had insisted on buying for her, saying, "It's my gift, Jo. You're my grandniece, after all! A daughter of this house!"—I was finally alone with Jo.

My mother was taking a walk around the garden. Jo sat on the armchair in the lounge, at an angle from where I was, on the sofa. Unlike the last time we were together alone, when she had been perched at the edge of her seat, ready to flee at the slightest provocation, she was relaxed, her back resting against the back of the chair, her hands and arms at ease, at her side, not clenched. "So—when did you learn Urdu?" I asked. "And how? And why?"

"When I started college, I was going to study African languages and be a missionary. Like my grandmother. But—right after I met you—*because* I met you, to be honest, I took Urdu instead. And Arabic."

"Arabic, too? I'm impressed. Your Urdu is very good. My mother—she said—at the airport—that this is not your first time in Pakistan?"

"No."

"You never tried to contact me."

"I came for work. I had no time for personal stuff."

"What kind of work? With the embassy?"

"No."

She told me, then, what kind of work learning Urdu had led her into. She didn't share all the details, but those she did were enough. I knew them already—knew, also, what she didn't say—from a different perspective. I had to check myself, to keep from shrinking away from her words, especially when she told me the story of a man she called Fuzzy—a man cared for by someone named Sharif Muhammad, who he called his uncle. When she was done talking, I put all her words together and realized that if she hadn't met me, her life would have been different. That whatever distaste I felt at what she had participated in, the fact of it could be traced back to learning Urdu, which, she'd said, she'd studied because of me.

I thought of what my mother had said. About the burden I carried and shared with those I met, with those I loved, and those who loved me. She had known this, what Jo was telling me, when she said it. Had known all of it—had seen the connection, had stepped away from the particulars of my story and Jo's, and noted the matching color of the threads that ran through both.

It took me a while to recover myself enough to ask her what I had already asked my mother—twice. I asked her why she had come.

"I ran away from you last time. It was just so inconvenient. The whole thing. To find out that I—the story of my life—wasn't what I thought it was. And I was too lazy to want to figure it all out. But running away didn't help. Your story—who you are—came back into my life in the weirdest way, through this man, Fuzzy. I mean, even if it turns out—that he's not—who it seems like he is, I had to come looking for you, to try and fix things that *I'd* broken. Inside of myself. And other people, too. I went to Deena because I couldn't find you. And through her, I got to know you better—I got to understand what I couldn't before."

"So—you are ready, now? To accept it? What you found inconvenient before?"

"More ready than before. I—I just want to be clear. I already *have* a father. Nothing is going to change that. But—I—get it now. That I have to make room in my life. For things that are true. Even when they don't fit easily into what I want to believe. Am I making sense? Probably not. Because I haven't figured it all out."

Instinctively, I said, "There's more. There's more you have to tell me."

She shook her head. "No. Yes. There is. But—I—let's just get this question answered first. This question about Fuzzy."

"Yes. Fuzzy. You—you want to meet Sharif Muhammad Chacha?"

"Yes. Deena told me that he lives with his sister now."

"Yes. They live together. I—I have been to visit them. And they come to visit me, from time to time." I didn't reveal what else I knew, for a moment. She'd assumed that my part in the life of the man she spoke of—the boy whose mother I had killed—remained what it had been when she'd come to see me in Chicago. "I'll take you to see him. You can ask him about all the missing years between my story and his. Those, I know little about. But the main question you've come to ask, I can shed light on that. That this man you call Fuzzy—whose name is Fazl—he *is* the same boy from my story."

"He—? How do you know?"

"Because I've met him. Since we last met, the story has progressed, Jo. I have changed. I see things, am able to see things, in a way I couldn't before. You said that you studied Urdu because you met me. As you spoke, I thought of all the negative consequences of that choice of yours—of how adversely I affected the direction of your life. But the same is not true for me, Jo. It's the opposite."

"What do you mean?"

"Did you know that I was engaged to be married when you came to visit?"

"Your mom told me."

"I was on my way back here, to Pakistan, for the wedding. It was arranged, the girl handpicked by my grandfather. She was young and pretty. Too young for me. I didn't realize that until I met you. That was a bit of a shock—you were like a midlife crisis come alive, knocking at my door, making me realize that, if I was lucky, nearly half my life was already over. And what had I done with it? Not the surface things. Going to college. Going into business. Making some lucky investments, with money given to me by my grandfather. Tech stuff, in Silicon Valley. And I was fortunate enough to have gotten out before the downturn there. I enjoyed the fruits of my success. I traveled. I met beautiful women. Living the good life, something I could afford because of who my grandfather was. Even my business success could be attributed to his wealth. What had *I* done? What had I *done?*

"There were two things I could think of to answer that question. One was the car accident. An accident that involved death. The other was you. Also an accident. Involving birth. That was what the effect of my life amounted to, in real terms, on others. A death I had never emotionally absorbed or atoned for—I'd never even spoken about it, the woman and the boy in my path that night, not until I told you. And a birth I'd had no idea about.

"I came back to Pakistan and broke off my engagement. I felt lost. Muharram came. Again, I remembered my meeting with you—all the childhood memories I'd shared out loud, for the first time. Going to *majlis*es with my mother, the sights, sounds, smells of a world I'd been shut out of when I joined this household, a world that was feminine and intimate. Suddenly, the stories of Karbala mattered, the way they had when I was a child—not as a sign of my identity, which is how I'd viewed religion for many years, as a way of defining myself, separating myself from others, from my mother, in particular, and from her husband—but as an experience in itself.

"Two years later, my grandparents went on pilgrimage, *ziarat*, to Karbala and Najaf, in Iraq. That was before the war. I went with them. It was—it was a life-changing experience. To be there. In places whose names were mythic in my mind. For years, grief and sadness were things I'd refused to acknowledge. The grief of Karbala helped me get in touch with other sources of sorrow that I'd never allowed myself to mourn. Losing my mother. What I'd done to another mother and her son at *fajr* time—at dawn—when I was a boy of fifteen. It was like a door opening.

"When we came back from Iraq, I asked my grandfather where I could find Sharif Muhammad Chacha, who had already retired. Dada was drinking tea, I remember. He seemed to know why I was asking. Without looking at me, his eyes on his newspaper, Dada said, 'Let it go, Sadiq. Let the past rest.' He refused to tell me what I asked. I had to find out where Sharif Muhammad Chacha lived from one of the other servants.

"One morning, I went to the address I'd been given—an extremely modest, cinder block dwelling in a part of town I had never before had reason to visit—and knocked on Sharif Muhammad Chacha's door.

"Macee opened it. She was shrunken in height, reaching up to embrace me with a shriek the moment she saw me. She spoke of my mother. 'Do you know, Sadiq Baba, that your mother has never forgotten me, since she went away to *Amreeka*? Her old Macee? She sends me money and writes me letters, which I ask the schoolmaster up the street to read for me, every month. Here, let me show you. The pictures. See? Here she is, my Deena Bibi. And her husband. And her daughter. My Deena Bibi has not forgotten me. And I? I will never forget her either. Or you, Sadiq Baba. How are you, *Beta*? And how is your dear mother?'

"'She is well,' I told her. 'I spoke to her last month.'

"'Oh, it is so good to see you, Sadiq Baba! Wait here, I will go and call Sharif Muhammad. He has gone to the neighbor's. I will just go and get him. Just a moment.'

"After only a minute or two, Sharif Muhammad Chacha came. His gray beard had turned white, his face more sharply scored by the lines that his hours in the sun had long ago defined. Neither one of us said anything. He stared at me, as if he was trying to read what he found on my face. Then he said, 'Come, Sadiq Baba. Come and sit. I have been waiting for you. For all these years. I knew that you would come, one day, to see me. To ask after the boy. That is why you are here, is it not?'

"I said, 'Yes,' and started to cry. Not the way I had cried before, when Sharif Muhammad Chacha had found me in my car, shaking with fear at what I had done. This time, I was not crying for myself. I cried, quietly, during the whole time that Sharif Muhammad Chacha took to tell me Fazl's story.

"'I've taken care of the boy, Sadiq Baba, from a distance, as best I could. His name is Fazl. Your grandfather gave me the money, a small sum, every month—more when I asked for it. But he never asked me any questions. Never wanted to know any of the details.

Of how much the child cried for his mother. Of how I found a school for him that would give him lodging. He was not a good student. And the masters there were harsh with him, so that I pulled him out and put him elsewhere. But the world was a hard place for Fazl, everywhere he went. We were never able to find out anything about who he was, about where he and his mother came from. Most likely from some village. He talked about fields and farms, in the beginning. He talked of his mother crying. Perhaps she was a widow. Perhaps a victim of some terrible injustice—how commonplace they are, these victims—that made her run away from the place she called home. Who knows?

"'He called me Uncle. I did what I could. But it was never enough. When he was grown, he found a job. And then another. I helped him with references, sometimes. But he was too simple. He was fleeced of any money I gave him, again and again. What I wanted to do was to bring him home with me. I asked your grandfather's permission. But he refused.'

"I asked, 'Where is he now?'

"'He is working again. As a servant. In a big house. I got him the job, knew the driver in that household, which was the home of very big people, like your grandfather. They are friends of his. Your grandfather has seen Fazl, many times, but he doesn't realize who he is. Do you want to meet him, Sadiq Baba?'

"I hesitated for a second. Then I said, 'Yes. I do. I want to meet him. To tell him who I am. To beg his forgiveness.'

"'I will arrange it,' Sharif Muhammad Chacha said. I left him, planning to go back the next day so that I could go with Sharif Muhammad Chacha and meet the boy. Fazl.

"When I came back, Sharif Muhammad Chacha was in some

distress. 'He is gone, Sadiq Baba. I don't know where. He left that house a month ago. He was fired. The driver told me that he had found him another job, through the cook there. But when I went to the new place, where the cook said Fazl was now working, he wasn't there, either. I've lost him. I hope he gets in touch with me. He has always counted on me in the past. Has come here when he needed me. We'll have to wait for him.'

"That's what we did. For many, many months. Finally, one day, Sharif Muhammad Chacha came to see me. 'I am afraid, Sadiq Baba. I was able to trace the boy through someone from the school that he attended. One of the teachers there, a mullah, found him a job. As a gatekeeper. When I went to inquire there, the house was empty. The neighbors told me that the police had been to the house some weeks before. That some very bad men lived there. Terrorists. The house had been raided, all its occupants arrested. I cannot do anything, now, Sadiq Baba. I am a poor man. With no power. You will have to take up the search. To find out what happened. To find out where Fazl has been taken. I am afraid for him. He has no one in this world to ask after him.'

"That, I knew very well, was my fault. I spent the next few weeks paying bribes to police officers, trying to find out what had happened to Fazl. I came to know that he'd been working for some big-shot Al-Qaeda people, wanted by the Americans. I think you found him, Jo, before I was able to. And you know what happened to him. Better than I. He was a simple man. An innocent one. They—you—shouldn't have taken him."

"I know," Jo said softly.

"In the process of searching for Fazl, I made many new friends. Human rights lawyers. Among them, Akeela, the woman who is to be my wife. She specializes in women's rights, but she was very helpful, hooking me up with people who were happy to assist. It was a long while before I found out. That he'd been taken to Guantánamo. I went to the States. I hired a lawyer for him there. But the case didn't seem to be going anywhere. They—the lawyers—hadn't even been allowed to see him. And then, suddenly, we heard that he had been released. Into Pakistani custody. Kept in prison here and treated badly. I paid more bribes. And finally got him out. He was so happy to see Sharif Muhammad Chacha, when we got him out of jail, that he paid little attention to who I was and the role I had played in his life. I tried to make him understand. But he is a simple man—a boy, really, incapable of holding anything against me. That doesn't make me feel any better. The opposite, in fact. But he is all right now. Safe. Living with Sharif Muhammad Chacha."

"Will you take me to see him?" Jo asked.

"Of course."

Two hours later, my mother and Jo and I were in Sharif Muhammad Chacha's humble home. I had explained to him—conscious of how incredibly unlikely it all was when I told him. Who Jo was. Who she was to me and who she had been to Fazl.

Fazl's eyes lit up when he saw my daughter. Clearly, he remembered her. But his eyes were gentle, smiling. "I told you," he said to her triumphantly. "I told you that Sharif Muhammad Chacha would save me. See? This is my uncle. Who is not really my uncle. And his sister, my aunt, who is not really my aunt. They take care of me now. I told you that he would save me."

Jo was crying.

"What did I say?" Fazl demanded of Sharif Muhammad Chacha. "I have made her cry. The American woman who speaks Urdu."

"Those tears are good tears, Fazl, *Beta*," Sharif Muhammad Chacha said, looking at my mother. "A wise woman that I know once said that the tears we cry for others are tears of sweetness—to be appreciated as a sign of God's love, and sorrow, for all of the injustice that we lowly creatures, human beings who have not yet learned to be human, all of us, inflict on one another. It is a good thing, when we cry those sweet tears, she said. It is a good thing."

By the rivers of Babylon, there we sat down,
yea, we wept, when we remembered Zion. . . .
For there they that carried us away captive required of us a song. . . .
How shall we sing the Lord's song in a strange land?

Psalm 137, v. 1–4

Jo

The tears I shed, in front of strangers, during that afternoon when I met Fazl, were the keys to an opening. Walking back to the main street with Deena and Sadiq, where Usama was waiting with Sadiq's car, through the narrow lanes of the area where Sharif Muhammad Chacha and Macee lived—a neighborhood only slightly better than the slum I'd visited outside of Nairobi so many years before—I could almost hear the squeak of the rusty hinges giving way, almost feel the stretch of it happening, the opening that came with a sense of relief all the more acute because I hadn't realized that anything had been closed to begin with.

Later in the evening, Deena and Sadiq and I went out for dinner—to a small, dark Chinese restaurant on Tariq Road that Deena remembered from her days in Pakistan. "You must try

Pakistani-Chinese food, Jo," she said. "It's very different—much tastier—than American-Chinese. The family that runs this place, Chinese, has been here, in Karachi, since before Partition."

At the restaurant, I could hear how different the sound of my own voice was, unleashed like it hadn't been for years. I talked and talked. The way I used to when I was little, without reserve.

Sadiq took advantage, asking the ton of questions he must have been holding in until the opening showed itself in my eyes and in the way I felt my mouth relax—about my childhood, my mom, my dad. And Chris. Even the questions about Chris I didn't hesitate to answer, describing my brother in detail in all the stories I told Sadiq and Deena about my childhood. I told them about PPSYC, making them laugh at some of my best camp memories. I told them about Grandma Faith—Wàipó-Lola-Bibi-Abuela-Faith. About the trip we took with her to Africa, about washing the feet of the kids who lived in the slum, and about how she was always riling up her own children—Mom and Uncle Ron—with her peculiar notions about faith and religion.

Once we'd ordered our food, the whole time I spoke—through dinner arriving, filling our plates, passing and eating—Deena kept mostly silent, letting Sadiq ask all the questions, watching and listening with those wise eyes and ears that seemed able to see and hear beyond the surface, straight through to what lay underneath.

"Tell us more about your brother," was the only thing she'd said to prompt me, right at the end of my monologue.

"He lights up a room. That's the only way to describe him. Without saying a word. When we were little, he hardly talked. Because I talked too much. But he didn't need to. His face said everything. Kids and animals and strangers tend to fall in love with him at first sight. He's the lead singer in a band that he started with his buddies in high school and has a beautiful voice." I lifted my chin up and said, "It's a Christian rock band."

Then Deena said the only other thing she said that night over dinner: "You love your brother very much," making the words a statement.

"Yes. Very much." I found myself blinking back more tears, when I thought I'd already cried myself dry, earlier, in front of Fazl. Deena put her hand on mine and squeezed.

We moved on, then, to talk about religion and politics and war. The only things I didn't talk about were Chris's accident and the tour in Iraq that led up to it. And the only time I was less than honest was when Sadiq asked me if I had a picture of my family. I did, but said I didn't, not yet wanting him and Deena to see the color of Chris's eyes. It was something that I knew I would have to share eventually. But I wasn't ready yet.

From that day forward, I started to enjoy myself, to really see, hear, taste, and touch the city of Karachi—with eyes wide open, breathing through my mouth, the way Grandma Faith had once said she liked to be when she traveled. But I was one up on her. I understood and spoke the language already. Still, I followed the spirit of how Grandma Faith had described herself on her journeys, letting the feeling of *I don't know* and *I don't understand* flow through me, so that I could let go and just take it all in, open, from one moment to the next.

I met Fazl a few more times, going back again and again just to listen, to hear the story of what happened to him after our paths crossed, to hear the story of others he had met at Gitmo, where, one day, I hoped to go. It would have been faster if I'd guided him with questions, but I tried hard to keep myself out of it, to only use my ears, like my dad had done with me when I was a child, letting him talk at his own pace, not wanting anything that passed between us now to feel like the interrogations he'd already suffered at my hands and others'.

I'd already been shopping with Sadiq's aunt and his cousin's wife, along with Deena, and had to resist their urgings to go again. With my new Pakistani wardrobe, they told me, I blended in.

"No one would even guess. That you're not Pakistani," said Jaffer and Haseena's daughter, Batool.

"A very fair, very beautiful Pakistani!" declared Asma, her grandmother. My great-aunt. She's the one who started the whole what-I-should-call-everyone thing.

"But—my dear! You cannot just call us all by our first names!" She was horrified when she heard me talking to Deena. "She's your *dadi,* after all! You can't just call her Deena!"

After that, I started calling everyone "auntie" and "uncle." Except for Deena. I asked her—if she didn't mind—whether I could call her Deena Dadi.

"Oh, Jo! I would love that! I must confess, it bothered me a little that you called Abbas Uncle *dada* without even thinking."

"Well. He's old. I kind of had to, didn't I?" It *had* been instinctive. I knew enough of the culture, from watching those old television dramas, to know that calling Abbas Ali Mubarak *dada,* the word for paternal grandfather—which could also be used for great-grandfather—wasn't about what he was to me. That older people were always given some kind of title of respect, something that implied a family relationship. In some ways, age trumped class.

That's why Macee was called *macee*, Deena had told me. "In some dialects, it means mother's sister. Your maternal aunt. Even servants, who are often unjustly treated as lesser humans, are still given respectful titles. *Macee. Amma,* which, you know, means 'mother.' You can't just walk up to someone older here and start using their first name. Age deserves respect. Or the show of it, at least."

So, everyone older became uncle and auntie. Everyone except Sadiq. Who stayed Sadiq. It was just too complicated to think of anything else to call him.

I called home, in Garden Hill, every other day.

When I did, Dad would say he loved me, in a hurry, before Mom grabbed the phone away from him.

I tried to reassure her, when she said she was worried sick. Every phone call, she complained, "As if I don't have enough to deal with, Jo. Right here. You being there—you're just adding to it all. I wish you would see that. I wish you would come home."

Whatever else she wanted to say or ask, she kept to herself. Chris was there, within earshot, waiting to speak to me, too. Always reluctantly, she would pass him the phone when he or I asked her to.

"Hi, Chris."

"Hey. So. Pakistan, huh?" he said, the first time I called.

"Yup."

"What are you doing there, Jo? Some kind of missionary work?"

I hesitated. "In a way." I didn't want to lie. I told myself that it was a good description. Only I wasn't here to save other people. I was here seeking my own salvation—the only kind of missionary work I still believed in. I was even more radical than Grandma Faith in the firmness of this conviction.

"Is it—is it safe there? I—I mean, is it a dangerous place?"

"Uh—"

"Isn't there a war going on there? Or—somewhere?"

I heard the confusion in his voice.

"No. No war. Not here. Where I am."

"Man, I'm ignorant! I've got to start reading some newspapers. I've been so wrapped up in getting better that I feel like the whole world has just been going on without me. I feel kind of left out, you know? Like I should get a job. Make a contribution to the world. Like you are."

"There's plenty of time for that, Chris. Just concentrate on getting better."

"I *am* better, Jo."

"I know, Chris. But—you've still got a ways to go. Just take it slow and simple."

"Easy for you to say."

"I know, Chris. Look, I've got to go."

"Oh, yeah. Must be an expensive call."

"Take it easy, Chris. Don't worry. You've got plenty of time to—catch up with the world."

He did, but I didn't. When I hung up, I remembered the conversation I'd had with Chris the day before I left him.

"Jo?"

"Hmm?"

"I—sometimes, I feel like—like Mom doesn't want me to remember. It kind of— freaks me out. Like there's something about the time I've forgotten that's bad. I'm—I—didn't do anything horrible, did I, Jo?" he asked with a laugh. "I mean, I didn't kill anyone, did I?"

My laughter, even more nervous than his, was my only answer. I was running out of time.

Sadiq introduced me and Deena to his fiancée, Akeela, and her two daughters, Samira and Tasneem. Akeela was the women's rights lawyer. She was very dignified, a little reserved, but friendly.

I went to church, something I'd never expected to do in Pakistan. Sadiq told me that his grandfather's nurse, Susan, was Christian. Presbyterian. My second Sunday in Karachi, I went to services with her. I was glad of the clothes that Haseena Auntie had helped me shop for, because all the women in church covered their heads, just like Muslim women, with their *dupatta*s. The whole sermon and service, a traditional liturgy—the prayers, quotations from the Bible, even the hymns—all of it was in Urdu. Deena came with me. She'd been to Mass once, she told me. When she was in school. But this was her first time in a Protestant church.

There was no choir and no organ. Instead, there was a little band, off to the side of the altar, made up of a keyboard, a couple of guitars, and a lead singer, who led the congregation when they rose to sing the hymns, the words for which were written in Urdu in hymnals called *Geet-e-Ibadat*—songs of worship, the same word for worship that Muslims use. They were all young, the musicians in this group. They reminded me of Chris and his band. At the end of services, I met the pastor, who shook the hands of all the men in the congregation and put his hand on the heads of the women. I wondered how many degrees of separation lay between me and the families that made up his parish, all of whom were originally from North India, where Great-grandpa Pelton had once visited during his missionary days.

I had been in Karachi for almost two weeks before I understood where I was being led next. I still thought of my life in those terms, in terms of providence and God's plan and how I must follow it, in spite of everything that had happened, in spite of all the evidence that might lead me to believe that what I'd thought of as God's plan before—back when I'd first met Sadiq—was really just a ghastly mistake, a long journey down the wrong path. Back then, God's plan was something I *thought* about, something I had to figure out. Like a puzzle. It was my hand that jammed the pieces into place. Now, it was something I waited for, without thinking at all. It just happened. I could fight it. Or, as Deena had talked about when she told me her story, I could surrender. Either way, it didn't require any effort on my part, no beliefs or judgments that I had to assume, defend, and rationalize.

It was a casual conversation, among all of the strangers who were my new relatives, in the car outside a sweets shop, that made the next step I had to take very clear.

Deena and I had woken up early to attend a women's *majlis* at Asma Auntie's house.

"You must come, Deena," Asma Auntie had urged Deena. "You will meet all kinds of women there that you haven't seen for years. The *zakira*—that's the woman who will preach, Jo—is Masooma, who is very progressive. Not like that Tayiba Khursheed, the fanatic who is so in fashion," Asma Auntie pursed her lips, "teaching all kinds of nonsense—that wives should give their blessings if their husbands wish to take a second wife, that women cannot leave their homes without their husband's permission, bullying everyone to wear the *hijab*. I don't know how anyone can stand her, but many flock to hear her. Incomprehensible!"

Deena was reluctant, at first. I understood. There'd been a lot for her to cope with on this trip. Staying in Sadiq's house, for one thing. He hadn't realized that the room he'd given her was hers and Akram's when they were first married. That she'd spent a lot of time there alone, when his dad wasn't well. When she asked me to share it with her, to keep the old ghosts at bay, I'd said yes, feeling even closer to her than I had become on the way to Pakistan, telling her things I hadn't before—about studying Urdu and Arabic and what I'd done with those skills. So that she knew those things already, before I told Sadiq. I hadn't talked about Chris, though. Not yet. It was a hard subject to broach. The more time passed, the harder it got.

When Deena saw how eager I was to attend the *majlis*, she agreed to go. It was like déjà vu, so accurate had Sadiq's imagery been. I thought of Chris. Is this the way memories would make their way back to the surface of his mind? Like old stories, someone else's, coming to life?

The sermon, in Urdu, was very different from what I was used to. Maybe because of the purely female congregation. The preacher talked about the power of the feminine, saying, "Women have gotten into the habit of underestimating their own power. Real change in the world, real justice, cannot happen without the participation of women. Paradise is under our feet. So we must be careful and deliberate with the steps we take. We must remember that without the sister of Moses, who watched over him from afar, and the woman of Pharaoh's house, who took him as her own, there would have been no Moses. Without Mary's womb, there would have been no Jesus. Without Fatima, there would have been no Husain. And without Zainab, no story of Karbala for us to remember." That was how she transitioned to the end of the *majlis*, the part I had been curiously waiting for—a distressing recitation of grief that the women around me responded to with tears and sobs, powerfully primal and impossible to resist.

Deena later said she surprised herself when she stood at the end, during the *matham*, and recited a *noha*, with no book in her hand, the words sounded out in a voice as beautiful as Sadiq had described, traced and recalled from memory.

"We, the humble," she sang, *"send our condolences for your loved ones. We send greetings of peace on the bodies of those slain, lying in the desert of Karbala, without shrouds; greetings of peace for the prisoners bereaved and mourning, looted and dishonored, driven out of burning tents, orphans and widows without shelter; greetings of peace for the one whose lap is still warm from the babe she cradled and could no longer nourish, snatched away by an arrow, still thirsty, the mother without milk; greetings of peace for all those whose wombs were betrayed by oppression and injustice, without their sons; greetings of peace for Zainab, the comforter of orphans and widows, the leader of the captives, the speaker for the destitute, whose voice still rings loud against the oppression of all tyrants, without the protecting arms of her brother. We are here, this year and next, and will be here in all the years to come, sending greetings of peace, we who will not forget, who will never forget, the stories of your grief and sacrifice."*

There was a prayer, at the end. *"Ya Illahi,"* it began. *"Oh, God, we pray that no grief other than the grief of Karbala should touch our lives or the lives of others. We pray for peace, we pray for solace. Ya Illahi, we seek refuge in our remembrance of you and those who sacrificed for you, we pray for justice over oppression, wherever it is found."*

Back at Sadiq's after the *majlis*, over lunch, Asma Auntie almost hugged herself as she said, "Deena! Do you know that no less than three women came to ask me, in whispers, how old Jo is?"

Deena paused with a bite of food halfway to her mouth, then put the fork down and laughed.

Asma Auntie saw my mystified look and explained, "Three women, Jo. Three mothers of eligible sons. They were making inquiries."

I frowned.

"During the Muharram season, prospective mothers-in-law scan and scope, looking for wives for their sons."

"But—I—oh," I spluttered.

"I'm not surprised," Deena said. "My granddaughter is beautiful."

"No doubt about that," said Jaffer Uncle. "Beautiful. Intelligent. Well-mannered and respectful. Who could resist all those qualities—topped off, as they are, with the bonus of her American passport."

"After Muharram and Safar, when proposals fly from families of young men to families of young women, you'll see. Offers for Jo will pour in," said Asma Auntie with a girlish giggle.

Later, in the night, Jaffer Uncle and Haseena Auntie invited us out for dessert. Like everything else I'd experienced in Karachi, it was an adventure, at midnight, like going to an old-fashioned drive-in, the kind you see in old movies and shows about life in America in the 1950s. Except, instead of Al's or Melvin's, the name of the place we went to was much more poetic—Rehmat-e-Shereen, which means "The Mercy of Sweetness." We stayed in the car—in three cars, actually, parked next to each other: one car where I sat with Jaffer Uncle, his two kids (who, they were happy to explain, were my second cousins, the first in my life that I'd ever met), and his mother, Asma Auntie; the second car containing Haseena Auntie, Nasir Uncle (who was Asma Auntie's rather quiet husband), and another cousin I'd just met; the last car holding Sadiq, Akeela and her daughters, and Deena—and waited until a server came to take our order, which he would then serve us in the car.

"What will you have?" Jaffer Uncle asked us all.

"*Kulfi!*" the kids shouted. "Are you going to have *kulfi*, Jo?"

"Is it good?"

"Oh, yes," the older one, Batool, said.

"Only if you don't get it with all the slimy noodles on it. Then it's like ice cream," said Zain, the younger, fussier one, who reminded me of Chris.

"What a way to describe it!" his grandmother, Asma Auntie, scolded.

"I'll try it," I said, with a wink at the children, "but without the slimy noodles."

When the plates of *kulfi* arrived, we were all quiet for a while, concentrating only on consuming our delicious, mercifully sweet desserts.

Then Asma Auntie said, "It was so lovely to hear Deena's voice again. In the *majlis* today. No one else has as much *dard* in their voice as Deena."

"*Dard?*"

"Yes. Pain."

"I understand. But— I'd never heard the word used that way before. It's a good thing?"

"Oh, yes. Like having spirit. Soul. You know what *humdard* is, Jo? In Urdu?"

"Sympathy?"

"More than that."

Humdard. A compound word. Us-pain. "More like empathy?"

"Yes. I suppose." Asma Auntie changed the subject. "So, Jo? You and Deena are leaving next week?"

"Yes," I said, feeling the dread rise up inside of me, dread of going back and facing the questions from Chris that I knew were only beginning.

"So soon? I wish I could convince you and Deena to stay longer. Maybe if you do, you will help me talk that reckless man, your father, out of going on his trip."

"What trip?"

"What?! You don't know? That he's going? And where?"

"No. Where?" I asked.

Jaffer Uncle answered for his mother. "To Iraq! For *ziarat*—pilgrimage. For Chehlum—which is forty days after Ashura. They call it Arbaeen in Arabic. He is going to Karbala and Najaf. He went last year. Has been going every year for the last few."

Asma Auntie shook her head. "No. He didn't go the year the war began. It was too soon after Baghdad fell. Too unsafe."

"And now? It's safe now?" Jaffer Uncle laughed.

"Of course it's not. You know, Jaffer, that I have been trying to tell him—tried to stop him last year, also. But he won't listen. Not even to Akeela." Asma Auntie turned from her seat in the front, to look at me. "Before the war, we all went together. Jaffer and Haseena, my mother and my father, also. Before his stroke. It was a wonderful trip. I understand why he wants to keep going. I wish

I could, too. And I will go again, *Inshallah,* when the war is over. But we must also be practical. There are too many reports of violence. It's too dangerous. You must convince him, Jo. I am tired of trying. He will listen to you. He has to. He's your father."

I was getting used to these assertions. I had no choice. Asma Auntie, when she spoke to me, always referred to Sadiq as "your father," not noticing the way I had shrunk from her words in the beginning. At the *majlis,* earlier in the day, she'd introduced me to everyone as Deena's granddaughter, Sadiq's child. For her, I couldn't just be Jo. Introductions had to be defined in the context of a wider circle that was feeling less and less strange to me.

What she said now was like a light shining out on the dark path in front of me, guiding my way forward. I didn't say anything then, just finished my *kulfi* and waited for my chance to speak with Deena, later that night. In bed, the giant one I shared with her, I waited until she turned out the light before I brought up the subject.

"Did you know Sadiq is going to Iraq?"

"Yes. He told me. He went last year, too. Something he forgot to mention in his monthly phone calls," she said with an exasperated sigh.

"I want to go, too."

"What?" Deena sat up in bed and turned the light back on. "What on earth for?"

It was the first time I voluntarily raised the subject of Chris. Not the part I had been unable, so far, to share. About the color of his eyes. Only what was relevant now. Only that I knew that Sadiq going to Iraq, my going with him, was a way to give Chris what I'd gained for myself in meeting Fazl. We spent a long time talking. She wasn't convinced.

The next morning, I told Sadiq what I wanted to do. He shook his head. "No. It's not safe."

"It's safe for you, but not for me?"

"It's not the same thing. For me, it's a matter of faith. For you—what is it that you want to go for, Jo? I don't understand."

So I told him what I'd told Deena the night before. About Chris. About his tour in Iraq. What he'd written in his journal. His "accident." And what needed to be done to make it safe for him to remember.

Sadiq tried to do what his aunt had wanted me to do to him, spending a long time convincing me that I shouldn't go. But I refused to take no for an answer.

"You said it's a matter of faith. For you. Can't you understand? That it's a matter of faith for me, too? I have to do this. I *know*. It's the reason I'm here. I *know* that. I have to do this for my brother."

In the end, after a lot more arguing and with a lot of obvious reluctance, Sadiq gave in, saying, "All right, Jo. Chris is your brother. Because of that, he is something to me, too."

That was when I should have said something. Like so many other times before. But I didn't.

Sadiq was still talking. "If this is something you feel you must do, for him, then I will help you. But if you're going, I'll have to get you a Pakistani passport. It won't be safe to travel as an American."

"Then you'll have to do the same for me, Sadiq," said Deena. "I'm not letting you two go without me."

Within a week, it was all arranged. I wasn't at all afraid. And now that she'd decided to go, too, Deena was happy.

She said, "I've always wanted to go to Karbala, since I was a little girl. You know, my grandmother, who I never met; is buried there. Ever since the war in Iraq began, with Karbala and Najaf in the news all the time, I have felt a peculiar calling. I think you're right, Jo. This is meant to be. I only hope you find what you're looking for there. For your brother's sake."

We traveled with a big group of pilgrims, most of us starting out from Karachi. On the passport that Sadiq had made for me—at no small cost in bribes, I'm sure—my name was Jamila Mubarak. That way, he said, they could still call me Jo. We stayed in Dubai for a night and met up with other pilgrims who would be in our group, all of them of Indian and Pakistani origin, hailing from Canada, Africa, and England. There were almost 150 of us altogether.

The flight from Dubai to Baghdad was a charter, the only passengers on it being those in our group. The mood among the other pilgrims ebbed and flowed, alternating between a reflective, meditative quiet and a kind of a festive spirit—like a bunch of kids on a school field trip, even though the pilgrimage was supposed to be a somber one. At those times, people handed around cookies, nuts, chips, and chocolates, sharing the foodstuff they'd brought. In the quiet moments, I would close my eyes and hear, as if he were speaking out loud, the words of Chris's journal, uncannily intersecting with what I experienced throughout our very different journey to the land where he had served and killed and suffered as a Marine.

One of the things I most remember about the trip was how much time we spent waiting. Waiting around at the airport in Dubai. Later, waiting to board the buses that would get us to where we were going, waiting to get off the buses, waiting for people at rest stops to use the bathroom, waiting to meet up with the others in the lobbies of our hotels and at meeting points in and around the places we visited.

Chris, too, had spent a lot of time waiting, months in Kuwait, anticipating a war that got more and more inevitable.

Waiting, still, here in Kuwait, he'd written. *There's no doubt about where we're going. Everyone knows the war's going to happen. It's just a matter of when. In the meantime, Ku-wait-wait-wait-wait!*

There was a man, Dr. Salman, and a woman, Mrs. Waleed, who were kind of the leaders of the group. People went to them with questions—practical and religious. Some of the people sitting together, toward the back of the plane, started reciting *noha*s almost as soon as we took off from Dubai. Soon, everyone joined in, beating their chests like they were clapping along. It felt like camp. Except the songs made people cry instead of laugh. In between, they'd chant the names of the martyrs and other imams, calling out the name of Ali—the first Imam, Husain's father—the loudest. Deena sat next to me, whispering explanations the whole time. Until someone requested a *noha* from her and she obliged, her voice having the same hushing effect that I'd already observed at the *majlis* in Karachi.

Chris had used his voice the same way when he was in Iraq. *The guys have started calling me the choir boy. Because of how many times I start to sing gospel songs and hymns without even realizing it. They tease me about it. But no one ever tells me to shut up. So I guess they don't really mind. I sing stuff from Christian March and old, traditional hymns, too. I also lead them in prayer sometimes, which some of them seem to really like, calling me Preacher March. Choir Boy and*

Preacher March. I laugh with them and tell them preaching runs in the family. Some of them have seen Uncle Ron on TV.

Landing in Baghdad was surreal. As soon as we got off the steps leading down from the plane, we were met by American soldiers. They ordered us to line up on the tarmac. It was the first time I realized how well I blended in with the others in the group. The soldiers looked at me the same way they looked at them. Not in a good way. They had dogs sniff at our bags and then at us. When we got on the bus that would take us to the terminal, one of the soldiers got on with us. Someone in the group shouted something loud and long, and everyone answered, *Ya Ali!*

The soldier with us on the bus yelled, nervously, his hands holding his gun as if he might need it at any second, "What are you guys shouting?!" and the male leader of the group, Dr. Salman, said, "We are calling out the name of our Imam."

The soldier's lips formed an *O*, as if he understood, but I wondered. I was going to get used to that chant over the next week. The more I heard it, the less strange it became, feeling more and more like people at church, in Garden Hill, shouting out hallelujahs.

At the airport terminal, there was a lot of hustle and bustle. Most of the people there were U.S. military. You could tell which ones were going home just by looking at their faces. And, I'm guessing, if you got close enough—which no one in our group tried to do, keeping as much distance between themselves and the soldiers and Marines as they could—by their breath, too. The ones going home looked and acted like they'd started celebrating a little early—the only shop in the duty-free was a giant liquor store, so it wasn't hard to guess how. The ones arriving in country looked pissed.

Our first destination was Karbala. It took twelve hours to get there by bus, even though it's only about sixty miles south of Baghdad. Dr. Salman said that part of the reason it took so long was because we had to avoid the most direct routes, which were the most dangerous, sticking instead to smaller, out-of-the-way roads, making the journey safer but more circuitous.

There were a total of six buses for our group. We had to go very slowly. The roads weren't very good and we stopped and pulled over a couple of times for U.S. convoys going by, many more times for checkpoints. Dr. Salman had warned the group about how to behave at those checkpoints. No cameras. No cell phones in sight. And if American soldiers boarded, he urged us not to stare at them, not to look angry or upset or scared, to do what they asked, to open bags and get off the bus if they ordered us to, without arguing.

We were boarded only a few times. When it happened, a small group of U.S. soldiers would walk up and down the aisle of the bus a couple of times, staring sternly into each of our faces, making everyone nervous. At the sight of them, I couldn't not think of Chris, who was the reason I was there. Again, I was struck by the fact that none of the soldiers recognized me as American. That felt strange. And scary, once, when one of them stopped and yelled, fiercely, at a woman in the group who had forgotten to put away her video camera. He nearly took it away from her. By now, she was crying. Dr. Salman came over, apologizing profusely, until the soldier got off the bus, still muttering angrily to himself.

Until that one soldier yelled, I had had the nearly irresistible urge to stand up and wave and say, "Hey, guys! Where are you from? I'm from California!" After that, I sank low into my seat, glad not to be noticed. If Chris were among those soldiers and Marines, would he recognize me?

On our way to Baghdad, Chris wrote. *Finally! We hardly see any women in the towns and villages on the way into Baghdad. Those we do are all in black. The people—men and women—look at us suspiciously. We look at them the same way. I guess they're afraid of us. I would be, too. In our uniforms and tanks, we must look pretty scary. Truth is, we're scared, too.*

I was wearing a black *abaya,* like the other women. We'd all had to practice wearing them, at Dubai, since it was an Arab form of clothing and none of the Indian and Pakistani people normally wore them. Most of the women in our group—other than Deena and a couple of others—did normally cover their hair, wearing the scarf they called *hijab,* but not the *abaya.* From what Deena said, this was an unusually religious bunch of people. Obviously. I couldn't see irreligious people wanting to go on a pilgrimage in a war zone.

Everyone in our group that I talked to said the same thing with regard to the danger, when I asked about it. They weren't afraid. They were at peace. The Imam would see to their safety. And God.

All the way to Karbala, we passed burned-out cars on the side of the road. And bombed-out buildings. There were gutted grooves in the road, too, that one of the translators on the bus said, darkly, were the marks of American tanks.

Almost there. It's been a mess getting there. We had to stop and clear the road a lot, from all the bombed-out cars, trucks, and debris. A lot of the buildings, too, are damaged. Our bombs got here before we did. We see people, too. A lot of them, waving white flags.

Also along the way, we passed other pilgrims, on foot, who were walking from other parts of Iraq to get to Karbala for the Arbaeen holiday. In every town and village we passed, there were tents set up for the pilgrims to sleep and rest in and stalls where water, tea, and food were served at no charge.

"That's the traditional *sabeel*," Sadiq said. "In Karachi, too, people line up on the sides of the Ashura procession, serving water and tea to the people walking in the *juloos*. Feeding the hungry and thirsty is a way people remember the thirsty children of Karbala."

There were a couple of translators on each bus that Dr. Salman had hired and arranged for, along with the buses, who had joined us before we left Baghdad. When one of them heard Sadiq explaining to me about the *sabeel*, he bitterly said, "This tradition wasn't allowed under Saddam. For Iraqis, none of the traditions of Muharram were allowed, though the regime allowed foreign pilgrims access to Karbala. It was a tourism thing—good for business. But it was different then. Government people were all over Karbala, limiting the interaction between the foreigners and the locals. The Shia in Karbala and Najaf were Saddam's biggest threat to power. And they suffered for it, too. But now, everything is different. The Americans saved us from the tyrant!"

"So—you're glad w—they came?" I asked.

"Of course! I used to give thanks for Mr. Bush every day, in my prayers."

"Used to?"

"Yes, sister. Not anymore. Now, it is clear why they came. With all their promises. They came for oil, they came for their own purposes. They knocked Saddam off of his throne, out of his palaces. And now they live there themselves. No one is fooled. It is long past time for them to leave. Thank you very much, Mr. Bush. *Yalla.* Now, go."

In Baghdad, on patrol, we get out on foot and walk the streets of the neighborhoods where Iraqis live. Sometimes, people come up to us and want to shake our hands. Some of them speak English. They say thank you. For getting rid of the tyrant. Some of them ask us how long we're staying. Not everyone smiles at us. I get it. I don't want to be here any longer than I have to, either.

When we got to Karbala, I was a bystander. I watched the others, participating when I had to, trying my best to blend in with the waves of black, billowing fabric of the women of our group. The sound of somber prayers and melodies, in Arabic, blaring out from street-corner speakers, alternated with more mundane program announcements, following us everywhere. As we elbowed our way through clumps of people, more private recitations, hard to hear over the PA system, reached out to our ears, swerving from Arabic to Urdu to Farsi and even English.

The entrances for all the shrines were different for men and women. "That is something new," Sadiq said. "Before the war, women and men came to the shrine together."

To get in to each one, we had to pass through four, five, sometimes six checkpoints, each of us frisked and wanded each time. It was all very organized. We checked our shoes in before entering. Everything around the shrine and inside of it was clean and grand and beautiful, the marble floors covered with richly woven rugs. Our hotel, the Baitul Salaam, the House of Peace, was right across the street from the grounds of the main shrine, the one with the golden dome, which was Imam Husain's.

Sadiq said, "This is a new hotel. There are lots of new buildings, lots of development. At least in the vicinity of the shrines. Before, you can't imagine how much poverty there was. I was overwhelmed by it. Though I come from Pakistan and am no stranger to the kind of poverty that is, well, distressing. There were children with outstretched hands everywhere you looked. And adults, too. I'm not speaking of homeless people and beggars. I mean our translators and guides and taxi drivers. The level of need, because of the shortage of goods from years of sanctions and also because Saddam deliberately kept these areas downtrodden, was obscene."

We pass out candy to the kids. They're cute. But some of them are dirty. They crowd around us when we go on foot patrol. They rip off the wrappers first thing and eat it up like they're starving. I gave away my stash of Hershey's bars. They were all warped and melted, anyway. I'm sticking to hard candy from now on. Gotta ask Mom to send me more. One of the other platoons, the one we call the Hard Ass Platoon, doesn't like it when we give the kids candy. They don't like them running up to 'em. To tell the truth, Sgt. Dixon doesn't like it much, either. He carries hand sanitizer around, rubbing his own hands with it, offering it to everyone around him, too, whenever the kids reach out and touch us, 'cause he thinks the kids carry germs that are gonna make us all sick. But at least he's not mean to the kids, like the Hard Asses are. I remember going to Africa with Jo and Grandma Faith. Washing those kids' feet. Don't think the sarge would make a very good missionary.

Speaking of which, some of the guys and I found out about an orphanage run by nuns—Iraqi Christians—in Baghdad. So, we've been trying to go once a week. Most of the kids there are disabled and abandoned. It's nice to just play with little people who don't look at you like you're an alien.

For the three days that we stayed in Karbala, we woke before dawn and made our way to Imam Husain's shrine for morning prayers. We entered the inner courtyard of the shrine through the gates of the exterior walls, geometrically adorned, accented in a shade of green that was dull compared to the brilliant blue borders of the main building inside the square. I followed what everyone else did—for the morning prayer and all the others—standing shoulder-to-shoulder in neat rows of black, bowing, touching my head to the ground, in my heart saying the Sinner's Prayer the way I had in church at Garden Hill, instead of the verses of the Quran and the prayers that everyone else was reciting. My ears pricked up at one of the prayers recited everywhere we went, a kind of salutation that had familiar names in it—Adam, Noah, Abraham, and Jesus—whose title was the Spirit of God. After morning prayers, we'd come back to the hotel for breakfast and make our way to other shrines around town, the most important of which was the one for Abbas, Imam Husain's brother. There were smaller shrines to visit, too, the markers for where each martyr of Karbala was killed. Returning to the hotel at lunchtime, most people would pray after lunch, nap, and then wake up again for all the evening prayers, making another round of the shrines, now beautifully lit up against the dark of the night sky.

Inside of the shrines, the sarcophagi were penned in with silver and golden screens, which the pilgrims went around, touching and kissing, rubbing them with cloth that they would take home with them as spiritual souvenirs.

By the actual day of Chehlum, or Arbaeen, the city was packed. Going outside of the hotel was like getting onto a six-lane highway, packed with bumper-to-bumper human traffic. The day started with the sound of loud drums beating through the streets, right after the dawn prayer, signaling the beginning of a day full of processions.

"They're different, in some ways, from the processions in Pakistan," said Sadiq. "Here, they do reenactments of the battles, too."

Accompanied by the drums, I saw the fake sword play in the reenactments, the men beating themselves with their hands, with chains, with knives—real ones. It was pretty gruesome. I understood why Sadiq had fainted when he was a little boy. The people in our group just stood on the sides, next to the palm trees, and watched it all like tourists—taking in a river of people instead of fish, black and white schools streaming, speckled with brilliant flashes of red and green, the colors of the flags and banners held high against the sand-colored brick that most of the buildings in Iraq seemed to be built of. I watched the blood flowing in the streets, not wanting to, but unable to turn my eyes away from the sight.

"Are you going to do that?" I asked Sadiq.

He shook his head. "I don't. Not anymore. I give blood instead. Like a good, enlightened grown-up."

Deena leaned close and whispered in my ear, "Are you all right, Jo? With all of this?" She waved her hand around. "It must be very—strange! To say the least. *I* find it to be so. I can't imagine what *you* must be thinking and feeling."

"It is strange. But I'm all right. I'm—I'm open. You know what I mean?"

She nodded.

As I spoke to her, my eyes followed the path of the blood on the pavement, saw the men who came to wash it up with hoses when the procession ended, getting the street ready for the next round.

We were patrolling the streets in the Dora neighborhood, on foot again, when it happened.

Such a stupid, stupid mistake. It's one of those things you shouldn't even have to think about—that you don't slam the cover on a live weapon. But Foley did. His M-16 discharged, hitting a kid who'd been playing in the street in front of his house. Foley was with Sgt. Dixon, way behind. Me and Phillips were on the other side of the street from where the kid was, watching him as he ran into the street, in our direction, probably wanting candy. He must have been eight, nine years old. Doc ran up and got down on the ground, took the kid's head in his lap, and tried to do what he could. The boy's dad came running out of the gate right after he heard the shot. He saw Doc working on his son, and stood there, shouting, "Allah! Allah!"

Then a woman came out of the house across the street, a bag in her hand. "I'm a doctor," she said, in English. She got down on the ground next to Doc, who looked at her and shook his head. When he pulled his hand away, I didn't have to be a doctor to see why. Some of the boy's brains were spilling out of the back of his head, sticky with blood, some of it stuck to Doc's hand. The woman closed the boy's eyes and stood up and spoke to his father in Arabic. He started screaming and yelling and sobbing. She put her hand on his shoulder and kept talking, her own eyes streaming. Sgt. Dixon called in for our captain to come.

After the first procession that morning, the women in our group gathered together in the dining room of our hotel to do a special prayer. Deena said, "This is the prayer of Ashura. It's like a regular prayer, but with some extra movements."

At the end of the prayer, we stepped forward as we said, *Innalillahi, wa inaa ilayhi rajiuna bi-qaz'aa-ihee, wa tasleeman li-amrihee.* Which means, "We belong to God and unto God we will return;

we are happy with the will of God and carry out the command of God." Then we walked backward again, back to where we started. We did this, back and forth, seven times.

"That is what Imam Husain said, over and over again, on that day when he lost his sons, his nephews, his brother. The last one he lost, before his own death, was his baby, Ali Asghar, who he carried, backwards and forwards, like this, already dead in his arms, unable to face the child's mother," Deena whispered to me.

The father of the boy pulled himself together, all of a sudden, and picked up his boy in his arms. He started walking back into the front gate of his house, then stopped, touched his forehead to his boy's, and shook his head, crying softly. The woman, the doctor, was still beside him, her hand on his shoulder. He took another few steps. And then stopped again. More steps. More stops. I didn't have to understand Arabic to know what was happening. He didn't know how he was going to do it. How was he going to take the boy back inside the house to show to his mother?

We stayed there, outside of the home of that dead boy, for a few hours. The captain came, he went in and talked to the family. When the captain came back out, the doctor woman from across the street was with him. She'd been translating between him and the family, which was a good thing, because we didn't have a translator with us. She told the captain that the boy's father wanted us all to come for the funeral the next day.

The captain didn't know what to say. Nobody did. This whole time, Foley was sitting on the side of the road. At first, he had his head in his hands. I'd gone over and sat down beside him for a while. Later, someone gave him a pack of cigarettes, which he smoked, one after another, until he made himself puke. Now, he looked up and around, but his eyes were dead. Like he wasn't with us anymore. The doctor lady said the father appreciated that it was an accident. He saw how we'd tried to help. And that we hadn't run away from what had happened. He wanted us to come to the funeral.

Our next stop was Najaf. We stayed there for three days, following much the same routine of prayers and shrine-hopping that we'd done in Karbala. In Karbala and in Najaf, in between visits to shrines, some people in the group went shopping, buying things like prayer beads and prayer rugs. There were food stalls running up and down every street. Business was booming in Najaf, as it had been in Karbala. The sheer number of pilgrims had a lot to do with that. We stopped in at a kabab restaurant a couple of times, for dinner, just me and Deena and Sadiq. It was a place recommended by one of the translators. His name was Qasim. The food was delicious.

Foley didn't go to the funeral. I did, with the captain and Sgt. Dixon. Some of the guys thought it was a bad idea. That the people there would be too hostile and that it could be a trap. But they were wrong. It was just a funeral. There were only men in the front room of the house. But we could hear the women in the back, crying. We figured the loudest of those cries must be coming from the mother of the dead boy. We'd tried to get a translator, but no one was available.

After a little while, the doctor lady who lived across the street came out from the back to translate for us. Through her, the captain told the family how sorry we were for what had happened. When we got up to leave, the doctor came outside with us, along with two men, one older, who I guessed was her husband, and another one who looked like he might be eighteen or nineteen, Foley's age. With them there was also a little girl, who hid her face in the doctor's skirt, and another boy, about the same age as the boy Foley'd killed.

The doctor told us her name was Sana and introduced us to her husband, Ali, whose English wasn't as good as hers. "My husband owns a kabab restaurant in Mansur. The Khalil Restaurant. This is our son, Ali Asghar. Our younger son, Uthman. And our daughter, Ayesha."

We all shook hands. Then Sana said, "Your friend didn't come? The other soldier? The one responsible?"

I waited for the captain to say something. But he was looking at me. I said, "He was unfortunately unable to come."

The woman sighed and shook her head, her ponytail swinging side to side. "What a pity. The boy is dead. Nothing can bring him back. But your friend was given a rare gift by the boy's father. To be invited to the funeral of someone he is responsible for killing. I am not sure I could have done the same in his place. Could you? He should have come. And shed a tear for the boy and his family. He should have come to say sorry. For his own good. Now, instead, he will carry the pain he caused home with him, a stain on his soul that he will bear for the rest of his life."

We all shuffled our feet, not knowing what to say.

Before we left, the captain said, "Again. We are very sorry for what happened. We'll be here again. To help the family fill out an application for some kind of compensation."

Most of the people in our group didn't stay for the last leg of our trip, in Baghdad. We would be staying in the Kadhimiya suburb of Baghdad, around the shrines of the seventh and ninth imams. Sadiq had spent a lot of time planning for this part of the trip, the end of it, which we had agreed would be the best time to pursue what I had specifically come for in connection with Chris. To do that, he had enlisted the help of the translator we'd spent the most time with, Qasim, who lived in Kadhimiya, near the hotel we would stay in. Qasim arranged for the car that would take us to the neighborhood of Mansur, where I wanted to go, where I hoped to find the address I needed.

"The neighborhood where we are going has become a dangerous one," Qasim said. "All of Baghdad is dangerous. Who you are can get you killed. Mansur is where the big shots live. And all the foreigners and journalists." Qasim shook his head. "I used to live in another area before. Until they drove us out, threatening to kill us. Because we are Shia. The same is true for Sunnis living in Shia neighborhoods. It's jungle law, now, in the great city of Baghdad."

We're scared all the time, now, when we go out on patrol. Especially after we lost Phillips. He always sang along with me whenever I did. His favorite was "Amazing Grace," but he liked "Onward Christian Soldiers," too, the Christian March version. He was from Missouri and used to joke about moving to San Diego and joining the band when we got home. He said he was really good on bass.

We don't go to the orphanage anymore. No one does. We feel too much like sitting ducks.

Every day, we hear about more guys getting blown up. Car bombs and IEDs planted by insurgents, there's no way to fight against them.

At night, we go on house raids. I hate it. Breaking down doors in the middle of the night, sometimes blowing them open with explosives, we burst in on people in their pajamas. Everyone screams. We round up the men. At first, it didn't feel so bad, 'cause we thought we were going after the guys who're trying to blow us up. That was when we still trusted the intel. But I don't anymore. We've torn up hundreds of houses and we never find anything. The men get treated rough, especially if they try to argue with us. Then we arrest all the men in the house and leave the women and kids behind, screaming and crying and begging us, on their knees, to let their sons, their husbands, their brothers, go.

The other night, Sgt. Dixon went too far. Not that anyone seems to give a crap. He beat up this old man with the butt of his rifle, because he wouldn't let go of his grandson, who we were arresting. I'll never forget the look in the old man's eyes. From the moment we entered his house. Terror. I looked at us from his point of view. A bunch of men in armored uniforms, with M-16s waving, busting in his door, terrifying his family. And him, helpless to save anybody. From us. We found out it wasn't even the house we were looking for. But there was a gun in the house and Sgt. Dixon wasn't in a good mood. So we took the grandson. I don't even think he was fourteen. We're not supposed to take kids younger than fourteen.

In the day, on patrol, the few people who come up to us only do it to complain. On the days we go out with a translator—our favorite is an Iraqi we call Slick Sam—we get an earful. About all the stuff that doesn't work. Power, water, sewage. We don't see any women anymore. When we first got to Baghdad, they were everywhere, a lot of them dressed in regular clothes, not like the ones we'd seen in the small towns and villages on the way into Baghdad. Now, the women in the city are all covered up, too. Slick Sam says it's 'cause it's not safe for women anymore. He says his sister used to go out shopping in jeans and skirts, but now he won't let her.

Things here are going crazy. Getting much, much worse. For the Iraqis. And for us, too. I can't wait to go home.

The Khalil Restaurant was still open. When we went in, we asked to see the owner. The waiters shook their heads and shrugged. Then, the cook came out from the back and asked us what we wanted. I spoke through Qasim. For some reason, Sadiq wanted me to keep my Arabic a secret. He said it might draw unnecessary attention. I told Qasim to ask about the owner named Ali.

The cook shook his head and said, "No, the owner's name is Abu Muhammad."

One week left to go! Can't wait to see Mom and Dad and Jo.

In Baghdad, life sucks, as usual. I just can't wait to get the heck out of here.

Every time we go by a restaurant, I remember the doctor. Sana. Truth is, I think of her and what she said every time I look into Foley's eyes. I see what she meant. He's messed up. Not just scared, like the rest of us. His eyes are still dead, even when he laughs or jokes around. After the boy's funeral, I heard the captain tell Foley not to worry about what happened. That it was a stupid mistake, but a mistake all the same. He told him to just brush it off, and get on with doing his job.

"The lady is asking about the old owner, whose name was Ali," Qasim explained again, patiently, for the third time.

"The old owner? I only just started working here. What do I know about the old owner?" the cook demanded.

I waited impatiently for Qasim to translate back to me, the pretense of not already having understood grating on my nerves.

"Ask him if there's anybody here who *did* know the old owner."

After a few minutes of this exasperation, an older man, someone sitting and eating in the restaurant, shuffled up to us. "Why do you want to know about Ali?"

I could barely stop from speaking to him myself, in Arabic. But I remembered not to, turning to let Qasim speak instead.

"Ask him if *he* knows him."

"Of course I knew him. You don't know that he's dead?"

TCP tonight. I hate Traffic Control Points even more than going on raids. Especially the kind we've been doing lately. Flash. Set up suddenly, so no one's expecting us. Hard Ass Platoon shot up a pregnant woman the other night. She was in labor and the husband was driving her to the hospital, driving too fast.

Just a few more days.

"Yes, the lady knows that he's dead," said Qasim. "She wants to know where he lived. She's an old friend of Ali's wife. Sana. She is trying to find her. Do you know where the family lives?"

"Of course! They live in Dora."

"Yes, yes. But *where*? She needs the address."

Bad night. The Hard Ass Platoon had a suicide car bomb hit them at the TCP. Couple of bad injuries. And Kirp's dead. Two more days and I am out of here.

We followed the old man's directions carefully. We passed through a militia checkpoint on the way into Dora. Qasim had said to let him do all the talking. After a few minutes of him explaining who we were—Shias on pilgrimage, from Pakistan, here to visit a friend—they let us in.

When we got to the street we were looking for, we knocked on what we thought was the right gate. A young man answered. Qasim told him we were looking for Sana.

The man frowned. "There's no Sana here. Who are you?"

Qasim said, "These people—this young woman—is an old friend of Sana. She wanted to visit her. Is this the wrong house?"

"I don't know any Sana!" the man shouted, looking around to see if anyone was watching before slamming the gate of his home shut.

We knocked on the gates on either side of the first one. No luck. Only more gates slammed in our faces. I glanced across the street, wondering which house could be the one of the boy Foley had killed.

After a few more minutes, we were starting to attract attention. A group of people gathered around us. Some among them were young men wearing black headbands, like the militiamen who'd greeted us at the checkpoint into the neighborhood. Someone said, very suggestively, "Oh, Sana, eh? The doctor? With two little children named Uthman and Ayesha?"

Qasim shot me a look. I nodded. After that, Qasim stopped asking the people around us questions, asking me, instead, in a whisper, "Is this woman a Sunni? The one you're asking about?"

I shrugged.

Qasim frowned. "If she is, you have put us in a bad position. This is a Shia neighborhood."

Then, someone in the group that had gathered around us, referred us to one of the houses across the street, saying softly, "Those people. They'll know."

I'm still shaking. I can't believe it. We set up a flash checkpoint tonight. A car was approaching, slowing down and still pretty far, no reason to worry. Then we heard a bang. It must have backfired. But that's not what it sounded like. Someone, one of us, yelled and fired and then we all joined in, round after round, until the car came to a stop, red mist coming out of its windows. In the silence that finally returned, I heard the sound of children crying. No one moved.

We knocked at the gate the man had pointed at. After a few seconds, someone answered it. Qasim started his spiel again.

The man at the gate said, "Dr. Sana? Why do you want to

know? She's a good woman! Isn't it enough that you fanatics have driven her away? Out of her home and out of her job! Leave her alone! She has suffered enough—more than any of us and we have all suffered plenty!"

It took a while, in the three-way conversation, to calm the man down. I took over, unable to contain myself, regardless of the warning look Sadiq tried to hush me up with.

I told Qasim, whose jaw was hanging open, "You just translate for Sadiq and Deena, so they can keep up, and let me do the talking here." The man whose house we were standing outside of was still looking at me with indignation. "We are friends of Sana. We are not here to hurt her. I— are you the man whose son was killed by an American Marine? In 2003? The very beginning of the war?"

He nodded.

"I'm so sorry. I'm so sorry for your loss."

He stayed silent for a long time, staring at me, and then moved aside, gesturing for us to come into his home. There, he served us tea and cookies. We met his wife. And his other children. We talked for more than an hour. At the end of our visit, I had Sana's address in my hand.

When we got back to the car, Qasim's voice was shaking. "You should have told me, Jo. That you speak Arabic. You were not honest with me. And now? Now, you want me to take you to Ad-hamiya? Are you insane? That is far too dangerous. For me. For you. *La, la!* There is no way, Jo."

On our way back to the hotel, a car bomb went off a block ahead of us. The blast shook our car, rattling my teeth and bones. We were stuck for two hours before we could move forward and get to our hotel.

It didn't seem to faze Sadiq and Deena, who went right back to the drawing board, helping me to figure out a plan for the morning. I watched them, wondering why they bothered. When it was all set, Sadiq used his cell phone to call Qasim and woo him back on board with what he and Deena had planned. Then Deena used the phone to call her husband, Umar.

"Don't worry, Umar. We're fine. I know. But this is something Jo has to do. For her brother. And I have to be with her. She's my granddaughter."

When they were both done with the phone, I told them, "I'm so grateful for everything you've done. But I can't let you come with me to Sana's house. Not now. What Qasim said is true. You saw how the people gathered around us in Dora. That was in a Shia neighborhood. In Adhamiya, it will be even more dangerous. Especially for you. I speak Arabic. I'll manage, somehow, with Qasim, by myself. But— you guys— it's too dangerous. I don't want you to come with me."

"Don't be ridiculous, Jo," Sadiq said. "I'm coming with you. Though I agree with you on one point. Amee, you don't need to be with us. You'll stay here. Jo and I will go and take care of this problem for Chris."

"Oh, no! You're not leaving me back here! As if I were some old woman, too fragile to take risks!" cried Deena.

I looked from one to the other of them and started to cry.

"Jo! What's wrong?" Deena asked.

"I— there's something— I— haven't told you. Something you have a right to know. I mean, here we are—in a war zone!—and you, Deena, you wouldn't even be here if it weren't for me! And Sadiq would have been home by now, with the rest of the group that left Baghdad yesterday morning. That bomb, today, went off a block away from us. If it had been a few minutes later, we would have been right on top of it. And—I've been hiding something from you both. I lied to you, Sadiq. When you and Deena asked me if I had a picture of my family."

Sadiq frowned. "What do you mean? Why?"

I went to my purse and pulled out the picture I was carrying, the picture I'd brought with the intention of showing him, but which I hadn't had the courage to do until now. I handed it to Sadiq. He looked at it for a second and then looked at me.

"Look—that's my brother. Chris."

Sadiq looked at it again and Deena pulled her reading glasses out of her bag and perched them on her nose, then stood beside where Sadiq was sitting, looking over his shoulder.

Deena said, "Chris. He—he has brown eyes?"

I nodded.

"He—I thought—he's your—"

I nodded again. "He's my twin brother. Younger than me by half an hour."

Sadiq's face paled. "He's—he's my son?"

"Yes. I promised my mother I wouldn't tell you—or him. He doesn't know. And I was afraid you'd—that you'd want to—talk to him—that he would find out. Before. But—after his accident, I decided I had to tell him the truth. Eventually. And that I had to tell you, too. You—he and you both—you have a right to know. You've—you and Deena—you've taken care of me on this trip. Letting me tag along. And I've been feeling terrible, thinking about Chris and why I'm here. I've put you both at risk. And I never told you the truth."

After a long while, Sadiq asked me all kinds of questions. About Chris. And then he got very quiet.

Deena said, "Well. It's good you told us. Don't feel bad, Jo. I knew. I knew there was something you weren't sharing. It— it was a difficult situation for you. And I'm glad you've cleared your heart now." She came over and gave me a hug. Then, wiping tears from her eyes, she gave a little skip. "Two grandchildren! Twins!"

"Can I— when will you tell him?" asked Sadiq.

"I don't know, Sadiq. I—I'm still trying to figure that all out."

"But you will tell him?"

"Yes." I got up and went and stood in front of him. Awkwardly, I gave him a hug. "I will. I—don't know when or how. But I will."

He put his hand on my face and wiped a tear off my cheek.

Then he said, "Are there any more of you I should know about?"

In the end, none of us could convince any of the others not to come the next day to Sana's house. In the morning, still a little miffed, Qasim didn't say anything when he came to pick us up, merely raised his eyebrows at the sight of all three of us waiting outside the hotel.

We took one taxi to the outskirts of Adhamiya and then another one to drive us through to the checkpoint, manned by Sunni militia, the way the one in Dora had been manned by Shia the day before. As Sadiq had asked him to do, Qasim brought his old ID, from before he was forced to move, so they'd think he was Sunni. His name was a neutral one, used by both Sunni and Shia. He told the guys at the checkpoint the same thing he'd said the day before, that we were old friends of someone who lived in the neighborhood, from Pakistan, and were just coming to visit. The men asked for our passports.

Qasim shook his head. "Sorry. I told my guests to leave them at my house, where they are staying. I told them they wouldn't need their passports. That the people of Iraq, despite all our troubles, still have big hearts and know what hospitality means." The men squinted into the car for a second and then smiled and let us through.

We had to stop and ask directions a couple of times. And then we were knocking—finally and rightly, I hoped—at Sana's door.

We all still had our rifles ready. Then, slowly, the rear door of the car opened. A little girl came out, covered in blood. Then a boy. Finally, a woman, shrouded in black, also came out of the backseat of the car. The woman gave her children a quick embrace, and pushed them away from the car, gesturing to them to wait, the high-pitched screaming of the girl unbearable to anyone who could hear it. It was dark. The mother went around to the front of the car and saw what we did when we advanced toward it, shining our lights in to see the front seat. She moaned. There were two men, the driver and a passenger in the front. No search needed to be conducted to know that there had been no reason to shoot. The driver—the father, the husband—had no face left. The front passenger moved, he said, "Ummi," and then his head fell forward. The woman opened his door and checked to see if he was breathing. Desperately, she gathered him out of the car and checked again. Then, she cradled his body in her lap and started screaming, "La! La! Ya Allah! La!"

The red mist that had sprayed out of the car seemed to have filled my head, because all I could hear, aside from the screaming and the sobbing, was something that sounded like a fountain. Or snow on a television. It was the sound of nothing. Or something—the sound of my blood flowing, the way the blood of those two men would never flow again. The woman left the body of her older son and went again to her younger children, turning her back, shielding them from the sight of us, but not before I got a look at the little boy. The loathing and terror in his eyes registered through the sound of the flow in my head. I did that to him, *I thought.* I did that.

Soon, an ambulance arrived at the scene. It loaded all of them up. Before the door shut, my eyes caught the eyes of the woman, shrouded in black, whose whole life I had just destroyed. It was like a shock, the spark that flowed from my eyes to hers, from hers to mine. The spark of recognition. It was Sana, the doctor, whose husband, Ali, and son, Ali Asghar, we'd shot and killed. It was her son, Uthman, whose eyes had simmered with hatred, her daughter, Ayesha, howling, drenched in the blood of her father and brother.

A woman answered the door. She was wearing jeans and a shirt. She looked afraid to see strangers standing there in front of her house.

I said, "Sana? Are you—are you Dr. Sana?" I'd spoken in English.

Looking confused, she answered in the same language, "Yes?"

"I—my name is Jo."

"Yes?"

"I—we've come to see you. To—talk to you. May we come in?"

She stared at me, the way the man in Dora had stared. She looked from my face to Deena's, Sadiq's, and then Qasim's. Like the man in Dora, she moved aside and gestured us in.

I sat in silence for a long time. She sat and watched me with a puzzled frown. I had known it would be difficult. But I hadn't realized that it would be impossible. How do you even begin the kind of conversation I was here to have?

"I—I went to your house in Dora to look for you. I met your

neighbor. The family across the street. The one whose son was shot by an American two years ago."

"Yes. I remember. I remember that day very well. That neighbor of mine—he is an incredible man."

"Yes," I said.

"Imagine. To invite the man who killed your son to your home. The very next day."

"But—the Marine, the man who shot the boy, he didn't come," I said gently.

"No. He didn't. Some other soldiers came. An officer. And two of them who were there when the boy was shot." Sana's eyes hardened a little, making me too afraid to continue for a while.

"You're American?" Sana asked.

I nodded.

"You're—you're here—because you're connected? To what happened?"

I nodded again.

"I saw one of those soldiers again. On the night—" Sana's voice broke off.

I picked up her sentence. "On the night your husband and son were killed."

"How do you know this? Who are you?" She looked frightened.

Quickly, because I didn't want her to be frightened, I said, "I know because the man you saw again is my brother. I—I came because I know what he—what he did. I know what happened. I know and I wanted to come—because—I had to come—" I felt my eyes begging hers, for some kind of sign, some kind of softening. And I felt guilty for what I was asking, knowing it was something I doubted I could give if I were in her place.

"Your brother? Your brother is that soldier? But I still don't understand. Are you also a soldier? Why are you here?"

"Because he can't be. Because he can't remember what he did. But he wrote about it. In his journal. And I know—I know how sorry he was. Is. Would be, if he remembered."

"You're telling me that he's forgotten? What he did to my family? That he is one of those who killed my husband and my son? He's forgotten?"

"He—my brother didn't forget. He wanted to. He—tried to kill himself. He crashed his car into a tree. And when he recovered from the accident, he'd lost his memory of the last few years. About everything that happened here in Iraq. But I wanted you to know that he was sorry. That he suffered for what he did. I don't know if that makes it any better for you. I don't think it does. But I wanted you to know."

She started to cry, very softly. I cried with her. So did Deena and Sadiq, and Qasim, too.

After a long, long time, Sana said, "You—you've come—just for this? Just to say this?"

I nodded.

"You know—I've thought about my neighbor in Dora many, many times in the last two years. I used to visit his wife and ask her—what kind of man is he? Is he some kind of saint? How could he have invited those soldiers into his home on such an occasion? How could she, his wife, have allowed it? She told me that he has always been like this. That he says anger is like milk. It doesn't keep. It becomes sour, bringing sickness and death to anyone who tastes it when its time has passed. Grief, she said he likes to say, ages better than anger. It is eternal. Her husband is a Quran teacher. He teaches his students that the *huẓn* of the Quran—that is, its voice—is one of sadness. I never realized this before she said it. That the voice of God is a sad voice. Now, I hear it all the time. The grief of God. The grief in the sound of the call to prayers. The sadness, the tears, it wells up in my heart every time I hear of the madness in the streets of Baghdad. When we don't understand this, when we trade our grief in for anger, bad things happen. No, they don't just happen. We do them. We do bad things to each other." She stopped talking for a while. Then continued, "If someone had told me—that I would feel what I feel, at your coming, I would have laughed. You think saying sorry will take away what has happened to me? I lost my husband, my son. I lost my home. Because I am Sunni and I lived in a neighborhood where Sunnis were driven away. If my husband had been alive, they would not have dared to threaten me, even sending me warning notes at the hospital where I worked. My husband was a Shia. Not that these things ever mattered to us. Look at the way we named our children! Deliberately, mixing Shia names with Sunni names. Because these things—the names of people, what we call them—shouldn't matter. But my husband was gone. And those thugs drove me out of my home and out of the hospital and the work I loved. Your sorry doesn't change any of that. It doesn't give me my son back. It doesn't give me my husband. What does your sorry mean? What can it mean? I'll tell you, Jo. It means everything to me." Sana started to sob. "It means everything. That my pain is something you recognize. That you share. It means everything, everything, everything and more."

I took a cab home from the airport in San Diego, because I hadn't called to give Mom and Dad the details of my flight. Mom had been unhappy when I'd called her from Pakistan, before Iraq, telling her I'd be home three weeks later than I'd planned, gone for six weeks instead of three. I'd said good-bye to Deena at the airport in Los Angeles before catching the flight to San Diego, promising, again, to stay in touch. The same way I'd promised Sadiq.

When I got home, Mom shouted with joy. She was glad to have me back. Relieved that I was safe. Dad hugged me. And kept tugging at my ponytail every time he was in reach. When I looked at Chris, I saw something in his face that made me worry.

He let two days pass before saying anything, waiting for Mom and Dad to go to sleep first, knocking on the door of my room, where I was folding laundry.

"Jo?"

"Yes, Chris?"

"I was—*am*—a Marine."

I sat down on the bed. "Yes. Are you remembering?"

"No. Yes. Someone said something. At church. And that made me start to remember."

"Does Mom know?"

"No. Not Dad either. I've been waiting for you to come home. You won't lie to me, will you, Jo?"

"No. I won't lie. Not anymore."

"The accident. It wasn't an accident, was it?"

"No."

"That's why Mom and Dad don't want me to remember."

"They're worried. They don't want to lose you. Neither do I."

"It would be easier, I think. Not to remember. When I first started to—a month ago, after you left—I'd have these flashes of scenes in my mind. I think— I think I tried to block them out.

Like there's a part of me that doesn't want to know. A part of me that wants to play along with Mom and Dad."

"What—what exactly do you remember?"

"Bits and pieces. Do you know, Jo? Do you know all of it?"

"I know why you— I know most of it, yes."

He sat down on the bed next to me. "You must be tired. Still jet-lagged."

"A little."

"Will you tell me, Jo? Will you tell me everything? So I can separate the truth out from all the stuff that's floating around in my head. It's scaring me, Jo. The stuff I've forgotten. And the scenes I remember."

"What if—what if you don't like the truth?"

"It's still the truth, isn't it? And the way things are—not knowing all of it, only flashes, like scenes in a movie I watched—I feel like I don't know who I am."

"I can relate to that, Chris. I've felt that way before in the face of truth. And I—I tried to run away from it. It doesn't work. You—you tried to escape it before, too. That's what Mom and Dad are afraid of. You have to promise, Chris. That you won't—that you won't try and escape it again."

"How can I promise that, Jo? When I'm not sure what I'm promising?"

I put my hands on his shoulders and squeezed. "Because you have to, Chris. You have to promise me. What's done is done. You can't go back and undo it. I'll tell you everything, Chris. But you have to promise me. That you'll stay with it. That you'll let yourself feel the pain. Feel it. Give into the grief. I've been learning to do that myself. But you have to promise. I can't lose you, Chris. Not again."

Chris closed his eyes. "I promise, Jo."

I took Chris's hand in mine. "Okay. But you started at the wrong end, Chris. I'm taking you back. When's the last time you remember going to camp?"

"We were there—uh—summer before senior year. After that—did you not go? After graduating high school?"

He was remembering. "That's right. We went to Africa. With Grandma Faith. I stayed behind and missed camp."

"Africa? Yes. To Kenya. We—washed those kids' feet. And gave them shoes. And Grandma Faith was mad. At Uncle Ron's people."

I laughed. "Yeah. You remember camp the summer after tenth grade? The year we had the Wall of Doubt?"

"Yeah. You had a hard time with it. And it bothered you. A lot." He grinned. "But you made it over in the end."

"It wasn't the wall that bothered me, Chris. It was the color of my eyes. Mine and yours."

They that sow in tears shall reap in joy.

Psalm 126, v. 5

Faith

Jo fluttered around the table, adjusting a fork here and a knife there. It had taken a lot for her to put this show together. Months of planning. Now, I saw, she was having a hard time doing the only thing left to do. Which was wait.

"Relax, honey," I said with a smile. "It'll be fine. You'll see."

Angie came out of the kitchen, her face even more scrunched up with stress than Jo's. Some of the creases on their faces—my daughter's and granddaughter's—lined up with each other. Some of them didn't. A miraculous blend of inheritance. I touched my own face, wondering which of the permanent lines there matched theirs, which didn't, and considered the role of experience in that blend. Tears, laughter, anger—how they leave their mark on the most visible part of us.

The doorbell rang. Jo stood at attention, smoothing down her skirt with a nervous smile my way, before heading for the door, having assigned herself the delicate job of making introductions for those who hadn't met each other yet.

Sadiq and his family were the first to arrive.

The most important introduction Jo had made already, in private, which was as it should be. So, when Sadiq arrived, with his wife and stepdaughters, Chris greeted him with a smile that was easy and comfortable enough. When Jake stepped up, I leaned forward, not wanting to miss a wink, like the worst kind of busybody.

Jo handled it beautifully, taking Jake's hand in hers, placing her other hand on Sadiq's shoulder, saying, "Daddy. This is Sadiq." With no hesitation that I could see, my son-in-law—who I hadn't much cared for when Angie first brought him home—pulled his hand free from Jo's, used it to give her hair a quick tug, that way that he always did, and offered it to Sadiq with a warm smile and no sign of the wariness I'd held my breath to see. Then, I held my breath some more and turned to look at Angie.

She said, "Sadiq. Welcome," putting her hand out.

"Angela. Thank you," he said, wrapping her hand in both of his and pausing for a moment, leaving me wondering what he was thanking her for, until he added, "They are beautiful." His eyes took Jake in, too. "Inside and out."

Angie's eyes filled and Jake nodded proudly.

Then, Sadiq turned to introduce his wife, Akeela, and her daughters, Samira and Tasneem.

After that, the doorbell rang a few more times. Jo spent the next half hour or so catching it.

When Deena arrived with her husband, Umar, their daughter, Sabah, and son-in-law, Habib—all names I'd brushed up on and memorized with Jo's help earlier in the day—she greeted Jo and Chris, and then turned to Angie, her arms wide open. "Angela! It's so lovely to see you again after all these years!"

Angie hesitated for less than a second, then some of the lines in her face smoothed out as she stepped in to hug Deena—finally surrendering, with that embrace, to the messy, complicated nature of truth.

The best arrival of all, for me, was my son's. Jo had put me in charge of getting Ron up to date. That had been fun.

I'd called him on the phone about a week earlier and said, "Ron, Thanksgiving at your sister's is going to be a little bit different this year."

"Why's that?"

"Well—" I began, and then gleefully launched into the story of Angie having had a lover, of that lover being the twins' father, of her having kept it all a secret from the twins and their biological father, and of how Jo had gone and found him and the rest of his family and now everyone was getting together at Angie's house for Thanksgiving. At some point, I let myself savor how quiet it'd gotten on the other end of the line. "Ron? Ron? You still there?"

"Uh, yes, Mom."

"Oh, good!" I exclaimed, because I'd saved the best for last. That the father was Muslim. That he was from Pakistan. That Jo had been there to visit. That she'd been to Iraq, too, on some kind of religious pilgrimage. Oh, I felt wicked for taking as much pleasure in his shock as I did. Of course, poor Ron hadn't wanted to come. And I'd thoroughly enjoyed delivering the lectures that had changed his mind. So, he came alright, bringing his wife, Lisa, and kids—Annie and Jack—with him. On the surface, he looked like he always did—skin glowing, not a hair out of place, as if he'd stopped by in the hair and makeup room of his studio before the drive down to San Diego. But the look on his face was priceless, like someone had smacked the smugness out of him—the open-mouthed uncertainty that seemed to have struck him dumb something I'd been waiting years to see.

When everyone had arrived, the house bursting at the seams, I popped my head into the kitchen and made my usual, perfunctory offer to help, but Angie knows her way around a kitchen well enough to know that I don't. She waved me out, and I obeyed—to my relief and hers. Jo helped her mother get the food out to the table. Sabah offered to help, too, but Jo shooed her away.

I could see how Jo had one ear tuned in to the family room. The game was on TV. Sadiq, Jake, and Umar sat and watched television with Chris—the picture of a happy, if unusual, family on Thanksgiving, all of them as relaxed as could be. Ron was with them, quiet as a mouse, still a little disoriented. So was his son, Jack, cheering a touchdown, taking it all in stride. Jo's other ear was tuned in to the dining room, where Deena and I and the rest stood around the table, exchanging opening pleasantries.

When Jo and Angie were done laying out the food and the fixings, buffet-style, they called everyone to the table. We stood in a circle and Angie asked me to say grace, instead of Ron. I did, thanking God for all the friends that had gathered, the new and the old, those with us and those who weren't. I took inventory of the former, calling names out loud. Angie, Jake, Chris, Ron, Lisa, Annie, Jack, Deena, Umar, Sadiq, Akeela, Samira, Tasneem, Sabah, and Habib, proud of myself for remembering all the new ones. Then I said, "Thank you, Lord, for revealing the power and love of the ties that connect us—these ties that we were unaware of and which you opened our eyes to—ties of blood and kinship, which we gratefully cherish and grasp with open hearts."

Jake carved the turkey. Ron, still having a hard time, spread his silence over the rest of us for a few moments.

Until Chris broke the quiet, loading his plate with stuffing and mashed potatoes, saying, "Oh, Mom, I forgot to tell you. I got an e-mail from Sana today. She said to thank everyone at church. They got the delivery of meds at the hospital. Started unpacking and using them right away."

Angie nodded with a smile. "I'm glad."

Jo loaded her plate and wandered around. She stopped next to Sadiq, where I heard her say, "Did I tell you? I'm going to Gitmo again next week. My fifth trip down there."

Sadiq gave Jo's cheek a touch and said, "I'm very proud."

My own plate full, I settled down in a chair next to Deena's. She said, "Faith. We have the same name. My maiden name is Iman, which means 'faith.'"

"Really?"

That got us talking about languages. A few minutes into the conversation, I knew that Jo was right. This was a woman worth getting to know. I hoped Ron would see that, too—someday anyway. I looked around and saw bad manners all around, everyone chewing with their mouths open because they were all busy chatting away, casually, like this was no big deal. Even Ron had been drawn reluctantly into a conversation with Sabah's husband, Habib.

Later, my eyes followed Jo, a plate of pie in her hand, as she went from dining room to living room to family room, taking stock, making sure no one was left out. Sadiq, pouring himself some coffee, said something that made Jake nod and smile and which lit up Chris's face with a laugh. Angie was right behind Jo, making slow rounds of her own, having stopped, now, to talk with Akeela and Sabah. Jo came over and stood in front of Deena and me, comfortably huddled together in the corner of the room we'd claimed, talking up a storm. Angie joined us a few minutes later, parking herself next to her daughter. She put her arm around Jo, gave a squeeze, and said, "Well, Jo. You did it. You pulled all these pieces together, from all over the world, and made it all fit." She looked from me to Deena, and back to Jo, and said, "Same time next year?"

I saw the plop of a tear fall on Jo's slice of pecan pie and said, "Jo! You're crying!"

Deena said, "That's okay. She's just sweetening her pie."

Acknowledgments

I could not have embarked on or completed this journey alone. First and always, I would like to express my deepest gratitude to Dr. Nahid Angha and Dr. Ali Kianfar, my teachers, for the guiding light that illuminates the path.

Also, my thanks to all the friends and family whose support sustained the effort—to Nuzha, Roya, Khaled, Michelle, Gillian, Fazila, Batool, Farah, and Sandy; to my friends at the Marin Interfaith Council; to the circle of wise women led by Sheikha Halima Haymaker, which meets and meditates regularly at the Institute for Sufi Studies; and, with love, to my Sufi family.

For the memories that informed this book, thanks to Mummy and Daddy, who helped me to imagine a Karachi before my time; to my cousins, Zohair, Imran, Soosan, Ali, Suroor, Mehjabeen, Zafar, Khadija, Azhar, Riffat, Abbas, and Rukkaya Apa, for the shared childhood moments that pop up, in modified form, here and there. Thanks to Sajjad Premjee, who generously gave me time and answers about a story that ultimately did not make it into this book—perhaps reserved for another one in the future. Thanks to Nusrat Auntie, Batool Mami, and Farah for sharing their detailed impressions of visits to Karbala and Najaf; to Azim Mamu and Mummy (Haji) for taking me on a tour of Karachi by night during the Muharram-Safar season; to Papa for taking me to Nishtar Park on Chehlum; to Alina for taking me to church in Karachi. And thanks to my grandfather, the author of a book, in English, which he wrote as a tribute in tears to the tragedy of Karbala.

Thanks to the truth seekers and tellers—all of the journalists, writers, soldiers, Marines, and civilians—who have the courage to share what they see, do, and suffer, among them: Clive Stafford Smith, Philippe Sands, Ron Suskind, Andy Worthington, Moazzam Begg, James Yee, Eric Saar, Chris Hedges, Laila Al-Arian, Aaron Glantz, Peggy Faw Gish, Mahvish Rukhsana Khan, Ashley Gilbertson, Farnaz Fassihi, Nir Rosen, Greg Mitchell, Tara McKelvey, W. Frederick Zimmerman, Ariel Dorfman, Rajiv Chandrasekaran, Dahr Jamail, Camilo Mejia, the Winter Soldiers, and so many, many others. Thanks to the works of Frank Schaeffer that reveal complexity and nuance on topics which others tend to reduce.

Thanks to BJ Robbins, my agent, for solid and steady confidence; to Laurie Chittenden, my editor, for wit and grace through the weeding and pruning process; to Trish Daly, Mac Mackie, Ben Bruton, Juliette Shapland, Brenda Segel, Tavia Kowalchuk, and all the hands at HarperCollins who gently shepherded the book on its way out to the world.

Finally, last but definitely not least, thanks to my brother, Hani, for the conversation that got me thinking; to my sister, Maryam, for listening and telling me, over and over, that this was a story that needed to be known; to my mother who, again, listened to every word along the way; to Khalil for rejecting every title until I found the one that fit best. And to Ali—my lover, my partner, my best friend—who is the reason.

Author's Note

The story "The Monkey and the Crocodile" is a tale still told, in many variations and versions, throughout Asia, Africa, and the Middle East, and can be traced back to the *Panchatantra*, an ancient Indian collection of fables written to instruct young princes on the subject of leadership. Scholars have also noted similarities with older stories, such as the Buddhist *Jakata* tales, as well as prior oral traditions.

Child custody laws vary widely in Muslim-majority countries. How they are interpreted and applied depends on the legal system of each state, whether secular or religious. In Pakistan, custody is determined by laws still on the books from the British Raj era and sectarian laws based on the faith of the individuals involved. While there are differences in the interpretation of custody rights among the major schools of Islamic jurisprudence, both within and between Sunni traditions and Shia, in general, maternal custody is favored for the period of early childhood—the definition of which ranges from age two to puberty—while financial responsibility remains a paternal obligation. Common to all the traditional schools of Islamic jurisprudence, preference shifts in favor of paternal custody in cases where the mother remarries. While the events of this novel are fictional and cannot be construed as a definitive representation of the laws of any one country, community, or sect, certain characters express views that are based on an interpretation of Shia (Jafari) jurisprudence, whereby custody may be granted to the paternal grandfather in cases where the father is deceased.

Glossary

Unless otherwise indicated, words are in Urdu.

abaya (Arabic)—cloak or robe, usually black, worn as an outer
   garment to veil the shape of a woman's body; traditionally worn
   in Arab cultures

abu—father

abuela (Spanish)—grandmother

achaar—pickled fruit or vegetable; most often, pickled, unripe
   mango

alhamdulillah (Arabic)—all praise to God

Allahuma sale ala Muhammad w'ale Muhammad (Arabic)—the
   salawat, which means, "Oh, God, bless Muhammad and the
   descendants of Muhammad"

amee—mother

amma—mother

anna—a sixteenth of a rupee, unit of currency no longer in use

Arbaeen (Arabic)—Shia holy day, forty days after Ashura,
   commemorating the end of the Muharram/Safar season for
   remembrance of the tragedy of Karbala

asalaam alaikum (Arabic)—greeting, may peace be on you

Ashura—tenth day of the month of Muharram, day of the tragedy
   of Karbala

azaan—call to prayer

ayah—nanny, children's nurse

baba—title of affection for a little boy

badaam—red, waxy-skinned fruit; also almond

baksheesh—token of thanks, tip

baraf-pani—lit. ice water; children's game of freeze tag

barkat—blessings, abundance

bas—enough

beta—son

beti—daughter

bhabi—sister-in-law, wife of brother; also used for wife of friend

bhai—brother

bibi (Swahili)—grandmother

bibi—lady; affectionate style of address rather than formal

biryani—rice dish cooked with spices and meat or vegetables

buddhi ka baal—lit. old-lady hair; term for cotton candy

burkha—head-to-toe garment for women, covering face and hair

cachumber—a chopped salad, eaten aside the main meal, made
   of onions, tomatoes, cucumbers, green chilis, vinegar/lemon
   juice, cilantro, and salt

chaat—savory, sour, spicy snacks

chacha—uncle, father's brother

chadar—lit. sheet; seamless cloth covering for hair and body but
   not the face

chai—tea

chakr—dizziness

chakram—fool, dizzy-headed person

Chehlum—Shia holy day, forty days after Ashura,
   commemorating the end of the Muharram/Safar season of
   remembrance of Karbala

chola—spicy and sour salad made with chick peas

chowkidar—watchman, guard

chutney—dipping sauce

dada—paternal grandfather

dadi—paternal grandmother

dard—pain

dho—two

dho pyaʒa—meat dish made with double the normal amount of onions

dupatta—long scarf, standard accessory for women's dress

ehsaan—obligation, social debt, to owe favors

ek—one

fajr—dawn; dawn prayer

faqa—half-day fast observed on Ashura

ghaʒals—poetic form in the Middle East and South Asia consisting of rhyming couplets with repeating refrains, usually expressing the pain of loss or separation and the beauty to be found in that pain

hai—lamentation, "Alas!"

hakim—traditional healer

halal—term for what is lawful in Islam, most often used in terms of dietary restrictions, specifically with regard to meat and poultry, whereby animals must be treated humanely (offered water, etc.), and the name of God is invoked before specific slaughtering methods, which are the same as those found in Jewish kosher tradition

hijab—head scarf covering all of the hair

humdard—lit. us-pain; one who shares one's pain

huzn (Arabic)—sorrow or sadness, a tone which professional reciters of the Quran aspire to express

ifthar—sunset meal to break the day's fast during Ramzan

Illahi—God

imam—religious leader or teacher; one who leads prayer

Imam—for Shias, one of the spiritual successors to the Prophet

imam zamin—armband for special occasions, with money sewn inside for charity

Independence—end of the British Raj in the Indian Subcontinent, establishment of the nation-states of India and Pakistan

Innalillahi, wa inaa ilayhi rajiuna bi-qaz'aa-ihee, wa tasleeman li-amrihee (Arabic)—"We belong to God and unto God we will return; we are happy with the will of God and carry out the command of God"

Inshallah (Arabic)—God willing

jamun—purplish red, ovoid-shaped fruit

jora—lit. pair or set; used for an outfit of clothing

juloos—procession, demonstration

jungle jalebi—fruit in a spiral, twisty pod, similar to tamarind but lighter in color and blander in flavor

jurwa—twin

kabab—meat dish—ground or cubed, roasted, grilled, or fried

kameez—long tunic, traditionally very long; for women, length varies according to fashion

khalifa (Arabic)—caliph; secular and religious leader who is in succession to the leadership of the Prophet

khorma—curried meat or chicken dish

Khudahafiz—good-bye; God be with you

kilona-walla—toy man, hawker of toys

kismat—luck, fate, destiny

kulfi—ice cream, usually flavored with cardamom

kurtha—loose, long tunic

la (Arabic)—no

lola (Tagalog)—grandmother

ma—mother

macee—mother's sister in some subcontinental dialects

madrassa (Arabic)—school

majlis—gathering or congregation

marsia—mournful, harmonious dirge for the remembrance of Karbala

masaib—tragedy

masala—spices

Mashallah (Arabic)—by the grace of God

masjid—mosque

masloom—victim of oppression or injustice

matham—ritual grieving in the form of self-flagellation to mourn the tragedy of Karbala—most typical form being an open-handed thumping of the chest

meher—prenuptial settlement given to the bride

mehfil—gathering hall

mehndi—henna; prenuptial ceremony when henna is applied in intricate patterns to the hands and feet of the bride and her female friends and relatives

mubarak—congratulations, felicitations on a happy occasion

muezzin—the one who gives the *azaan,* the call to prayer

Muharram—first month of the Islamic calendar (the Islamic calendar being lunar and unaligned or adjusted, so that it slides

backward in relation to the Western calendar approximately
ten days each year)

mullah—religious preacher or scholar

mushk—water bag

mut'a—temporary marriage

naan—slightly leavened bread, usually baked in a clay oven

namak—salt

namaz—prayer

nikkah—Muslim wedding ceremony

nikkah-nama—wedding document indicating prenuptial
agreements, such as gift to the bride, and conditions of
marriage, etc.

noha—mournful, rhythmic dirge to accompany the beating of the
chest (*matham*) ritual in remembrance of Karbala

oof—an expressive utterance indicating dismay or displeasure

paan—betel nut wrapped in leaf, spread with lime paste and
assorted flavorings

pakora—deep-fried fritters, often made with vegetables, battered
in lentil flour

pallo—loose end of a *sari,* typically worn over the shoulder or
drawn over the head

Partition—the division of the Indian Subcontinent at the time of
Independence from the British into the nations of India and
Pakistan (East and West, the former of which later became
Bangladesh)

phupi—aunt, father's sister

phupijan—aunt dear, *jan* being a term of endearment—"dear" or
"darling"

pyas—thirst

Raj—rule, as in British Raj or Rule

Ramzan (in Arabic, *Ramadan*)—the ninth month of the Islamic calendar, the month of fasting

rickshaw—motor tricycle taxi

roza—lit. day; the word for the Ramzan fast, abstaining from food and drink from sunrise to sunset

rupee—currency note in Pakistan, India

sabeel—lit. spring; refreshments offered to pilgrims and mourners in commemoration of Karbala

sabzi mandi—vegetable market

sadhu—ascetic, one who renounces worldly life

Safar—the second month of the Islamic calendar

sajda—position of prostration in prayer, forehead to ground

salaam—greeting, peace

salan—curry

salawat—call for blessings on the Prophet and his descendants

samosa—triangular, pastry-wrapped pocket of meat or vegetables, fried as snack or appetizer

sari—woman's clothing comprised of yards of fabric wrapped and pleated over an underskirt and blouse

sayt—boss, master

shaami kabab—lightly fried kabab made of ground meat and lentils, battered in egg

shaheed—martyr; one who bears witness

shalwar—loose, baggy pants for men and women

shalwar kameez—outfit comprised of loose, baggy pants and matching tunic top

sharbat—sweet, cold drink, often made with milk and nuts

Shia—follower of the sect of Islam that traces the spiritual succession to the Prophet down from his cousin, Ali; minority sect in Islam

Sunni—follower of the sect of Islam that follows the tradition of the Prophet and accepts the spiritual leadership of the first four caliphs as successors to the Prophet; majority sect in Islam

tasbeeh—prayer beads, rosary

teek heh—it's okay; it's all right

tonga—two-wheeled horse carriage

ummi (Arabic)—mother

Wahabbi—follower of eighteenth-century Abd al-Wahab; a term, often used pejoratively, for a conservative religious worldview intolerant of anything contrary to what is considered a purist view of Islam, including Shia practices and beliefs and Sufi practices. A prevalent form of Islam in Saudi Arabia, Wahabbi ideology has been exported elsewhere, fueled by oil money, in the form of schools and missionary work

wàipó (Mandarin Chinese)—maternal grandmother

ya (Arabic)—oh

yalla (Arabic)—expression for "let's go," or "come on"

ẕakir—one who remembers, male; in Shia, Indo-Pakistani usage: one who remembers and recounts the story of Karbala

ẕakira—one who remembers, female; in Shia, Indo-Pakistani usage: one who remembers and recounts the story of Karbala

ẕanjeer ka matham—ritual grieving, self-flagellation in commemoration of Karbala, involving chains and blades

ẕiarat—pilgrimage; offering a spiritual salute to the departed, whether in person at the grave or through recitation and prayer

A+

AUTHOR
INSIGHTS,
EXTRAS &
MORE...

FROM

**NAFISA
HAJI**

AND

Wm
WILLIAM MORROW

Mining Memories

Several threads of personal and collective memory were mined and processed while writing the story of *The Sweetness of Tears*.

When I was nine years old, my father accepted a two-year foreign assignment in the Philippines, and my family moved from Los Angeles to Manila. Among the many wonderful memories I collected there, two left an impression deep enough for me to want to explore in *The Sweetness of Tears*. On our first Good Friday in the Philippines, their curiosity piqued by what they heard about how the Passion of Christ was commemorated by some on the Catholic-majority island of Luzon where we lived, my parents took us on a drive into the countryside. There, I remember seeing somber processions of men engaged in self-flagellation like that practiced by Shia men during Muharram, something I had heard of but never seen. I saw chains and blades swinging, blood dripping down bare backs, and I heard my parents marvel at the similarity to sights they had witnessed as children in Pakistan, only here as the expression of a faith and culture very different from their own. The brutal acts of self-inflicted pain, rituals of atonement and remembrance of long-ago suffering, were the expression of something I spent years trying and failing to understand. The two tragedies they evoked—the Crucifixion and Karbala—were forever linked in my imagination.

About a year into our time in the Philippines, Islam and Christianity intersected again in an unusual way, closer to home. A colleague of my father's, another expatriate, invited our family over for dinner. He was a devout Christian, the quintessential family man. I remember the long drive to his house, away from the swanky suburbs where most expatriates lived, into a neighborhood that was more authentically local. It was a lovely evening. The man's children, older than me, kept me entertained, lending me a favorite book that I came to love, too. The dinner at their home was followed by an unusual request. The man and his family were returning to the United States earlier than they had planned and would be unable to fulfill a promise to host some guests from their church back in the States. Instead of asking another (Christian) colleague, the man asked my father (a Muslim) if he would be willing to put up the visitors, missionaries on their way to work farther north in Luzon. He believed that our home would be more "wholesome," he said, alcohol-free and removed from the high-flying social engagements of others in the expatriate circle of coworkers he might have asked. My father, flattered by the confidence implied, agreed. The missionaries, two young women, stayed with us for only a few days, but the memory of their visit—their friendliness, their curiosity about our family and the country they were visiting, the mystery of what they were there to do, Protestants in a Catholic land—seeped into some of the characters of *The Sweetness of Tears*. Religious faith in general has played a significant part in recent public discourse, to the discomfort of many. Islam and Muslims—to some extent understandably, in light of how little they are known and understood in the United States—have become the object of intense fear, anger, and sometimes even vilification. But in certain circles there is also a high level of contempt directed at the Evangelical Christian community. Through the March/Pelton family in *The Sweetness of Tears,* I hoped to go beyond stereotypes about people of faith, to explore religious complexity through the stories of two families from different faiths.

Some of my fondest childhood memories are set in circles of wise, older women—my mother, aunts, grandmothers, great-aunts. I remember shocked squeals as particularly juicy snippets of gossip were exchanged, laughter accompanied by winks and waggling eyebrows as suggestive jokes sailed over my head when I was younger and then educated me about the mysteries of reproduction as I matured, tears shed at the recollection of past tragedies. My place in those feminine circles was assured— merely because I was female. Years later, I would come to understand the exclusive nature of that membership in a conversation with my younger brother. He recalled those moments of feminine solidarity from the outside, as someone who was told to leave the room, who heard the laughter and the squeals from the other side of the door, and noted the hushed fall of silence when he tried to break in, an unwelcome intruder whose outsider status became even more pronounced as he grew into the masculinity of adolescence and manhood that barred him forever from the confidences of those circles.

That conversation with my brother made me sad. It made me feel guilty about my access to a treasure of collective memories and sense of self that he and my male cousins were denied. It gave me a perspective on the balance of power between male and female that is far more complex than the one that typically defines women as victims. I saw, for the first time, that gender imbalance can be as painful for men as it is oppressive to women—even more so where legal and cultural norms are stacked against the feminine. This wasn't a new idea. When yin and yang, male and female, are out of balance in any context, personal or public, everyone suffers. This was something else that I tried to explore in the character and story of Sadiq, who is traumatically severed from his mother and her world of song and stories—left adrift, alone, out of balance, and dangerous to anyone in his path. In the same way, he is cut off from the existence of his daughter, his biologically feminine legacy to the world. Sadiq is a man twice exiled from the feminine.

Something else on my mind that made its way into the themes of *The Sweetness of Tears* was war and its consequences. In

A + AUTHOR INSIGHTS, EXTRAS & MORE...

the run up to the Iraq war, antiwar views were hard to hear in the mainstream media—among them cautionary comparisons, issued at whisper volume, with the Vietnam War. The nature of those comparisons, often derisively dismissed, was subject to interpretation, reflecting a historical divide in how the failures of Vietnam were perceived. Was Vietnam a failure because of how we had "cut and run"? Was it in how homecoming veterans had been treated? Was it in how the war had been conducted? Or was it in the fact that we had been defeated? The answers were unclear because this was a chapter of American history, among others, which we had never reckoned with honestly, our present and future still held hostage to the unresolved issues of the past. When the war began, I found myself glued to the coverage of "shock and awe" and later the dramatic scenes of Baghdad falling. Throughout, I winced at the way the names of places in Iraq were butchered in the mouths of newscasters—Karbala and Najaf—badly mispronounced, with no regard for their legendary significance for millions of people around the world. Karbala, that city synonymous with a 1,400-year-old tragedy, the inspiration for poetry and art, alive and vivid in the religious rituals and shrines located there, was witnessing tragedy again, on a massive, modern scale. I wondered whether we would ever have the fortitude to mourn our mistakes, whether we would again forget those who served, some of whom would come back permanently scarred, whether we could summon the empathy and attention that the widows and orphans we would one day leave behind deserved. For the characters in *The Sweetness of Tears,* reconciliation with the past requires a commitment to remember and mourn, honestly, the tragedies of their own making.

Soundtrack for Writing

When I'm writing, songs pop into my head. One of my favorite forms of procrastination entails spending inordinate amounts of time tracking down the tunes and putting together a playlist—sort of like a "soundtrack" for whatever I'm writing. This is helpful, too, for keeping track of the emotional threads running through the story. Certain songs get tied to certain moods, characters, or scenes that I'm working on. Just listening to them helps me find my place again, like opening the page of a book I'm reading to a favorite bookmark I've tucked into the pages.

The playlist for *The Sweetness of Tears* was ridiculously extensive:

1. "The Mission," Ennio Morricone
2. "On Earth As It Is In Heaven," Ennio Morricone
3. "Paradise City," Guns N' Roses
4. "Don't It Make My Brown Eyes Blue," Crystal Gayle
5. "Brown Eyed Girl," Van Morrison
6. "Knockin' on Heaven's Door," Guns N' Roses
7. "What Am I to You?," Norah Jones
8. "Sweet Child O' Mine," Guns N' Roses
9. "Love Me Tender," Elvis Presley
10. "Ya Hussain Ya Hussain" ("Oh Hussain Oh Hussain"), Nusrat Fateh Ali Khan
11. "Ali Da Malang" ("Disciple of Ali"), Nusrat Fateh Ali Khan
12. "Dil-e-Nadaan" ("Naïve heart"), Jagjit Singh and Chitra Singh (poem by Ghalib)
13. "Boys Don't Cry," The Cure

14. "Superman (It's Not Easy)," Five for Fighting
15. "Hairaan Hua" ("I was shaken"), Abida Parveen
16. "The Long Way Home," Norah Jones
17. "Where the Streets Have No Name," U2
18. "People Are Strange," The Doors
19. "Seven Years," Norah Jones
20. "Come Away With Me," Norah Jones
21. "Bohemian Rhapsody," Queen
22. "I Wish I Knew How It Would Feel To Be Free," Nina Simone
23. "America the Beautiful," Buffy Sainte-Marie
24. "I Am a Patriot," Burns Sisters Band
25. "My Country Tis of Thy People You're Dying," Buffy Sainte-Marie
26. "The General," Dispatch
27. "Ave Maria Guarani," Ennio Morricone
28. "People Like Me," K'naan
29. "Wavin' Flag," K'naan
30. "Jailhouse Rock," Elvis Presley
31. "Hound Dog," Elvis Presley
32. "Don't Be Cruel," Elvis Presley
33. "Teddy Bear," Elvis Presley
34. "Wooden Heart," Elvis Presley
35. "All Shook Up," Elvis Presley
36. "Can't Be Still," Booker T. & the MG's
37. "Until It's Time For You To Go," Buffy Sainte-Marie
38. "Dil Hi To Hai" ("It's only a heart"), Jagjit Singh and Chitra Singh (poem by Ghalib)
39. "Aree Logo" ("Oh people"), Abida Parveen
40. "Bazeecha-e-atfaal Hai Duniya Mere Aage" ("The World Before Me Is a Children's Playground"), Jagjit Singh and Chitra Singh (poem by Ghalib)
41. "I Am a Patriot," Jackson Browne

42. "Yeh Jafa e Gham ka chara" ("The solution for this oppression of grief"), Abida Parveen (poem by Faiz Ahmed Faiz)
43. "Allah Hoo" ("The Divine is"), Nusrat Fateh Ali Khan
44. "Illahi Aansoo bhari Zindagi Kisi Ko na De" ("Lord, please give no one a life full of tears"), Mehdi Hassan
45. "19 Miles to Baghdad," Lizzie West & the White Buffalo
46. "Ya Ilahi" ("Oh Lord"), Shaam
47. "Universal Soldier," Buffy Sainte-Marie
48. "Rock the Casbah," The Clash
49. "Killing an Arab," The Cure
50. "Rivers of Babylon," Boney M.
51. "100 Years," Five for Fighting

In addition, on my playlist was a selection of *noha*s and *marsia*s, including:

"Shabbir Ka Pursa" ("Condolence for Shabbir"—a title for Husain), recited by Asad Jahan
"Ghabraye Gi Zainab" ("Zainab will be distraught"), recited by Nasir Jahan
"Salaam e Akhir" ("The final salutation"), recited by Nasir Jahan
"Hussain Hai, Hussain Hai" ("Hussain, alas, Hussain"), recited by Nusrat Fateh Ali Khan
"Hussain, Hussain" recited by Noor Jahan

Most of the above *noha*s and *marsia*s can be heard/seen on youtube.com. The biggest surprise was finding a scratchy old recording of a *marsia* by Mir Anees, recited by the famous Lata Mangeshkar.

Robert Stewart

Nafisa Haji

I was born and mostly raised in Los Angeles, California—"mostly," because we moved around a lot and spent some time in other countries, too, including Pakistan, the Philippines, and England. I have a habit of bragging that I never spent more than two years in one school, until I taught at one for seven in inner-city Los Angeles. Before my son was born and after I finished my doctorate, my husband and I resumed the Gypsy lifestyle of my childhood, living in Boston and Chicago for a couple of years each before running away from the snow and home to California, this time to the Bay Area, where we are now settled.

I am the eldest in my family, with a brother behind me and a sister who keeps me feeling young because she's a good number of years younger than I am.

I live with my partner, Ali, who, even better than over-looking my faults, seems to be truly blind to them; with my eleven-year-old son, Khalil, a budding musician, spelling bee champion, and very sweet guy; and my dog, Giovanni, who I had to get to prevent myself from being a smoth-ering mother to my suddenly independent middle-school son—the added bonus with Giovanni is that he loves being cuddled and never talks back.

In between frenzied bouts of research and writing, I am honored to represent the International Association of Sufism as a member of the board at the Marin Inter-faith Council, which is a haven for friendship, community, and understanding in a world where faith is too often the source and object of hostility and violence.

BOOKS BY NAFISA HAJI

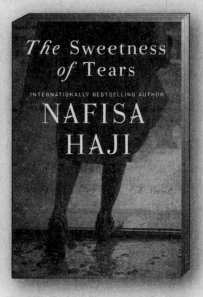

THE WRITING ON MY FOREHEAD
A Novel

ISBN 978-0-06-149386-7 (paperback)

A brilliant, internationally bestselling debut novel describing one woman's struggle with the Indo-Pakistani traditions of her family and her own independence.

"This book . . . will go a long way toward deconstructing stereotypes about American Muslims, and that, on top of its value as a work of fiction, makes it a treasure."—*Minneapolis Star Tribune*

Finalist for the Northern California Independent Booksellers Association Book of the Year Award!

THE SWEETNESS OF TEARS
A Novel

ISBN 978-0-06-178010-3 (paperback)

Nafisa Haji's highly-anticipated second novel, *The Sweetness of Tears*, is a deeply profound story in which a young Christian woman, Jo, uncovers the secret her mother has been keeping from her: that her biological father is Muslim. On a journey from California to Pakistan and Iraq, Jo must find a way to reconcile her faith with family secrets and the role political culture can take in our lives to find compassion and love.

Visit www.NafisaHaji.com and www.AuthorTracker.com for up-to-the minute news on Nafisa's books.

Available wherever books are sold, or call 1-800-331-3761 to order.

WI JUL 8 2011